keeps the tradition in the family and writes under her maiden name. Although she always wanted to be a novelist, she worked in London as a graphic designer for a couple of years while scribbling fiction in her spare time. To her delight, in 2000 she won the Romantic Novelists' Association New Writers' Award. However, when she realised that she would have to make a speech, her delight wavered momentarily.

She lives in Essex with her husband, but no cats, because unfortunately he's allergic to them. Valerie-Anne hopes that he won't develop a sudden allergy to dirty nappies, as that would be far too convenient.

About the author

Valerie-Anne Baglietto was born in Gibraltar in 1971. Her grandfather and great-grandfather were both writers, so Valerie-Anne [illegible] a novelist, she [illegible] as a graphic designer for [illegible] the Romantic Novelists' Association New Writers' Award. However, when she realised that she would have to make a space [illegible]

She lives in Essex with her husband [illegible] Valerie-Anne [illegible] but it would be far too convenient.

The Wrong Sort of Girl

Valerie-Anne Baglietto

coronet

CORONET BOOKS
Hodder & Stoughton

First published in Great Britain in paperback
in 2000 by Hodder and Stoughton
A division of Hodder Headline

A Coronet Paperback

10 9 8 7 6 5 4 3 2 1

A CIP catalogue record for this title
is available from the British Library

ISBN 0 340 76801 0

Typeset by Hewer Text Ltd, Edinburgh
Printed and bound in Great Britain by Clays Ltd, St Ives plc

Hodder and Stoughton
A division of Hodder Headline
338 Euston Road
London NW1 3BH

To my parents . . . this one's for you

ACKNOWLEDGEMENTS

A big hug of gratitude goes to all my family and friends, near and far, who will probably be miffed that I haven't mentioned them individually, but you all know who you are!

A huge thanks . . . To the RNA, for the invaluable role it performs, and to Hilary Johnson for her pearls of wisdom. To Dinah Wiener, for putting up with me and teaching me a few hard lessons. To Kirsty Fowkes and everyone at Hodder, for pulling a rabbit out of a hat, metaphorically speaking, and giving me my big break.

And then – in a niche all his own – thank you to Tim, for everything else.

ACKNOWLEDGEMENTS

[illegible]

[illegible]

[illegible]

'When a young lady is to be a heroine, the perverseness of forty surrounding families cannot prevent her. Something must and will happen to throw a hero in her way.'

Jane Austen, *Northanger Abbey*

One

There had to be worse predicaments than this, thought Meg, glumly chewing the end of her plait, which with every passing second was drawing closer to its appointment with the executioner's block.

If only she could stretch her legs out, but either they were too long or the room was too small. Drat, damn, hell. The end of her plait now soggy, the ragged chestnut strands having turned a darker shade of brown, she spat it out and rested her chin in her hands and her elbows on her knees, drumming her fingers impatiently against her jaw.

'Don't worry, Meg,' appealed a female voice, stifling a giggle, 'we'll have you out in no time.'

'Libby, you said that half an hour ago!'

'*Chérie* . . .' A burgundy-rich Parisian accent filtered reassuringly through the solid wood door. 'Marguerite, *mon ange*, do not worry about this. You worry too much. It is not good for your 'art!'

She ground her teeth in irritation. Thierry had told her he was doing his best, but that didn't mean he wasn't trying it on with Libby in the meantime, oozing Gallic charm all over her wipe-clean plastic pinny.

'I've got to get back to the kitchen,' Libby was apologising. 'I've a café to run and my meringues need checking. Thierry will sort you out, Meg.'

Thierry had already sorted her out, the most significant occasion being eleven and a half years ago, when they'd first met in Montmartre. Too much Pernod and not enough good sense, sniffed Meg. She recalled how her hands had trembled as she'd tried to translate the pregnancy test instructions into English by torchlight because the bulb in the small communal bathroom had blown. She'd been too scared to ask the dour old concierge to replace it.

She sighed incredulously at the memory – how naïve could a girl get? Meg replaced her own blown light-bulbs these days.

'*Mon petit chou*,' she wheedled, hoping Thierry would speed up the locksmith routine if she called him her little cabbage in his native language, 'don't you love me any more?'

'You know I will always love you, Marguerite. But I am not Superman.'

Funny though, how he had X-ray vision when it

came to women's clothing. He always seemed to know what kind of underwear they had on.

'What happens if there's an emergency?' wondered Meg, aloud. 'Like a fire, or—'

'You will have to climb out into the back alley.'

Meg looked dubiously over her shoulder at the only exit apart from the door. She could easily climb on to the loo seat and the cistern, but she wasn't sure her bust would make it through that slit in the wall which had pretensions of being a window.

She checked her watch again. 'How much longer is this going to take?' She had less than ten minutes to spare.

'We are nearly there,' Thierry assured her, rattling something metallic in the revolving lock.

A screwdriver, Meg hoped, who knew all about his unconventional methods, which sometimes worked, but more often than not . . .

'Oh drat,' she moaned, hitching up her chunky green jumper. 'I need to wee again. Keep the door shut till I tell you.'

Thierry pushed the door open an inch.

'You sod!' howled Meg.

'And you have the – how do you say it? – dodgiest plumbing I have ever come across.'

A few seconds later, grumbling under her breath, she leaned down heavily on the flush lever, dashing out of the lavatory before she was sprayed by the dodgiest plumbing *she'd* ever come across. Once the cistern had calmed down, Meg returned to wash her hands in the tiny sink. 'I'll never lock this door again,' she vowed. 'I'll just have to sing and hope no one's as perverted as you are.'

Thierry laughed. 'I think, Marguerite, you are more strung-up than usual.'

'Don't be daft.' She smiled, but it was forced. 'Why should I be strung-up?'

'Because of your rendezvous with this man whose name you will not tell us tonight.'

Meg didn't want to discuss her 'rendezvous', or the fact that Thierry's sentence wasn't grammatically correct, so she pecked his cheek to distract him. 'Thanks, Frog.' He'd never turned into her prince, no matter how many times she'd kissed him. Even when he had followed her back to England from France, it still hadn't been enough.

He looked at her mournfully. 'Is this all the gratitude I get?'

'Cheeky beggar! Who did I lose my virginity to when I was only sixteen?'

'That was so long ago . . .'

'Didn't you keep the Polaroids? What's the problem?'

He feigned horror. 'Marguerite! You have such a mouth on you!'

Before she could help herself, she was hugging

him. His hand slid down to her bottom. She giggled, trying to take a step back, but found that her scalp hurt when she moved. Thierry had twisted her plait around his brawny wrist.

'Oi!' she spluttered. 'Let me go!'

'Not until you promise not to cut off this lovely hair of yours. Libby told me what you are planning.'

'Oh bugger. I promise.'

'I know that look in your eye, you are lying to me.'

'As if I would!'

'The way you didn't lie about loving me all those years ago . . .?'

'I did love you, Thierry. I still do.'

'No.' He shook his head. 'You have never cared for any man the way they cared for you. But, perhaps, this new man you keep a secret . . . he has the power to touch your soul, no? For once, Marguerite, you will be the one to suffer for *amour*.' With an odd look on his stubbly face, Thierry let her go.

Pessimism. Great. Just what she needed. 'I don't know about touching my soul, but he's definitely got to my kidneys!' She thrust the joke into the suddenly strained atmosphere for the same reason she always squeezed the last bit of toothpaste out of a stubborn tube, because she hated to let it go to waste.

Thierry smiled and stroked her cheek with his grubby hand. 'I cannot stop you doing what you must do, so go on, *mon ange*, run. Or you will be late.'

She glanced at her watch again. 'Hell, you're right.' Landing another kiss on his cheek, she grabbed a thick woolly cardigan, a scarf and a rucksack which were all hanging on a peg in the corridor. 'See you down the pub tomorrow night?'

Thierry nodded.

Meg turned and hurried out through the café, heads swinging in her direction as she called out to Libby, her friend as well as her boss.

'It's amazing what thirty-five minutes locked in a loo can achieve.'

Libby looked up expectantly from serving table two. 'Are you all right now, Meg?'

'Never better. I actually came to a decision.'

'Decision?'

Meg nodded gleefully as she pulled on her cardigan. 'I'm definitely having it off!' she grinned, leaving every face gaping after her as she breezed out of Best Bib and Tucker and set off at hurricane speed down the High Street.

Oh blimey, what had she done?

The man reflected alongside her in the mirror was staring at her hopefully, eagerly, fearfully.

She would be a louse if she let him down. Scrabbling up the sleeve of her jumper for a tissue, Meg couldn't find the one she had tucked away earlier. In all probability, it had taken refuge in her armpit by now.

'I – I don't know what to say,' she said, sniffing loudly and swiping at her tears with the back of her hand. 'It looks great. Honestly. Doesn't it look great, Aggie?'

'Great?' The old woman in the adjacent chair groaned. 'It's one thing after another with you, Margaret Oakley. You'll never learn. Never.'

Learn what? wondered Meg, ignoring the scathing glances being aimed at her green and purple striped leggings and cherry-red Doc Martens. Anyone would think she walked around Yarleigh stark naked except for two strategic tassels and an extra-large fig leaf (waxing her bikini line had always been a sore point).

'Clients sometimes get rather emotional when they go for a dramatic new look,' explained Savannah Maurice, who had actually been named Suzanna Morris by her parents and was the owner of the only beauty parlour the village had to offer. 'And you have no idea how many poor women treat us as though we're psychiatrists and psychoanalysts. The tears that have been shed over this very floor . . .' As if she didn't want to have to mop up any more, she dumped a tissue box on the shelf in front of Meg's chair and made a nifty crab-like movement towards the till.

Meg looked down at the floor and could have sworn that the snippets of chestnut hair that had fallen to the tiles were reproducing in a B-movie sort of fashion even as she sat there snuffling into her first tissue, then her second. Just as she was reaching for her third, she dared to raise her head and meet her own gaze in the mirror again.

Victor, proud of his position as Savannah's top stylist, had been in seventh heaven when Meg had told him how she wanted her hair cut. He had made the obligatory snorts, of course. 'Are you quite, quite certain, Margaret? It's a very big step; perhaps a chin-length bob first? No? The full monty? The whole hog? Well, sweetheart, if you're *sure* . . .'

'Sophistication' had been the key word throughout, but the only word that had come to mind since it was all over had been 'short'.

She gulped.

Extremely short, in fact. Shorter than it had ever been since she'd been in nappies.

Her long, glossy, annoying hair was now a springy crop, which seemed to have altered the entire shape of her face as well as the length of her neck. She looked nothing like Audrey Hepburn, although, on closer inspection, there was something almost chic about it, something which had started off by whispering 'elfin' but was now exclaiming at the top of its lungs that she ought to have taken the plunge years ago.

'This cut wouldn't work on just anyone,' Victor was saying, covering his tracks admirably, 'but with a skull like yours, you carry it off to perfection!'

'Perfection? Really?' She was suddenly overcome by a rush of euphoria which swept up to heat her face and neck and then trickled down into her fingers and toes until every part of her seemed to be tingling with anticipation.

It was almost lunchtime. She had a million and one things to do before this evening. If her life was about to change for ever, she wanted to make sure the freezer was stocked up and the laundry basket empty.

Victor darted forward to help her off with the PVC robe, flicking away stray hairs from beneath her ears. Meg, who was more than just a little bit ticklish, writhed in the chair and caught Aggie's disapproving gaze once again. She stood up, chin poked audaciously in the air as she dragged on her cardigan and tossed on her scarf.

'Thank you, Victor, I'm indebted to you for all eternity. Or at least until my next visit. You've got wonderful hands, the best in the business!'

Aggie's brow darkened to North Sea grey.

'Well,' said Meg, 'he has.'

'If anyone would know, it would be you.'

'I'll take that as a compliment, shall I?'

Coughing pointedly, Savannah dragged Meg back to the most important matter. 'That'll be seventeen pounds fifty,' said the beautician, adjusting her tights in a practised fashion, without even having to hitch up her suede skirt the one extra inch that would have made the whole procedure a doddle.

Meg unzipped her purse. Instantly she ceased radiating defiant joy at the thought of her new look and her big date, and flushed to her follicles with embarrassment. 'Could I owe you a fiver? I can pay you back tomorrow . . .'

Savannah sighed. 'I suppose I can stay solvent another day without it. Don't you have a cheque-book or credit card on you, though?'

'Cheque-book!' There was a derisive snort from the remaining client in the salon. 'Haven't you heard yet? Margaret Oakley only deals in hard cash!'

Meg headed for the door, looking back over her shoulder and offering the blue-rinsed septuagenarian a forgiving smile. Sometimes, even after twenty-seven years, it was all too easy to forget that Aggie Widdicombe was her godmother.

A lime-green body, of the cotton and Lycra variety, flew out on to the landing. It was closely followed by a pair of skin-tight jeans that Pug Heybridge had thought were tacky long before the kitchen scissors had been taken to them in a frenzy of Beaujolais and PMT.

'Meg!' she yelled, poking her head round her half-sister's door. 'Watch it, you almost—' Her jaw plummeted. 'Meggy, *your hair!*'

'What about it?' Meg, kneeling on the floor, put a hand up to her head. 'Oh dammit, did you see where it went?' She lifted a velour hat in mock panic and peered beneath it. There was nothing there. Shuffling about on all fours, she blundered around her usually tidy bedroom, rummaging through jumpers and skirts until finally she lifted the lid off a shoe box and brandished the missing hair in relief. 'Thought you'd got away from me, did you?' The plait made no reply. 'Well you thought wrong, buster,' she hissed, giving it a shake. 'Nothing and no one gets away from Margaret Hermione Oakley!'

'I could murder you! Why did you do it?' Pug blinked as if to clear her vision, because everything about this room was crazy tonight. It was swamped by a jumble of uncoordinated clothing. The drawers from the tallboy were lined up on the bed, their contents in small mounds all over the floor – like multi-coloured mole hills, Pug thought dazedly, having been praised only the other day by her creative writing tutor for her 'lively' similes and metaphors.

Meg straightened her face. 'Why did I do it? That's easy. I couldn't bear the thought of my crowning glory reincarnated as hair-extensions or a paint-brush. I told Victor I wanted to keep as much as I could as a souvenir.'

'Don't be fatuous!' Pug was always being caught out by Meg stubbornly refusing to be serious when she really ought to be. 'You know what I mean!'

'Fatuous? I used to think that had something to do with Weight Watchers.' Casting a swift glance at her alarm clock, Meg pulled off the figure-hugging ribbed top she was wearing and deftly tugged on another. 'Eeek!' she cried, when she saw the result in the mirror. 'My boobs look like giant peas!' And she pulled off the green top and dived under the bed, mumbling something about a psychedelic silk shirt she'd been meaning to get rid of.

A few moments later she reappeared – minus the shirt. 'I can't find the bloody thing!'

Pug shook her head. 'Well I haven't seen it.'

'Bugger.' Meg stood shivering with exasperation in her best satin (nylon) underwear.

'Why didn't you warn me you were going to have your hair lopped off?' demanded Pug, making it as hard as possible for her sister to be evasive.

Meg frowned. 'You're sounding very school-marmish today. Don't you like the new look? I think it's great, although I didn't decide to go the whole way until I went round to Best Bib and Tucker beforehand to discuss it with Libby, even though it was my day off and I knew she would have tried to talk me out of it. But you'll never guess what happened . . .' Meg narrated the story of the jammed lock. 'At least it gave me a chance to think things through properly for myself. After all, I realised, it is *my* hair. So anyway, I popped in to see Libby on my way home and she loved it! She really couldn't pretend—'

'Oh, shut up!' Pug had heard enough. 'I could have killed for your hair before, but some people just don't appreciate what they've got.' She swallowed her dismay, sweeping back a greasy tendril of her own hair. It was chin-length and mousy, and whatever shampoo or conditioner she used, however much cash she invested in an ad-man's promise, there was never any body or lustre to it. 'I'm sorry,' she said at last. 'It's just . . . it'll take some getting used to.'

'You're telling *me*. I still have a minor identity crisis every time I look in a mirror.'

'At least it's only minor. Unlike mine.'

'You're still not putting on make-up like I taught you,' Meg said brightly. 'If you made more of an effort—'

'I'm not allowed to wear make-up at St Dominic's.'

'That never stopped me when I was your age.'

'By the time you were my age you weren't actually *going* to school.'

'I was!'

'Turning up for registration and then bunking off doesn't count. You missed the whole point by giving up when you did.'

Meg shivered again. 'I was a no-hoper. Everyone at St Dominic's kept telling me so. Why sit exams just to prove to them that they were right?'

'What about proving them wrong?' Pug was annoyed that they'd wound up having this old argument which never got anywhere. 'You're brainier than I am, and I'm supposed to be getting "A"s and "B"s in nine GCSEs this year.'

But Meg had conveniently vanished into her wardrobe. 'Brains are wasted on me,' she muttered, loud enough for Pug to hear.

'So that's why you're learning all that computer stuff then? To prove how thick and useless you are?'

Meg didn't reply. After a moment she reversed into the room with what looked to Pug to be a wide black velvet scarf, slightly out of shape. 'I haven't worn this dress in years! Do you reckon it might still fit?'

'A dress? Is that what it is? Maybe you *are*

stupid.' Pug watched as Meg lay on the bed and proceeded to wiggle into it. 'You're not seriously going to set foot outside the house like that?'

'Why not?' Meg sat upright and reached for a pair of seven-denier hold-ups in Soft Charcoal. 'It still fits. And the moths haven't got to it.'

Pug curled her lip. 'If I were a moth I wouldn't go anywhere near it. I'd have too much self-respect.'

'I got this dress for my twenty-first. You were ten at the time, so you probably wouldn't remember. You used to tuck yourself up in bed by nine o'clock and switch your light off by half-past, even on special occasions.'

Pug pouted sullenly. Her earliest memories were of her half-sister. Of soft cascading hair brushing her cheek and warm, gentle lips kissing her forehead. Of a spindly teenager in the shortest school uniform Pug had ever seen outside of *Neighbours,* striped tie askew, shirt untucked, blazer ripped, half a centimetre of black kohl smudged around her eyes and two or three crusty layers of electric-blue mascara.

This woman before her, skilfully applying the rest of her make-up, was tall and rounded in all the right places, moving with the enthusiasm of a puppy; there was something almost Peter Pan-ish about her now that her hair was short and curly like a young boy's. Her skin was glowing, as if she'd swallowed the moon. Pug had read something like that, but she couldn't remember where.

'Meg,' she said, her voice small, 'I'm sorry for being such a grouch . . .'

Meg grinned at her in the mirror. 'Who said you were being a grouch?'

Right, thought Pug, here's my chance – nab it. She wet her lips. 'So who *is* the lucky bastard tonight then?' she asked, trying to appear nonchalant but sounding as if her life depended on Meg's answer.

'No one special.'

'Oh yeah! You could have fooled me! Is it—'

'There are about a hundred men living in Yarleigh. You can list them all, if you want, but I never said he was local. Did I?'

Meg's laughter, thought Pug – knowing that she ought to take her writing tutor's advice and jot down her best ideas as they came to her – was like a dozen crystal goblets tinkling companionably in a dishwasher. Provided you could put crystal goblets into a dishwasher, and that the sound of the water whooshing about didn't drown out the tinkling.

'Meggy, please, why won't you tell me who your latest bloke is? You blurt out the other day that you're seeing someone new, and then you won't say who he is. Why make such a big deal—'

But Meg was giggling too much for Pug to get any more words in edgeways, nothing except for, 'Bloody hell, have it your own way then!', before stomping out of the room towards the cupboard that was politely known as her study.

Reverend Baxter, thought Meg, skimming down the list of Yarleigh's menfolk, or at least the ones she could recall off the top of her head – now that was a hilarious prospect! He was distinguished in a grizzly sort of way, but he'd be pushing up daisies in less than five years, unless he had one of those longevity genes everyone was going on about. Even if he did, Meg was sure he wouldn't survive long if she went anywhere near him in this dress.

Sliding into her square-heeled black mules, she cursed the current fashion trend and wished she'd been able to afford the classic pair of evening shoes she'd seen in Tockley last weekend. She swayed towards the door, realising she would have to practise walking around the house to get used to the feeling that the floor wasn't exactly where it ought to be.

Unable to stop fondling her hair – running her fingers through a tenth of what they were so sure they would find, as if her brain hadn't transmitted the update to every part of her body yet – Meg went to find Pug.

The girl was in her study with her nose in her homework.

'Listen,' said Meg. 'I made enough lasagne yesterday for leftovers today. Enough for you and Dad. Just pop it in the microwave and fish out some veggies from the freezer . . .'

Rewarded with a look that would have heated the lasagne in five seconds flat, Meg shot a fiery glance back. 'Don't wait up for me,' she said. 'I'll see you when I see you. Probably tomorrow evening. I'm working at Libby's till six.'

Pug frowned. 'Are you trying to tell me you won't be sleeping in your own bed tonight?'

'That's the gist of it,' Meg muttered with a sigh. 'Look, I'm not exactly sure what my plans are . . .'

'If you're not doing anything you shouldn't be doing, and if you're not seeing anyone you shouldn't be seeing, why the big secret?'

Meg couldn't look her in the eye. 'It won't be a secret for long, it just has to be for now. It's more fun that way too, like Romeo and Juliet. And he is available – sort of. It's just that we can't tell anyone yet, but when he says it's OK you'll be the first to know, I promise.'

Pug scowled. 'So keeping it secret was *his* idea?'

'Yes!' snapped Meg. 'Oh, why can't you be an insatiable romantic like any normal little sister?'

And with that she turned too quickly, her heavy shoes a couple of manoeuvres behind her feet. Swiftly regaining her balance and her composure, she clomped off indignantly to hunt out a jacket. Clearing away the rubble in the bomb-site of her room would just have to wait.

Downstairs in the lounge, her gaze settled on the mantelpiece. She had received five valentine cards, and there they stood in a neat row. Three from ex-boyfriends she would rather forget and whose writing she still recognised, and the other two from ex-boyfriends she'd remained on friendly terms with, one of them being Thierry.

Not one of the cards was from the man Meg was meeting tonight; the man who didn't need to be kissed before he turned into her prince. No one had ever put a spell on him; it was far more likely he was the one with the magic wand. Sending a card would have been far too cheap a gesture for someone in his league, Meg reminded herself. But still . . .

'Oh, sod it!' This time she was going to give her all. Heart, soul, body, the lot.

As she shrugged into her jacket, she relived the glorious moment when the 'lucky bastard's' countenance, nut-brown from all that skiing, had appeared like a tantalising mirage from behind his tinted car-window. With a toss of his hair, adorable in its floppiness, his lazy smile had broadened into a lazy grin and he had offered her a lift into Tockley. Her beloved Mini had been in the garage for servicing, yet again. Shivering and cursing in the deepening dusk as she'd waited at the deserted bus-stop on her way into town from Thierry's, she had been too cold to play hard to get. Feeling safe with a man she had known all her life, if only from afar, she had thought nothing of climbing into the dark leathery interior beside him.

Nothing, that is, but disbelief, rapture and awe.

And so it had begun. She hadn't said yes immediately when he'd asked her out – there was a major obstacle, after all – but he'd been charming and persuasive and, if she had to be honest, she'd wanted him to notice her for too long to throw it all away on a technicality.

Now, slamming shut the front door of 26 Chaffinch Lane, Meg greeted the first blast of icy wind with a jittery smile, empathising with the White Rabbit of *Alice in Wonderland* fame as she glanced at her watch. She would have broken into a whistle in an effort to calm herself, but the idea was to blend into her surroundings like a shadow. Ducking her head, she slunk in and out of the amber glow of the streetlights until she came to the end of the narrow road and, with just a moment's hesitation, plunged stealthily into the inky darkness beneath the trees. Her lungs took a long drag of frosty air and refused to let it go.

An engine revved into life. Headlights flicked on and the window whirred down. 'You look stunning . . .' He whistled appreciatively.

Her lungs let go. A silvery cloud streamed out towards him. 'I wasn't sure you'd be here. I wasn't sure you'd come.'

'I was certain *you* would. I'm even more certain you still will . . .' Without smiling, lazily or otherwise, he reached out through the window and stroked the back of her hand with the tip of his finger. The tiny circles of sensation rippled upwards, constricting her throat.

Meg felt drunk, even though she hadn't been drinking. 'So,' she managed to rasp, 'what now?'

'Hop in and find out,' he dared her, his voice just as raspy.

How strange love was, she thought, as she stood there trembling uncontrollably. Strange that she should want to shrivel up and die of panic when all her wildest dreams were so close to coming true.

Two

The dozen roses which Matthew Potter had laid on the grave the day before yesterday, the fourteenth, were covered in the frost that had blanketed the countryside last night like a snowfall that hadn't quite come up to scratch. Most of the students in his creative writing class would have said the frost was like icing sugar, because 'creative', Matthew acknowledged for the hundredth time, was rarely applied as a synonym for 'original' by his more mature pupils, who wrote with their heads and not their hearts.

As for the kids in the primary school . . . The majority of them were so full of adventure still, like little buccaneers. Even a mouthy brat could fill a couple of pages of his or her exercise book – albeit grudgingly – with such bizarre originality and acute perception that Matthew, when he was marking it later, was compelled to take off his glasses and rub his eyes as if the verbal picture pained him.

Pushing those silver-framed glasses further up his nose now, he hunched into the long greatcoat that had once belonged to his father. It was shiny and worn around the edges and at the elbows – not unlike its current wearer, reflected Matthew drily, reaching down and pulling at the scarf looped around his own son's neck. The small boy squirmed and stamped his wellies into the hard earth beside the gravestone.

'Daddy,' he sniffed, 'I want to go to school.'

Matthew straightened his shoulders. To a teacher, hearing those words made all the effort worthwhile.

'Timothy Arundel's bringing in his Virtual Zapper laser game,' the boy went on impatiently.

Matthew snorted, and ruffled Freddy's hair, which was the same texture and colour as Polly's had been. Very fine and very fair. Polly would have smiled at her son's lack of guile. Polly, who had loved roses on Valentine's Day, would have laughed and hugged the boy.

Matthew stared down at the flowers until his vision blurred.

'I'm cold,' said Freddy. 'I'm cold and I want to go to school. I sit beside a radiorater.'

With a jerk and a hot rush of apprehension, Matthew hitched up the sleeve of his coat and shook his wrist. His watch slid down to where he could see it. The first bell at Yarleigh County

Primary would be ringing in less than fifteen minutes. If they didn't make a move soon they would both be late.

'You mean a radiator,' he said.

'A radiorater,' Freddy insisted.

Just a few seconds more and then they would go. Matthew lifted his gaze from the grave and glanced around the churchyard of St Dominic's, the oldest Catholic church in the diocese, deserted so early on a week-day morning, especially a morning as bitter as this one. The air was motionless and clear, carrying the slightest sound, but as Matthew had moved through it earlier – from the house to the car, from the car to the churchyard – the ice had smoothed itself like butter on to his face, sinking into his pores until his jaw felt frozen and stiff. He was almost afraid to move towards the car again.

Rubbing a hand across his face, the scuffed leather of his gloves catching on his hurriedly shaven skin, he closed his eyes.

'Daddy,' said Freddy, 'there's a strange lady just fallen out of the woods.'

Frowning, wrenched away from his misery before he was ready, Matthew turned and looked towards the trees at the far end of the churchyard.

The dishevelled young woman heading in their direction was having difficulty walking.

'Hiya!' she cried as she came closer. 'You can't even begin to imagine how glad — Sod it. These flaming shoes!' She bent to rub her ankle. 'Still, never mind.' She looked up with a grin. 'You're a sight for sore eyes. Like a bottle of Optrex in fact!'

Matthew glanced over his shoulder, but she was definitely talking to him. Freddy was gawping. Matthew grabbed his hand and pulled him closer. There was something familiar about the young woman, but right at that moment he couldn't place it.

'I – I'm sorry,' he said, 'do we know each other?'

She had to be on the verge of hypothermia, dressed in an inadequate velvety dress and a thin black jacket, her long legs attractively encased in very sheer, dark tights. Or were they stockings? Or those hold-up things Polly had sometimes worn to parties?

'I'm Meg Oakley,' she said, her teeth chattering. 'And you're Matthew Potter. You teach at the primary school. And you run an evening class on a Thursday. Creative writing. My sister Pug goes. Pug Heybridge. Well, she's my half-sister really.'

He slipped off his coat and started to unwind his scarf. 'Here, take these, you must be freezing.'

'Just a bit,' she laughed, snatching at the coat. 'Keep the scarf or I'll feel guilty.' The greatcoat was slightly too large for Matthew; it made the girl look as if she'd shrunk in the wash, and she wasn't even petite like Polly had been. 'This is so kind of you,' she chattered on. 'I must look a real sight.'

'Not at all,' he lied. 'Um – can I ask you a stupid question?'

'Go ahead. The stupider the better.' The manic grin had obviously frozen to her lips.

'What are you doing out here this early in the morning dressed like—' He startled himself by almost voicing his thoughts.

'I was abducted by aliens,' she said, 'for experiments. You know the sort, the embarrassing kind. But I've got to give them some credit. At least the little green buggers came prepared.'

An excited Freddy broke out into a jig, but Matthew was well aware that they were having their legs pulled. For some indefinable reason, he went along with it.

'Prepared?' he repeated blandly.

'Well, it seems they even have to use condoms on Mars. Or was it Jupiter? Or Herpes?' She waved her hand dismissively. 'If you've seen one planet you've seen them all.'

If she'd mentioned UFOs in front of Freddy, Matthew wouldn't have minded, but she'd gone too far by bringing STDs and condoms into the conversation.

He scowled. 'Miss Oakley—' (He assumed

from the lack of a wedding ring that she *was* a Miss.)

'Call me Meg,' she insisted. 'And I'll call you Matthew, if you like. Or do you prefer Matt? Pug says that they call you Matthew in the writing class, because it's for adults, sort of. But personally—'

Polly had always called him Matt. Sometimes, in his dreams, she still did.

'Miss Oakley,' he interrupted, 'I haven't got time for this. If you're not going to tell me what you're doing out here . . .'

'I can't.' Her grin was now a beam. 'Apart from the fact that I was planning to catch a bus, it's all got to be kept hush-hush. But even though I can't tell you, could you possibly give me a lift back to the village? I'm running late.'

For a moment, Matthew wondered if he was still asleep and had only dreamed that he had got up this morning. Everything about the scene was surreal, as if the milk in his cornflakes had been spiked.

Meg Oakley took a step closer and dipped her head towards the gravestone.

' "Polly Angela Potter," ' she murmured, ' "beloved wife, mother and daughter. Fell asleep, aged twenty-seven, on the sixteenth of February . . ." '

Why was she reading it aloud? How did she

dare to in front of him? How could she spell it out so plainly, in spite of the euphemism?

POLLY IS GONE. POLLY IS NEVER COMING BACK.

'I'm sorry,' Meg was saying now. 'She was your wife, wasn't she? Polly Hancock, before she married you. I remember her from school. She was in Sister Assumpta's typing class with me. I used to call her Pollyanna. You know, from the book, and that film with Hayley Mills.'

A wave of recognition hit Matthew. This was Polly's old tormentor, although Polly had never actually called her that; but she'd spoken about their schooldays at St Dom's often enough. Meg Oakley: the rebel without a clue, let alone a cause. The troublemaker from Sister Assumpta's typing class who years ago had dared to flaunt nail-varnished hands over the antiquated machines and had chewed bubble-gum and sneered mockingly in Polly's small, sweet face.

'Are you all right?' she was asking. 'You look—'

'Come on, Freddy.' Matthew tugged his son towards the ancient Volkswagen Golf parked a few yards away.

Meg hurried round to the passenger door. 'Please, Mr Potter,' she gabbled, 'I'm—'

'What?' he snapped. 'Haven't you said enough?'

'Oh hell,' she sighed. 'I ought to have been immunised against foot-in-mouth at birth.'

Matthew took off his gloves and tossed them on to the dashboard. After a pause, a moment's hesitation, he said, 'Get in. I can take you as far as Yarleigh Primary.'

'My hero!' She smiled warmly again, wrestling with the car door.

Her sincerity annoyed him further. He hadn't been expecting it, hadn't asked for it. He wanted to resent her for Polly's sake, but somehow she wasn't making it easy for him. There were moments when she was straying perilously close to the space inside him where his sense of humour had once been. Actually, to be fair, it was still there – not like his appendix or tonsils, which were no longer with him – but it seemed to Matthew that his taste for the absurd resembled a deflated balloon by now.

'Oh!' Meg halted with one foot in the car and one foot out. Matthew followed her gaze, dreading how late he was going to be if he lost his cool with the manual choke and flooded the engine. 'Is something the matter?'

'You've, er, got a baby in the back . . .'

Matthew craned his neck round further. Georgina Ann was still fast asleep in her car seat. The only part of her that was visible among the coat, hat and blanket was her saucer-shaped face – beautiful to him because of those long gold lashes, just like Polly's, and the simple fact that he was her father.

'Don't worry,' sighed Matthew, 'she's mine. I didn't nick her. And she was one year old in December.'

Meg didn't look reassured. 'She's still a baby though.'

'Do they bring you out in an itchy rash or do you just start sneezing uncontrollably?'

'What?'

'Are you allergic to them, Miss Oakley?'

'Don't be daft!'

'Well what then? I promise you Georgie won't bite. Not unless she's provoked.'

Casting dubious glances over her shoulder, Meg climbed into the car and fastened her seat-belt. 'I forgot you had a daughter. You didn't say anything.'

'I wasn't aware I had to.'

They crunched off across the gravel and pulled out into the empty country road, Matthew changing gears with exaggerated emphasis to prove he was in control.

'Don't you like babies?' he demanded, when the silence became unbearable.

'I don't know,' she admitted. 'I'm not sure. I'm still trying to make up my mind.'

'Daddy,' piped up Freddy from the back, 'what's a condom?'

Meg's face was swallowed up by the large flapping collar of the coat as Matthew turned to glower at her.

'See what you've done now? I take it you're not a parent yourself, Miss Oakley?'

'Not so I've noticed,' she said, her head still bowed. 'Not in a conventional sense anyway. My step-brother William was only little when my mum married Dad – my step-dad, I mean – and I was already eleven by the time Pug came along—'

'Daddy,' Freddy interrupted again, 'Timothy Arundel, at school, he said his Uncle Jake had a whole box of them—'

'Freddy!' warned Matthew. 'Not now.'

There were odd sounds coming from beneath his greatcoat. He wasn't sure if they were sniggers or sobs.

'Daddy' – Freddy was as obstinate as Polly had been – 'are they like sweets? Or are they more like chewing-gum? Timothy's uncle said that Timothy was too young to have any. And you're always saying that I'm too young for your chewing-gum because I might forget it's just for chewing and swallow it instead—'

'Freddy,' Matthew's voice wasn't loud, but the message was ominously clear, 'will you please be quiet. I'd rather you didn't wake up your sister.'

'OK.' The boy sighed resignedly, raising his eyes to the grubby car ceiling, splattered with Ribena.

Meg lifted her head, cocking it slightly, reminding Matthew of the terrier his grandmother had owned when he'd spent his school summer holidays in the old cottage by the loch . . . But he couldn't help reliving more recent memories as well: his honeymoon nine years ago. Hiding away from the world with the only girl he'd ever loved in that very same—

'Mr Potter, WATCH OUT!' Meg's hand lunged for the steering wheel. A split second later Matthew spotted the bollard, lurid and yellow, emphatic as an exclamation mark. The car missed it by millimetres, heading instead for a ditch on the other side of the crossroads.

His reflexes woke with a start, and his shaking hands finally regained control. His rubbery foot found the brake pedal and pumped it, the Volkswagen shuddering to a halt in a symphony of not-quite-new tyres skidding on slippery Tarmac, baby waking up outraged and screaming, older child whooping with panic and delight, and there in the seat beside him, Matthew could scarcely believe his ears, the young woman laughing as if she'd just climbed off a particularly thrilling ride at Chessington World of Adventures.

'What's so funny?' he demanded, in a tone he

rarely used, even on his pupils at the primary school. 'What the *bloody* hell is so *bloody* funny?'

'I always laugh when I'm scared,' she explained, wiping tears from her eyes with his scarf, the one he was still wearing. 'I'm sorry. You just seemed to lose your concentration so I grabbed the wheel. It seemed like the right thing to do at the time . . . Damn, my heart's going to pop out!' She was clasping her chest, which wasn't exactly flat; it looked to Matthew as if there were two hearts within it struggling to thrust themselves free. Polly had never been bigger than a 34B, not even when she'd been pregnant or breast-feeding.

'This is so *bloody* funny!' Freddy chortled from the back, wiping tears from his little sister's face with the paper napkin from his lunchbox.

Matthew wrestled his trailing scarf back from Meg's quivering hands. 'Thanks for nothing,' he said, so low that Meg instinctively leaned closer to hear him.

'Well it's not my fault you can't drive for toffee and your son's a flipping parrot,' she retorted, just as quietly, so that he leaned closer to her and they almost bumped heads.

'Oh, for pity's sake!' He grated the gears as he scoured them for reverse, backing the car on to the correct side of the deserted road, his voice nearly drowned out by the plaintive whine of the engine. 'Do you realise how late I am? It's the third time in two weeks.'

'That's still not my fault,' she said primly, staring out of the window as he shot off again with a kangaroo-hop in the direction of the village. 'And you should watch where you're going, Mr Potter. Someone could get hurt next time.'

'Next time', he thought, was much closer than she imagined. For if his hands left the wheel as they were itching to do and formed an ever-decreasing circle around her slender white neck . . .

If it wasn't for the children, murder wouldn't have been entirely out of the question.

They made it to Yarleigh Primary intact. Instead of turning into the staff car-park, Matthew kept the engine running outside the open gates and jumped out to help his son down.

'Freddy, you'd better get a move on. I've got to drop Georgie off at Mrs Carter's. If you see Mr Nugent tell him I won't be long.'

Mr Nugent was the headmaster. Frederick Andrew Potter suspected that his father was secretly afraid of him, but Freddy knew that Mr Nugent's bite wasn't half as bad as his bark. At least that's what he'd heard Mrs Nugent saying to Mrs Santa Claus at the school jumble sale last Christmas.

He held on tightly to his red and blue rucksack. 'Bye, Dad,' he said, and then turned to smile at the strange lady who had fallen out of the woods and was wearing his father's coat. 'Bye.' She had wound down the window and was tousling his hair.

'Goodbye, Master Potter. It was very nice meeting you.'

'It was very nice meeting you back,' he replied politely, looking up at his father for approval. Instead, his dad, wearing another huge frown, bobbed down and smoothed Freddy's hair back into place, pressing firmly on the bit that Grandad called a cowlick.

'Now go on, laddie, scoot. And remember, Mrs Carter will pick you up at ten past three. I've got a meeting after school so she'll be making you tea.'

'Yuck.' Freddy stuck his tongue out. 'Fishcakes and mashed potato.' He looked up at the strange lady. 'I hate fishcakes,' he confided in her. 'Mrs Carter makes them too slushy, and she puts peas in them too.'

'It's a tough life, kiddo,' Meg sympathised.

In other circumstances, she would have been more helpful. But she was finding it hard enough to stay on the right side of the boy's father, and if she was to impose herself on Matthew Potter a while longer and beg him to take her as far as Chaffinch Lane, she couldn't advise Freddy to be frank with Mrs Carter and tell her exactly what he thought of her culinary delights. Somehow, she didn't think Mr Potter would approve.

'Sorry,' he was saying, tugging open her door after making sure his son had run in through the gates and disappeared into the main building. 'You can't get out unless someone pulls at the handle from the outside. It's always jamming.'

Story of my life, sighed Meg.

'Look,' she began, well aware that Matthew Potter had been kinder to her than she deserved, 'Muriel Carter lives in Larkspur Road, doesn't she? And Chaffinch Lane, which is where I live, is *virtually* round the corner—'

He slammed her door shut without a word, rounded the car and jumped back in. But did he have to rev the engine so aggressively? And had he remembered to check his mirrors properly before pulling out like that, without even indicating? What was it about men and cars? And this particular man was worse than most, probably sulking because he didn't have a Ferrari or a Porsche. But just for today Meg had to be a beggar. She hadn't the time to be choosy, and all things considered, the coat he'd lent her was so wonderfully warm.

'You can drop me off at the bottom of Chaffinch Lane, if that's best for you,' she said, almost going on to inform him – as an independent observer – that he would be quite a pleasant human being if he'd just loosen up and smile every so often. And while she was at it, to egg him on she could say that those spectacles really suited him. He didn't look the least bit nerdy. In fact, he was very—

She experienced a sudden sinking sensation as the penny dropped.

Oh no! It had dawned on her tired little mind, miles too late – today was the sixteenth, the sixteenth of February. Exactly a year ago . . .

She waited as long as she could, having no idea what to say. 'Mr Potter,' she began at last, deliberately husky and reverential, 'I'm so sorry. It's the anniversary of your wife's . . . I didn't realise . . . I would never . . .' Bugger.

Matthew couldn't bring himself to answer. If he did, he would cry. He kept what little composure he had left by vowing to himself that no one, *no one*, especially not this airhead of a female with the conspicuous chest and the long, rather shapely legs, would ever again get away with calling his son 'kiddo', or daring to tell Freddy that life was tough.

Even if it was, thought Matthew bleakly.

Three

Agnes Widdicombe didn't consider herself an old cow, despite what that snotty-nosed ten-year-old from two doors away had said when she had caught him hiding her freshly delivered milk bottles in her herbaceous border. After all, she was only seventy-two, and had stopped remarking that she was 'old' around the same time everyone else had started implying that she was. As for being a cow . . . Agnes 'humphed' in indignation.

This particular morning, on her way to the general store in the High Street for her daily provisions (a walk a day kept the doctor at bay), she was forced to set a slower pace than normal. Irregular patches of frost glittered wickedly on the pavement, and the last thing she needed was to slip and shatter her hip as well as her theory about doctors and walking. There was far too much going on right now to find herself incapacitated in Tockley Hospital, even if it would mean people bringing her presents.

The first letter had arrived a fortnight ago. The second today. Another blue envelope lying on her door-mat, and again the tears had prickled behind her eyes when she'd read and reread the message enclosed. Now though, as she neared the south-west end of Chaffinch Lane, all thoughts of broken promises flew straight out of her head at the sight of a familiar blue motor vehicle parked at the bottom of the road.

Odd. That was definitely Matthew Potter's Volkswagen; she could tell by the number plate and the layers of grime. But what was it doing here when he ought to be in school by now?

There was a stirring by the car; someone was getting out of the driver's side. Agnes shuffled behind a nearby hedge, peering around the edge and stiffening in surprise when she saw Matthew himself rather than a joy-riding yobbo. Then she sighed, unable to help herself.

Such a sublime young man – a hunk they would say these days, if they had any taste. He was so tall and dignified. And the fact that his past was so tragic only seemed to make him more handsome. Losing his parents in a sailing accident when he was just a boy, and then his wife to cancer . . .

He couldn't be older than thirty-two, and the way he wore his wavy light-brown hair, short at the back and long on top, unkempt, uncombed, in need of a woman's touch . . . Agnes sighed again, her spinster's heart swelling with something not purely maternal.

Matthew had darted around the car and was now opening the front passenger door. How gallant. And everyone said chivalry was dead these days. A pair of feet appeared in plasticky looking shoes, rapidly followed by a long dark coat and—

No! Impossible. It couldn't be, it simply couldn't!

And yet . . .

All that talk going on lately in the village, huddled little conversations about Margaret's love-life, folk wondering who the next victim was going to be, most wives and girlfriends clinging to their husbands and boyfriends like jungle vines.

Agnes's scalp tingled in shock as she watched her god-daughter slip suggestively out of the coat and hand it back to its owner with a wistful shrug. It was obvious. Clear as day. From the way the girl was dressed . . . *Oh,* moaned Agnes, Margaret ought to be shot! A man like Matthew Potter belonged on a pedestal with a halo welded to his head.

Suddenly, leaning towards him, Margaret kissed his cheek. Then she spun around and set off at an ungainly trot up Chaffinch Lane.

A few seconds later, as Matthew drove off in the direction of Larkspur Road, Agnes emerged shakily from behind the hedge only to collide with a sensible tweed skirt and matching jacket.

'Miss Widdicombe! Goodness! Are you all right?'

She blinked up at Mrs Spencer, whose husband was a local solicitor and one of the governors of Yarleigh Primary. 'No,' she said dazedly.

'Are you ill?'

Agnes shook her head.

'Would you like to come in and sit down?' asked Mrs Spencer. The Spencers' mock-Tudor semi was only two doors away. 'I've just been stocking up on Earl Grey. We can have a nice brew together.'

Agnes was already behind schedule for the day. She was due to meet Father Holmes at ten o'clock to start going over plans for the Easter Bazaar, even though it wasn't quite Lent yet. But her mind was full of steel wool. A quick cup of Earl Grey would help clear it and put everything back in perspective.

'That's very kind of you,' she nodded.

Mrs Spencer smiled benevolently. 'Nonsense, it's my pleasure, but you have to tell me what it is that's upset you . . .'

There wasn't really time for a shower, but Meg knew she couldn't go out again without having one. Her only claim to hygiene so far this morning had been to spray herself with perfume, and that didn't count for much after the gymnastics of the previous evening.

Beating her own record, she was out of the bathroom in five and a half minutes. Dammit. What was she going to wear? Her room was still a mess, obviously – unless fairies had cleared up in the middle of the night – but she couldn't do anything about it now. And she couldn't pick out her undies until she knew what she would be wearing on top.

In the end she settled for a caramel-coloured chenille dress (once a jumper, before it had stretched) on top of a grey bra, yellowing thermals and woolly tights. She slapped on a tinted moisturiser, blusher, lipstick and mascara, but there was no time for a full make-over today. After a quick blast with a dryer, her hair – despite the fact that there was less of it – was still damp and crispy from the styling gel. She pulled on a fake leopardskin hat and dragged out her warmest jacket, the one she would have worn last night if her common sense hadn't been on strike.

'Hell, hell, hell!'

She was starving, but she'd grab a muffin or two at work, provided Libby was feeling charitable. Meg hated to be in a hurry, but always seemed to find that she was. Strange, she thought now, how her life was still chugging along on the same old tracks. Had she honestly expected a radical transformation in a matter of hours? There would be other nights like last night, she was sure of it, but meanwhile there would still be days just like the rest of this one was bound to be: boring, uneventful, samey. Although, to be fair, the morning so far hadn't been lacking in drama – except that something inside her curled up and died in horror when she thought about her blunder with Matthew Potter.

She finally dared to remove her hat a quarter of an hour after arriving at Best Bib and Tucker.

'Your hair doesn't look anything like it did yesterday,' said Libby.

'I've gone for the tousled look today,' explained Meg, defensively. 'It's an extremely versatile cut!'

'I can think of other things to call it, but I've customers waiting.' Libby sashayed out of the kitchen with a full tray, leaving Meg to deal with the clearing up as a reward for being late.

Best Bib and Tucker had first come into being four years ago, when an archway had been knocked out between a hardware shop and a greasy spoon café. Meg had worked there from the start, fitting it in around various other part-time jobs, none of which she'd managed to keep hold of. Libby Fielding, she often thought, must be a saint to put up with her.

The café had long since lost its greasy image and now smelled of chocolate, coffee and vanilla rather than burnt fat, chips and vinegar. The Formica tables and plastic chairs had been replaced by dark wood trimmed with red and white gingham, and the babywear and gift section of Best Bib and Tucker – where the hardware used to be – was constantly stocked to the brim with clothes from talented local seamstresses and industrious knitters. Meg had even persuaded her retired step-father, who enjoyed woodwork, to set up a small line of traditional toys, including pull-along jungle animals and old-fashioned building blocks. It only brought in a tiny bit of cash but anything was a Godsend. His pension wasn't too bad, and it was a blessing that the mortgage was paid off, but Meg – who added most of her own wages to the family pot – seemed to find there was never much left over at the end of the month after the bills had been paid and the groceries bought.

That morning, in the kitchen at Best Bib and Tucker, Meg flaked out almost immediately, an hour earlier than usual. She helped herself to a mug of steaming caffeine.

'So,' began Libby, who had left her other assistant in charge out front, 'how's things?'

'Things?' Meg raised an eyebrow. 'Be more specific.'

'All right. Heard from Yasmin lately?'

This wasn't the line of interrogation Meg had been expecting. She couldn't decide whether to be miffed or relieved. 'I got an apple-shaped postcard from Manhattan the other day. She went there for the weekend.'

'You mean she hopped on the Subway,' said Libby sniffily.

'She'll be back in the UK sometime before Easter, anyway.'

'Mmm. What about you though? Are you going to be jetting off to seek your fortune in the near future?'

'As if! And Yasmin's hardly earning a fortune,' Meg pointed out, in defence of her friend. 'She's only teaching European history.'

'Which reminds me, how are your studies going?'

'Slowly. My PC can't even run the latest version of Windows. Sometimes I wonder if there's any point to this "self-improvement" lark.'

Libby poured herself a coffee and topped up Meg's mug. 'Well you can't work here for ever.'

'Can't I?' Meg stiffened automatically, her survival instincts on stand-by. 'Why not?'

'Because only last month you told me you didn't want to. Apparently you were cut out for better things, like slaving your butt off in an office.'

'I'm mad. It's only because of the money. I like working here.'

'Do you?'

'Sometimes, especially when we're closed. No, look, I'm only kidding. This has nothing to do with you, you're a brilliant boss. No one else would let me get away with half as much.'

'Don't I know it!' Libby smiled. 'Actually, I'm humouring you this morning. I really only want to find out how last night went.'

Meg couldn't suppress the grin that always seemed to be getting her into trouble. 'I haven't had a chance to go over the details in my head yet. Not properly. It's all still a big haze.'

'That "big haze" probably explains why you're only wearing one earring.'

Meg put a hand up to her ear. 'Oh ha ha! Very funny!'

'The other side, dipstick.'

Libby wasn't joking. 'Blast!' The small silver stud in Meg's left ear was missing. 'I only put them in last night!' They weren't worth much, but Meg hated losing anything, especially jewellery. It wasn't as if she had it coming out of her ears. At least, not yet. She brightened up a second later when she caught up with her inadvertent pun.

Libby frowned. 'You weren't smoking anything funny, were you?'

'You know I don't smoke. And I can't remember the hippy era – unlike you. But I did drink champagne.'

'Out of your shoe, I suppose, you hussy.'

'Out of a glass, although there was an ice-bucket involved.'

'Even worse. Can't you tell me where you went, at least?'

Meg shook her head. 'Not even on pain of death.'

'How about on pain of redundancy?'

'You wouldn't!'

'Well there's not much point making bets on your love-life if you won't tell anyone who it is you're seeing. How do we know who's won?'

Meg wasn't a gambling woman, and didn't derive any pleasure from being the subject of a wager, however popular it made her. She wished she had kept her mouth shut from the start and never blurted anything out about a mystery man.

'All things come to those who wait,' she said enigmatically.

'Bollocks!' Libby scrunched up a dirty tea-towel and tossed it into the laundry basket.

Just then, the other assistant came hurrying into the kitchen. 'Help, you two!'

'What's wrong?' Meg looked in concern at the

young woman who had skidded to a halt by the industrial oven. Beatrice was her oldest friend; they had known each other since as far back as infant school.

'Gwendolyn Arundel and the Honourable Miss Aurora Lloyd! That's what's wrong.'

'Sounds like something out of an Oscar Wilde play,' quipped Meg, to disguise the jolt that had passed through her.

'What about them?' asked Libby.

'Aurora looks like a stuck-up cow in my opinion,' said Beatrice, 'and we all know Gwendolyn's a real pain in the—'

'*What About Them?*' Libby punctuated her words sternly.

'They've just swanned in and ordered two espressos, and you know what I'm like . . . You know what happened when Jake Arundel tried to turf poor Billy Tomkins out of that farm cottage last year . . .'

'Oh, fu—' Libby paled. 'Fudge. You ran the protest campaign.'

'The worst bit was when I wrote "Capitalist Pig" on Jake's windscreen. Bloody stupid. They don't make that shade of lipstick any more. It was my favourite!'

Libby glanced down at her own faded corduroy ski-pants. There was only one thing for it. 'Meg, you're going to have to serve them.'

'What? I can't!'

'Why not?' Beatrice began to busy herself with the coffee machine. 'I'd probably pour it into their laps, and then they'd sue me or poor Libby and she'd have to close this place down, and then we'd all be out of a job!'

Libby shoved a tray into Meg's hands. 'Just serve them their coffee, smile politely, and come straight back. There's nothing to it.'

'Well why can't *you* do it then?'

'Just look at me. I'm a mess. And your dress is gorgeous.'

'Gorgeous? You mean short and trollopy?'

'Casual and cosy. Now go on, it isn't the done thing to keep them waiting.'

'Here's the coffee.' Beatrice rattled the cups in their saucers as she put them on the tray.

'I shouldn't be doing this,' winced Meg, the cups still rattling.

'You'll be OK.' Libby held the door open. 'Easy peasy.'

Meg managed to dodge a couple of pushchairs and hold on to both her equilibrium and the tray until she reached the table by the bay window. One of the women sitting there was staring out through the leaded panes into the High Street; the other was playing with a twinkling boulder on her left hand. They looked up as Meg forced her lips into a smile and tremulously placed her load on the table.

'Milk?' said the older of the two women, blinking down at the coffee which had slopped over the edge of the cup into the saucer.

The younger woman was ransacking the bowl of sugar sachets which stood beside a vase of silk bluebells. 'Do you have any low-calorie sweeteners?'

Meg bolted back to the kitchen to tell the others they'd cocked things up already.

As Libby handed over the milk, Beatrice turned a drawer upside down searching for the Sweetex, grumbling that Aurora Lloyd was already as thin as a Pepperami.

Meg dashed back to the table, splashing milk up her sleeve. The quicker this was over with, the better. Thumb-screws couldn't be any worse a torture than being confronted with that obscenely huge engagement ring.

She hadn't intended to speak, but her tongue had other ideas. 'Would you like anything else? Passion cake? Treacle tart? Is that coat real cashmere?'

Aurora Lloyd twitched visibly in her chair. 'Pardon?'

'Er—' Meg's tongue, having had its say, packed up on her. 'Your – um – coat. It's very . . . nice.'

'Oh.' Aurora flicked back a tendril of her sleek saffron bob. 'Thank you.'

'It's her own design,' said Gwendolyn Arundel, with a proud smile.

Any person in their right mind would have put an end to the conversation there and then, but . . .

'Her own design?' said Meg.

'Gwendolyn' – Aurora's blush clashed with the freckles on her nose – 'there's really no need—'

'There's every need! You're far too unassuming, darling, which is terrible PR when you run your own boutique.'

'You run your own boutique?' Meg already knew this, but there was a comforting rhythm in regurgitating Gwendolyn's words.

'I'm a designer too,' said Aurora, playing with the Sweetex.

'Golly,' said Meg, who had never said 'golly' out loud before. 'How thrilling for you.'

'I wish my father was as enthusiastic. Most men don't seem to approve.'

'Don't they? What about your – um – fiancé?' The word almost never made it out.

Aurora looked down at the table. 'Of course *Jake* approves . . .'

Turning to Gwendolyn again, Meg searched for a resemblance between this elegantly coifed woman and her floppy-haired son. Apart from the same warm colouring, like gold mixed with honey, there were no striking similarities.

Up until his death three years ago, Howard Arundel, Gwendolyn's husband, had been the local squire, or so Agnes Widdicombe and virtually everyone of her generation had referred to him. His family had owned most of the farmland in the Yarl Valley since the turn of the century, but Howard had been the Arundel who had boosted their fortunes through a series of inspired international investments. Howard and Gwendolyn's two children, Jake and Jacintha, had been sent to Harrow and Roedean respectively, followed by Oxford for the boy and an élite London secretarial college for his twin sister.

'Jake's a sweetheart about it all really,' Aurora added. 'Only yesterday he told me I ought to spend more time up in South Ken keeping an eye on things.'

'How understanding,' smiled Gwendolyn, sipping her espresso. 'Because it is lovely for him having you staying at the hall, you know.'

Meg turned to go.

'Don't rush off, dear.' Gwendolyn called her back. 'This is such a charming place you have here.'

'I'm not the owner,' Meg corrected her, 'just the hired help.'

'Really? Is this a full-time job?'

'Gwendolyn, you're far too nosy for your own good.' Aurora smiled up at Meg, who was irritated by the fact that, as smiles went, this one was genuine.

'I wish it *was* full time,' frowned Meg. 'But at the moment I have to take what I can get.'

'Do you have children to support?'

Meg felt like some sort of museum exhibit labelled: 'How The Other Half Live.' Any minute now, Gwendolyn would whip out a magnifying glass from her Gucci handbag.

'No,' said Meg grimly, 'I don't have any children. I'm not married. But I've got ties, all the same. Working isn't a choice, it's a necessity.'

'How admirable of you, dear.'

Remembering all those times she had pored over *Hello!* or *Tatler*, Meg realised that she could hardly cast stones at these women for regarding her with an equal amount of compulsive fascination.

'My daughter Jacintha has a child,' sighed Gwendolyn. 'Timothy is such a cherub. He'll be eight in a few weeks.'

Meg caught up with her faux pas, but it was too late. Illegitimacy wasn't confined to the lower classes and never had been. 'Oh, yes,' she said quickly, 'Timothy.' The little 'cherub' currently leading Matthew Potter's son down the road to ruin.

From what Meg had heard, Jacintha Arundel had been eccentric from an early age, and this matter of becoming an unmarried mother had simply been another addition to her long list of caprices. Her late father had indulged her modernist views, and had backed her staunchly, if a little dazedly, when she'd announced not long after her return from a year on a kibbutz that she intended to be a single parent and live off the State.

And Jacintha had been true to her word, it seemed. Only one letter out, in fact. By 'State' she had basically meant 'Estate'. The one her brother was running these days with such dynamism and skill.

That could hardly count as failure, thought Meg magnanimously. It was more of a verbal typing error. If the stories were true, then Jacintha had never been a model secretarial student. She probably still thought Qwertyuiop was a place in Wales.

'Such a shame if the powers-that-be close down that darling village school,' Gwendolyn was now wittering. 'That's the main reason Jacintha sent Timothy there – as a form of protest. She doesn't want him to lose touch with reality. And my son feels the same. He insists that we support as many local causes as possible. So today it's your turn.'

Meg arched an eyebrow. Best Bib and Tucker was now a cause, was it? And two espressos counted as support? How reassuring. Libby would sleep so much sounder tonight.

'Jake's quite an entrepreneur,' continued Gwendolyn. 'But he never loses sight of the smaller cogs in the wheel. Always does his bit for the village, in between all his other pursuits. He has such energy, such vitality . . .'

Meg would have added 'stamina' to the list, but it was bound to raise awkward questions.

'He has his fingers in so many pies,' agreed Aurora, 'it's hard to keep track.'

Gwendolyn toyed disconsolately with her Cartier watch. 'I worry he'll turn into a workaholic and burn himself out like his father.'

'He had to fly up to London yesterday at such short notice,' sighed Aurora. 'But at least we got to spend the whole of Valentine's Day together. I shouldn't be so hard on him. Business is business, as I'm sure you'll appreciate.' She smiled at Meg, who couldn't look her in the eye.

'Fly? Up to London?'

'Oh! You know what I mean.' Aurora laughed, sipping her coffee. 'His car. It seems to just take off at times.'

'Yes . . .' Meg adjusted the turtle neck of her dress, wishing she *could* vanish into it like a turtle retreating into its shell. 'I've seen it around the village. I imagine it must have a slight kick.'

'To put it mildly.' Aurora looked amused.

'Master of understatement, that's me.' Meg shrugged, sizing up her escape route.

Gwendolyn tapped a varnished fingernail against the side of her tiny coffee cup. 'Surely you mean mistress?'

Meg was speechless.

'To be fashionably and politically correct,' explained Gwendolyn, 'you're female, therefore you're not a master.'

Enough was enough. 'Will you – um – excuse me? Before they send out a search party . . .' Meg fled back to the kitchen.

'I told you it would be easy!' Libby was flushed with triumph and the heat from her boiling fettuccini. 'I took a peek and you were getting on with Gwendolyn and Aurora like a house on fire, as if you actually had something in common! What on earth were you talking about for so long?'

Meg collapsed on to a stool. 'The weather,' she lied, feeling rotten.

Only last week, she'd given up a parking space seconds after she'd nipped into it (her Mini being marginally faster than the Robin Reliant approaching from the other direction). The couple in the three-wheeler had still glowered at her as she'd backed out and beckoned them into her space, but those extra minutes spent circling Sainsbury's car-park looking for another place to park had made her feel warm and fuzzy and worthy of the Maltesers she'd treated herself to after filling the car up with petrol on her way home.

She wasn't feeling warm and fuzzy now. Far from it.

And yet, she'd already been through it all with Jake. OK, so he was still engaged to Aurora – but not for much longer. He'd confided in Meg that he'd been pressured into the relationship by his family. Rory – as he called her out of habit – had been at school with Jacintha. He'd known her for years before they'd started going out together. It wasn't going to be easy to break up with her at any stage, but – and here he had reached out mournfully to Meg for comfort – what kind of a man would he be if he waited until *after* they were married?

He'd been so earnest, so desperate for affection . . . so gorgeous.

'Your eyes are glazed,' said Libby, waving a hand in front of Meg's face.

'I'm fine,' blinked Meg. 'Really.'

The tip Gwendolyn and Aurora left her was nearly three times more than the bill itself. They'd bickered over who was going to pay, and both ended up leaving cash on the table.

'Keep the lot,' Libby told Meg. 'You deserve it.'

On her way home that evening, Meg dropped into the beauty salon and settled her debt in full.

'I see you've opted for the just-got-out-of-bed look today,' sniffed Savannah.

Meg quickly pulled on her hat, to demonstrate why she was treating Victor's handiwork in such a cavalier fashion. 'It's nippy out there,' she winked. 'I don't want to end up with chilblains on my ears.'

Victor looked mollified. Savannah wanted to know where she'd got the fake leopardskin hat from. 'It would go really well with the new skirt I bought last Saturday . . .'

With a spring in her step, and having lent Savannah the hat for a few days, assuring her that chilblains were really the least of her worries, Meg popped into Chan's Newsagent's to buy a copy of the *Tockley Evening Gazette.* Aggie Widdicombe and her staunch ally Edith Sopwith were deep in conversation beside a revolving rack of greetings cards, fluffy pastel tea-cosies on their heads (cloche hats they called them), and handbags so bulky dangling from their elbows that a potential mugger would have to think twice before striking.

Both women lapsed into a stony silence when they saw Meg.

She smiled and nodded, but neither of them nodded back. A smile would have been too much to hope for. Meg couldn't remember having seen one of those on Aggie's lips since Jurassic times.

'Come along, Edith.' The old ladies bustled out of the shop, apparently without making any purchases, Aggie at the helm as usual.

Meg shrugged and sighed, counting out her coins to pay for the newspaper. She flashed Mr Chan her best smile. 'Can I owe you a penny?'

Certain he was about to say, 'Have it on me, sugar lips,' like he normally did when she ran short, she picked up the paper, only to have it whisked out of her fingers by Mrs Chan as the little lady swooped out from the back of the shop.

'We don't serve anyone on tick here!' she crackled, flaring her nostrils to drive the message home.

Meg blinked in surprise. Mrs Chan was normally so tolerant, especially when Meg made a point of admiring her window displays. 'But it's only—'

'All those "pennies" of yours mount up, missy! You've taken enough liberties over the years!'

Meg sympathised with Mr Chan as she made her exit, although he hadn't spoken up in her defence.

As for Aggie and Edith, they had been positively icy. The two old biddies could be unapproachable at the best of times, but Meg preferred it when her godmother at least spoke to her, even if it was just to hurl insults. When Aggie didn't snap that Meg's neckline was too revealing, or her dress too clingy, or her skirt too short, Meg worried about her.

Of course, if they had found out what she had been up to last night . . .

But Meg wasn't paranoid enough to imagine for more than just a moment that they *had* found out. Jake had been so careful; his plan had gone so smoothly.

As she trudged home, the spring having left her step, Meg decided she must have done something trivial to offend her godmother yet again. Or maybe it was all still to do with cutting her hair. If it was, then Meg knew that in a few days – or weeks, knowing Aggie – the fuss would have blown over. Yet she found herself trying to work out for the thousandth time how her mother could have been such good friends with someone as stodgy as Agnes Widdicombe.

By the time Meg opened her front door, her confused spirits were at a dangerous low. They nose-dived even further when she realised someone had turned up the central-heating to tropical greenhouse proportions. In summer, her family did nothing but moan and whine that they were too hot. In winter, they were only content when the thermostat was turned up high.

As she passed Pug's bedroom, doing her best

not to feel suicidal about the next gas bill, she spotted her sister curled up on the bed, reading.

'Do you fancy tuna bake tonight, Pug?'

'If you like.'

Meg tried to remember if she herself had spoken in code when she'd been a teenager. This particular sixteen-year-old was looking at her coolly over a paperback of *Lady Chatterley's Lover*.

'Is that on your syllabus?' asked Meg, trying not to bat an eyelid.

'No.'

'Can I read it when you've finished?'

'You're kidding, aren't you? It might give you ideas.'

Meg poked her tongue into her cheek and was about to retreat when Pug said, 'Before I forget, have you seen your remuneration for last night's performance yet? It's on the kitchen table. A standing ovation, I'd say.'

'What?'

'You'd better go look for yourself. I don't want to spoil the surprise.'

'Surprise? What kind of surprise?'

'If I told you it wouldn't *be* one, you divvy,' sighed Pug, rolling her eyes towards the ceiling, which needed a fresh coat of paint.

'Well sod you then!' Meg snapped, without meaning it, excitement getting the better of her as she pounded down the stairs and into the kitchen, skidding short of the table with a gasp.

'Oh my . . .'

Four

Meg cooked dinner in a daze, so it was hardly surprising that her dolphin-friendly tuna bake ended up being made with the tin of best quality red salmon she'd been saving for a special occasion. No one seemed to notice though, so Meg didn't bother drawing attention to her mistake. Although she was sitting next to Pug as usual, the girl was miles away. And with the aid of an old portable black and white television, her step-father and step-brother were cheerfully propping up the bar at the Queen Vic in Albert Square, seeing as Meg had failed to buy the local evening paper they sometimes enjoyed squabbling over.

She didn't mind having no one to talk to; she was perfectly content to push food around her plate and shuffle her thoughts into some semblance of order.

'Meg,' said William, when he'd stuffed his face and clearly couldn't manage any more, 'd'you want a hand with the dishes?'

For the first time she wondered what her step-brother was doing at home today. 'Why aren't you at uni?'

He clattered his plate into the sink and pointed to a scrap of torn paper flapping from the fridge door. 'My timetable,' he said, before slouching out of the room; economical with his words, as always. A minor miracle that he'd offered to help with the clearing up, but too much to hope that he'd stick around long enough for her to take him at his word.

Pug scraped back her chair. 'I've got home-work to do.' And she followed William out of the kitchen.

Meg looked at her step-father, expecting him to make a run for it too. But he didn't budge. As he'd already had a second helping of tuna (sal-mon) bake, and never ate thirds, Meg knew that something fishy – apart from the food – was up.

'Coffee?' she offered.

He shook his head.

'Tea?'

'Meg . . .' She was already on her feet when his hand shot out and coaxed her down again. 'We need to talk.'

'We do?' She adjusted the turtle neck of her dress, a gesture that was becoming something of a habit. 'What about?'

'Don't treat me like a fool, pet.'

Meg hadn't known her real father and had never felt disloyal calling Robert Heybridge Dad. He had been a part of her life for eighteen years; she couldn't imagine anyone else in his place.

'No one's ever sent you flowers like that before,' he said, nodding towards the dresser.

Meg looked at the vase spilling over with tiger-lilies and orchids. She had always been a sucker for flowers. In the past, though, if they hadn't been the cheapest the local florist could supply, then they'd come from garage forecourts, almost as if they had grown there in between the petrol pumps.

'So,' said Robert Heybridge, 'who is he this time?'

'Dad, I'm sorry, I can't say anything about it yet.'

'You were out all last night.'

'I'm a grown woman,' she reminded him. 'A consenting adult.'

'I have noticed, pet. It's just . . .' He shifted uncomfortably and jabbed a hand through his thinning hair. 'If Kathleen were here . . .'

Meg stood up and turned her back to him, running hot water into the sink and giving the Fairy Liquid bottle an over-generous squeeze. She rolled up her sleeves as suds billowed towards her elbows.

'I appreciate your concern,' she said at last,

rather stiffly, 'but I do know what I'm doing. I can take care of myself.'

'Yes, but who's going to take care of the rest of us?'

He was teasing, but Meg sensed an underlying fear. She took out her frustration on a fork, scrubbing strenuously between each prong.

'I'm not going anywhere just yet, Dad. And whatever happens, I won't leave you in the lurch, I promise.'

She had practically taken over the running of the household when her mother had left. But it wasn't gratitude or appreciation she was after now, just trust. Trust that she wasn't going to fail them too. Like mother, like daughter . . .

No! she thought fiercely, attacking an innocent teaspoon with a Brillo pad. I'm not like that! I'm not like her!

A hand crept on to her shoulder. She jumped, then relaxed.

'I'm sorry, Dad.'

'So am I. I shouldn't expect so much of you. You work hard enough as it is.'

'I don't mind.' She let the teaspoon go free. It landed on the draining board with a tinkle of relief.

'Are you going out tonight, pet?'

She nodded. 'I said I'd meet Thierry down the pub. Some of the others might be there too.'

He pushed her gently aside, rolling up his shirtsleeves. 'Let me finish the washing-up. You get going.'

Meg stared at him. He only normally offered to help at the preparation stage of any meal, knowing full well that she would consider him a hindrance unless there were spuds to be peeled.

Caught up in the touchy-feeliness of the moment, she kissed his cheek, catching a whiff of stale cigar smoke. A grandfatherly sort of smell, like the kind described in books. Sometimes she forgot that he was in his sixties already. She ruffled his grey hair – what was left of it – and grinned.

'Thanks, Dad, you're a poppet.'

'Oh, go on, get off with you!' He smiled sheepishly and picked up a sponge and a dirty plate, regarding them as if he wasn't sure what to do next.

Meg made her getaway, knowing that her stepfather was only buttering her up. His inability to cope with everyday life wasn't a problem, just as long as she was there to act as a buffer.

He was scared of losing her, and she was scared of letting him down.

The Spread Eagle public house was a fifteen-minute walk away when Meg was sober. When she wasn't, it could be anything from half an hour to an hour's meander to get back home again. Usually Thierry or one of her other friends meandered along with her, chatting in a desultory fashion about politics, religion, TV, the past, the present, or the progress of the local rowing team. The highlight of the sporting calendar in the Yarl Valley was Yarleigh Regatta, held every year in July. Hardly on the same scale as Henley, but a good enough reason to crack open the Asti.

Unfortunately, it wasn't July yet. It was only February, and the evening was so chilly Meg made it down to the Spread Eagle in nine minutes flat. Out of breath, and with lungs that felt as if they were full of ice cubes, she picked her way across the smoky room and slumped against the bar beside Thierry.

'That's the last time I jog anywhere,' she gasped.

'You look like a crab,' he said, smiling at her red cheeks.

'You mean a lobster.' She pulled off the woolly hat she'd been wearing and crammed it into her jacket pocket.

'*Sacre bleu!* Your hair!'

The pub fell silent. Even the juke-box seemed to freeze in shock.

With an impish grin, Meg tousled her flattened curls back to life.

'Stop doing goldfish impressions and buy me a

drink,' she ordered, prodding Thierry in the ribs. 'I'm skint.'

Two double brandies later, the ice cubes in Meg's lungs had melted and she was curled beside Thierry on a faded tapestry window seat. He was stroking her hair, with the excuse that he was trying to get used to it. Meg was too lulled and comfortable to protest.

'Anyone would think you two were still an item!' said Beatrice, bursting upon the scene. She whisked off her coat and scarf. 'I suppose you think this is a brilliant smoke-screen, Margaret Oakley?' Her hands on her hips, Beatrice arched an eyebrow at Thierry. 'And *you*, I thought you had more Gallic pride.'

'Only when it suits me,' he replied calmly.

Meg frowned at Beatrice. 'Smoke-screen? What are you on about?'

'I'm getting a vodka and Red Bull first, girl. You've got a head start and it's not fair!' Without offering to buy anyone else a drink – it would spoil her chances of catching up – she swept off to the bar.

Meg looked at Thierry. 'Whose round is it?'

'Mine.' He stood up. 'It's been my round all evening.'

'Sorry.' She stared into the bottom of her glass. Thierry worked as an odd-job man for the

Arundels, living in a three-roomed cottage on the edge of their estate. Like her, he wasn't made of money, but at least he only had himself to support.

'Do not worry,' he said, digging deep into his pocket.

'I know, I know, it's not good for my 'art.'

He went off to the bar. Meg nursed her empty glass and waited for her friends to return.

As soon as they did, Meg sat up straight. 'Bee, what did you mean when—'

'I've only got one thing to say to you,' said Beatrice, holding her chin up defiantly. 'Matthew Potter!'

Meg wrinkled her brow. 'That's two things.'

'Don't be so mulish.'

'Matthew Potter? What's he got to do with anything? I don't know what you're on about, Bee.'

'Play the innocent then. It doesn't wash with me, I know you too well. You probably saw him as a challenge, didn't you? But someone like Matthew deserves a lot more consideration.'

'What do you mean?'

'Oh, don't give me that. I may not have known about all this earlier today, but I know very well *now*.'

'Know *what*, for goodness' sake?'

'That you spent last night with Matthew Potter!'

Meg sprayed brandy back into her glass.

'Deny it then,' challenged Beatrice.

But Meg was too stunned to speak.

'You see! You can't!' Beatrice was adamant.

'Beatrice,' said Thierry, 'who is this man?'

'You don't know who he is?' She launched into a description that would have made a saint seem like a drug-pusher by comparison.

Thierry nodded. 'Mr Potter the teacher, *non?* His wife died last year—'

'A year ago today, actually,' said Meg, finding her voice again.

Beatrice's eyes grew wide. 'Do you realise how much worse that makes it?'

Meg was getting a fair idea. 'Look,' she began, gearing up to deny the absurd accusation. But then anything remotely intelligent that she had been about to utter catapulted straight out of her brain again.

Over Beatrice's shoulder, Meg had spotted Jake Arundel and Aurora Lloyd ordering drinks at the other end of the bar.

Jake's gaze met hers across the crowded room. Meg wanted to run into his arms. But just one witness would have been one too many, let alone a pubful. She had always kept her feelings for him to herself. Feelings which had started blossoming in adolescence really, at a time when a 'secret love' seemed the most wonderful thing in the world. Something to be cherished, not giggled over. Something that would lose its sacredness if she revealed it to anyone. Now, even though she wanted to yell about it from the rooftops (frustrating because she knew she couldn't), perhaps – perversely – there was still a small part of her that worried that the thrill and sheer wonder of it would vanish if people knew.

'So,' Beatrice was demanding, 'what are you planning to do about this mess then?'

'Mess?' croaked Meg.

'Matthew seems a really lovely guy. I don't think anyone would say otherwise, even if he does keep himself to himself. And I love you to bits, you know that. I just don't think you're right for each other. He needs someone—'

'Sane?' said Thierry.

'Someone who'll understand him,' Beatrice went on, 'who'll always be there. Someone—'

'Safe.' Thierry hit on the word he'd been after.

Beatrice nodded. 'Exactly! Someone nice, safe and dependable. You're nice, Meg, we all know that, but you're far too . . . *dizzy* for someone like him. He needs an anchor, not a boat without oars, or sails, or even a rudder . . .'

As Meg listened to herself being likened to little more than a very basic dinghy, an idea was stirring to life . . .

'And what about what *I* need?' she sniffed. 'You

haven't even stopped to look at it from my point of view, except to take it for granted that I'm always the one who ruins things, and that I'll do the same with Matthew. I don't mean to cock things up with men. I haven't had much luck, that's all.' For once, her tissue hadn't crawled out of reach up her sleeve, it was exactly where she'd left it. She blew her nose for effect.

'But—'

'I can't say anything more about it right now, Bee, I'm sorry. I don't even know how you found out about last night.'

'Agnes Widdicombe spotted you getting out of his car this morning.'

Of course. Meg should have guessed that it was something along those lines. It would explain what had happened in the newsagent's that afternoon.

'I found out from Mrs Chan,' continued Beatrice, 'when I popped in to buy— Oh, Meggy . . . Don't take it so hard, I'm sorry.'

'It's OK,' Meg muttered, feeling sick as Aurora snuggled up to Jake five tables away.

'I've been insensitive.' Beatrice bulldozed Thierry out of the way and sat on the window seat beside Meg. 'I just hope you know what you're getting into.'

Thierry had been silent for a while. Now he stared at them gravely. 'Will you see Marguerite home, Bee? I must go. I have an early start tomorrow.'

Beatrice nodded.

Meg mumbled goodbye. She felt even sicker. What *was* she getting herself into?

'Matthew Potter!' sighed Beatrice. 'Who would have thought it? It's a difficult position for him to be in. I just hope things work out the way you both expect.'

Meg already felt hungover, and it wasn't even morning yet. 'I think I'm going to go home myself. I don't feel too great.'

'Really? Sorry I was such a cow. I'll call us a cab, how about that?'

'Don't you want another drink?'

Beatrice shrugged. 'There's not much point now. Besides, I've got an early start tomorrow too. And Tom will be waiting up.' She smiled the smug smile of a newly-wed. 'He should have nearly finished the ironing I left him,' she added, going off to use the public pay-phone.

Meg glanced over at Jake again. He caught her eye and winked over Aurora's shoulder.

Meg looked away.

'We're in luck,' said Beatrice, on her return. 'There's a cab just dropping someone off down the road.'

As they headed for the door, Meg couldn't

resist one last glance. Jake was winding his way towards the bar. Edible in Aran and Levi's, he was well over six-foot and slender as a palm tree. But beneath that oh-so-casual apparel, Meg knew from first-hand experience that his muscles were strong and rippling from the frequent work-outs in his personal gym, which was apparently right next door to the sauna and the heated indoor swimming pool.

To Meg, Arundel Hall was a story-book palace with an irresistible mystique. Somewhere in its cavernous Victorian depths there was probably more than just one closed door with a missing key. Years ago, when Meg had been a knobbly-kneed kid with grubby cheeks and tangled hair, she had trespassed on to the Arundel Estate countless times with her equally knobbly-kneed playmates, each time as if it were a covert operation from those black and white war films they'd loved so much. Climbing the trees in the orchard and the spinney, they had spied on the individual dramas unfolding on the lawn behind the house with a passionate fascination.

When she considered it now, nothing much seemed to have changed. Except that I don't go around climbing trees any more, she thought with relief, tumbling gratefully into the cab which pulled up outside the pub. And I don't have knobbly—

She peered downwards, cursing under her breath.

'Meg Oakley,' frowned Beatrice, 'what the hell are you squashing your knees like that for?'

Five

'Georgie! Georgie, *let go.*' Matthew Potter, bent over the safety seat in the back of the car, grabbed at his glasses before his daughter could pull them off and snap them like the last pair. Her small hands gripped the metal frame with determined glee, and Matthew, who had been caught unawares as ever, gently tried to prise her fingers away. 'Georgie,' he grumbled, 'I'm warning you . . .'

Freddy looked on in silence, wondering why his dad always fell into the same trap.

It was tiredness and boredom rather than anything else that finally induced the toddler to let go. Matthew straightened up, narrowly escaping a bang to his head. 'Right, young lady . . .'

Georgie yawned and turned into a dead weight as her father lifted her free of the straps and the buckle. Her eyelids fluttered and closed. She proceeded to dose off against his shoulder, making his job even harder.

'Freddy,' Matthew held out the house keys, 'take these for me, will you?' Adding swiftly, so as not to be a hypocrite: 'Please.'

The boy was trailing his rucksack across the small patch of front lawn. 'Do I have to?'

'Frederick Potter—'

'OK.' Freddy complied, but made certain his father knew it was grudgingly.

'Right, what did I do with the car keys?' Matthew patted his trouser and jacket pockets with his free hand. Then he bobbed down and saw that they were still dangling from the ignition. His briefcase was in the boot, with his mid-week shopping; he'd have to come back for it all in a second. He left the children in the house – Freddy watching Children's BBC and Georgie asleep on the sofa. Returning to the car, he collected his case and four plastic bags, and was just nodding to an elderly neighbour, Edith Sopwith, when he heard the front door slam shut.

'Oh shit.'

He'd forgotten to put the latch on, and the house keys were lying on the hall table.

Edith Sopwith waited beside Matthew, nervously guarding his briefcase and watching him shout through the rusty letter-box.

'Freddy! Freddy, come and open the door for me, there's a good lad.'

'I don't think he can hear you, Mr Potter.'

'Of course he can. He's not deaf.'

'But the telly is on rather loud . . .'

And getting louder, if Matthew wasn't mistaken.

It was hanging around with hell-on-legs Timothy Arundel that was making Freddy such a rebel at times. Invariably the worst times, but Matthew could forgive his son for that. It was Timothy Arundel he was shouting at in his mind's eye; Timothy Arundel, who for some nightmarish reason had latched on to Freddy like a leech, even though they weren't even in the same class at school.

'I understand Timothy has been a little disruptive lately,' Edward Nugent, the headmaster of Yarleigh Primary, had said only this afternoon, broaching the subject with a diplomacy reserved for favoured pupils, or in Matthew's opinion, the children of favoured parents.

'That's putting it mildly.' Matthew couldn't stand the way everyone was so willing to bend over backwards to accommodate the Arundels. 'He ripped a wall display and threatened to eat the class pet alive. Just an average morning.'

'The gerbil . . . ?'

'I don't think it would be a good idea to let Timothy take Nibbles home at the weekend. I know it's his turn, but . . .'

Edward Nugent had been far more ruffled than usual, fidgeting with papers on his desk and waggling his jaw about as if his dentures were a poor fit. 'I like to think of myself as a man of the world, Matthew,' he had said suddenly. 'And far be it from me to interfere in your . . . private affairs—'

'Has Freddy been playing up?'

'I wasn't referring to your son.' For some strange reason, Edward Nugent had crimsoned right up to his receding hairline. 'I won't say anything more, except . . . it would be in everyone's best interests if you were discreet from now on. I know it's been a difficult couple of years for you, and it isn't my place to judge you out of school hours, but I do expect a certain level of behaviour from my staff . . .'

Edward was renowned for speaking in riddles, even in assembly. Matthew, tired and fed-up, hadn't attempted to wrap his mind around this latest conundrum.

'Something has to be done about Timothy,' he'd interrupted. 'We can't leave it for much longer, it's only getting worse.'

With a sigh, Edward Nugent had leaned back in his chair. 'Very well. As you seem to know best, in all matters, what do you propose to do about it?'

Matthew all too vividly recalled the last time he

had crossed swords with Jacintha Arundel. 'I think' – he had hesitated – 'I think that someone ought to talk to Miss Arundel again.'

'Well, why don't you make an appointment to see her?'

'Me? Wouldn't it be better coming from—'

'Timothy is in your class. It makes sense that you should be the one to speak with his mother.'

Matthew had run a finger around the inside of his collar. 'All right,' he had nodded, wishing he could just say, 'Not on your nelly.'

Now, shouting through his letter-box, he was aware of a familiar coldness seeping into his veins and marrow; a sensation that life wasn't worth the struggle, and that a man could only bang his head against a brick wall for so long.

Closing his eyes, he leaned against the door. A second later, he toppled oafishly into the hallway. Freddy was standing with his hand on the latch, calm, collected, and finishing off a packet of crisps.

'Didn't hear you,' he said.

'Really?' Grinding his teeth, Matthew gave his son the benefit of the doubt.

'Georgie's crying,' said Freddy. 'She rolled off the sofa and woke up.'

Matthew rushed into the lounge to find his daughter sitting on the floor with her face screwed up in a fit of angry, silent tears and her fists flailing wildly. It wasn't a long drop from the sofa, and the carpet had a deep pile which was lethal when it came to crumbs, but handy for cushioning little bones. At fourteen months old, though, Georgina Ann Potter was already a drama queen.

'I think she's hungry.' Matthew scooped her into his arms and tried to remember how Babe the piglet had managed to round up those sheep in the video Polly's parents had given Freddy for Christmas. Matthew needed that very technique now to negotiate Edith Sopwith out of his lounge, back into the hallway and through the front door. She was aiming for the kitchen when he stepped smartly into her path. Every room needed a thorough tidy-up, but the kitchen in particular resembled Armageddon.

'Thanks for your help, Mrs Sopwith. It was very kind of you.'

She looked disappointed. 'Isn't there anything else I can do? Pop something in the oven for your tea, or—'

'No! No, thanks again. I can manage. Honestly.'

Not without effort he couldn't spare and tact he thought he didn't have, he succeeded in steering her out of the house, closing the front door behind her with a shudder of relief.

'Can we have chicken nuggets for tea?' asked Freddy.

'We had chicken nuggets yesterday.'

'So what?'

So what exactly. Matthew was too drained to rustle up anything more imaginative. 'If you promise to eat all your veg, all right?'

'So long as it's not peas,' agreed Freddy.

Later that evening the boy showed his father his most recently acquired treasure. Georgie was fast asleep in the nursery, and Freddy, bathed and in his pyjamas, had come downstairs to curl up on the sofa beside his dad.

'Do you like it?' he asked, unclenching his fist and proudly showing off the small silver earring. 'I'm going to put it in the treasure chest Granny gave me.'

Matthew picked up the silver knot. There was no butterfly attached. 'Where did you find it?' he asked.

'In the front of the car.'

'Our car?'

Freddy nodded. 'This morning. Can I have it back?'

Matthew frowned. 'I'm sorry, Freddy, but do you remember we gave that lady a lift yesterday?'

'You borrowed her your coat.'

'I lent her my coat, yes. Well, I remember she wore earrings just like this one.'

'So did she lose this?'

Matthew nodded. 'She must have.' He prayed that his son wouldn't start going on about finders being keepers.

'Will I get a reward?'

'Sometimes you have to do something because it's the right thing to do, not just because you expect a reward.'

'Do I have to give it back to her then?'

'I can give it back for you, if you like.'

'But that means *you'll* get the reward.'

'Somehow, I don't think there'll be one. But I promise, if there is, I won't keep it all to myself.'

'Sometimes,' pouted Freddy, 'you're as bad as Mr Nugent.'

Matthew tossed the earring in the general direction of the coffee table. 'Right, you're in for it now, laddie!'

Freddy giggled hysterically as his dad tackled him to the floor.

There was a new boy in town.

Or rather, he was about twenty. Which made him a man, thought Pug Heybridge dreamily, studying his square jaw and the mop of streaked blond hair from her vantage point one table back in the creative writing class. And strictly speaking, if you wanted to be pedantic, Yarleigh wasn't a town.

Perched on the edge of the large desk at the

front of the classroom, Matthew Potter had introduced the stranger as – he had hesitated, glancing down at the name in front of him as if he didn't believe what he was reading – Giles Augustine. An aspiring poet.

Everyone had sat up more attentively, if that were possible. Except for Pug, who had leaned her chin in her cupped hands and decided that Augustine was a heaven-sent name for a poet, even better than Shelley or Keats or Byron, although Wordsworth still had a lot going for it.

The class was drawing to a close now, and Matthew was setting a new project. Something to do with antagonists. 'And I'd like you to get as far away from the stereotypes as possible.'

'So no moustache-twirling arch-villains?' piped up Mr Christie, who went around telling everyone he was related to Agatha.

'Definitely not,' said Matthew, wiping the board clean.

'No Mafia Dons?'

'Or Cruella de Vil types?'

Matthew shook his head. 'Something mind-blowingly original, please.'

A toughie, thought Pug, who embraced a challenging assignment with a passion bordering on the obsessive.

The school caretaker was looming in the corridor, dangling his mammoth set of keys. Poets, playwrights and storytellers slipped back into their everyday guises: the butcher, the baker, the woman who owned the little candle shop at the northern end of the High Street.

Pug was just slipping her notebook into her bag when a voice close to her ear made her jump. 'Hello.'

She tilted her head, only to be confronted with the collar of a denim shirt casually poking out of the V-neck of a cricket jumper. She tilted her head back further and swallowed at the sight of the square jaw and a smile crammed with teeth that were reassuringly crooked but sparkling white.

'Oh,' she said faintly, 'hello.'

'You're Elizabeth, aren't you?' He held out his hand.

'Yes. Well, no. I'm only Elizabeth in class.'

The smile widened, the teeth dazzled. 'Who are you out of class then?'

It wasn't the first time she'd wished she could say something like Lizzy, or Beth, or even Betsy.

'Pug,' she muttered. 'Everyone calls me Pug.'

'Pug?' The vision of manhood wrinkled his brow. 'What's the story behind that one?'

Shrugging, she said, 'Virtually everyone's called me that for as long as I can remember.'

'Maybe you had a squashed nose when you were born?'

Pug hesitated, certain that her nose was still squashed but finding nothing unkind in Giles Augustine's tone, or even in his eyes, which were the colour of flint but ten times softer. 'Maybe,' she mumbled, looking down and zipping up her bag.

'Well, it's great to meet you, whatever you're called. I'm Giles – in and out of class. My family moved to Yarleigh last week. We used to live near Cambridge.' He shrugged. 'You know what it's like, it can be a real drag making friends in a new place. I used to go to a creative writing class back home – my old home – so I thought I'd give this one a go.' He lowered his voice. 'Thought there'd be more people our age here, though.'

So that was why he was talking to her; there was no one else in the class under twenty-five. Pug swung her bag on to her shoulder and looked at her watch. 'You'll have to excuse me,' she said. 'I've got to—'

'Elizabeth, sorry to interrupt.' It was Matthew. 'Could you give this to your sister for me?' He took a silver earring from his inside jacket pocket and handed it across.

Pug blinked down into the palm of her hand, recognising the earring as Meg's, yet totally baffled as to what Matthew Potter was doing with it.

'Tell her I had a quick look for the butterfly but I couldn't find it.'

Pug looked up at him. 'I don't understand . . .'

'Sorry, I've got to hurry. I said to the babysitter I'd be home by ten.' And gathering up his brief-case, he dashed from the room.

Pug stared at the earring. Giles stared at Pug. 'Something wrong?'

She shook her head. 'I don't know.'

The caretaker was looming closer now, jangling his keys pointedly.

Giles touched Pug's sleeve. 'Listen, Elizabeth – Pug – can I give you a lift anywhere?'

She looked up, forgetting that she was supposed to be annoyed with him. 'You've got a car?'

'I nick my dad's whenever I need to,' he smiled.

'I normally just walk if Meg can't pick me up.'

They were trudging along the echoing corridor now, towards the main exit.

'Meg?'

'My sister. Well, she's my half-sister really.'

'I can give you a lift, it's no trouble . . .' He tailed off. 'On the other hand, you've only just met me. I'd understand if you said no.'

They stood outside beneath a glaring white spotlight. There was only one vehicle in the car-park, a Peugeot, but just at that moment a Mini came trundling noisily through the open gates. In daylight it would have been a bright tomato-red, but at night – even under a garish security beam – the paint-work was mercifully easier on the eyes.

Meg wound the window down as the small car crunched to an abrupt halt beside Pug and Giles. 'Hiya! Who's this?' She looked at Giles with undisguised interest.

He shook her hand and introduced himself.

'Well,' Meg twinkled up at him flirtatiously, 'any friend of Pug's is a friend of mine. Do you want a lift home or . . . ?'

Giles explained the situation. Pug was circling the car to the passenger side when he called out to her, 'Before you shoot off . . . would you fancy going to see a film in Tockley this weekend?'

She ducked behind the car, picking up her bag, which she'd dropped in shock. 'Er . . .'

'I'm sorry.' Giles hugged his folder and note-book to his chest. 'If you've got a boyfriend—'

'She hasn't,' said Meg.

But Pug had recalled the real reason behind Giles's friendly overtures. 'I'm busy,' she fibbed, climbing into the car and slamming the door.

Giles bent down, looking in through the open window. 'Look, don't worry about it. See you next Thursday then?'

'If you don't have anything better to do,' mumbled Pug under her breath, giving him an affected little wave.

Meg began executing a three-point turn. 'That guy is one seriously—'

'Meg Oakley, shut up!'

'Don't you think he's cute?'

'Of course I do. I'm just not a nymphomaniac like you.'

The Mini slowed down and then speeded up again. Pug knew she ought to apologise, but she felt too miserable to bother.

The sisters didn't speak until they were back home. Meg was pouring Baileys into a mug of coffee, her face pale and drawn in the fluorescent light of the kitchen. On sunny mornings this was the best room in the house. Facing east, it showed off its sunflower-yellow walls and cornflower-blue cupboards as if it was modelling for a DIY magazine. Tonight, though, it just seemed cold and annoyingly bright.

Pug let the earring drop on to the work-surface.

Meg suddenly perked up. 'That's mine – you found it!'

'Not exactly. Matthew Potter had it, for some odd reason.'

Meg didn't reply. She just frowned.

'Well?'

'This isn't as bad as it seems, Pug . . .'

'Oh really? He said to tell you he'd looked for the butterfly, but he couldn't find it. Where exactly would he have conducted the search, do you reckon? In his bathroom? Under his pillow?'

Meg was guzzling the contents of her mug as if there was no tomorrow.

Pug shook her head. 'Do you have any idea what you're doing this time?'

'Frankly, it's no one's business except mine and his,' said Meg, after a pause. 'I've never felt this way before, and I don't know where it's leading. But I refuse to be treated like a criminal.' She tossed her head and puckered her lips into an offended rosebud. 'You'd think I was a corrupting influence or something!'

Pug almost choked on the irony of it all. 'Go look at yourself in a mirror and say that,' she huffed, stomping out of the kitchen and making as much noise as possible on her way upstairs.

Meg stared warily at the ceiling and waited for silence to fall. When at last it did, she put her mug in the sink and went out into the hall. Her stepfather would probably be in bed with his Walkman, listening to Glenn Miller, or Ella Fitzgerald, or the Rolling Stones if he was feeling daring and in need of being a moody youth again. As for William – the genuine moody youth of the family – he'd gone back up to university, taking half the contents of the fridge with him.

Kneeling on the floor beside the hall table, one ear trained for the creak of the top stair, Meg flicked through the local telephone directory to the 'P's.

There were eight Potters listed, sandwiched between the Poskitts and the Pottingers. Only one M. A. Potter living in Yarleigh, though. Twelve, Peachtree Crescent – which rang a small bell of recognition.

Her mind racing at full throttle, Meg sat back on her haunches and slapped the directory shut.

Six

The night was as high as the stars and as cold as Siberia. Meg, naked and curled in a foetal position beneath the duvet, blinked out through the curtainless window at the moon. It was large and low, veined by the criss-crossed branches of winter trees. She shivered, and felt vulnerable again, as if it was only here in this cottage in the middle of the woods that she could begin to understand how mind-bogglingly huge the universe was.

Jake had ruffled her hair when she'd tried to explain. 'I need the lav,' he'd said, dashing her hopes of profundity as he'd slipped into his jeans and shoes and pulled a Ralph Lauren sweater over his head. 'Keep the bed warm for me.' He'd grinned and tucked the duvet under her chin.

Now, Meg turned drowsily away from the window and watched Jake's return. He tore off his clothes and dived to join her beneath the lumpy quilt. 'Didn't even need the oil-lamp or the torch,' he whispered, his breath hot in her ear.

'The moonlight's amazing tonight . . .' He kissed her neck and sent his hands, erotically glacial at first, on a walkabout of her body. 'You're not tired, sweetheart? You don't want to go to sleep yet?'

She desperately wanted to say, 'I am' and 'I do', but even though this was only the second time they'd spent the night together, she knew that he would only shrug and turn his back on her, sulky and petulant and hungry, as if he hadn't eaten for hours.

'*You* may not have to work as hard on Saturdays,' she said, hoping he'd take the hint.

'No rest for the wicked,' he grinned.

'Oi! What are you implying?' She tried to clobber him, but he fought her off, pinning her beneath him.

'So what *do* you have planned for the weekend, Cinders? Think you can slip away here on the Sabbath for dessert after you've cleared away the roast? Forget about Yorkshire puds though, you've got those built in.' He made a grab for her breasts, but she wriggled away.

'Jake, you're awful! I can't come here on Sunday. I've got business elsewhere.'

'Oh?'

Earlier that evening Meg had told him about the assumptions people were jumping to about her mystery lover. 'I actually feel a bit sorry for Matthew

Potter,' she had been swift to add, because she'd wished Jake could have shown the teensiest trace of jealousy rather than just laughing, even though there was nothing to be jealous about.

Now, she detailed how she was planning to go round to Matthew's house on Sunday with a home-made shepherd's pie – to thank him in person for the return of her earring.

'Priceless!' Jake laughed again. 'Make sure people see you going in and out.' He trailed a hand teasingly down Meg's thigh, switching to Casanova mode. 'In the meantime, sweetheart, you still haven't thanked me properly for the flowers I sent . . .'

In Meg's estimation she had thanked him more than enough, but men seemed to work on a different value system to women.

'How do I know it was you who sent them?' she asked playfully, stalling for time, even though his hand wasn't. 'After all, they were . . . Oh!' She closed her eyes and arched involuntarily, her body severing all ties to her mind, which was telling her she needed to get some sleep.

'You're so bloody beautiful,' gasped Jake.

His breath thundered in her ear as he took the lead as consummately as the last time.

By the time Meg woke in the morning, the sun had replaced the moon and a hurriedly scrawled note on the pillow beside hers had replaced Jake's head.

Sorry, had to rush. See you next Friday, maybe sooner. I'll be in touch. Good luck with the 'smoke-screen'.

X.X.

Meg leaned over the side of the bed and retrieved her clothes from the floor, writhing into them beneath the duvet. The trouble with using the old Gamekeeper's Lodge on the Arundel estate as a love nest was the lack of running water, gas, electricity and an inside loo. Why couldn't it be summer already? She glanced at the empty bottle of Krug in the ice bucket on the flagstone floor; no need for ice, even if they had a freezer. The romance of the past – including an old iron bedstead and authentic oak beams – was all very well; a power-shower and central-heating would have been handier.

All right, she conceded, so the two-roomed cottage had more elbow and knee room than Jake's car. And, admittedly, it was more discreet than a hotel. It was unlikely anyone would stumble upon them here in the middle of the night. When Jake picked her up at the quieter end of Chaffinch Lane, near the river, he would take the longer route to Yarleigh Woods. It was a more roundabout way, but a whole lot safer than driving down the High Street.

Unfortunately, unless they could bring themselves to struggle up while it was still dark, Jake couldn't give her a lift back. Which meant that she had to use the footpath which brought her out by St Dominic's Parish Church. It was too much to hope that Matthew Potter would be there again to give her a lift back to the village, even if his driving *was* white-knuckle edge-of-the-seat stuff.

Of course, Margaret, she told herself, now that you're sure you know the way off by heart, you can bring your own car next time and meet Jake here. That was a more logical solution. But, for today, she would have to make do with the methods of transport at her disposal – her feet, and then a bus.

There had never been a reported rape in Yarleigh, not in living memory; and only one flasher, who, according to the story, had had nothing worth flashing. Still, Meg wished she was in possession of a handy Doberman, just in case. But as that wasn't feasible, she'd have to make do with the few disabling manoeuvres she'd picked up at self defence classes. (Or rather, class. She had only ever gone the one time, bullied into it by Beatrice.)

Outside the cottage, high in the trees, the birds that dared to risk a grim British winter were chirping merrily away as if they knew it was the weekend and that spring wasn't far off.

'Some of us still have to work,' Meg confided in them, her voice reverberating eerily. She glanced at her watch. Plenty of time. She didn't have to be at Best Bib and Tucker until twelve, to help with the lunchtime rush.

By the time she emerged at the edge of the woods by the churchyard, she was no longer on Arundel land but on church property. The marble gravestones glittered ominously in the watery light. Meg shivered. Walking fast with a deafening crunch, crunch, crunch, in the boots she'd wisely brought with her this time, she made for the busstop in front of the church. Suddenly she stopped, in the very spot where Matthew and his son had been standing the other morning. She looked down, recalling her gaffe and biting her lip at the sight of the withered roses.

'Listen,' she frowned at the gravestone, 'I made a prat of myself the other day and I'm sorry. Really I am. But that's why I'm going to make up for it.'

Polly's name, chiselled so neatly into the marble, seemed to arch a cynical eyebrow at her.

'It's true!' Meg defended herself. 'I'm not just doing it for me. I want to apologise to Matthew and thank him. You were a lucky woman to have a man like that,' she said, while thinking in truth:

poor you. 'I know we never got on when we were at school together, Pollyanna, but you made more of a success of your life when you were alive than I'm making of mine.'

The marble seemed to soften – but only a fraction.

'Oh, fine!' said Meg. 'You win! I can do better than shepherd's pie. People are always telling me I make a mean stroganoff.'

With a determined toss of the head, she crunched off towards the bus-stop.

Sighing, Matthew pushed aside the Sunday newspapers and supplements and took off his glasses. He rubbed his eyes and wondered what he ought to do first: make a dent in all that marking piled on his desk, or ransack the freezer in the vain hope of finding something interesting for lunch.

He was saved from making a decision by the doorbell. It was just about audible above the racket of Pinocchio telling another outrageous whopper.

'Freddy,' said Matthew, 'could you turn that down, please?'

The boy snatched the TV remote control away from his sister and lowered the volume the tiniest fraction of a decibel. Georgie screamed. Matthew wanted to join in. He rammed on his glasses and went to answer the door instead.

'Hiya!' grinned the young woman jiggling about on the doorstep, a large saucepan cradled in one arm and a Sainsbury's bag with a bottle of wine poking out in the other. 'Hope I'm not interrupting anything?'

'Er . . .' Matthew scratched his head. 'Miss Oakley . . .'

She glanced quickly over her shoulder, then turned back to him and leaned closer. 'Meg, remember? Miss Oakley sounds so formal, and we're past that stage now.'

'We are?'

'Aren't you going to ask me in? It's bloody freez—'

Freddy appeared. 'Hello again. Have you brought me my reward?'

It was Meg's turn to look confused. 'Reward?'

'For finding your earring in the car. Daddy said there might be a reward.'

Matthew's eyebrows rocketed upwards. Freddy should seriously consider joining the legal profession when he grew up; he had the genes for it.

'I never said—'

'I have brought a reward as a matter of fact,' smiled Meg, stepping into the hall.

Matthew had no choice but to close the door behind her, nodding a cursory greeting at Mrs Sopwith, who was replenishing the seeds on her bird table.

Meg was already picking her way across the sea of primary-coloured toys littering the lounge. Georgie had stopped screaming and was looking on in curiosity.

'I suppose your kitchen must be this way,' said Meg, arriving at her destination before Matthew could stop her.

She jerked to a halt in the doorway.

'I've been meaning to clear up.' Matthew sidled past her and retrieved a stained tea-towel from the floor. The room was largish and square, with the fitted pine units Polly had chosen. Of course, she would never have let it get into this state, the pale work-surfaces stained beyond hope (he'd told her they should have opted for dark) and the filthy lino crunchy beneath Matthew's old brown socks, through which his toes were beginning to show. Suddenly, it all seemed worse than ever. He stared down at his porridge-splattered jumper and jeans and had to screw the tea-towel into a tight ball to stop himself lashing out and breaking something which until then had managed to remain miraculously in one piece.

Meg recovered and headed for the hob, which she guessed might be ceramic. Depositing her load on a spare section of work-surface, she moved aside plates and saucepan lids from beside a row of grimy knobs and saw that her guess had been correct.

'You shouldn't leave things lying on top, you know,' she scolded, relieved to see that at least it was switched off at the mains. 'You haven't made anything for lunch yet, have you? Because you can always leave what I've brought for tomorrow. It'll keep. On the other hand—'

'Miss Oakley,' began Matthew, but she shot him an aggrieved look. 'Meg,' he surrendered, looming over her as she fought off the plastic bag clinging to the wine bottle. 'I don't understand what all this is in aid of.'

'I wanted to say thank you for returning my earring. Where's your fridge?' She glanced around and spotted it. The top door was virtually obscured by novelty magnets; the entire alphabet set out in higgledy-piggledy rows, and numbers one to ten vying for space beside shopping lists and postcards and . . .

The wine almost slipped from Meg's fingers. A pretty blonde in her early twenties beamed at her from a Polaroid snapshot, green eyes sparkling, long straight hair tossed by an unseen breeze. Looking protectively down at the girl from his great height was a young man who obviously worshipped the ground she trod on, his lips stretched into a grin: broad and genuine and startlingly handsome.

He *could* smile, thought Meg, and he did it so well, too.

Although the wine was already chilled, she tentatively opened the fridge and popped it inside, relieved when the iffy smells she'd been afraid might assault her nostrils failed to materialise. 'Oh, look! You've got lettuce and a tomato. I can make a salad.' She held up a single lettuce leaf and a cherry tomato.

Matthew was chewing on his lip as if that was all he'd been planning to eat today. 'Like the feeding of the five thousand,' he muttered, grabbing his son as Freddy tried to peer into the Sainsbury's carrier bag.

'Where's my reward?' demanded Freddy.

'Well, let's have a look, shall we?' Meg came back around the table and dug her hand into the plastic bag. 'Ooh, what have I got here?' She pulled out a box of chocolates just as Georgie toddled into the kitchen.

'*She*'s not having any!' yelled Freddy, making a grab for them. 'They're mine!'

Matthew saved Meg from being crushed against the oven and grill. He swung Georgie on to his hip and hauled his son into the lounge. 'Now, laddie, sit here and watch your video, and if I hear so much as a peep . . .' He returned to the kitchen, still holding Georgie, who had rammed her fist into her mouth and was making loud slurping noises.

'I'm sorry about that,' he said, looking as if he

wanted to retreat into a shadowy corner and fall apart quietly, without any fuss.

'No, it's me who should be sorry,' said Meg quickly. 'You were so kind giving me a lift the other day, and I rabbited on like a complete numskull. If I upset you . . .'

Matthew shook his head. 'We both said things we shouldn't have.' Depositing Georgie in her high-chair, he stared gloomily at a stack of bills on the kitchen table.

'Maybe I ought to get going,' Meg muttered. 'When you're ready you can heat up the stroganoff slowly on a mediumish heat. It's not too spicy. I made it milder because of the kids—'

'Stroganoff?' Matthew twitched back to consciousness.

'Er, yes, you know, it's a Russian dish. There's some soured cream in the Sainsbury's bag – add that at the end and—'

'I used to joke that the height of Polly's culinary expertise was bangers and mash.'

There was silence for a moment, then they both spoke at the same time.

'I really ought to leave—'

'After the trouble you've gone to—'

Matthew's words hung in the air. He was obliged to finish the sentence. 'Why don't you stay and eat with us?'

It was the invitation Meg had been angling for.

'That's very kind of you . . .' She eyed him sceptically as he fished out a corkscrew from beneath a mountain of old newspapers.

'The thing I can't stand is pity,' he said, fetching the wine from the fridge. 'When Polly was in hospital, and then after she . . . There seemed no end to the people coming round here with hotpots and shepherd's pies.' He snorted sardonically, wrenching out the cork. 'I know this probably sounds odd, but I couldn't cope with all that sympathy. What I really wanted, what I needed, was someone to act out of pure unadulterated guilt. But there was only one person who was guilty then.' Matthew poured out the wine. 'And I always will be.' He advanced on Meg with a full glass. 'You don't know what a change it is to find I'm not the only one feeling like such a—'

Freddy poked his head around the door. 'Daddy, I'm *starving*.'

Matthew smiled, but Meg noticed that it never went further than his lips. 'We'll be eating soon. Go finish your video.'

Meg had already demolished half her glass of Chardonnay. Matthew's eyes were glittering with that strange feverishness that mad people's eyes were reputed to glitter with, the words coming out of his mouth in a stiff, bitter way. He topped up her glass. She immediately threw most of it down her throat to join the rest.

'People are always so kind,' he said, knocking back his own wine in a similar fashion. 'And I know I should be grateful, I know it's only right. But when you're angry, nothing makes sense except your anger.'

Meg blinked down at a tiny piece of cork floating in her glass.

'You came here because you felt bad about the other day,' Matthew went on. 'The earring was as good an excuse as any. You felt guilty, and you wanted to make up for it. Oddly enough, I can respect you for that.'

I can't, thought Meg. If he knew the truth, Matthew Potter would send her packing. She might as well do the job for him.

'Thanks for the wine.' She finished it off and slammed down her glass, forgetting she'd brought him the bottle of South American Chardonnay in the first place and that she ought to have brought something red to go with the meal, like a claret, or that Valpoli-Italian-stuff. 'I've actually got to be off. I'm supposed to be somewhere else,' she lied.

Why, oh why, hadn't she taken Jake up on his suggestion that they get together today? Was it too late to ring him on his mobile? Would Aurora—? Meg stalled herself in mid-thought. Jake would only be annoyed with her for botching things up.

'Bugger,' she whispered, 'why do I have to complicate everything?'

Matthew looked up from investigating the contents of the saucepan.

Meg manhandled him out of the way and rolled up her sleeves. She had to go through with this whether she liked it or not. 'Leave this to me. If you want to clear some space on that table, you might find room for cutlery and place mats.'

He stood staring at her. She busied herself with turning on the extractor-fan. 'I normally have creamed spuds with stroganoff, but if you'd prefer rice or pasta . . .'

'There's instant mash in the cupboard by your head. I thought you had to be somewhere else?'

'There's no hurry. It can wait. Besides,' she looked over her shoulder and smiled tersely, 'it's just struck me that I haven't worked off all my guilt yet. There's a bit left. Right here, in fact.' She waggled her little finger. 'See? Guilty as sin. I'm even going to go as far as to do the washing-up later.'

'Would your remorse stretch to ironing a few shirts?' he joshed.

'Pour me some more wine and I'll think about it,' she quipped back, casting a surreptitious frown at the demon toddler as Georgie started banging a plastic spoon like a gavel on her high-chair tray. But Matthew had left the room. There was no need to be surreptitious.

'Don't you dare start judging me as well!' she whispered to the child, conscious of Polly Potter's eyes boring into her from the fridge door. 'It's bad enough with your mother—'

Matthew came back into the kitchen with a set of smart place mats that looked as if they'd hardly been used.

Meg nodded. 'Won't be long now.'

True to her word, within ten minutes they were sitting around the pine table, Matthew shovelling morsels of meat and potato into his daughter's mouth, in between cramming larger pieces into his own. As if he hadn't eaten for days, thought Meg, who'd distanced herself as much as possible from the high-chair, suspecting the only angora jumper she possessed might end up looking like a table cloth in an Indian restaurant. She should have worn something old and tatty, along the same lines as the gear Matthew had on. Never mind. She would know better next time; because, of course, there would have to be a next time. There was no dodging the fact, not if she wanted to divert attention away from her relationship with Jake.

When it was time to put the kettle on for coffee, Meg opened the chocolates. Freddy plunged straight in.

Meg smiled feebly. 'Maybe it wasn't such a good idea.'

'I wouldn't say that.' Matthew elbowed Freddy out of the way. 'Oh no you don't, that's *my* toffee crunch.' The boy giggled and elbowed him back, grabbing the Turkish delight instead. Matthew looked at Meg. 'Aren't you having any?'

'I can't. I've given them up for Lent. It would be awful if I caved in after just a few days.'

'Are you a Catholic? I mean, I know you went to St Dom's, but you don't have to be Catholic to go there.'

'Well I am. Baptised and everything.'

'I wouldn't have put you down as a practising one though.' The toffee crunch made a mound out of Matthew's right cheek. Meg stared at it, but quashed the temptation to make her own mound with a hazelnut whirl.

'There are one or two habits from childhood I just can't break,' she explained. 'Lent's one of them.' Her mother's doing.

'I always thought women and chocolates were inseparable.' He twitched an eyebrow, then sighed. 'Maybe that was just Polly . . .'

Meg jumped up. 'I'll make the coffee, shall I?'

Once the kids had been wiped clean, they scuttled off into the lounge to wreck a few toys. Meg and Matthew sat studying each other, while pretending not to, over two mugs of instant decaff.

'I suppose this is what's known as a truce,' he said. 'Or maybe it's a stalemate.'

Meg preferred the sound of the former. 'I hate falling out with people, even those I don't know very well.' And by now she had realised that she hardly knew anything about this man. What would happen if he found out what people had been saying since last Tuesday? reflected Meg, who had so far unwisely ignored the possibility that he might.

'Polly used to talk about you quite a bit, you know,' he said. 'Apparently you were the bane of St Dominic's Convent Grammar School for well-behaved young ladies.'

Charming, thought Meg. 'Glad to hear she painted me in a good light.'

Sarcasm wasn't lost on him. 'Sorry, that was harsh. It's just that Polly used to describe you as the kind of girl who would have scared the living daylights out of me . . .' He tailed off awkwardly.

Meg sighed. 'I wasn't the nicest person when I was at school,' she admitted, frowning at the knowledge that she was no better now. 'But, you see, my side of it is that girls like Polly always scared the living daylights out of *me*. They were the form prefects, the boffins, always so well organised, every teacher's pet. I was just . . .'

She frowned harder, standing up and heading for the sink. 'Have you finished with your mug?'

'Daddy!' wailed Freddy from the lounge. 'Georgie bit me!'

Meg pulled a face and started running the hot water. 'Go and play referee. I promised I'd do the washing-up.' But when she looked round, Matthew had already left.

Having so much practice, Meg whipped through the dirty dishes in what seemed like seconds, which gave her enough time to wipe down the table, flick a few crumbs away from around the toaster, clean the hob and still feel as if she hadn't been overworking herself. There was lots more she was itching to tackle, but she didn't want to go too far on this first visit and dent Matthew's pride.

Breezing out into the lounge, she stopped short. The children were sprawled on the floor in front of the TV, apparently hypnotised by Mary Poppins, like generations before them. Matthew, however, was slumped in an armchair, his head to one side, mouth slightly open, his eyes shut. So this was why Meg hadn't heard anything out of him while she'd been busy on her own in the kitchen. From the moment she'd arrived today, she'd noticed how exhausted he looked, and after all that food and wine she couldn't blame him for dosing off. He had probably only intended to sit down for a few minutes.

She edged nearer. His glasses were sliding down his nose. Should she take them off? As she drew close enough to attempt it, he stirred and shifted. Meg leapt back as his feet swung round.

'Like that, is it?' she muttered softly, perching on the sofa. 'The kind of bloke who kicks a woman in his sleep!' But he looked so peaceful, so innocent, she could forgive him without any effort.

Freddy twisted his head round and grinned at her. Meg grinned back. He climbed on to the sofa, getting comfy beside her. Spontaneously, she put her arm around him. Then Georgie looked round too, showing six tiny front teeth in a smile that could almost be called cute. Seconds later, she'd clambered on to the sofa herself, sticking her head in Meg's lap and her bum in the air.

Meg hardly dared breathe, let alone move. This wasn't her idea of an idyllic Sunday afternoon, but sacrifices had to be made.

I'm still not sure I like you, baby, she thought, staring warily down at Georgie.

A dubious smell wafted upwards.

Now I'm certain I don't! scowled Meg, wondering where Matthew kept the nappies.

Seven

The lounge was in darkness by the time Matthew woke up. Groggy and disorientated, he pushed his glasses up from their precarious position on the tip of his nose and heaved himself to his feet. The TV was off, but there were sounds coming from upstairs. He followed the laughter all the way to the nursery door. It was ajar, and he could just make out Meg Oakley on all fours with Georgie on her back and Freddy holding his sister steady so that she didn't topple off.

'Daddy!'

The boy spotted his father first and let go of Georgie in order to wave. A startled Meg turned too sharply in mid 'Eeyore'. Georgie lost her balance and tumbled off Meg's back. Matthew was by his daughter's side in two quick strides, sweeping her into his arms and checking her head for bumps or cuts.

'Is she OK?' Meg looked mortified. She climbed stiffly to her feet, tugging her skirt down.

It was a mercy those black tights were opaque, thought Matthew, trying to avert his eyes but finding they refused to respond.

'I'm so sorry,' Meg was saying, 'I thought Freddy was holding her steady . . .'

Matthew, who always woke up in a foul mood, knitted his brow and finally managed to peel his gaze away from Meg Oakley's legs. He concentrated on checking Georgie over again, but it didn't look as if there was anything wrong; her eyes were focusing properly and she'd stopped crying after squeezing two lustrous fat tears out, one for each cheek.

'Is that the time?' He glanced at the Jack and Jill nursery clock. 'You should have woken me up.' He turned accusingly to Meg, who was taking refuge on the other side of the rocking horse.

'I'm sorry,' she muttered. 'But you looked as if you needed that nap.'

'Nap? I've been asleep for over two hours! I've got a stack of paperwork to get through.'

'Haven't you got half-term—'

'I hate falling behind schedule.'

'Oh. I'll get out of your way then.' Meekly, she inched sideways. 'Unless you want me to carry on playing with the children while you—'

'No!' he said, too quickly.

She bombed out of the door and down the stairs without appearing to care if she tripped and broke her neck. Freddy was hot on her heels.

Still holding Georgie, Matthew took his own descent more cautiously. 'Miss Oakley – Meg—'

Freddy pulled at her arm imploringly. 'Don't go! I haven't shown you my T-Rex yet.'

'Another time, kiddo.' She flicked her gaze towards Matthew, as if to insinuate that she'd had enough of large reptiles for one day. Freddy pouted. Meg stroked his hair, pressing down on the cowlick.

In spite of the fact that she'd just called his son 'kiddo' again, it was Matthew's turn to be sorry. Jumping down her throat was no way to repay her for the meal, the chocolates and wine, and most of all the grown-up conversation. Lately, Matthew had begun to feel as if he spent ninety per cent of his waking hours talking to under-tens, and although he thought children remarkable and fascinating creatures, there was a point when his mind screamed out for something on his own level. This young woman with the unfortunate dress sense wasn't as giddy as he'd initially assumed, but right at that moment he was simply grateful that she was an adult. An adult from his own generation – suddenly the most important factor.

'I overreacted just now,' he began. 'I ought to be thanking you . . .'

Meg shrugged. She seemed glued to the welcome mat.

'Georgie's always falling off things,' put in Freddy. 'It wasn't Meggy's fault. At least she was playing with us. Sarah-Jane never plays. She just watches TV or reads magazines.' Freddy's eyes grew bright. 'Why doesn't Meggy babysit for us on a Thursday instead of Sarah-Jane? I like her better, and she's—'

'Probably far too busy,' said Matthew firmly.

But Meg seemed as animated as his son all of a sudden. 'I'd love to babysit for you,' she said.

Matthew was taken aback by her alacrity. 'It wouldn't be worth your while, really. Sarah-Jane's still at school; she only helps me out for a bit of extra cash . . .'

'Making my first million isn't the issue,' said Meg. 'I enjoyed playing with the kids today. And I probably wouldn't be able to do every Thursday night anyway. The best thing might be if you call me on a Tuesday or Wednesday to find out if I'm free.' She pulled a pen from her bag and grabbed his hand, scrawling a row of numbers across his palm. 'If I'm not home, try Best Bib and Tucker.'

'Mega!' cried Freddy.

Matthew looked wistfully at the notepad on the hall table.

Meg was about to make her exit when he remembered the saucepan. He went off to the kitchen to fetch it. He returned, swallowing any last trace of ill-temper.

'Thank you for cleaning up in there,' he said, avoiding her sapphire eyes. 'There was no need,' he added, knowing that someone would have had to do it before the penicillin started to thrive.

'It was nothing.' She smiled, zooming in to drop a kiss on his cheek, catching him by surprise as she had the other day.

The neckline of his jumper feeling two sizes too small, Matthew closed the door behind her and slid the chain across in record time.

'Are you all right, Daddy?'

Matthew blinked down at Freddy. 'Yes,' he snapped. 'Why? Don't I look it?'

'No,' said Freddy calmly. 'You don't.'

The following Tuesday, Meg waited for Matthew to call her. On Wednesday, she waited again, glancing impatiently at the phone in the kitchen at Best Bib and Tucker. She knew the writing class was on because Pug had said so, but Matthew Potter didn't get in touch.

In the end, Meg spent Thursday evening sifting through her belongings for old clothes or knick-knacks that she could donate to St Dominic's for the Easter Bazaar.

She was more ruthless than ever this year, still unable to find her psychedelic silk shirt, but finally giving up the fake crocodile-skin stilettos she'd been hiding under her bed out of pure embarrassment, although she was still attached to them for sentimental reasons. Pug poked her head around the door just as Meg was about to shove them into a bin-liner along with a red satin basque.

'Getting rid of your stock in trade?' enquired the teenager. 'Is that wise?'

'This stuff was only ever for fun,' said Meg coolly. 'Remember Bee's Vicars and Tarts party?'

'How could I forget? You must have been the only guest there who didn't need to dress differently from normal.'

Pug removed herself from the firing line just as Meg threw one of her huge Rudolph the Reindeer foot-warmers at the door.

Meg turned to the bobbly pink cardigan that was next in line waiting to hear its fate. She buried her face in its soft folds, knowing that, bobbles or no bobbles, nothing could induce her to part with a single item of clothing she'd been wearing on the day Jake roared out of her dreams and into her life in his shiny black coupé. She laid the cardigan reverently into her pile for keeping.

Over two hours later, her wardrobe and drawers had been blitzed back into order and Meg turned her attention to the little jewellery she owned. Anything made of plastic, namely an imitation amber necklace and a sparkly bangle, would have to go, she decided. She was also swift to discard an eighteen-carat gold ring she'd been given by an ex-boyfriend which, curiously, had started to turn black.

The clockwork ballerina in her childhood trinket box had long since stopped working, but Meg could still hear the music in her head. At the bottom of the box she found a silver rosary and a small gold crucifix. Both items had belonged to her mother, and Meg had proudly worn the cross when she'd made her First Holy Communion, aged eight.

She'd worn it too when she'd been Confirmed, although Mum hadn't been around then to witness the momentous occasion: the last time Meg had set foot in St Dominic's Parish Church, all of twelve years ago. In a surge of adolescent rebellion, everything had seemed complete, a chapter closed. Every pew, every stone, every echo within St Dominic's had reminded her of Mum. Meg couldn't bring herself to go back inside.

Fingering the rosary beads now, she tried to remember how she'd prayed with her mother every night before bed; tried to recapture her mother's face, her touch, her voice . . . But it was all so misty, so veiled . . .

Gently, she laid the rosary back beside the crucifix and closed the box. How would she have felt if she'd never even had the chance to know her mother? What would treasures like this have meant to her then? She thought of little Georgie Potter, and acknowledged that some allowances had to be made for a child who had only known a mother's love for a few short weeks but would never be able to recall it.

Sympathy welled up within Meg, and however sincerely she understood Matthew Potter's point of view, she couldn't help but think that he'd been unfair to expect anything less of her. She had as much right to feel pity as the next person.

'People can be so generous, don't you agree, Ag— Oh!' Father Ben Holmes suddenly turned pink. His shock and embarrassment prompted Agnes Widdicombe to ram the scarlet satin undergarment back into the bin-liner. 'Is it' – Father Ben hesitated – 'someone's idea of a joke, do you think?'

Agnes pursed her lips, looking in dismay at St Dominic's parish priest. He was in his mid-sixties, bald and stout, and Agnes had taken him under her protective wing from the instant he had set foot in Yarleigh five years ago.

'The other items in that sack were suitable though, weren't they?' he said hopefully, when she didn't reply. 'At least, I thought they were all right. For the bazaar, that is. A touch on the colourful side, but that will only liven up your stall . . .'

'I'm not having any of these things flashed about in public, Father. I'm sorry.'

'Oh.' The bemused priest looked around at the boxes and bin-liners filling the rear parlour of the presbytery, and then back at the sack Agnes was tying a knot in. 'It was on the doorstep this morning with a couple of others,' he explained. 'I never imagined there was anything untoward about it. There's something so harmless about an ordinary black bin-liner, except when you see it on one of those crime serials on TV. Then you know there's something sinister going on . . .' He tailed off with a sigh.

'I'm taking it back first thing tomorrow morning,' frowned Agnes. 'She can't seriously expect anyone to buy this rubbish.'

Father Ben leaned closer, the embarrassment now replaced by concern and curiosity. 'Are we talking about your goddaughter here?' he ventured.

Letting the sack slip from her fingers, Agnes sank into the nearest armchair. It was no good. She couldn't carry on without telling someone. 'It isn't just Margaret,' she began. 'I've received letters . . . from Kathleen.'

'Kathleen . . . ?'

'Oakley.' Agnes felt herself grow pale. 'Kathleen *Heybridge*.'

'Oh.' The priest's mouth formed an 'O' shape long after the word had been uttered.

'I hadn't heard anything in fourteen years,' continued Agnes. 'And then suddenly, in January . . . So unexpected. I don't think I wanted to believe it was real. I was so angry. But then – then I realised I'd failed her as much as she'd failed everyone else. I was supposed to be looking after Margaret . . .'

Father Ben laid a gentle hand on her sleeve. 'Where is Mrs Heybridge now? Did she explain why . . . ?'

'She's in North Yorkshire.'

'I only know the story through you, Agnes, and even then . . . I don't think you've been entirely honest with me.' His eyes were kind, not condemning. 'Does her family know you've heard from her?' he asked. The most terrifying question of all.

Agnes hesitated. 'No,' she said at last, shaking her head, which weighed down on her shoulders like lead. 'Not yet.'

From far away, somewhere in the tropical rain forest, a bell started ringing. Suddenly, Meg was no longer sharing a hammock on a lush desert island with Jake. The pina colada in her hand had turned into a leaky fountain pen, and Matthew Potter – menacing in mortar-board and flapping academic's gown – was looming over her ink-splattered desk, cane raised above his head.

Meg woke with a jolt.

From much closer now, the ringing became the doorbell, not a schoolbell. She threw off her duvet and reached for her towelling robe. Who the hell was calling at the crack of dawn on a Sunday morning? She groped her way along the landing, down the stairs and into the porch, where she opened the front door.

'Margaret Oakley, it's gone nine o'clock. Were you still in bed?' Agnes brushed past her into the house.

Stabbing her fingers through her knotted hair, Meg staggered into the kitchen after her god-mother. She wondered why she felt so grotty . . . then she remembered. Last night she had gone to Beatrice and Tom's house-warming party. They had mulled copious amounts of wine as if it were Christmas again, and dumped anything edible and small enough into the fondue Meg had given them as a gift. Battered prawns, sausage rolls, miniature chicken kievs. It was an experiment which had led to Bee being horribly sick and Meg briefly joining her.

Agnes plopped into a chair at the kitchen table and stared pointedly at the kettle.

'Good-morning, Mademoiselle Widdicombe. Is it not a heaven-like day?'

Oh bugger. Meg closed her eyes at the sight of Thierry in boxer shorts, leaning casually against the door frame. She'd forgotten he'd walked her home, and that she'd lent him a blanket and pillow so he could crash out in the living room.

'How was the sofa?' she asked, looking at him again and willing him to take the hint. 'Not too uncomfortable?'

He strode over to the window, his muscular form instantly bathed in a golden glow. 'A heaven-like day,' he repeated, stretching and yawning and failing to answer her question. The sod.

'Good-morning, Mr Duval,' said Agnes, managing to look outraged and smug at the same time.

Meg reached the end of her tether, which was always at its shortest when she had a hangover. 'Aggie, don't you *dare* assume the worst of me again. Thierry's a friend of mine, and sometimes, if it's late, I let friends sleep on the sofa. There's nothing wrong with that!'

'Marguerite,' Thierry turned from the window, the dark patch of hairs on his chest glistening with sweat, '*mon ange*—'

Agnes snorted.

'My angel,' persevered Thierry, 'there is no need to wind yourself up like this.' He turned to

Agnes. 'I crashed into the sofa. Marguerite was very kind to let me stay.'

'Perhaps you ought to put some clothes on though,' suggested the old lady tersely. 'It may be a "heaven-like" day, but it's not sunbathing weather yet.'

Thierry grinned and bowed, sweeping gallantly out of the room. Meg checked there was enough water in the kettle and then slammed down the switch. 'Aggie,' she said briskly, 'what do you want? You hardly ever come round here any more, not without an invitation, and even then you usually manage to dream up some excuse to get out of it.' She turned to face her godmother. 'Oh . . . are you OK?' She could have sworn there were tears glinting in the old woman's eyes.

Agnes opened her Tardis of a handbag and extracted the red satin basque. 'Father Ben persuaded me that everything else would be suitable enough for the bazaar, although I still have my doubts about those preposterous high-heels, but as for this . . .' Aggie waved the lace-up contraption in the air just as Thierry stuck his head around the door.

'Would it be an impediment to use the shower, *chérie?*'

Meg sighed. 'The clean towels are on the top shelf in the airing cupboard. Help yourself.'

But Thierry didn't budge. His eyes glazed over as he stared at the basque.

'Shower!' Meg reminded him crisply.

He disappeared. She busied herself making the tea.

Aggie seemed lost for words rather than just deliberately silent – an unprecedented situation which Meg wasn't sure how to handle.

'Maybe you ought to apologise to Father Big—' she pulled back the reins on her tongue, 'I mean, Father Ben. On my behalf, that is.' Meg grabbed the basque, pushed her foot down on the pedal bin and was ridding herself of the unfortunate undergarment for ever when her sister entered the room.

'There's a naked Frenchman in the bathroom,' said Pug. 'Is it Thierry? He had his back to me, I couldn't tell.'

'How do you know he's French then? Did he have the national flag tattooed on his bum, or was he whistling the Marseillaise?'

'I think he said, "Don't mind me," with a French accent. But he was trying to gargle at the same time.'

The morning so far had been like an old-fashioned farce, thought Meg, pouring out cups of tea until the pot ran dry and the strainer was clogged up. One, two, three, four . . . But who knew how many people might traipse through that door at any moment? The Pope and his entire Vatican entourage probably. A second later, Meg bit her lip for being flippant. Slopping milk into a jug, she deposited it on the table beside Agnes and the sugar bowl. 'You'll have to excuse my slovenly ways,' she said tensely, 'but I can't help acting in character at nine-thirty on a Sunday morning.'

'Is it half past nine already?' Agnes glanced at the clock. 'Oh, not quite.' She seemed anxious about something. 'I have to be at Mass by ten.'

'Any excuse not to drink my tea.' Meg slumped at the kitchen table. 'Did you come here just to return—' But Agnes was extracting something else from her handbag. A sparkly plastic bangle. 'Why did you bring that back?' asked Meg. 'How can there be anything offensive about a—' She stopped at the expression on her godmother's face. 'Oh Aggie . . . I'm sorry . . .'

Another memory came flooding back. When Mum had been in hospital having Pug, Aggie had taken Meg and William to the fair in Tockley Park.

'You won this for me, didn't you?' muttered Meg. 'It was so long ago, Aggie. I *had* kept it all this time. But I was in such a filthy mood when I was clearing out my stuff, I just . . .'

'There's no need to explain, Margaret. If you don't want it, I quite understand.'

Instinctively, Meg's fingers closed over it. 'I do. I'm sorry.' She gazed at her godmother and felt as if the moment might have become sentimental, significant almost, when her step-father came shuffling into the kitchen.

'Why is it I can't even use my own bathroom any more?' he sighed, squinting at Agnes and nodding a good-morning at her before turning to Meg. 'Do you fancy a fry-up, pet?'

Meg was beginning to feel ill again. She wished her step-dad had refrained from mentioning a fry-up. Last night's unorthodox fondue obviously hadn't finished making its mark.

She blinked at Aggie. 'Will you excuse me? There's something I've, er, got to do . . .'

Moments later, Thierry was poking his head around the shower curtain as she threw up into the toilet. 'You should put a lock on that door, Marguerite. It is like Charing Cross Station around here.'

She wiped her mouth and sat back wearily on her haunches.

'You are not . . .' Thierry hesitated '. . . with child?'

'No,' she said truthfully, squeezing the tips of her fingers against her throbbing temples. 'I'm not pregnant, Thierry. I only ever had one scare, and that was with you.'

He grinned. 'That is because I am more of a

man.' And he pulled back the shower curtain unashamedly, reaching out for his towel.

Meg looked away, inclined to agree with him. 'You're not trying to make a pass at me in my step-father's bathroom, are you?'

The towel wrapped around his waist, he bobbed down beside her. 'Not when you're feeling unwell, *mon ange.* I would never take advantage of you like that.'

'Only when there's Pernod involved.' She smiled, her first one of the day.

He smiled back, stroking her hair. '*Exactement.* You were too drunk and beautiful to resist.'

'Do you know how much I adore you, Thierry?' She put her arms around him fondly, even though he was dripping wet.

'Not enough,' he whispered into her neck as he hugged her back.

Meg didn't know whether to pretend that she hadn't heard him or simply turn it into a joke, but just then there was a bang on the door.

'Hurry up!' called Pug.

'Your sister is not her sweet earnest self these days,' observed Thierry.

'She's lovesick,' sighed Meg. 'A guy from her writing class. Only she won't admit it.'

'And what about you?' Thierry leaned back to study her face. 'Will you admit it?'

'What?'

'That you, too, have your own guy from the writing class. There is a glow about you these days, even when you are hungover.' Thierry stroked her cheek softly with his thumb and had a stab at mimicking Beatrice. 'You put a whole new slant on an apple for the teacher. Isn't that what Bee would say?' He laughed, but it was too forced for Meg to join in.

Her relationship with Jake was as blissful as it could be under the circumstances – hence the glow. Unfortunately, not having heard from Matthew since she had turned up at his house a fortnight ago, the smoke-screen plan was starting to go awry. Now though, an idea was forming, triggered by Thierry's teasing.

Figuratively speaking, an apple for the teacher might be just the thing she needed, thought Meg.

Eight

Matthew, who disliked Wednesdays, knew that this particular one would probably be worse than most. Driving through the open gates of Arundel Hall, he negotiated the winding drive until eventually he came to a halt between a shining Mercedes and an equally shiny black coupé. He climbed out of his own car – in need of a good waxing – and slammed the door.

He'd put off this meeting with Miss Arundel as long as he could. In normal circumstances she would have come up to the school like any other parent, but Edward Nugent had suggested that an exception could be made in this case. Perhaps Jacintha Arundel would feel more at ease on 'home turf', as it were.

The crunch had come yesterday, when Matthew had been forced to admit that burying his head in the sand was irresponsible when children's futures were at stake. Timothy Arundel had proudly admitted to scribbling obscene words in felt-tip pen in the boys' toilets, and had then been spotted looking up the girls' skirts during a game of hopscotch. These weren't the kind of habits Matthew wanted his own son to pick up.

He shuddered now and turned up the collar of his coat. The sun was fading from the March sky, veiled by a thin blanket of cloud on the horizon.

Approaching the stone steps leading to the main portico, Matthew slowed his pace. There was a gardener in wellingtons, a mud-splattered anorak and patched cords sitting on the bottom step beside a concrete jardinière. The plant in the jardinière appeared to be dead, and the gardener was smoking a thin hand-rolled cigarette and staring into space as if he really didn't give a toss. Suddenly, though, he jerked his head up, as proprietorial as a guard dog.

'I'm Matthew Potter,' Matthew felt compelled to explain. 'From Yarleigh Primary. I've come to see Miss Arundel . . .'

The gardener, eyes like jet, stared up at him with a frown. 'Mademoiselle Arundel is in the conservatory, I think.'

Matthew nodded his thanks, surprised by the French accent. He proceeded up the steps to the double oak doors and pulled the bell cord.

A few moments later, the doors swung open with a protesting creak. A fair-haired young man as tall as Matthew stood in the parquet-floored hall, tailored blazer in one hand, mobile phone in the other.

'On my way out.' He grinned, as if he was in on some joke Matthew wasn't privy to. 'You're just in time for tea. My sister's in the conservatory. Follow that corridor to the end, you can't miss it.' And, slipping into his blazer, he bounded down the steps towards the black coupé, bleeping it open from a distance with his remote.

Trying not to imagine what it would be like to stride along in Jake Arundel's privileged shoes, the world at your feet, Matthew stepped into the immense hall. He closed the doors behind him and trod diffidently down a corridor lined with dour ancestral portraits and smaller paintings of bloodhounds, who looked as though they could have done with a visit from the RSPCA.

'Mr Potter,' cooed a dulcet voice, 'in here . . .'

He entered what was akin to the Glass House at Kew Gardens. Timothy Arundel's mother was sitting demurely at a white wrought-iron table in a floral print dress. Her hair fell sleekly around her puff-sleeved shoulders, her blue eyes sparkled up at him from behind dark-gold lashes.

'Tea?' She smiled at him flutteringly. 'Wonderful,' she went on, before he could answer. 'Please, take off your coat. We have to keep the temperature up in here – understandably.'

Matthew glanced around, already beginning to sweat.

'Milk, Mr Potter?'

He nodded.

'Splendid,' said Jacintha, pouring it out. 'Now – may I call you Matt?'

'Um—'

'I know we didn't quite see eye to eye at that parents' evening, Matt,' she swept on, tilting her head coyly. 'But I do hope we can put that little altercation behind us. We are both adults, after all. Sugar?'

He shook his head. 'No, thank you.'

'And there I was thinking you were the kind of man who would appreciate a little sweetness in your life.' She smiled again. 'Do sit down. You don't have to stand to attention.'

Sinking into a chair beside a huge ugly plant which dwarfed him, he smiled back stiffly. 'Miss Arundel—'

'Call me Jacintha.'

'This isn't a social visit.'

She sighed. 'More's the pity. I'm sure you'd be very good company.'

'We've got serious matters to discuss,' he said firmly, aware that he was being buttered up. 'About Timothy.'

'Timmy *can* be rather excitable at times,' she admitted.

Matthew almost choked on the tea. 'I, um, rather think it goes deeper than that.'

'Deeper?' An edge crept into her voice.

Now that he had come this far, Matthew refused to be daunted by the memory of her shrewish temper. He recounted Timothy's latest 'exploits'. 'I'm sure your son's behaviour isn't malevolent,' he was quick to conclude. 'I think it's just a severe case of attention-seeking.'

Her cheeks filled with colour. 'Are you telling me I neglect my son?'

Matthew thought of the nanny who dropped Timothy off at school every morning and returned to pick him up every afternoon. Jacintha didn't work, not even part-time.

'Are you implying that I'm a bad mother?' she continued. 'You weren't *quite* as brutal the last time . . .'

'I'm sorry.' Matthew couldn't reconcile himself to the idea that she was neglectful on purpose. Perhaps she was raising Timothy with a restricted view of what parenting was really about. After all, she had probably been brought up by a nanny herself. 'Miss Arundel . . .'

But she was looking past him, her cheeks suddenly pale again. He turned round, following her gaze. The French gardener who had been slouched on the front steps was now standing by the conservatory door which opened on to the terrace. He was staring in at them quite blatantly.

'Excuse me for a moment.' Jacintha rose to her feet in one elegant movement, moving quickly towards the door and closing it behind her.

Matthew couldn't help watching. She was pretty in a doll-like way, and she obviously had class. It was a shame she was so highly strung, though. He couldn't hear what was being said, but he could see that she was even getting worked up with the gardener now, who was scowling through a cloud of smoke from his cigarette. Mind you, thought Matthew, you wouldn't have caught one of the staff arguing back and smoking in front of his employer in the old days. It would have been more a case of doffing one's cap and tugging at one's forelock; not that this employee had a cap to doff, but still . . .

Matthew watched as the gardener strode off across the terrace.

Jacintha came back into the conservatory. Her movements were jerky now, and nervous.

'I'm sorry, Mr Potter, I'm going to have to ask you to leave.'

'What?' Matthew was caught off guard.

'Yes, I'm sorry, but I'm beginning to feel a migraine coming on—'

'Miss Arundel, aren't you the least bit concerned about your son's welfare?'

Her eyes flashed. 'My son is the most important thing in my life, and you have no right to come into my house and tell me that I don't care!'

'I didn't—'

'Mr Potter, I can't talk about this right now.' There was a tremor in her voice. Matthew wondered if she was faking it. 'I must ask you to leave.'

Feeling as if he was being dismissed like a servant, he grabbed his coat, struggling to put it on. Why was it the sleeves always vanished when he was agitated? 'Maybe we can continue our discussion another time. If you want to make an appointment to come up to the school one day—'

'Yes, yes.' She waved him off. 'Another time.'

'Fine,' snapped Matthew, heading for the corridor. There was no point trying to continue with this now. He knew about women and their moods; he'd lived with Polly for nine years. Apparently a man was never allowed to get angry on the flimsiest pretext. Whereas a *woman* . . . it seemed a woman could act pre-menstrual whenever she bloody well felt like it.

Frederick Andrew Potter, super-sleuth, aged seven and three-quarters, was quick to deduce that his father was in a lousy mood.

For starters, there was a new dent in the car. And secondly, the level of whisky in the bottle Granny and Grandad had given Dad in a hamper for Christmas had gone down again. Freddy vaguely understood why drinking and driving was bad, but in this case the two weren't connected. The car was dented because Dad had reversed into a concrete plant pot when he was leaving the Arundel estate yesterday. Timothy had seen it happen with his own eyes and told Freddy at school first thing this morning. As for the drinking, Dad hadn't had any breakfast today because he'd said he had a headache; it was then that Freddy had noticed the whisky bottle on the Welsh dresser. Timothy said his mother always had headaches after she'd been drinking a lot, and she nearly always drank a lot when she was in a bad mood.

Opening the front door now because his father was in the bathroom, Freddy looked up in surprise at the lady on the doorstep who had just rung the bell.

'Hello, Master Potter,' she grinned, ruffling his hair and then rapidly smoothing it down again.

'Hello.' He smiled back. She was pretty and funny and not an old fuddy-duddy like those other women who used to come round with saucepans and casserole dishes. They were all as ancient as Granny, and they pulled his cheeks as if he were a baby. Freddy hated having his cheeks pulled; what if they stretched? 'I thought you were Sarah-Jane,' he said.

'Oh!' Her face lit up. He liked the way it did that. 'Well, that's why I'm here, you see.' She stepped into the hall carrying a large plastic bag. Freddy loved it when people came to visit with large plastic bags; they nearly always had presents.

Matthew appeared at the top of the stairs, a toothbrush sticking out of his mouth. As his jaw dropped, he fumbled to catch the brush before it fell to the carpet. Toothpaste was a bummer to clean up.

'Hiya,' said Meg brightly, waving up the stairs. 'I'm back again, like the proverbial bad penny.'

Matthew criss-crossed his brow.

Uh-oh, thought Freddy.

'Sarah-Jane Elliott came into Best Bib and Tucker today,' Meg went on. 'I happened to overhear her talking with her friend Sam, or was it Sal? Well, whatever, they wanted to go to see a film in Tockley tonight, only showing once, an arty type, not the rude sort. Anyway, Sarah-Jane was saying that she had to babysit, so as I was serving her strudel – Libby does a really wicked strudel, with apricots and sultanas rather than apples – I happened to ask who it was she was babysitting for . . .'

'Heck,' mumbled Matthew, through a mouthful of froth. He thumped off into the bathroom again, coming back a few seconds later. 'Are you trying to tell me *you're* here in Sarah-Jane's place?' He thumped down the stairs. 'Why didn't she call and let me know?'

'Well,' said Meg, 'I told her I'd call you myself.'

'But you didn't.'

'Actually, I did. You must have been out or something. So I thought I might as well come straight round. It would have been too short notice for you to get anyone else.'

'How convenient.' Matthew seemed more confused than angry.

'I don't see what the problem is.' Meg pouted defiantly. 'If you're worried I haven't any experience, you're wrong. I'm always having to entertain the kids when Libby has her Mother and Toddler mornings.'

Freddy looked from his dad to Meg. They were staring each other out. He knew which of them he wanted to win.

Matthew looked away first, scowling at his watch. 'OK. I should be home by ten.'

'Don't worry,' she smiled, 'everything will be fine. And could you do me a small favour? I'd feel a lot happier if you gave Pug a lift back here after the class. I don't want her walking home on her own when she can come back with me.' She gestured towards a Mini parked in front of Mrs Sopwith's bungalow.

Matthew didn't bother to reply properly; he just grunted and nodded.

Meg closed the front door behind him and grinned down at Freddy. 'Well, kiddo, I think I'm going to have to call your father Thumper. That's who he reminds me of.'

In the blink of an eye, she rose even higher in Freddy's estimation. And if she let him stay up after nine, like he planned, she'd be his friend for life.

Meg tucked Freddy up in bed at nine-fifteen and dropped a kiss on his forehead.

'Now *sleep*, it's a school day tomorrow. And apart from that, you've worn me out.'

'Thank you for my present,' he said drowsily.

'Don't mention it.' Meg smiled and clicked off the bedside lamp.

As she was checking on Georgie in the nursery, the telephone rang. Meg followed the sound to the main bedroom, which had to be quicker than dashing downstairs. The phone was on the bedside table furthest from the window, the one with the radio alarm clock and a photograph of Polly which Meg did her best not to look at.

'Hello?'

'Meg, it's me.'

'Jake!'

'Don't worry, sweetheart, I withheld the number.'

Meg lowered her voice. 'Why are you ringing me here?'

'Why do you think? I was missing you, wondering when we could get together again . . .'

She was missing him too, but: 'It's only been a couple of days,' she smiled. 'And I only spoke to you this afternoon.'

'I know, I know. How about meeting up tomorrow?'

'We'll see,' she said archly. 'I'll think about it.'

'Usual place, usual time?'

Meg couldn't tease him for long. 'You know I'll be there. Listen, Jake . . .'

'Yes?'

'About Aurora—'

'We've got to be patient. I'll explain tomorrow, and you can tell me how the babysitting went . . .' He said goodnight softly, as if they were sharing a pillow rather than a telephone line, and hung up.

Meg sighed, and had just replaced the receiver in its cradle when it made her leap out of her skin by trilling a second time. She flopped on to the bed, hand to her heart, or as close as it could get.

'Yes?' she gasped.

'Pardon . . . ?'

Blimey. It was the Queen. 'Er . . .' said Meg.

'Do I have the wrong number?'

'I don't know,' said Meg. 'Do you?'

'Is that the Potter household?'

'Ya-ars. I mean, yes. Do you want Matthew? Because he's not here. He's at—'

'Oh! Oh, of course, it's a Thursday. How silly of me. I forgot about his little writing class. This is Daphne. You must be the babysitter.'

'Sort of, I'm—'

'You don't sound like the usual girl.'

'That's because I'm not,' retorted Meg, adding, because she couldn't resist it, 'I'm the unusual one.'

'Oh!' exclaimed this Daphne character, clearly taken aback. 'Who exactly—'

'I'm Margaret Hermione Oakley,' said Meg sweetly. 'May I take a message? Can I get Matthew to call you back? He shouldn't be long.'

'Well . . . Perhaps you could just . . . The thing is, Hugh's gone to bed. I'd rather Matthew didn't call back tonight . . . he's such a light sleeper.'

'Matthew?' Meg snorted. 'You're kidding! He sleeps like a log.' She recalled his 'nap' that Sunday. 'Oh, hang on, are we still talking about Hugh here?' Who was this Hugh bloke anyway?

Daphne was beginning to sound strained and faint. 'Matthew? Like a log?'

'Could you bear with me a mo?' Meg glanced around the room for a pen and paper. 'If you're going to give me a message I'd better write it down. I've a brain like a sieve.' She pulled open the bedside table drawer. 'Great – a Biro!' She pounced on it with glee. 'Oh sugar.' It slid from her fumbling fingers on to the bed, not a Biro after all but a rather slim fountain pen. With the phone tucked under her chin, she apologised for keeping Daphne waiting. 'I'm sorry! I'm such a butter fingers! I've just got ink all over the duvet. Oh bugger, he's going to kill me! Hello? Hello . . . ?' The line had gone dead.

'Meggy?' Freddy appeared in the doorway, yawning.

She put the phone down with a mystified shrug. 'That was the Queen. Or at least it sounded like the Queen, but she turned out to be called Daphne. Bit of a disappointment really.' Meg was picking up the fountain pen as carefully as possible when Freddy made her drop it again in dismay.

'Granny called?' he said, rubbing his eyes sleepily. 'What did she want?'

Nine

Why was it, Meg mused disconsolately, once Freddy was tucked up in bed again, that the nightmarish part of the dream she had had (the one Aggie had interrupted) was the bit that was now coming true?

Instead of Jake, the hammock and the pina colada on the desert island, she was faced with a leaky fountain pen and the prospect of a far from pleased schoolmaster. The ink-splattered desk had turned out to be a duvet, but so what? That was just a minor detail.

And as for the imperious Daphne! Meg cringed.

It simply hadn't clicked. She hadn't associated her with Polly, 'beloved wife, mother and *daughter*', even though, looking back, she could recall meeting Daphne Hancock once at a parents and pupils function at St Dominic's. In fact, she had done more than meet her, she'd called her a snooty cow – within earshot.

Ohhh . . .

Groaning, Meg sunk her head into her hands and slumped at Matthew's kitchen table. She had never intended matters to get so out of hand. Fate had appeared to be on her side, in fact. While planning a way of approaching Matthew again, she had had such a lucky break she'd bopped around the kitchen at Best Bib and Tucker until a sternly bemused Libby had threatened to fire her for being a health hazard.

Meg hadn't been able to help herself. When that girl at table three had started talking to her lunch companion about babysitting and then mentioned the Potters . . . The perfect excuse! Meg hadn't been backward about coming forward. She'd butted right into the conversation. Sarah-Jane Elliott had been surprised yet easily persuaded.

But now . . .

Meg was still hunched dejectedly at the kitchen table when Matthew came home – minus Pug – at five to ten. With a sigh, he put down his briefcase and eased off his shoes.

'Elizabeth already had a lift,' he said.

'With that Giles Augustus bloke?'

'Giles Augustine.' Matthew hit the switch on the kettle. 'Elizabeth didn't seem her usual self though.'

The knot of apprehension tightened in Meg's

stomach. Remembering how grown-up and sophisticated she had thought herself at sixteen, Meg hoped Pug wasn't going to do anything rash.

'Do you know how old Giles is?' she asked Matthew.

'Nineteen. He got straight As at A-level, but he took a year off before university to concentrate on his writing. He's off to Warwick in the autumn.'

He sounded nice enough, but Meg was now cursing herself for having encouraged Pug to notice how attractive Giles was. Admittedly, this self-reproach was rather odd, since she'd always wished her sister could make more of an effort with her appearance, to lighten up and not take everything so seriously, to be as interested in boys as she was in her books. Now Meg realised that the last thing she'd wanted was for Pug to grow up as fast as *she* had.

Sighing, she scraped back her chair. 'I hope you don't mind, but I helped myself to a Jammie Dodger.'

'No, of course not,' said Matthew. 'Did the kids give you too much hassle?'

'They were cherubic.'

He raised an eyebrow. 'Are we talking about the same two children, or did you swap them while I was out?'

'Well,' she squirmed, 'maybe not cherubic. But I survived.'

'Would you like a coffee in that case? I'm afraid I'm short of medals at the moment.'

She shook her head. 'Thanks, but no thanks. My kidneys won't be able to cope. I'll be on and off the loo all night like a flaming yo-yo.'

'What's this doing here?' He'd caught sight of a brightly coloured wooden toy under the table.

'It's a diabolo.' She watched as he bobbed down to retrieve it. 'Freddy played with it for about two seconds; it couldn't quite compete with his PlayStation.'

'I had one of these when I was his age. Where's the other part?'

They found it on the floor in the lounge. Two thin green sticks joined together by a long yellow string.

Within seconds, Matthew was a boy again, bouncing the wooden hourglass-shaped weight along the string without dropping it. 'I'd forgotten how good I was at this,' he grinned.

Meg looked on in fascination. 'You're miles better than me. I'm hopeless.'

'Where did it come from?'

The expression on his face had her mesmerised. 'My step-dad made it.'

'Your step-dad?'

Please keep smiling, she thought; don't let me wipe it straight off again. 'I wanted to bring the kids something,' she said. 'A present each.'

'There was no need . . .'

'I . . .' Come on, Margaret, she told herself. Don't just stand there. Explain yourself. 'I suppose . . .' she stammered, because she could hardly tell him Thierry had inadvertently given her the idea. 'I suppose, I thought . . .' Next time, Margaret, please do think, it might make a pleasant change. 'Well,' she snapped, the mental strain making her huffy, 'why not? Why shouldn't I bring them presents? It wasn't as if they cost me anything. My step-father makes them for Best Bib and Tucker. Georgie's got a new pull-along toy he's designed, shaped like a rabbit. It sort of . . . hops.'

'Like a rabbit?'

'Exactly.'

'So, what you're saying is that you've been using my children as guinea pigs?'

Guinea-pigs? she frowned. 'Oh! You mean did my step-dad ask me if I knew any kids I could try out his new designs on, and I said, "Yes, as a matter of fact, I do"?'

'So?' Matthew looked quizzical. 'Did he?'

She had to nod. 'Yes. Sort of. But it's not as if the toys are dangerous or anything. He just wanted to know how they measured up in the entertainment stakes.'

'And what's the verdict?'

Meg thought it was time to try for another

smile again. She targeted Matthew's lips and waited for his reaction. 'I'm afraid I'm going to have to tell Dad that the diabolo, at least, rates better with the father than with the son. In fact, I may even have to ask the father for lessons.'

Rather than the lips twitching, a forefinger did. It beckoned her towards him.

'I want you to show me your technique,' he said.

'You what?'

'Here.' He passed her the diabolo. 'Go on. I bet you're not as bad as you think you are.'

Of course not. She was worse.

Matthew shook his head in despair. 'I'll have to charge you for lessons, I hope you realise that,' he said, grabbing her hands from behind and breathing down her neck as he tried to show her how to keep the weight balanced on the string. Ever the teacher, she thought, as her palms grew clammy and her throat constricted. He was so totally preoccupied with the diabolo, it probably hadn't crossed his mind that he was practically hugging her.

'This isn't going to work,' he complained, his breath hot in her ear.

'What isn't?' she muttered.

'You're too stiff. How am I supposed to show you how to do this?'

'You really don't have to,' she murmured

politely, attempting to extricate herself. But her wriggling turned out to be successful in a way she'd never imagined.

'That's more like it!' he cried. 'See?' The weight was rolling along the length of the string as if by magic. 'All you need is a bit more practice.'

Suddenly, his closeness wasn't so disquieting. She could sense his smile on the back of her neck. Normally, when she stood this close to a bloke, their intentions were strictly dishonourable. Laughing, mildly embarrassed, she dropped the diabolo – on purpose this time – and half-turned towards him, feeling silly for her earlier discomfort.

'So,' she grinned broadly, 'what do I owe you for today's lesson?'

Matthew's face was less than three inches from her own. He blinked down at her from behind his glasses, his eyes growing wider. 'I . . .' He stepped back, colliding with the TV cabinet.

Meg backed away herself, crashing into an armchair. 'Well, anyway, joking apart, thanks for showing me how to . . .' She gestured towards the diabolo. 'But I really ought to be off, it's getting late . . .'

'Yes,' he nodded, looking relieved. He followed her out of the lounge. 'Of course.'

'Oh drat!' she said, smacking her forehead,

harder than she'd meant to. 'I was forgetting!' A clear case of wanting to. Which was a far more reasonable excuse, she told herself, than the notion that Matthew had distracted her.

'What?'

'Your mother-in-law rang, and—'

'Daphne? What did she want?'

'Well, you see, I was trying to jot down a message when I dropped the pen on the bed.'

'On the bed?' Was it the light in the hall or was he turning green?

'I'd just put Freddy to sleep – well, not in the veterinary sense, but anyway, the phone rang' – Meg remembered in the nick of time not to mention Jake's call – 'so I thought it would be quicker to answer it on the upstairs extension. And at first I thought it was the Queen, because your mother-in-law sounds quite posh, in a royal sort of way. But of course it wasn't. So I was about to take a message down, like I said, when I happened to drop your fountain pen – sorry, but I had to go through your drawer – and when I apologised for keeping Daphne waiting because I'd got ink all over the duvet, she, er . . . We must have been cut off.'

Surely Daphne Hancock wouldn't have hung up without saying goodbye? Well-bred people didn't do things like that.

Matthew opened his mouth and then slammed it shut again.

'I'm sure if you explain . . .' said Meg. 'Maybe it might have sounded a bit . . . odd, but . . .'

He was shaking his head. 'It doesn't matter,' he said, his voice strained. 'Please thank your step-father for the toys.'

'Oh, yes . . . Well, of course I will.' Bizarrely, thought Meg, she was wishing that Matthew *had* got annoyed about her 'chat' with Daphne, and about the ink stain, rather than just looking depressed. 'About next Thursday . . .' she ventured.

'What?'

'Would you, um, like me to babysit again?'

'Oh . . . Er—'

'Maybe I can bring some dinner with me,' she heard herself say.

He blinked at her, his hand against the front door, preventing it from shutting behind him.

'For the kids,' she went on quickly. 'I usually have some leftovers. Meatballs, spaghetti . . .' In case he thought she meant slops or gruel.

'That would be kind of you.'

'I'll be seeing you then.'

He wasn't even looking at her, but at his shoe-less feet. They were on the large side, she observed again, although at least today the socks weren't in need of darning. At the rate she was going, she would probably have offered to do it for him.

She hurried towards her car without looking back.

Without questioning his reasons this time, Matthew stared at the Glenfiddich bottle for a long while before pouring – just a drop – into the first mug which came to hand. As he sat in semi-darkness in the lounge, he realised he wanted to stop being able to think, especially about how time had come between him and Polly. Over a year. Thirteen months. All those days when, inevitably, other memories were being formed.

Matthew put his empty mug on the small round table beside him, but didn't get up to pour himself another. He could hardly believe he'd been such an idiot over that diabolo business. He'd simply wanted to show Meg where she was going wrong. It was a natural instinct. After all, he was a teacher. He'd never meant . . .

Frowning, he stared into the imitation open fire, listening to the gas jet hiss gently and watching the flames flicker hypnotically through the mesh of the fireguard. Years ago, as a boy, he'd sat in front of his grandmother's crackling and sputtering log fire, cross-legged by the flagstone hearth, hugging her little dog and making up all those stories which had never been captured on paper, never been given life except in his head.

Now the stories were other people's, like Elizabeth Heybridge's *The Enemy Within*. The most original of the creative writing class's efforts at inventing an antagonist, in this case self-delusion. The plot revolved around a young woman searching for a meaning to her life, throwing herself indiscriminately at one man after another as she listened to the voice of desperation rather than that of reason.

Matthew had felt as if Elizabeth was speaking to him personally as she'd read it aloud. He was convinced that everyone in the class had felt the same though, it was that kind of story. Giles Augustine had certainly been attentive; then again, he had his own reasons. Elizabeth wasn't conventionally pretty, but she had the same sweet seriousness that had first attracted Matthew to Polly. He could understand why Giles was drawn to her; she was only months younger than Polly had been when Matthew had first met her.

Even though he wasn't sure he could endure it tonight, Matthew relived the moment again, as he had a thousand times. A studious young man in round owlish spectacles, sitting at the same table in the same London library as a pony-tailed blonde with her freckled button nose buried in Tolstoy's *Anna Karenina*. Tears glistened like diamonds on her lashes. Matthew had been hooked. Polly had looked up to find him gazing at her. 'I'm sorry,' she'd murmured, moving her bag and her folder, 'am I taking up too much room?' The same question she'd asked when they'd first shared the same bed, on their wedding night . . .

Now, in agony, he dragged himself free from the memory and reached for the phone. He coughed to clear his voice as he punched out a number he knew off by heart.

Eventually, a familiar voice answered. 'Hello?'

'Hello, Daphne. How—'

'Matthew? Is that you? Is something the matter? Are the children all right?'

'They're fine.' He frowned. 'Why shouldn't they be?'

'It's almost midnight. I thought . . . I expressly said that you weren't to phone back tonight. Hugh's having such trouble sleeping, and when he finally does go off the slightest little thing wakes him up.'

'Meg never said . . .' He sighed. 'I'm sorry, I didn't realise it was so late.' He took off his glasses and rubbed his eyes with the heel of his free hand. 'I'm sorry if I've woken Hugh.'

'Well, yes, you did wake me as a matter of fact, but that's beside the point. It's Hugh I'm worried about.'

'No.' Matthew rubbed his eyes harder. 'I meant—'

'This "Meg", would that be the girl I spoke to earlier?' Daphne was definitely wide awake now. 'She said her name was Margaret.'

'Margaret Oakley. She was at St Dominic's with Polly.'

'Really?' said Daphne. 'I can't recall having heard the name. Oakley . . . Oakley . . . Who are her parents?'

'I, er, don't think she's got any.' Matthew hadn't thought too much about the fact that they had this in common. 'She lives with her step-family. The Heybridges.'

'I don't know them either,' said Daphne, with a 'tsk' tagged on the end. 'I thought your babysitter was the Elliotts' daughter. What's her name again? Such a sweet girl. Selina? Sarah?'

'Sarah-Jane. And she *was* my babysitter. Still is, I suppose . . . Anyway, Meg steps in when Sarah-Jane can't manage it,' he said finally, keeping the explanation simple.

'Is she a friend of yours?' His mother-in-law made it seem as if it wasn't the done thing for him to have any. 'Only you've never mentioned her.'

'I haven't known her long at all,' he answered quickly. 'We just sort of . . . bumped into each other in the village and got talking,' he lied. 'She works at Best Bib and Tucker.'

'Oh yes,' said Daphne. 'I know the place. Very . . . quaint.'

'She was babysitting for me tonight, and just happened to be checking on the children when you rang, so she answered on the upstairs extension—'

'And managed to make a mess of your duvet.' Daphne was growing cooler by the second. 'I do hope it was washable ink.'

Matthew was growing audibly cooler himself. 'She's great with the kids, especially Freddy.' As he said it, he realised it was true. Amazingly.

'For their sake, I hope you're right. As for the reason I called earlier this evening, it's about Easter.'

'Oh?' The thought of spending a long weekend in the Hancocks' Chelsea townhouse, watching Freddy and Georgie like a hawk, filled Matthew with unspeakable dread. There were too many valuable antiques just begging to be broken, and the garden was microscopic. He also resented having his every move monitored by his mother-in-law, and being obliged to make small-talk with the Hancocks' stuffy, patronising friends.

'There's been a change of plan,' said Daphne. 'Don and Patrice have asked us to join them at their villa in Corfu.'

Matthew perked up. This was a different

kettle of fish. The kids would love it. There would probably be a pool. He could start teaching Georgie how to swim, the way he'd taught Freddy during that week in Portugal six years ago.

'If only Don didn't need peace and quiet to recover from his operation,' Daphne went on, 'I would have suggested that you join us. With the children, naturally. Frederick and Georgina would have loved it. There's a swimming-pool, you know. A huge thing apparently. But it wouldn't be fair to poor Don.'

Poor Don? Matthew swallowed his disappointment, his frustration that the grandchildren didn't come first with Daphne and Hugh, especially with their only child, their perfect, beloved daughter, gone. Besides, they were the only Granny and Grandad the kids had; not that they would have been Matthew's first choice, but that hadn't been Polly's fault.

'No, of course not,' he muttered obediently, thinking about Freddy and Georgie's godfather – also not his first choice. 'I didn't realise Don had had surgery . . .' He had visions of a heart transplant or by-pass.

'It was just a small hernia,' said Daphne. 'But Don's so brave, he's coming along in leaps and bounds. Only last weekend we went down to the country club, and he ordered the most enormous steak with all the trimmings. And then he had strawberry soufflé for dessert!'

'Really?' said Matthew, swallowing more than just disappointment and frustration. 'I'm so glad to hear it.'

Ten

Gazing out of the window into the Mediterranean-style courtyard, Meg rested her chin in her hands and drummed her fingers impatiently against her jaw. She heaved a sigh. There were some things a girl could only confide to her Number Two Best Friend, and when that Number Two Best Friend had been working abroad for six months . . .

'Meggy!'

'Yazza!'

'Have you been waiting long?'

Squealing and giggling, they hugged effusively before flopping down at the rear window table in the Cappuccino Café in Tockley, their favourite pre- and post-shopping haunt before Yasmin had jetted off to the States to teach European history.

'So, how *are* you, Yaz?'

'How are *you*? Look at your hair! Where's it all gone?'

More giggling ensued.

'Oh, Meg, you'd just *love* America!' Yasmin was emphatic. 'And you'd go wild over New York! It's just the sort of place you've always dreamed of. I can see you now – gazing out over Central Park from your penthouse on Fifth Avenue . . .'

'Tell me more,' groaned Meg.

They chatted for nearly an hour, ordering a constant supply of cappuccinos and two large portions of tiramisu.

Meg slumped back in her chair. 'I'm stuffed!'

Yasmin twitched a thin eyebrow. 'That doesn't sound like the Meg I know. You always wanted to finish up with a zabaglione. Don't tell me you're watching your figure? Unlike Bee! I could hardly believe it when I heard. She always said she was waiting until her mid-thirties.'

'Accidents happen,' shrugged Meg. 'In fact, she thought it was a dodgy fondue to begin with, seeing as I was ill as well. When it carried on, she convinced herself it was stomach flu. *Then* she realised it was ages since her last period.'

'I'll bet Tom's chuffed.'

'He'll make a great dad. Bee can't complain.'

'What about you, though? Met any "great dad" material lately?'

Meg had never really thought of Jake that way. And yet . . . She smiled. 'Maybe.'

Yasmin leaned forwards. 'Who is he? You didn't mention anything in your letters.'

Meg thought about the underwear she was wearing: cream-coloured, the sheerest silk edged with the softest lace. Jake gave her a different gift each week, none of them cheap. 'One day . . .' he'd said, implying he could buy her the world. It always seemed that way, or at least when she closed her eyes at night and lived the fairytale from the safety of her pillow. In Meg's dreams, no one got hurt. In Meg's fantasies, Aurora Lloyd was swept off her Bally heels and straight into a Lamborghini by a Ray-Banned Romeo who would shower her with true love and financial support, in such a way, of course, that her pride wouldn't be hurt. She would appear in *Hello!* showing off an even larger engagement ring than the one she had now. Meg wanted every girl to be a princess. She wished there could be enough fairytales and true love to go round.

'If I don't tell someone soon, I'll burst!' she cried suddenly.

Number One Best Friend Beatrice would never have understood. She had found her cosy little niche, her cubby-hole in life. She would tell Meg to wake up to reality and smell the freesias because the kind of roses she was dreaming of didn't exist. But Beatrice wasn't there when Meg was with Jake; she couldn't know how intense it was, how electrifying, how . . .

'Are you all right?' asked Yasmin.

'Mmm?'

'Who is he? Before I give you a Chinese burn or pull all your toenails out!'

'OK, OK . . .' Meg leaned closer to her. Beloved, wild, intellectual little Yasmin, whose Barnsley accent, as warm and wholesome as freshly baked bread, hadn't lost any of its charm over the years. 'You're the only one who can know about this. Apart from the fact that you never blurt my secrets out, even when you're plastered, you're the only one who'll understand.' Beloved, wild, romantic little Yasmin, who'd spent her whole life proving cynics wrong.

'Jake Arundel!' she yelped unromantically a moment later, her hazel eyes boggling.

'Ssshhh,' hissed Meg. 'Keep your voice down.' She instantly regretted not having waited until they were alone, ideally in a locked sound-proof booth with blacked-out windows in case anyone looking in could lip-read.

'You're shagging Jake Arundel and you expect me to keep quiet about it?'

Meg looked fearfully over her shoulder then turned back to Yasmin and explained why the affair had to be clandestine. 'And,' she concluded, 'it's more than just shagging. Jake and I love each other.'

'Now, let me see, is that love on his part as in "just a quickie, darling, and I'll be off", or as in "you haven't shaved your legs in weeks, you've put on two kilos – darling, I think you're beautiful!"?'

'Huh?'

'Don't pretend to be thick. You just said yourself that he hasn't broken off his engagement yet. Remember when you swore you'd never get involved with a married man? Well, this is almost as bad.'

Meg bit her lip, bewildered by Yasmin's reaction to the bombshell of the century.

'Put it this way, Meg, would you classify it as a relationship? In the fullest sense of the word.'

'Ye-es.'

'Right. So where do you see yourself a year from now?'

'With Jake, of course. It's just . . . Aurora's having some financial difficulties at the moment. That's why Jake hasn't told her yet.'

'Very conscientious of him, I'm sure.'

Meg frowned at Yasmin's sarcasm. This wasn't exactly what she'd been after; it was only making her feel worse in fact. Her spirits had been sagging a bit lately. Even when she was with Jake, she couldn't quite shake off the cloud clinging to her. It wasn't just to do with Aurora; there was something else. Meg had never felt as if life was piling in on her quite this way before. She had always been able to plod on, chin up. But ever since she'd met Matthew Potter, she'd felt as if a part of his pain, his tragedy, was rubbing off on her. She'd taken the risk of exposing herself emotionally to Jake, but somehow a little of Matthew's despair had crept in along with Jake's passion.

'Yaz . . . when you did that stint as a substitute at Yarleigh Primary, was Matthew Potter working there?'

'Matt?' Yasmin raised an eyebrow. 'He still is, isn't he? Working there, I mean. And what's this got to do with Jake Arundel?'

'So you do know Matthew?' Meg couldn't help noticing with a pang of annoyance that Yasmin had called him Matt.

'Course I know him. He's a really nice bloke. Why do you want to know?'

Meg pulled a face. 'Yaz, there's, um . . .' she looked out of the window at the daffodils and crocuses bobbing in the small flower-bed in the centre of the courtyard '. . . something else that maybe you ought to hear . . .'

Yasmin listened, stunned. Once she had the facts more or less straight in her head, she sat back and ordered another cappuccino. By this point, Meg had moved on to camomile tea.

'I didn't mean to get so involved,' she said, in a last ditch attempt to justify her actions.

'Involved?'

'I feel really sorry for him, but then I find myself wanting to tell him to just get on with his life and stop moping about. It's been over a year since Polly died—'

'You think he should just snap out of it? Forget her and find someone else?'

Meg stared down at the table. 'No. Yes. Oh God,' she groaned, 'I don't know. I don't think he should ever forget her. I know how he feels. I still think about Mum every day . . .' Meg hesitated. She'd never told anyone how she honestly felt about her mother and she wasn't about to start now. 'I just think Matthew should begin living again,' she said quietly. 'And I don't know how to make him see that. If I knew what he'd been like before . . .'

Yasmin stirred the foamy milk floating on top of her coffee. 'Matt isn't your responsibility, and you're not the only one who's tried to help him through this.' She rested her spoon in her saucer. 'I was working at Yarleigh Primary when Polly's cancer was diagnosed. I was friends with her as well as Matt. She was the school secretary. She'd just found out she was pregnant again. Matt was over the moon. So was Polly. They'd been trying for years for another baby, a brother or sister for Freddy.'

Meg froze, the camomile tea half-way to her lips. She could literally feel the colour draining from her face. It was one thing to have cannily extracted a version of the story from Beatrice while pretending to know it already, but village hearsay wasn't the same as this I-was-right-there-when-it-happened perspective.

'And then,' Yasmin continued, 'it all crashed down around them. Polly found a lump, under her arm . . . The specialists wanted to operate, give her chemo, the works . . .'

'Georgie,' breathed Meg. 'She was carrying Georgie, wasn't she?'

'It would have meant terminating the pregnancy.' Yasmin was matter-of-fact. 'But Polly refused to have an abortion, and she refused any treatment that might have harmed or affected the baby. I wasn't working at Yarleigh Primary by then, I'd moved to Tockley. Matt and Polly seemed to lose themselves in this weird cocoon. I hardly saw them. I tried to keep in touch, but after that . . . It was as if they didn't need friends any more. As if, by depending on each other and no one else, nothing terrible could happen.'

'They thought fate wouldn't be that cruel.'

'Possibly. I don't know.'

'But, Yaz . . . why didn't you ever talk about this at the time? Why didn't you tell me about it?'

Yasmin stared at the bubbles in her cappuccino. 'Don't you compartmentalise your life, Meg? Don't you tell some people one thing and other people something else? I don't mean lying exactly, I mean sifting the truth. And then there are the things you never tell anyone . . .'

Meg shifted uncomfortably. Yasmin had hit the nail rather accurately on the head, and knew it.

'Steer clear of him, Meg.' Yasmin narrowed her eyes. 'Matt just needs time to get over this.'

'Is it that simple?'

'I thought you'd have more sense. Can't you see what you're doing? You can't play with someone's life like that.'

Whatever Yasmin thought, Meg knew she couldn't just leave Matthew alone. She wanted to help him. Her motives weren't entirely dubious any more. And if he had heard rumours about their 'romance', he'd never mentioned them to her. She knew she was taking a risk, that he might try to quash them by distancing himself from her, but that was unavoidable. He would probably deny it emphatically if anyone confronted him on the subject, but that wouldn't count for much in a village like Yarleigh where gossip seemed to be the only 'truth'.

And so, thus far, she concluded, no harm had been done. In fact, maybe she had done some good.

'Meg . . . Have you ever wondered what might happen if Matthew starts to like you too much?'

She sat up and blinked at Yasmin. 'Don't be silly! The only person he's wrapped up in is Polly.'

'But you said yourself, he should move on . . .'

'I'm not his type,' Meg pointed out. 'He'd be more likely to go for someone like you. You've got loads more in common.'

Yasmin paused a moment, fiddling with her empty coffee cup. 'Basically, he's convenient to you because he's still too busy grieving to become romantically attached.'

Meg didn't reply. It was only now that she recalled how Yasmin could be a bit too much of a schoolmarm at times, instead of simply a friend.

Football, reflected Matthew, shifting his squelching wellie-clad feet and keeping a vigilant eye on his daughter's efforts at making mud pies, wasn't at its best at ten-thirty on a damp grey Sunday morning, even if it *was* the greatest game ever invented.

Suddenly, he was jolted from his brooding by a cry of excitement to his left.

'GO-AAAL!'

Looking round, he saw Meg Oakley bouncing towards him. Some parts of her, he couldn't help noticing, bounced more than others.

'Crikey!' she gasped. 'Did you see that? Your son's a proper little Michael Owen.'

'Mmm. He does enjoy his crisps rather too much,' said Matthew, deciding from the way Meg was dressed that she must have been out jogging, and wondering – from a purely scientific viewpoint – how the elastic of a certain undergarment could stand the strain.

She giggled, adjusting a green and pink striped woolly hat over her ears. Her legs, he noted with a worrying sense of disappointment, were hidden beneath faded baggy jogging pants. Gesturing towards the junior footie match being played on the field behind Yarleigh Rowing Club, she said, 'I've missed most of it, haven't I? My blasted alarm didn't go off.'

'There's about fifteen minutes left.'

'Oh well, I've managed to keep some of my promise then. Hopefully he'll forgive me.'

'Your promise?'

'To Freddy. I told him I'd be here, to cheer him on. And before you ask, I'm still babysitting on Thursday.'

Twitchy and uncomfortable, Matthew looked back towards the game. Freddy was running their way, caked in dirt, emerald eyes shining. 'Meggy,' he gabbled breathlessly, 'I saw you coming. I scored that goal for you! Did you see it? Did you?'

'For *me?*' Meg clapped her gloved hands, her voice crackling with delight. 'Thank you, kiddo. No one's ever scored a goal for me before!'

Freddy ran back to join the game. Matthew burrowed his hands deeper in the pockets of his coat, watching the match and wondering where spring had vanished to overnight.

'Oh wow!' yelled Meg. 'Did you see that? He was so close!' Matthew looked down. Her hand was on his arm, her fingers digging into him. This, he corrected her silently, was 'close'; missing the goal by a mile wasn't.

He caught the eye of Patrick Sherfield, whose son was in Freddy's class. Patrick raised an eyebrow at Matthew and inclined his head towards Meg, as if nodding his approval.

Hell.

Matthew shifted away from Meg automatically, but the damage was done.

She was holding out a paper bag of aniseed balls. 'Have one,' she urged, and then said rapidly, 'After the match is over, I thought I could take Freddy and Georgie to see the ducks on the pond. I mean, you could probably do with an hour to yourself to catch up on things, couldn't you?'

'Meg—'

'Oh go on, you know it makes sense.'

The pockets of her jogging pants were apparently bottomless. After her aniseed balls had been put away, she pulled out a small plastic bag full of chunks of bread. 'For the ducks.

I'm not a secret Hovis addict.' She smiled. 'Listen, I promise to throw myself in after the kids if they fall in the water. I won't let them drown.'

'And you always keep your promises – in part.'

'If alarm clocks aren't involved, I try to keep them in full.'

He couldn't stop himself smiling.

Meg took it as a yes. 'Great,' she smiled back.

Matthew could hardly turn around and say no now.

'We won! We won!' Freddy came running up to them as soon as the match was over and the coach had congratulated the team. 'Three-nil! And one of them was mine!'

'Down with Tockley Rovers!' whooped Meg. 'Up Yarleigh United!'

Oh heck, thought Matthew, she'd be buying a team strip next.

'By the way,' she said, after Freddy had been made to look a little more presentable and Georgie was safely buckled in her buggy, 'do you have any plans for Easter Sunday?'

'Easter Sunday?'

'You know, the one after Good Friday.'

'I haven't any firm plans,' he admitted grudgingly.

He didn't have any plans at all now that Daphne and Hugh were going to Corfu.

'Great,' said Meg. 'Then you and the kids are

the last of my invitees. Any more and there won't be space around the table.'

'Sorry, I'm not with you.'

'I hope you will be on Easter Sunday though,' she smiled cheesily. 'I always have a big bash. After all, it's meant to be more important than Christmas. It's round at Aggie's this year, although I'm doing most of the cooking. She's got the room for it, and if the weather's nice her garden's gorgeous to sit in. I thought I could hide eggs around it for the kids to hunt.'

Freddy took her hand and grinned.

Matthew knew he would be the spoil-sport villainous dad if he refused. Meg had cornered him again. 'Who else is going to be there?' he asked.

'Just a couple of friends, and my family, and Pug asked if Giles Augustine could come. Aggie's always a firm fixture, even if she does just sit and sulk, but seeing as I managed to persuade her to let me hold it at her place for once . . .'

'Aggie?'

'Agnes Widdicombe. My godmother. She lives at the other end of Chaffinch—'

'Yes,' Matthew nodded, 'of course.' She had been one of the kind souls who had tried to smother him after Polly's death. He'd known her before that though, when Polly had sung in the church choir. Agnes Widdicombe was an accomplished organist. He had given her a lift a couple of times to the White House, as Polly had playfully called Agnes's home, Linden Trees Villa, the largest house in Chaffinch Lane, built in 1928 according to the plaque above the door.

'I'd forgotten she was your godmother,' he said. 'Polly did mention it once.'

'I think Aggie would love to forget it too. But I've decided to be extra nice to her from now on.'

Matthew – busy dodging the last of the glances being cast in their direction – had a sudden defiant urge to give his fellow villagers something to really talk about, but his imagination cut off as if fused when trying to picture what that something might be.

'Well, see you later,' Meg called back to him, pushing the buggy across the bumpy ground towards the road. As she started chattering animatedly to Freddy, Matthew remembered what day it was.

A cold needle seemed to pass through his heart. Although he had a thousand things to get on with at home, he didn't want to return to an empty house – even if it meant he could put his feet up for a moment or two to skim through the papers in peace. It held too many memories of past Mother's Days; of breakfasts in bed and vases spilling over with roses . . .

He decided to go for a walk along the river,

glancing back because Meg had said something to make his son giggle. The boy was practically walking on air alongside her.

That was the most dangerous thing about the woman, realised Matthew, as he stared at Meg Oakley over his shoulder, transfixed: not the fact that she *was* a woman and couldn't conceal it even beneath a grungy oversized sweatshirt, but that she made him want to laugh as uninhibitedly as Freddy.

Really laugh. Not just pretend to.

Eleven

The vast attic of Linden Trees Villa was crammed with three-quarters of a century's worth of bric-a-brac. Meg had looked on as her step-father had brought down a wooden high-chair covered in dust. 'Did I ever really fit in that?' she'd murmured, arming herself with cleaning accoutrements as if going to war.

Now, a couple of hours later, Agnes stood watching her god-daughter lay the finishing touches to the dining table. A small Easter egg by every setting, and a fluffy yellow chick on the high-chair. Such attention to detail, marvelled Agnes. And miracle of miracles, Margaret was even wearing a dress which just about covered her thighs.

'I was reading an article in the *Tockley Evening Gazette* last week, full of tips on how to make Easter celebrations extra special,' explained Meg, standing back to survey her handiwork.

'Really?' Remembering there was a turkey in

the oven that needed checking, Agnes bustled out of the dining room.

Meg, already panicking that something was going to go disastrously wrong, fished about in the side pocket of her dress and pulled out one of her many lists. What, she wondered, was the sudden attraction of list-making? Did she feel any more organised? Running a finger down the piece of paper, she figuratively ticked off the 'things to do'. Everything that she had remembered to write down was done. What remained now was for her guests to arrive. She couldn't understand why she was so jittery and eager. It wasn't as if Jake would be turning up. He wasn't in Yarleigh for Easter, and even if he had been around . . .

It was true, thought Meg, that she'd been close to quite a few men in her life, and sometimes she had actually tried to fall in love, to see what all the fuss was about. But she had discovered that that kind of love wasn't about trying. It couldn't be forced, especially by a heart as well insulated as hers. She had never given as much as she could all in one go, but now, with Jake . . . this had to be IT: the emotion the world was supposed to revolve around.

She only wished it didn't hurt so much.

Ten minutes later, the doorbell chimed 'Auld Lang Syne' and Meg rushed out from the bathroom where – in need of the distraction – she had been touching up her make-up. As she came down the stairs, she saw that Aggie was already at the door. Thierry had arrived, but Matthew and family were hot on his heels. Both men were carrying flowers. Each had a bunch for Aggie and another for Meg. Thierry handed his riotously colourful mix of blooms over first, lavish with his cheek-kissing. Matthew, casting curious and surprised glances in his direction, was rather more reserved.

'Hello,' he said, handing Meg the all-yellow daffodil and freesia mix.

Before she could thank him, his son stepped forward holding a gigantic Easter egg complete with glossy purple ribbon. 'This is for you too, Meggy. Daddy said it was OK. You wouldn't feel guilty because Lent was over.'

Thanking him, she took the egg in her free hand as she juggled both bouquets in the other. 'You remembered,' she beamed at Matthew.

He shrugged it off while still shooting curious glances at Thierry, who had his arm around Aggie and was smiling down at her charmingly.

'Um,' said Meg, 'Matthew, this is my good friend Thierry Duval. Thierry, this is—'

'We've met,' said both men at once.

'In a manner of speaking,' corrected Matthew. 'Up at Arundel Hall.'

'You knocked over my jardinière with your automobile.' Thierry flashed him a heated look.

Meg raised an eyebrow at the accused. 'You knocked over a plant pot?' It wasn't hard to believe, but out of courtesy she acted surprised.

Freddy answered before his dad could. 'Honest to God,' he said, with just the same intonation he'd heard Timothy use. 'There's a dent in the car this huge to prove it.' And he demonstrated with his hands, exaggerating by an inch or ten.

'Remind me never to hire you as my barrister,' snorted Matthew, ruffling his son's hair so that the cowlick stuck straight out.

Meg glanced at her watch in irritation.

'Pug and Giles are late,' she said crossly to Aggie as they stood over the table in the kitchen, Meg fussing over the cake, which was for dessert, and her godmother sprinkling cheese on some cauliflower. 'I don't know what's the matter with that girl these days—' Meg broke off. 'What? What are you looking at me like that for?'

'The term "role model" springs to mind.'

'Are you saying it's my fault?'

'Isn't it?'

Meg couldn't work Aggie out. One minute the old woman was insisting it was only right that she paid for all the food being laid on today, seeing as it was being laid on in her house; the next she was dishing out insults.

'Aggie,' said Meg, wanting to return to the previous subject, even though she had been the one to change it in the first place, 'listen. I can't possibly accept your money. I feel guilty enough for suggesting we hold lunch here this year. After all, if I hadn't gone around inviting people the way I did—'

'Most of them would have sat at home, miserable and bored and wishing someone *had* invited them to a big family get-together like this.'

Meg looked up from decorating the cake, which was shaped like an Easter bunny. 'Half of them aren't family though. You're not. Not biologically.'

Aggie stood watching her. 'You don't need the same blood to be a family, Margaret. You of all people should know that. Now, are you going to let me foot the bill or not?'

Meg felt uncomfortable saying 'yes please', so instead she came out with, 'No thank you. I couldn't possibly accept. I can easily work an extra shift to cover it. You've only got your pension to fall back on.'

'Margaret, have you ever wondered how I manage to live on my own in such a large house when I could do just as well in a modest bungalow like Edith's?'

Meg put down the icing syringe. Honestly, her

fossil of a godmother was cracking up. 'You've lived here all your life, Aggie. It's always belonged to your family. Why live anywhere else?'

'A house this size though . . . There may not be a mortgage to pay, but have you never asked yourself how I manage to run it?'

'I know you're careful with money. You do a lot of budgeting and that kind of thing. Mum always said so . . .' Meg shrugged.

Linden Trees Villa didn't look anything like her idea of a villa, in spite of its colour. Villas belonged in much hotter countries, close to a beach, or at least a swimming-pool. Meg had to concede, though, that it wasn't the house's fault that it had such a fussy, dated feel to it, as if no one had revamped it since it was first decorated. Aggie's parents sounded like the sort of people who would never have dreamed of going to IKEA – if IKEA had been around in those days. Aggie's father had been a country doctor, and Aggie herself had risen to the rank of chief librarian before the small village library had closed down. Meg couldn't really visualise her godmother going along to Homebase or B&Q, or sitting down in front of the telly to pick up some tips from *Changing Rooms.*

'Are you trying to tell me you've got a few grand stashed under the floorboards?' Meg asked cheekily.

'Not under the floorboards, Margaret. Don't be infantile.'

And that was that, Meg realised; she had been hooked, but not reeled in. The conversation was over. Her godmother drifted into the pantry, and Meg returned to decorating the cake, although her mind wasn't on the job.

Ooops . . . Oh dammit. Would anyone notice that the Easter bunny had acquired a navel?

When Pug and Giles finally tramped through the front door, an irate Meg hustled them out into the garden. 'What took you so long?'

'It's such a gorgeous day, we decided to go down to the river.'

Meg stared at the psychedelic shirt Pug was wearing (rather baggily). 'That's mine! That's *my* shirt. You had it all the time!'

'I didn't, actually. I found it last week. Behind the sofa.'

'How did it get there?' Meg was confused.

'Well,' flung back Pug, 'you tell me. How do items of clothing normally end up behind sofas?'

Meg suddenly became conscious of the fact that Matthew and Thierry had drifted over to join them. She stared miserably at her feet, thinking back. She must have been absolutely plastered if she couldn't recall how her shirt had got there – or who might have relieved her of it in the first place.

'As I remember,' said Thierry, 'it was a night of Trivial Pursuit.'

Meg looked at him in shock.

'Oh,' Pug nodded, as if the light had dawned, 'so that's what Meg's calling it these days.'

'You don't understand, little one,' said Thierry, a patronising edge to his voice. 'It was the night in January when a few of us had drinks and played board games.'

'Boring games, don't you mean?' yawned Pug.

Phew, thought Meg. Nothing dodgy had gone on.

'Strip Trivial Pursuit, was it?'

She jerked her head towards Matthew. 'What?'

'Yes, Meg, why exactly did you need to remove your shirt?' Pug cocked an eyebrow expectantly.

'She was hot,' said Thierry, making it clear by his tone that he wasn't talking about her sexual prowess.

'Really?' Meg sighed in relief. It was just the sort of thing she was likely to do if she'd had one drink too many. Thierry was speaking the truth, she could tell. His left eye tended to twitch when he wasn't.

'Any normal person,' said Pug, 'would have turned the heating down.' She fixed her gaze on Matthew. 'What do you think? You're always going on in class about what's plausible and what isn't.'

To Meg's surprise, Matthew replied, 'We're not in class now, Elizabeth.'

Meg stared at him. Then a thought struck her. 'Pug, what were *you* doing behind the sofa?' It was too much to expect that her half-sister had been moving the furniture to vacuum thoroughly.

'I – er – dropped something behind it myself,' said Pug, grabbing Giles's hand. 'Come on, let's go find something to drink.'

'Pug—' Meg called after her, but the cosy twosome had scuttled off.

'Do not worry, *chérie*, the little one is teasing you something chronic.'

Meg frowned at Thierry. 'How do you know?'

'Because all her life she has taken lessons from her sister.' And with a sad little crease to the side of his mouth, he strolled off across the lawn.

'Thierry,' said Meg, finally managing to catch him on his own a short while later. 'Do you know what he was doing up at Arundel Hall in the first place?'

'What? Who?'

'Matthew. When he knocked over your jardinière.'

'Would you like some assistance with that crockery, Marguerite?'

She blinked down impatiently, having forgotten

she was carrying it. 'Don't change the subject! Why was Matthew at Arundel Hall?'

Thierry frowned. 'He was seeing Jacintha. About Timothy.'

'He went to see her at home? Why didn't she go to the school like any ordinary parent?'

'Because, *chérie*, Jacintha is not an ordinary parent. She is not ordinary at all. Only the other day—'

'Take these to the dining room for me, please.' Meg thrust the warmed soup bowls at him and rushed back to the kitchen to help Aggie with the soup itself.

'Grub's up!' she shouted from the French windows a while later.

Really, tutted Agnes. The girl had been doing so well.

Meg caught her look of disapproval. 'Sorry,' she said defensively, 'you haven't got a gong.'

By the time everyone had gathered around the table, the soup bowls had cooled down.

'Tuck in,' Meg urged, 'you don't have to be on your best behaviour. And there's plenty of food to go round.'

'Why is this chair beside me empty?' asked Thierry.

'Yaz called to say she was running late and not to wait for her.'

'Yaz?' echoed Matthew.

'Daddy,' interrupted Freddy, 'why have those grapes got red bits in them?'

'They're not grapes. They're stuffed olives.'

'Oh, gross!' The boy curled his lip in distaste. He'd heard olives were good for you. They must be yuck.

Matthew frowned. 'Don't say "gross".'

Meg offered the vexed father a bread roll. 'Yaz is Yasmin Bradley. She says you know each other.'

'We worked together.'

'That's right. Yaz has just come back from America.'

'I wasn't aware that you two were friends. You didn't mention it.'

'Didn't I? Oh well. Do you want a roll or don't you?'

Matthew blinked at her. 'Er, no. No thanks.'

'For what it's worth, kiddo,' Meg shot the sulking Freddy a conspiratorial look as she finally sat down herself, 'I don't think much of olives either.'

'But you always remember I adore them,' smiled Thierry. 'They remind me of home.'

He popped two into his mouth at once, a dreamy look on his face.

The second the meal was over for Freddy – when the grown-ups were on the boring coffee bit and he hadn't been allowed a third slice of Easter bunny cake – he asked to be excused, and bolted outside into the fresh air.

This place was so cool, masses larger than his own garden. Granny had called that tiddly, even though hers in London was even tiddlier. But here there was a huge tree you could climb, with a rope swing, and the lawn was large enough to set up a goal net on, or play rounders.

Freddy made for the tree and scrambled easily on to the first branch. He went up to the next one, and sat and stared at the large white house. He thought about his dad, who didn't thump about as much lately and was smiling a lot more, except when Meggy was around, when he smiled a lot less. Freddy thought that was weird, especially as Meggy was so funny.

He hugged the tree trunk as the man who spoke in the silly accent came out into the garden. His name was Terry, but everyone said it in a silly accent, as if they were foreign too. Terry saluted him. Freddy giggled and saluted back, then watched as the man started rolling a cigarette. He knew that that was what Terry was doing, because he'd seen Grandad do it last Christmas.

Dad was coming out into the garden too now. He wandered over to where Terry was perched on the low wall around the patio.

Freddy closed his eyes and pretended to be invisible – just in case.

Matthew nodded at Thierry. 'It's too fine a day to be stuck indoors.'

Thierry squinted up at him. 'I do not like to smoke inside. I am the only one here who has the habit.'

Matthew paused, glancing around the garden. 'You were saying earlier that you rent one of the old farm cottages on the Arundel estate.'

'I have no choice. My penthouse apartment overlooking the Seine is in refurbishment at the moment.' Thierry flashed him a smile. 'A small joke.'

Matthew hazarded a small laugh, his mind racing. 'Is the cottage near Yarleigh Woods?'

Thierry nodded. '*Oui*, the woods are my back garden. The cottage comes with the job. I pay pecan nuts for it.' He shrugged. 'A man cannot complain when he has work and a roof over his head.'

Matthew agreed in part, but didn't say so, also neglecting to point out that Thierry had his nuts mixed up. 'So, how long have you and Meg been . . .'

'Friends?' Thierry flicked ash on to the crazy-paving. 'For less time than we have been lovers. We are not lovers now, of course, but we were once, a long time ago. *Tu as l'air* . . . offended? But, Mr Potter – Matthieu – you must remember, the French are more philosophical about these things . . . As I see it, if Marguerite herself has not told you—'

'It's not as if it's anything to do with me,' said Matthew stiffly.

Thierry paused, staring at him. 'Is it anything to do with me if I ask how long you and Yasmin have known each other? She is pretty, *non?*'

When she had finally arrived, *oui.*

Matthew had always thought Yasmin Bradley was attractive. Polly had loved winding him up about it. Setting eyes on Yasmin again today though, after so long, had only dredged up the past as painfully as when she'd gasped at Freddy, 'Just look at you! You're the image of your mother!'

It was Meg who had smoothed over the awkward silence by asking if Yasmin wouldn't mind lending a hand in the kitchen. Which was typical of her, Matthew was beginning to appreciate. Meg seemed unable to sense a single bad vibe without immediately having to do something about it.

Matthew looked up now as William, Pug and Giles ambled out into the garden, heading for a blanket spread out in the sun. They were laughing, and obviously looking forward to an idle hour or two while other people took care of the clearing up. Robert Heybridge was close behind, heading for a bench in the shade of a small apple tree.

Something in Matthew snapped. Meg shouldn't have to worry about washing-up; she'd worked hard enough as it was today. Stiffening his spine into schoolmaster mode, he made his excuses to Thierry and strode over to the three young people making themselves comfortable on the picnic blanket.

'Right,' he said briskly, 'you're all coming with me.'

Twelve

Pug looked down at the mountain of dirty crockery and frowned.

'I'm supposed to be on holiday,' groaned William.

Giles was too busy in the dining room to complain.

'Don't be such whingers!' scoffed Matthew.

Meg, chivvied to one side along with Aggie and Yasmin, gazed at him in amazement.

'Your sister and Miss Widdicombe have both worked extremely hard today,' he was saying now. 'The least you can do is get off your backsides and do something to help.'

Pug swivelled back to face the sink, her head bent.

Meg continued to stare at Matthew. He took her arm, steering her out into the garden, Aggie and Yasmin following close behind.

'Meg,' he turned her to face him, 'you've bent over backwards for that girl today, and all she's done is be rude to you. Now I don't know how you two normally get along—'

'It's between Pug and me!' said Meg, bridling at Matthew's interference. Her relationship with her half-sister, or any other member of her family for that matter, was no one's concern but her own.

'I don't want to get involved—'

'A bit late for that!'

'But it seems to me you're pandering to her. That's the wrong way of going about it.'

Thought he knew everything, did he? Just because he was a schoolteacher.

'I am *not* pandering to her—'

'Meg Oakley, you are and you always have!' put in Aggie.

She spun to confront her godmother. 'You – you called me Meg. You've *never* called me Meg!'

'There's a first time for everything . . .' Aggie faltered. 'And I need to talk to you . . . It's important.'

'Go on then!'

'Not now.' The old woman grew pale. 'This evening, when everyone's gone.'

Meg looked at her godmother, suddenly concerned. 'Are you feeling all right?'

'I'm fine. Really. Please excuse me . . .' She drifted off towards the bench by the apple tree. Meg watched her progress, until Matthew spoke again.

'Listen . . .'

She raised an eyebrow. 'What?'

'I'd be a hypocrite if I didn't help clear up as well. I'm sorry for sticking my oar in where it evidently wasn't wanted.'

Meg and Yasmin both stared after him as he strode into the house.

Yasmin let out a low admiring whistle. 'Wow, talk about heroic!'

'Are you implying I needed rescuing?' demanded Meg. 'As if I'm some sort of wimpish damsel in distress?'

'No, I just—'

'Are you saying I let my family trample all over me? That that's all I am to them – a skivvy? Someone who mops up after them, who clears up their messes, who—'

'Meg, whooaa, keep your hair on. I was just going to say that if I were Matt I wouldn't risk going back into enemy territory quite yet.'

Meg wasn't sure why she needed to slip away and snatch a moment to herself, but it was short-lived anyway. Thierry found her upstairs, cross-legged on a bed, staring at the patchwork counterpane.

'You do not look happy, *mon ange*.'

She took Thierry's hand and drew him down beside her, tracing the lines on his palm with her index finger. 'I just felt a bit down, that's all. It's silly, I know. Today's supposed to be all about celebrating.'

'But you are not religious.'

'So?' she sniffed. 'Even a Buddhist has every right to enjoy Easter. It's supposed to apply to every single human being after all, not just to people like Aggie who go to church every Sunday. It affects everyone – even you, Thierry.'

He chuckled. 'I forget sometimes that you are a convent schoolgirl.'

'Well, how do you think I ought to remind you? Bash you over the head with my autographed-by-the-Bishop Sunday Missal? Or was it my Bible he signed?' She reflected a second. 'It was so long ago. All I remember was that he told me I had very healthy rosy cheeks, and I said that was all thanks to Max Factor. Mother Mary Bernadette thought I meant some bloke. She nearly burst a blood vessel.'

Thierry laughed again, gazing into her eyes so intently she had to bow her head and pretend to laugh too. And as she stared into her lap, an idea started forming. Thierry could be quite a fount of inspiration at times.

'If I tell you something, could you keep it to yourself?' She lifted her face. 'Please . . . it's important.'

'Of course.' He squeezed her hand. 'Marguerite,

you can tell me anything. I will repeat it to no one.'

Unless, she thought shrewdly, you've got six pints of lager inside you.

'The thing is,' she began, her voice barely above a whisper, 'Matthew and I – we haven't . . . we've never actually—'

'Made love?'

It sounded so much more romantic in a French accent. But that didn't blunt the frisson of shock that passed through her, along with something she couldn't define, something that caused her to blush when normally she wouldn't. 'How – How did you know?'

'I am a man, I am from Paris. I know you, and I know what it is I must look out for.'

'Do I look at him too platonically? I do, don't I?' It had to be a dead give-away to someone who knew her as intimately as Thierry.

But his reply cut through her logic like a knife through margarine. 'It is not so much you, as him, Marguerite.'

'Matthew?' Meg jerked back in surprise. 'You can tell just by looking at Matthew?'

'He is a man surveying a beautiful woman and not comprehending what it is he sees.'

Meg screwed up her brow. 'Huh?'

'You want me to explain the unexplainable.' Thierry twisted his lips ruefully. 'Something I see with my eyes, yes, but which I understand here.' He pressed his hand over his heart.

'Thierry—'

'It is like this with you, Marguerite: men see your face and your body, and by the time they see your soul it is too late. You 'ave given all you think you have to give all it is you think they crave. And then you run, you hide, because most of them find they want something you do not feel you have.'

Oh goodie – riddles. 'Thierry, please talk English. Or French. Anything's better than the crap you're coming out with.'

He gave up gracefully. 'What I do not understand, Marguerite, is *why* you and the fine Matthieu have never—'

'If you hadn't jumped the gun, I would have told you.'

'*Oui.* I spout "crap". So tell me now.'

'Well,' she said, 'he's Catholic. A proper one, not like me. He doesn't believe in, um . . .'

'In what?' prompted Thierry.

'Sex before marriage,' she mumbled quickly, feeling herself blush again.

It wasn't fun lying to friends for a reason such as this. Even worse lying to your own family. Although, weeks ago, she had only set out to 'bend' the truth by not correcting certain assumptions people were making, she had found herself having to tell whoppers. She couldn't stop now that she'd dug such a deep hole for herself. The most she could do was try not to make it any worse.

She had no proof that Matthew didn't agree with sexual relations outside of marriage, but to protect him to a degree, she had said that he didn't. It made him sound more noble, she thought, and not entirely at her mercy.

Most of her friends were under the impression that she was reluctant to discuss her burgeoning relationship because she might be tempting fate. After all, her track record was nothing to write home about.

When she'd invited Matthew to Aggie's, she'd been confident that no one – not even Pug – would confront him directly about the 'affair' because they respected him too much. No one would feel comfortable teasing him, would they? Especially not with his background.

So far, she had got away with things, but today she'd taken a big risk. She'd wanted to invite Matthew for his sake as well as her own, though, so that he'd have some adult company and not be stuck in that little house of his, moping.

She had dealt with the last lie – the one to Thierry – in such a canny way, she felt, that it wasn't going against Jake's smoke-screen plans; Meg was reassured that the man she loved wasn't going to jump down her throat. Jake was perfectly free, she contemplated dreamily, to jump down it in other, more delicious ways when he came back from his skiing holiday. She had never met such a fabulous smoocher. Just thinking about his kisses made her melt inside.

As she zigzagged across the garden, pretending she had no firm destination in mind, she studied Matthew standing at the foot of the oak tree. He was talking to his son, who had grown rather attached to the second branch up.

'Why did Jesus Christ get risen today?' she caught Freddy saying, as she approached Matthew quietly from behind.

He paused a moment. 'So that people like your mother could have a special place in heaven.'

'What about people like me?' asked Meg, and then promptly bit her lip.

Matthew jumped and turned round. His eyes were a dark caramelly brown, and however much they might glower there was something about them, Meg noticed now, that could never be menacing.

'People like you?' he repeated archly. 'I suppose so that you might at least have a chance of actually getting in.'

She grinned.

'Can I hunt for my eggs now?' asked Freddy.

Meg pulled a face. Another thing she'd left off

her list! She'd forgotten to hide the damn things. Only yesterday she had painted a dozen free-range chickens' eggs in bright jewel colours *à la* Fabergé. She should have pricked holes and blown out the contents first, but that had seemed too laborious, so she had hard-boiled them instead, feeling sure the mother hens would understand it was all in a good cause.

'Do you like climbing trees, Freddy?' she asked.

'Timothy Arundel has lots of trees,' he nodded, obviously forgetting all about the eggs; children could be distracted so easily. 'He says one day he'll show me his tree house. Terry built it for him because his Uncle Jake was too busy, and anyway, Timothy says his uncle's no good with his hands.'

Meg was blushing. She felt as red as her old basque.

'Please, please, *please* can I hunt for my eggs now?' begged Freddy.

'If you close your eyes and count to one hundred,' sighed Meg. 'You *can* count to one hundred, can't you, kiddo?'

'He's my son,' said Matthew drily, 'what do you expect?'

With a huge sigh dripping with melodrama, Pug flopped on to the picnic blanket beside William and Giles.

'Meg's ruining that man,' she lamented, gazing forlornly at Matthew and her sister darting around the garden hiding painted eggs. 'He used to be so mild-mannered, so—'

'You mean he never raised his voice at you till today.'

William was deceptively perceptive, thought Pug, scowling at him because she didn't want to admit that he was right.

Giles reached for Pug's hand, but she whipped it out of his grasp.

'I think your sister's great,' he said.

'You're a man,' said Pug, with a 'humph'. 'You would think that.'

'I don't know why you're so hell-bent on giving her a hard time.'

'I wouldn't expect you to understand.' She snatched at a clump of clover on the lawn. She wasn't sure she entirely understood herself.

'You're making out that you and I are more than just friends.' Giles was propped on one elbow, staring up at her, willing her to look at him. 'I think that means I have a right to an opinion.'

Half of Pug had come to accept that Giles was genuinely interested in her company, but the other half kept repeating over and over: 'He must be mad!'

'I didn't hear you complaining,' she said, on a

high from her own cleverness and audacity, and hating the other things, the feelings and circumstances all conspiring to pull her back down.

He tried to hold her hand again, but she shook him off. 'That's because I'm not,' he said. 'I'm not complaining.' His cheeks were filling with colour. 'I really do want—'

'I'm not like my sister,' snapped Pug, her own cheeks glowing hotly.

'He didn't say you were,' corrected William. 'And how *did* you find Meg's shirt behind the sofa? I keep meaning to ask.'

'I was hoovering,' she admitted truthfully. 'A mad moment of guilt for being so off with her lately. It didn't last long, I only ended up doing half the lounge.'

Giles was chuckling in a complimentary manner. Pug frowned at him. Ever since she'd been a little girl, she had dreamed of how it would be when romance entered her life. Even as a child, she had imagined her Prince Charming to be as mature, generous and intelligent as Giles. But the adult feelings he evoked, his amazing good looks, the warmth in his gaze . . . This was beyond anything Pug had envisaged; this was *Heavy* with a capital *H*.

She watched as he closed his eyes and rolled on to his back.

'It's about time Meg took responsibility for her actions,' Pug stated emphatically.

'Shush,' hissed William. 'She's coming over.'

Meg was breathless from racing around the garden. 'Can I hide an egg under the blanket, please?'

Pug didn't answer. William nodded. 'Go ahead.'

'Great.' Meg blew him a kiss and rushed off again.

'. . . ninety-nine, one hundred. REA-DY!' yelled Freddy.

Georgie, who had only recently woken up from her afternoon nap, toddled around the garden, rubbing her eyes and chattering away to herself until she spotted a squirrel and decided it would be fun to play with it. This consisted of chasing it and shrieking at a hundred decibels while she did so. Yasmin ended up having to chase Georgie before the little girl tumbled head-first into the goldfish pond. Freddy, meanwhile, hunted for eggs with all the undiluted energy of a seven-year-old boy.

Meg sank down on a plastic patio chair beside Matthew. 'Today feels as if it's been a week long,' she groaned.

'Mmm.' He sounded distant. She risked a sidelong peek. He was staring pensively at the house.

'Penny for them?' she smiled.

'I was just thinking . . .' he said.

Meg was hesitant about prompting him, but she didn't need to.

'I used to live in a house like this once,' he went on. 'Well, not exactly like this, but it was white, and about this size. A family house, except that I was an only child, so it always felt huge and empty. My parents weren't rich by today's standards, and they spent their money as quickly as it was earned. They used to go abroad a lot. Sometimes they sent me to stay with my grandmother in Scotland, when they went away during school holidays. Most of the time, though, they went on their trips during term-time, when I wasn't at home anyway.'

'Did you go to a public school?' Meg was surprised. She thought of Harrow and Eton and Rugby, wondering why Matthew hadn't turned out like Jake, and then wondering what exactly she meant by that.

'It wasn't anywhere well-known. Just a small place, decrepit and Dickensian. Some boys were boarders and others weren't. I hated it.'

'You hated school?' Meg found this hilarious. 'But look at you now!'

'I know.' He glanced at her and smiled. 'I think that's why I became a teacher. I wanted to prove I could do it better than the ones I'd grown up with.'

'And are you better?'

He shrugged modestly and looked back at the house.

'What about teaching in a secondary school?' she asked. 'Doesn't that appeal?'

'Not really. I prefer children's minds when they're between the infant and the adolescent stage. When they're just starting out and everything's an adventure. Perhaps it isn't as ambitious as certain people would like . . .' He tailed off.

'Oh?' Meg was intrigued. 'Who?'

Matthew shook his head. 'It doesn't matter.'

'Maybe if I'd had a teacher like you when I was Freddy's age, I might have turned out differently,' she said, after a pause.

He swung his head round. 'Why? What's wrong with you?'

The question threw her. 'A lack of qualifications, for starters.' She laughed, to disguise her awkwardness. 'A lack of common sense, others might say.'

'That's a heavy burden to lay on my shoulders.'

'Your shoulders?' Meg squirmed in her chair. His shoulders were nice and wide, but what was he insinuating?

'With the kids I teach – I only try to light a spark. For about a year I do what I can. After that, it's out of my hands.'

'Oh! Oh, I see.' This made more sense. He was talking generally, not specifically.

'You know,' he hesitated, 'I wasn't entirely honest about the things Polly told me about you.'

'You weren't?' He had probably held back the worst. 'Go on, I'm bracing myself.'

He gave her a wry smile. 'It's nothing awful. Polly once said that – in spite of everything – she liked you. She thought you'd end up being a famous comedy actress, like Lucille Ball. In the end, when she left St Dominic's, she really missed you.'

'Oh right!' This had to be a joke. 'A simple "thank you" for today's meal will do.'

'I'm not making this up.' He looked miffed. '*I* was the one who thought badly of you after the stories I'd heard. Polly and I came to Yarleigh when Freddy was two. She'd hated having to leave when her parents moved up to London and she'd always planned to come back. So when I applied for a job at the primary school and got it . . .'

'. . . Polly's wish came true.'

He paused for a moment to contemplate his hands, lying tense in his lap. Meg stared at them too, until a preposterous urge came over her to hold one.

'About a month after we moved here,' Matthew continued, 'Polly came home from shopping one day and said she'd bumped into you in the supermarket. You'd picked up one of Freddy's toys and handed it back to him.'

'Really?' Meg couldn't remember the encounter at all.

Matthew nodded. '"Oh hi!" you said to Polly. "How are you doing?" And then you grinned.'

'Did I?'

'"Been busy I see," you added. "Cute kid. Wouldn't mind one just like him one day – maybe!" And that was it, off you went up the cereal aisle in a mad rush.'

'The "mad rush" bit sounds familiar.'

'I always remember Polly telling me about it. I said to her she was crazy to be so happy.'

'Happy?'

'I couldn't understand her logic either. I suppose people just want to be liked.'

'A bit like dogs when they start licking the one person in a group who they sense isn't keen on them.' The words were hardly out of her mouth before Meg wanted to kick herself for comparing Polly to a dog, or for making it seem as though she'd disliked Polly, when in truth she'd been in awe of her. 'Did you know "prefect" is an anagram of "perfect"?' she said, sounding distant herself now. 'I was only ever a mouthy cow when I felt intimidated, and Polly was so—'

'Intimidating?'

'You know what I mean! I told you this before.

She was in the goody-goody set, and I was . . .' Why did baddy-baddy not sound right?

'You know,' said Matthew, 'if she hadn't been so shy, I think she would have actively tried to make friends with you. I probably would have insisted she had a screw loose, but now . . .'

Meg twisted her mouth sardonically. 'Now you're the one with the loose screw.'

'Perhaps . . . But it's beginning to dawn on me,' he said, 'that maybe Polly liked you because . . .'

Answers rattled in manic fashion through Meg's brain: Because I bribed her. Because she was delusional.

'. . . Because it's impossible to know you and *not* like you,' stated Matthew quietly but firmly, as Freddy ran up to them with half a dozen eggs in the basket Aggie had lent him.

The boy was ecstatic. 'I've found six, but Georgie hasn't found a single one! Are there any more?'

Meg was staring at Matthew, who was acting as if he hadn't said what she thought he had said. Maybe she had misheard him. Maybe she had wanted to mishear him. Oh crikey, which was worse?

'Yuck! Bloody hell!' A wail from across the lawn made them all look round.

William and Giles were both rolling hysterically on the grass. Pug was holding up the picnic blanket in fury and disgust.

'Meg, you divvy! I thought you said you'd hard-boiled ALL the bloody eggs before painting them!'

Meg had never known an Easter Sunday like it. By eight in the evening, all she wanted to do was go to sleep. Thierry had hitched a lift home with Giles nearly twenty minutes ago. Dad, William and Pug had set off for home too, only a short walk down the road. As for Matthew, he had just finished bundling the kids into their jackets, the evening having turned chilly. He kept trying to zip Freddy's up, but Freddy – an obstinate little lad – wanted it undone.

'Would you like me to stay and help you finish up here?' Yasmin asked Meg at the front door.

'No, it's all right, you get home. Most of it's done anyway.'

'Thanks to Matt.'

Meg didn't need reminding.

She was too drained to bother kissing his cheek today as she said goodbye, although he hovered, as if expecting it. Freddy wasn't going to be put off by her lack of enthusiasm; he gave her a hug. She felt obliged to return it.

For good measure, she pecked Georgie's cheek.

Matthew thanked Meg and Aggie again, then turned to Yasmin. 'I'll walk you to your car.'

She beamed. 'That's very chivalrous of you, Matt. Don't you agree, Meggy?'

Meg smiled stiffly. She thought it totally unnecessary; she could see the car from where she was standing.

'You *are* coming to Meg's birthday party, aren't you?' Yasmin asked Matthew, as they went down the garden path running straight between the two lime trees which gave the house its name.

Meg bit her lip. She hadn't wanted to expose Matthew to her friends *en masse.*

'Um,' he was saying, 'her birthday? When exactly—'

'Not this Friday coming, the one after. She'll be twenty-eight.' Yasmin grinned wickedly. 'We're going to give her one last bash she'll never forget, before she gets too old to enjoy them. I'm surprised she hasn't mentioned it yet. It must have slipped her mind.'

It did, thought Meg. Deliberately.

'I'll have to see,' said Matthew. 'I'm not sure if I can make it.'

Yasmin didn't look as if she was going to take no for an answer.

By now, Meg was convinced that her Number Two Best Friend fancied her chances with Matthew.

'Do your best, Yaz,' Meg called after their retreating backs, her voice strained, 'but don't twist the poor guy's arm. If he can, he can. If he can't . . .'

Thirteen

By the following afternoon, Matthew had decided for certain that he wasn't going to Meg's birthday party. If it were just going to be a bring-a-bottle type evening at her house, he might have thought differently, but her friends were planning something that would involve a lot more cash. He was just conceding that he ought to at least send a card, when all thoughts of birthdays flew straight out of his head. The Ford Fiesta he was a passenger in was about to plough into a hedge at the side of the road.

He jerked at the steering-wheel.

'Sarah-Jane – *careful!*'

'I'm sorry.' The girl seemed to be having trouble with the pedals. Her face was screwed up in concentration and dismay; any second now, the water-works would start.

Matthew had known this was a bad idea ever since Sarah-Jane's mother had brought it up, but he'd been expertly press-ganged into saying yes.

'Polly wouldn't have minded,' Mrs Elliott had said, smoothing a crease in her linen suit. 'She always said you had the patience of a saint. I think she would have talked you into doing this little favour for Sarah-Jane, don't you?'

And so here he was, on Easter Monday of all days, because 'there isn't much time until her test, and she really needs as much practice as possible.' Mrs Elliott had been downright Machiavellian. 'Don't worry about the children, they can stay with me. I'm sure it would be a break for you, Matthew.'

A break? He'd be lucky if he ever saw them again.

'Sarah-Jane,' he groaned, 'you should have turned off back there.'

'Should I? I'm sorry! Shall I do a three-point turn?'

He shook his head weakly. 'Not on a dual carriageway, no. Just take the next exit.'

She did as she was told, although the tyres screeched and she forgot to change down a gear. They were now on a much quieter stretch of country road. The speedometer crept up to forty-five . . . Matthew hadn't planned an emergency stop, but when he caught sight of a car he recognized, and told Sarah-Jane to hit the brakes, he should have tagged '*gently!*' on the end. The Fiesta shuddered to a halt. Fortunately, it hadn't rained recently.

Matthew clambered out and hurried towards the tomato-red Mini he'd spotted parked at an angle on the grass verge. He looked in through the open window. 'Are you OK?'

Meg frowned up at him. 'I'm fine.'

'Are you sure?'

'Yes,' she snapped, climbing out and closing the door rather forcefully. 'Of course I'm sure!' But she didn't look it. Instead, she kicked one of her tyres and swore.

'Have you got a puncture?' asked Matthew, a certain inevitability at running into her again creeping in around the edges of his world.

She shook her head. 'No. The car just conked out.'

'Is it still conked out, or have you tried starting it again?'

'There's no point.'

'But have you tried?'

Her face about six inches from his own, she snapped, 'It's bloody petrol, isn't it? I haven't bloody got any!' And her gaze burned into him as if it was all his fault. Then she stared over his shoulder, her eyes widening. He looked round. Sarah-Jane was getting out of the car.

'Don't just leave it in the middle of the road,' he yelled, striding back.

Once the Fiesta was on the verge, and Sarah-Jane had been placated with a grudging apology, Matthew turned to Meg again.

'Aggie give you a hard time last night after the rest of us left?' he asked jokingly, trying to lighten the atmosphere. 'Heck, you've got me calling her Aggie now, too.'

Meg scowled. 'Well, I'm sure she wouldn't mind. After all, she reckons the sun shines out of your—'

'Jerrycan,' said Matthew quickly. 'That's what you need. Do you have one?'

'No,' said Meg.

He glanced at Sarah-Jane.

She shrugged coolly. 'No idea.'

Matthew ground his teeth. 'Well, would you mind checking?'

The girl rolled her eyes and went off to open her boot. 'Do you mean this?' She held up a bright yellow and green one.

'That's it.' Matthew nodded.

'It's empty.'

'They're meant to be,' said Meg. 'I think it's a safety regulation.'

Sarah-Jane frowned. 'Then how are we supposed to—'

'We'll have to go to the petrol station and fill it up,' explained Matthew. 'Come on, there's no point dawdling.' He gestured to Meg.

She shook her head and leaned against her car. 'I'd rather wait here.'

'Oh come on, it's the middle of nowhere. I'm not leaving you here on your own.'

'Save your concern, Mr Potter, for people you really feel it for.'

Perturbed, he walked back towards her. He had never seen her so gloomy. 'Meg . . . what's wrong?'

'Nothing. Just go get the petrol, please. I'm in a really big hurry.' She reached into the car and pulled out her purse. 'Here, take this.' She attempted to hand him a tenner.

He refused to take it. 'We'll settle up later. Where are you on your way to then?'

Sure enough, *that* made her head snap up. 'None of your bloody business!'

'No,' he sighed. 'It probably isn't.'

She kicked at a pebble lying beside her foot. 'There's no "probably" about it.'

Matthew shifted before she could get around to kicking him too. He turned to Sarah-Jane. 'Your mother said I could drive your car if necessary, didn't she?'

'Ye-es.'

'Well then, you stay here with Meg.'

'But—'

'And here's your mobile.' He grabbed it from

inside the Fiesta and handed it across. 'In case of any *other* emergencies.'

Twiddling a finger in her hair, Meg leaned against the back of the Mini. Sarah-Jane leaned against the bonnet. They didn't speak for a minute or two, until Meg remarked casually, 'There were L-plates on your car. Is Matthew teaching you to drive?'

'Just a few extra lessons.' Sarah-Jane seemed to perk up. 'It was Mummy's idea. Mr Potter – Matthew – will take me out for an hour or two whenever he can, up until my test, and in return I'll do some babysitting for free.'

'Oh,' sighed Meg. 'What's Matthew like as an instructor then?' She rubbed her eyes, which were beginning to feel too large for their sockets. She was exhausted. Hardly surprising considering her lack of sleep the night before. 'I mean,' she went on, 'his driving doesn't exactly inspire confidence.'

'I'll tell him you said that, shall I?'

Meg shoved her hands into her pockets to stop herself whacking the girl.

'No, really,' smiled Sarah-Jane, 'he's great. So incredibly patient.' She paused a moment. 'It's so sad, isn't it? What happened to his wife. Mummy says she doesn't think Matthew will ever get over it. He has his needs like any other man, but she doesn't think he'll actually marry again.'

It was obvious what Sarah-Jane was playing at.

'You can tell your mother from me,' said Meg, 'that I have no intention of becoming the second Mrs Matthew Potter.'

'Oh, but I didn't—'

'Anyone would be a fool to try, and that includes seventeen-year-olds with crushes as huge as the Millennium Dome!'

Sarah-Jane blushed furiously.

Oh bugger, groaned Meg inwardly, me and my big mouth.

Matthew was as quick as he could be without breaching the Highway Code. When he returned, Meg and Sarah-Jane looked as if they hadn't exchanged a single word. The pouting teenager was playing with her mobile phone, and Meg was staring out broodingly over the patchwork valley.

'Right,' said Matthew, 'shall I do the honours or do you want to?' He was going to give Meg as little cause as possible to launch into a feminist rant.

She shrugged. 'You can do it.'

Which probably meant that she'd never done this before and didn't want to make a fool of herself.

'Here.' He pulled out a packet of sweets from his jacket pocket. 'I got them in the garage shop, help yourself.'

Meg stared at them. 'Jelly beans? How old do you think I am?'

'I always grab them automatically when I pay,' he said. 'For Freddy. But he's had more than enough teeth-rotting substances lately. If you don't want them—'

'She didn't say she didn't want them,' said Sarah-Jane, who obviously fancied a few herself.

'Now share nicely, children,' he smirked, as both females made a lunge for the packet. But a moment later, Matthew almost dropped the Jerrycan in surprise.

Sarah-Jane was flapping at her mouth as if it had caught fire.

Meg was doing a war dance around the car.

'What's wrong?' demanded Matthew.

'Those!' hissed Meg, pointing at the sweets.

Sarah-Jane picked up the packet and waved it in his face.

'What?' He read the label. '*Chilli-flavour Jelly Beans – Extra Hot!!!* Oh heck.' He looked at Sarah-Jane. 'They must have swapped them about on the shelves. I'm sorry . . .'

'They're hor-*ren*-dous.' She wrinkled her nose and shook her head, as if convinced he had made a deliberate mistake.

He glanced at Meg, who had transferred her war dance to the sloping field next to the road, except that now she appeared to be trying to shake something off her foot.

'Listen,' he said to Sarah-Jane, 'I'm going to go talk to her. Wait here.'

Sarah-Jane tapped her watch. 'Mummy expected us back a quarter of an hour ago.'

'Well, why don't you call her on that little phone of yours and tell her that if you hadn't missed our turn-off, we would have been back on time.'

'But it's not *my* fault your girlfriend's like a bear with a sore head.'

Matthew looked back at Sarah-Jane. 'She is not my—'

The girl was oozing bravado now. 'Whatever,' she shrugged.

Shaking his head in exasperation, Matthew trudged over to Meg, who had flopped on to the grass in a dejected huddle.

'Right.' He sat down beside her, the way he approached the kids in class when they had a problem – at eye-level, so that they wouldn't feel too threatened. 'What is it? What's bothering you?'

'Cow pat.'

'Sorry?'

She pointed at her shoe. 'Cow pat. Just my sodding luck.' And her head drooped even further.

'Actually, I'd call it lucky. At least it's dry, not a steaming wet one.'

With a sharp intake of breath, a smile crossed her lips, albeit reluctantly. 'I'm such a wally,' she said. 'A sentimental prat. I try to go on as if everything's normal, but—'

'Slow down, I haven't a clue what you're on about.'

'The bazaar. At St Dominic's. I went there to see Aggie, to tell her nothing had changed. But she'd got a headache and Edith Sopwith was running her stall.'

'I always used to think a Sopwith was a kind of camel.'

She regarded him sceptically. 'A Sopwith Camel is an old plane with two wings.'

'Well of course it is.' He didn't dare point out that most planes had two wings. 'But it would have explained why Edith always has the hump.'

Meg sank her head into her hands. 'Careful, that almost sounded like a joke.'

He stared down at her red-brown curls. 'So, why did you want to tell Aggie nothing had changed? Why should it have?'

'Do you know what I did, Matthew?' She looked up at him again. 'I only went and bought back everything I'd donated, didn't I? It was all still there on the stall. No one wanted it. I'm so bloody sentimental!'

He grinned. 'At least it's in a good cause.'

She winced. 'I knew you were going to say that!'

'Well then why—'

'Oh shut up. Shut *up!*' She pressed her hands over her ears and shook her head.

Matthew scrambled to his feet. 'If you're going to be like this—'

Meg's hand shot out, coaxing him down beside her again. Her pale face filled with contrition. There was desperation in her eyes. 'I'm sorry. This isn't your fault.'

'Meg, what *is* it? What's wrong?'

She hesitated. 'Can I ask you something, Matthew? Something personal.'

'If you want.'

'Your parents . . .' she hesitated, her brow furrowing '. . . they died in a sailing accident, didn't they?'

He nodded. 'I was twelve. They went on a trip around the Far East and never came back.'

Meg nodded too, but slowly, thoughtfully. 'My mum went to Sainsbury's, which is a lot nearer, I know, but she never came back either.'

'I'm sorry.' Matthew paused. 'What happened exactly?'

'I was fourteen, Pug was three, William was five. Mum said she was going for the weekly shop. It wasn't till gone eight that Dad really started worrying. He went to look for her, but it was too late.'

'Too late?'

'She didn't want to be found. Dad was going to call the police, but then he saw the note on their bed. It just said that she was sorry.'

Matthew snatched at his breath. 'Suicide?'

'No.' Meg stared into the distance, at the winding River Yarl. 'She'd walked out on us. Left us. She wasn't going to come back.'

'Oh . . . I – I don't know what to say. Polly never mentioned . . .' Out of the corner of his eye, he spotted Sarah-Jane venturing within earshot. He arched a forbidding eyebrow at her. She wandered back to the road, looking pointedly at her watch.

Meg hadn't noticed; she was too wrapped up in the past. 'At first, people couldn't stop talking about what my mother had done. But then . . .' She sighed and shrugged. 'After a while, some other scandal erupted, and a woman abandoning her husband and children became old hat. Yesterday's news. We were left to get on with it.'

'It couldn't have been easy.'

Meg smiled darkly. 'If Mum had died . . . been run-over or something . . . If there'd been a body to bury . . . This probably sounds twisted, but it would have made things simpler. You can get over something like that, because most of the time you know they didn't leave you on purpose—' She jerked her head up. 'I'm sorry . . .'

He took her hand, holding it limply. 'Meg, listen, you don't have to apologise. I understand. Honestly.'

'You're a good man, Matthew.' Her long, slim fingers, soft and warm and trembling with life, slid away from him. 'And I've been such a bitch to you.'

'Don't be a divvy.' He grinned dismissively. 'I haven't exactly been at my best with you either.'

She smiled again, but it was an ominous sort of smile. Matthew could sense a mass of heartache behind it, hammering to get out.

'Last night,' she said, 'after you'd all gone, Aggie told me something . . . Something I didn't want to hear.'

'About your mother?'

Meg nodded. 'Aggie and my mother used to be close. I never knew my grandparents, they died before I was born. So did my real father. My mum met him at a dance. Colin Oakley. Tall, dark, handsome, a real heart-throb by all accounts. Mum managed to lose the few photographs she had of him. She didn't live around here then; he was no one local. Anyway, he got her pregnant, but managed to stick around long enough to do the decent thing by her.'

'A heart-throb with a conscience,' said Matthew dryly.

'Exactly. But he had a motorbike. He crashed it a month before I was due to be born. He was dead by the time they got him to hospital. Mum came to stay with Aggie, who was like an aunt to her. I popped out prematurely a fortnight later in the middle of dinner at Linden Trees Villa. It was a Friday, Mum said, because they were having fish.'

'So you're loving and giving,' put in Matthew, before he could stop himself. 'Friday's child . . . according to the nursery rhyme.'

Meg blinked at him. 'Don't sound so surprised.'

'I'm not! I'm just trying to get my head around this.'

'There's more.' Meg swallowed. 'Aggie's been getting letters for weeks now – letters from my mother . . .'

'Oh God . . .'

'My mother sent them to Aggie because she didn't know how I'd react, and she didn't want the rest of the family to know. Aggie was supposed to "test the waters" or whatever, but she hadn't wanted to tell me. "Protecting me," she said. But then last week she found out something that put a whole new perspective on things. My mother hadn't wanted to mention it before. She hadn't wanted me to agree to see her only out of pity.'

'Your mother wants to see you? What about Elizabeth and your step-father?'

Meg shook her head dully. 'Just me. Everything's always up to me . . .'

'But why would you only do it out of pity?'

Meg was silent, staring out across the valley, snatching at clumps of grass around her feet.

Matthew put a finger on her cheek and turned her to face him. 'Meg . . .'

Tears were welling. She struggled to sniff them back.

'Meg,' he persisted, 'tell me.'

Jerking her head away, and with a final almighty sniff, she snapped despairingly, 'Because she's dying.'

Fourteen

Before she had run out of petrol, Meg had been on her way to see Aggie. Now, alone again in her car, she dropped her head against the steering-wheel and allowed self-pity to wash over her.

Matthew had been . . . amazing, she realised, when she finally rammed the car into gear and headed off towards Yarleigh. He had listened, and said virtually all the right things – until he had warned her that she would regret it for the rest of her life if she didn't go and see her mother now, while she could. Meg hadn't wanted to hear that. She had wanted to hear exactly what she was telling herself – that nothing had changed.

And so she had worked herself into another strop over it, because she didn't want to give him the chance to make any sense.

'I don't need your advice,' she'd snapped, among other things.

His face had darkened, but he hadn't raised his voice. 'We'll talk another time, Meg. This isn't the right place, not with Sarah-Jane hanging around. And you're working yourself up. When you've had time to think . . .'

I don't want to think. I don't want to admit that you might be right! Meg had tried to ignore him as he'd finished filling her car with petrol. He had asked her to start the engine, to check that everything was OK, then she had paid him what she owed. He had tried one last time to offer some discreet word of comfort but she had brushed it off, and so, frowning, he had driven off in the Fiesta with Sarah-Jane.

Now, Meg parked her Mini in front of the old bell-tower, opposite Best Bib and Tucker. She was no longer possessed by the need to tell Aggie how she felt. The urge had been eclipsed by Matthew's hand touching hers; she didn't understand how or why, it just had.

She wasn't supposed to be working until tea-time, but keeping busy could be the distraction she was so desperate for. Libby wouldn't mind if she came in early.

In fact, Libby practically pounced on her as she walked through the door. 'Am I glad to see you!' She hustled Meg into the kitchen. 'I've been trying to get hold of you. Bee hasn't come in today. She's not feeling up to it; another bout of "morning" sickness. I've been tearing my hair out. The weather's so nice for once, townies are obviously jumping into their cars on the spur of the moment and descending on the countryside like a mob of marauding Vikings! I mean, what on earth do they think Hyde Park is for! Can't they descend on that instead?'

'Aren't you glad of the business?'

'Only when I cash up.'

'Well, listen.' Meg could already see a solution. 'It doesn't matter that we're nowhere near Devon, but how about Devonshire teas? We can do a Bank Holiday Special. It keeps things simpler. We make a big batch of scones and—'

'Whip up some cream . . .'

'And we've still got plenty of that strawberry jam you made the other day.'

'You're a genius!'

'So,' broached Meg, her heart – despite its heaviness – thumping as she tied her apron on, 'does that mean you're still all right about my having Friday to Sunday off then?'

'Mmm? Oh, that computer course in London.'

Meg couldn't look her friend in the eye. 'That's right. Is it still OK for me to go?' She held her breath. She *needed* to get away; it wasn't just a case of wanting to.

' 'Course it is,' said Libby. 'You've given me enough warning. I'll find someone to cover in case Bee can't come in. You just go and brush up on your bytes.'

'Bites?' Meg's hand flew to her neck in alarm, but Libby, humming 'I Will Survive', had already bustled off to the larder.

'I thought you said you were taking me to a hotel?' Meg peered over the top of her new Jackie-O-style sunglasses at the three – no, *four* storey – townhouse that loomed up from a row of virtually identical houses. 'Where are we? Whose place is this?'

'I thought you'd be curious to see where I stay when I've got business in town.'

'Jake!' Meg nearly knocked her sunglasses off. 'This is your place? But it's humungous!'

'It's not just mine, sweetheart. It's Mother's and Jacintha's too.'

Meg took a step back. 'They're not here now are they?'

'I'm not completely insane. We've got the house to ourselves. Happy Birthday, darling. You're queen of the castle for a whole forty-eight hours.'

'It's not actually my birthday till *next* Friday.'

'Well, think of this as an early present then.' He stretched out his hand to her. 'Come on, don't dawdle.' He grinned meaningfully. 'We're wasting valuable time out here.'

As he led her up to the shiny black front door, Meg glanced furtively over her shoulder. 'Aren't you afraid someone might see us?'

'Darling,' he explained patiently, 'this is Belgravia, not Yarleigh. Even if curtains twitch now and again, neighbours have a marvellous habit of keeping things to themselves. Besides, you're carrying my briefcase; you look like a PA.'

Meg was doubtful. 'But I read newspapers and magazines. They're always full of gossip.'

Jake was searching for his keys. He looked up and scanned the quiet leafy square. 'I don't see any paparazzi about today.' He smirked. 'Maybe I'm not as important as you seem to think.'

'You're important to *me*,' Meg murmured, deciding she would prove it to him the second they were through the door.

'I thought,' said Meg, 'that we might have gone out somewhere.'

It was dark outside, and they still hadn't budged from Jake's bedroom except to use the en suite bathroom.

'And I thought,' said Jake, lighting yet another cigarette, 'that we'd just stay in tonight. I want you all to myself.'

Meg couldn't bear lying there any longer. There was a danger she might fall asleep earlier than she had to, and her dreams the last few nights had left her feeling depressed and confused. She didn't want to revisit her childhood again, as if watching an old cine film.

'How about a Jacuzzi?' she asked. 'I've never been in one before, except in a showroom, and there wasn't any water in it.'

'I thought you said you couldn't swim?' he pointed out sarcastically.

'I can swim enough not to drown,' she retorted. 'Come on.' She tugged at his hand. 'I'll let you scrub my back.'

That seemed to change his mind. By the time they were on dry land again, Meg was starving. 'So,' she said, as she landed on the bed, wrapped in the fluffiest towelling robe ever, 'are you a good cook too?'

'Is that a hint?'

It appeared that she ought to make the most of the fluffy white robe while she could; she might not be in it for long.

'Jake, I'm hungry,' she protested.

'So am I, sweetheart.'

'No.' She pushed him away. 'I mean hungry as in "feed me".'

'It's still early . . .' He untied her robe and buried his face in her stomach. Right on cue, it emitted a deafening rumble. He lifted his head. 'Talk about romantic.'

Meg sat up and pulled the robe around her. 'I'm going to go down and raid your kitchen. Are you coming or not?'

'I'd rather be coming up here, preferably in

the near future, but as you've left me no option . . .' Scowling, he pulled on his jeans and reached for a jumper.

A couple of glasses of wine later, he was sufficiently mollified to help her lay the table.

'So what are we having?' he asked, trying to drag her on to his lap.

'If you give me a chance – spaghetti carbonara.'

'Is that all?'

'The spaghetti is from Fortnum and Mason's, and the carbonara sauce said Selfridges.'

'Mother likes to splash out a bit when she's up in town.'

Meg thought wryly of her 'Own Brand' economy shopping back in Yarleigh, trying not to dwell on the fact that he'd said the word 'mother'. A small part of her wanted to confide in him as she had in Matthew. But the part with more of a say was determined that she shouldn't; not just because it wanted to ignore the problem, but because it seemed so convinced that Jake wouldn't understand. That, in itself, would be opening another can of worms. Wasn't a lover supposed to be a confidant as well?

She dished out the pasta. Jake scoffed – and scoffed really was the appropriate word – every last morsel on his plate. So, thought Meg, he hadn't been hungry in a 'feed me' sort of way, had he?

'Shall we open another bottle of wine and chill out in front of the telly?' she suggested, as she cleared up the dishes, thankful for the effect of the alcohol on her brain. If she was comatose by the time they went to bed again, perhaps she wouldn't dream. Failing that, perhaps she wouldn't remember her dreams when she woke up. That would be the next best thing.

'I have no intention of letting you chill out,' said Jake, finally succeeding in pulling her down on to his lap. He peeled back the towelling robe. The wool of his jumper scratched erotically against her bare skin.

'Jake,' she rasped, 'we haven't any you-know-whats down here . . .'

He pulled one out of his pocket. 'Always be prepared for any eventuality. That's my motto, darling.' And he kissed her, whispering roughly against her lips, 'Isn't that why you're so crazy about me?'

It was almost three a.m., and Georgie had woken up crying again.

As an exhausted Matthew carried her back to his room, Freddy appeared. The minute both children were tucked up in his bed, Matthew watched them drop off to sleep again. So much for his intended Saturday morning lay-in. His little darlings would be awake at seven on the dot, clambering all over him. On weekdays when he was running late they were horrors to get up.

He gazed down at the two angelic golden heads peeping out above the duvet. The curtains were open slightly, and moonlight sneaked in and tip-toed across the bed, illuminating the faint blue stain on the duvet cover that still hadn't washed out completely. Shivering in his boxer shorts, Matthew sat down and traced the shape of the stain with trembling fingers.

He didn't mind the children sleeping in his bed, although he knew he was being too soft, that it was going to be harder to get them out of the habit in the long run. But he missed the warmth of another human being beside him. When the children slept straight through in their own rooms, Matthew would wake up and reach out automatically to find that the other side of his bed – the side nearest the window that had always been Polly's – was cold and empty and . . . dead.

Matthew turned to the photograph of his wife on the bedside table, but even as he stared at her, all he could really see was the outline of the ink stain.

'Oh, Poll,' he moaned softly, 'what the hell am I going to do?'

* * *

When Meg had accepted Jake's invitation to come up to London, she had expected to see a lot more of it than various ceilings. Now, finally, at seven o'clock on Saturday evening, she was fully clothed and intending to stay that way until long past midnight. Standing back to survey herself in the mirrored wardrobe doors, she sighed with relief. She'd almost forgotten what she looked like dressed.

Jake strolled out of the bathroom and wolf-whistled. 'Wow! You look sensational. I could almost ravish you all over again before the others arrive. In fact—'

'I don't think so!' She shoved him away. 'There's no time. Your pals could be here any minute.'

'Hardly likely,' sulked Jake. 'They're always late for everything.'

'Get dressed, or I'm off back home.'

'Don't you get shirty with me, Madam!'

'OK,' she smiled, finding it impossible to stay cross with him for long, '*you* get shirty.' She pointed towards the wardrobe. 'And don't forget your trousies and shoesies too.'

As he dressed, she went into the bathroom to preen on her own. She did look fairly good, even if the outfit had been cobbled together on a small budget. The black PVC hipsters clung to her legs, accentuating each sleek curve; the cream sleeveless body (she felt a bra underneath was definitely necessary, whatever Yasmin had said) set off the glow of her skin; while the floaty chiffon blouse she wore open over the top, complete with wide ruffles, lent a romantic, feminine touch.

'You're going to make everyone envious of me tonight, aren't you, darling?' grinned Jake a short while later downstairs in the lounge, as he headed for the drinks cabinet.

'I'll do my best,' she assured him, suddenly nervous about meeting his oldest friends. 'Make that a large brandy, please,' she gulped, starting as she meant to go on.

'So, how much is this house *really* worth?' she was demanding, three large brandies later. She prodded Pip Holland-Smith in the chest, right bang in the middle of his silk tie, which reminded her of a painting by Picasso, darned if she could remember which one.

'Meg,' sighed Jake, 'hurry up and finish your drink. The table's booked for eight-thirty.'

She threw him a stroppy look which more or less meant: shut it. Then she turned back to Jake's friends. 'One of you must know how much this house is worth. Jake here won't tell me. I mean, are we talking hundreds of thousands, or thousands of hundreds, or—'

'Millions,' sighed Jake. 'Just plain old millions.'

'Italian lira, right?'

'No, darling.'

'French francs then?'

'Oh come on, Meg.'

She gulped. 'Pounds? Millions of . . . *pounds?*'

Pip flung his arm around her shoulder. 'Meggikins – you don't mind if I call you Meggikins, do you? – I have to say that you're a refreshing change from Jake's usual—'

'Another small whisky before we go, Philip?' asked Jake, through what appeared to be clenched teeth. 'Although we haven't really much time. Better leave it, hmm?'

Meg didn't think that was any way to talk to guests. She flashed Pip, Frank and Edmund her best assuaging smile. It was, she felt, her duty as gracious hostess. She drained what was left of her drink. 'I'm ready whenever you lot are.'

They trooped outside. Meg wanted to flag down the taxi herself. '*Please.* I've never done it before.'

Jake threw his hands up impatiently. 'Go ahead.'

'Just like they do in films?'

'If you want.' Jake shrugged.

They trooped off to the main road, and as a black cab appeared around a corner, Meg stuck two fingers in her mouth and let out a piercing whistle, which instantly sent Pip, Frank and

Edmund into snorts of laughter. The cab screeched to a halt as Meg looked ready to hurl herself off the pavement in front of it. She waited for one of the gentlemen escorting her to open the door and help her in.

Frank, who was very frank about his interest in her, did the honours, squeezing her knee playfully as they sat down on the wide leather seat.

'Can we go the scenic route?' she asked. 'I'd love to see the river by night. It won't take that much longer, will it?'

'Anything for you, Meggikins,' Pip assured her, tapping the glass partition and informing the cabby.

Meg sighed, revelling in being the centre of attention, Jake's girl for the first time ever in public, in the heart of a vibrant city like London. She could almost believe that she was . . . happy.

'Oh look!' she cried. 'There it is!' And she flung herself across Frank to get a better view of the magnificent iridescent Thames, only dimly aware that Frank was getting a better perspective himself of the view down her top.

They ate in a Greek restaurant somewhere behind Tottenham Court Road.

'We still have to be discreet,' explained Jake. 'It wouldn't be much fun for Rory to find out about us through the grapevine.'

Meg looked at Jake's three chums. Old Boys, they'd said. Jake would have trusted them with his life. Met at school fagging, whatever the hell that was. She didn't dare ask.

'So where *is* Rory this weekend then?' asked Pip.

'Visiting the old man down in Kent.'

Pip was cynical. 'Keeping him sweet, you mean.'

Meg thought it wasn't really tactful of them to be discussing Aurora in front of her. She coughed, to remind them she was there.

'Cigarette?'

She looked at Edmund and shook her head. He lit up, without asking if she minded, blowing smoke in her face as if he thought it was sexy. Still, he *had* held her chair out for her as they'd sat down. Meg stared into the flickering flame of the candle on the table as the gentlemen changed the subject and started droning on about portfolios. She wasn't naïve enough to think they meant designer leather briefcases, but when they started going on about 'footsie', she did think they were referring to the under-the-table flirting game.

'No,' murmured Pip, his breath hot in her ear, 'F,T,S,E.'

'Oh. Oh right.' Made even less bloody sense. She peered broodingly out of the window, needing an alcohol fix to pep her up again.

The waiter soon arrived with the wine. Meg pounced on her glass.

'Darling,' said Jake, 'steady on.'

But she didn't want to. If Jake intended to be a damp squid – or was it squib? – Meg wasn't going to stop him.

'A squid would be damp already, wouldn't it?' she said. 'It lives underwater, so—'

'Meg, sweetheart, please eat something.' Jake thrust a basket of pitta bread under her nose.

She ate grumpily, dipping the bread into the taramasalata and screwing up her face in disdain when Pip offered her the olives.

'Will I like this "dolmades" thing you've ordered for me?' she asked Jake.

'Stuffed vine leaves,' he translated. 'You'll love them.'

And she did. But it was hardly surprising; anything that might have some connection with wine and wine-growing was bound to go down well tonight.

As the meal drew to a close, Meg became conscious of an urgent tweeting noise, like a bird in pain. Concerned, she leaned back and lifted the tablecloth slightly. Nope, nothing there. Across the table, Frank was patting his jacket as if searching for something. He pulled out a slim mobile phone from his breast pocket.

Meg scowled and took refuge in her wine,

embarrassed by her gaffe. Why couldn't those flipping mobiles sound like normal phones? Why couldn't—

Frank was standing up. 'I've got to shoot off. That was my little brother. He's up to his neck in the proverbial again.'

'I don't know why he just doesn't dump his girlfriend the normal way,' snorted Pip.

'He thinks knocking her about *is* normal.' Frank slipped the phone back into his pocket. 'And if she's stupid enough not to take the hint . . .' He nodded at Meg. 'I would have liked to become better acquainted with you, Miss Oakley, but I'm afraid you're going to have to excuse me.'

Meg was still trying to work out exactly what was going on. All she could be certain of was that Frank was very annoyed and in a rush to leave. 'I'm sure we'll bump into each other again,' she called after him.

He faltered, glancing back at her and then at Jake. 'Er, I'm sure we will.'

'He hasn't paid his share,' Meg pointed out after he'd gone. She couldn't help noticing things like that.

'Don't worry.' Jake laughed it off. 'The bastard always gets out of paying somehow.'

'Looks like it's just the four of us now,' said Pip.

Meg frowned as a hand squeezed her knee. Jake had both of his on the table, fiddling with his cigarette lighter. The hand crept up her thigh. By her reckoning, it had to be Edmund, who was closest to that particular leg. It was rather a strange feeling, stirring up contrary sparks of emotion. If she hadn't been pickled up to her eyeballs, she would have shooed the hand away. As it was – although she seemed to know that she shouldn't – she was enjoying the sensation.

'So,' Pip glanced around, 'are we going on to a club?'

'Not tonight,' said Jake. 'Don't fancy it.'

'Killjoy.'

Jake sighed. 'You can come back to mine if you want. I've stacks of booze.'

'Sounds good to me,' proclaimed Edmund.

Meg gasped as his hand roved further upwards.

The instant they got back to the house, she sped off to the downstairs toilet. She took ages, and by the time she swayed out again, her mind was steadier than the rest of her body. Unwelcome thoughts about her mother, and about Matthew Potter, of all people, were beginning to sneak in again.

'We were on the verge of coming to look for you,' said Jake, as she teetered into the lounge and landed with a plop on the sofa.

'Bloody body popper things,' she moaned.

'Actually, I think they make things a lot easier,' grinned Pip.

'Depends which angle you're approaching from.' Meg was adamant; the men agreed she had a point. Edmund handed her a brandy and sank on to the sofa beside her, brushing her frizzing curls off her face. 'Needs a trim,' she said absently, pulling away slightly. She decided she would try to get an appointment with Victor this week, before her birthday party, because she wanted to look extra nice, just in case—

Her head dipped hastily towards the brandy glass. Think about Jake, she told herself. Think about the here and now and the fun you're having. You *are* having fun, Margaret, she stressed. I absolutely insist on it.

'Do you like playing polo?' she asked Edmund, in an attempt at scintillating conversation.

'I prefer cricket.'

'Oh right.' She nodded. 'The one without the horses.'

Edmund and Pip laughed.

In an attempt at a sophisticated pose, to impress Jake's friends rather than just entertain them, Meg tried to prop her elbow on the back of the low sofa. Instead, she miscalculated the distance and rolled with a giggle into Edmund's lap, spilling brandy all over her blouse. 'Sorry!'

'I'm not complaining,' Edmund laughed.

'I wasn't apologising to you.' She carried on giggling uncontrollably. 'I meant this poor chiffonything. The brandy'll probably burn a hole in it.'

'Why don't you take it off?' said Pip. 'Before you get hypothermia.'

'Hypo . . . ? Is that the one where you turn blue?'

More laughter. Blimey, this was getting predictable. She held her glass out to Jake. 'Another drinky, please. I'm parched.'

'I think *you've* had enough,' he said stiffly.

Pip and Edmund turned to him in surprise.

'Give the girl a drink, Jake.'

'I'm not going to throw up or anything,' Meg assured him. 'I don't do that with alcohol. Well I do, but only if it's cheap and nasty, and I'm very very sure your brandy isn't. You could afford to get something exhorb–exhorb–' She frowned. 'Not cheap.'

Jake ignored her. He fumbled for a cigarette. 'Shit, I've run out. D'you have any, Ed?'

'Nope. None left.'

'Think I've got some upstairs . . .' He strode out.

Why was he being so sullen and stuffy? wondered Meg, suddenly noticing that her face was being turned ninety degrees. She found herself nose to nose with Edmund, whose eyes were curiously glazed. Before she could even squeal in protest, his tongue was in her mouth. Pushed to the back of her mind was the realisation that if she hadn't been so drunk, she would have squirmed to get away. Her limbs were paralysed though, her senses reeling in a thousand different directions . . .

And then she heard Jake's voice, furious and tortured, and suddenly Edmund was being yanked upwards, landing with a perplexed grunt on the floor.

'Are you deaf?' spat Jake. 'I told you to get *off* her!'

Pip leapt up from an armchair. 'Come on, old chap. No need to take it so personally—'

'*Personally?*'

Meg had never seen Jake this angry before. He was taller, wasn't he? And terrifying.

But Edmund seemed angry and terrifying too. 'I don't know what you're getting so worked up about. It's not as if you *care* about her. She's just like all the others . . .'

The lounge was losing its fashionably bright acid tones and becoming very grey and strangely blurred. The voices were getting further and further away. Meg held her head in her hands and fought to listen, to make sense of it all. Jake was somewhere in the hall, shouting and throwing something that made a smashing sound. 'Get the fuck out of my house!'

Meg brought her knees up, curling on the sofa like a defensive hedgehog. The slam of the front door sent a shock-wave through her quivering body. Her arms sprang up in goose-bumps.

And then, there was Jake, framed in the doorway, but he had shrunk back to his normal height. He was standing very still, just staring at her, his face the colour of ashes in a grate.

'Meg—' His voice seemed to stick in his throat.

She stretched out a shaking hand. The world speeded up again. Suddenly he was kneeling on the floor, dragging her into his arms, burrowing his face in her neck.

And then she heard him moaning, 'Oh God, Meg,' over and over, but without trying to slip his hands into her underwear for once.

'Rather sleepy, darling,' she muttered, an instant before the world grew ominously dark and started spinning in the wrong direction. 'Don't feel too—' And the stuffed vine leaves made a shock reappearance over his pale-aqua Armani shirt.

Fifteen

Matthew rushed to fish Georgie out of the toilet after she'd tried to climb into it the moment his back was turned. Freddy watched from the bath, splashing about with laughter. Matthew popped his daughter back in the tub with her brother and knelt on the mat beside it, rolling up the sleeves of his jumper, which kept slipping down and were already soaking. At this rate, he was going to have to get himself a wet-suit. And why were bathtimes always worse when he was in a hurry? He unhooked the shower attachment and rinsed the kids off while they shrieked in outrage.

'Yes,' he agreed grimly, 'I'm the worst dad ever. Any minute now Social Services are going to come charging through that door and beat me to a pulp with their clip-boards.'

The moment he turned the shower off, the kids shut up. He whisked Georgie out first, bundling her into a towel complete with hood. Freddy wanted to stay in the bath longer, playing with his toy boat.

'Not today,' said Matthew. 'Look, see this.' He grabbed the boat from his son. 'It's just been torpedoed.' And he filled it with water and sank it. 'Right. Out you get, laddie.'

As soon as Freddy and Georgie were dried off and in their pyjamas, he checked the toddler-proof gate at the top of the stairs and left the kids playing in the nursery. Freddy ought to be old enough to keep an eye on his sister, but Matthew left the bathroom door open anyway while he took a quick shower. He shaved just as hastily, and for the first time in ages, opened his only bottle of aftershave and actually used it.

A minute later, he was standing in front of his wardrobe. Polly had always enjoyed helping when he hadn't been in the mood to choose his own clothes for an evening out. She'd been brought up with an unfailing awareness of how to dress to impress. He couldn't help wondering what she'd seen in him when she could have had the pick of those expensively tailored bankers, lawyers and brain-surgeons her parents had frantically tried to introduce her to.

He pulled out a rugby shirt from his chest of drawers. Would this be too casual? He knew he wasn't supposed to wear trainers or jeans, but . . . Matthew stuffed the rugby shirt back in the drawer. Ten minutes later, when the doorbell rang, he was tucking a dark-claret cotton shirt into old stone chinos, which fitted him provided he used a belt. Running his fingers through his still-damp hair, beginning to wave in its usual all-over-the-place way, he hurried downstairs.

It was Sarah-Jane. He started pelting her with instructions of where to get hold of him in an emergency.

'Pilgrims?' Her eyes widened. 'You're going to *Pilgrims*? In Tockley?'

'I'll be there from about ten, maybe sooner. It's over twenty-fives tonight, isn't it? Hopefully I won't feel too out of place.'

The doorbell rang again. This time it was Yasmin, in an ankle-length green dress. He smiled down at her. She still didn't quite come up to his shoulder, even in platform shoes. 'You look great, Miss Bradley.'

Out of the corner of his eye, he noticed with wry amusement that Sarah-Jane was gaping in surprise.

Meg leaned against the bar in the Spread Eagle, taking comfort in a rum and coke. The phenomenal hangover she had nursed last weekend had been due to the dodgy Greek wine, or so she'd convinced herself. If she didn't mix her drinks from now on, she'd be fine.

Yet the weekend hadn't been *all* bad, even though bits of it were patchy in her memory. She could distinctly recall an argument because a drunken Edmund had tried to take his flirting one step too far. That hadn't been . . . nice. But Jake had seemed different after his friends had gone. Quieter. More affectionate. Even when Meg had asked if he thought Edmund or Pip would spill the beans to Aurora, Jake had just stroked her hair and told her everything would be fine. And when he'd flagged down a taxi for her on Sunday, he'd called her an innocent and told her to go home, where she was safe, where no one could hurt her.

She'd smiled. 'Don't be silly. I like it here in London.'

'You wouldn't survive two minutes up here on your own. And if you don't get going right *now,* you'll miss your train.'

She'd pouted. 'Are you saying I'm not sophisticated enough for you, Jake Arundel? That I'm some sort of country bumpkin?'

'Meg Oakley,' Jake had smiled wretchedly, 'you're my downfall and my salvation.'

He said such strange things sometimes, thought Meg, lifting her head as a familiar group entered the pub. She waved, hurrying to greet them.

Thierry broke her skid. 'Ooof! *Sacre bleu!*'

'Sorry!' She kissed his rough jaw. 'How are you doing?'

'I am doing well, *mon ange*.' He pecked her cheek. 'Many happy returns of the day.'

She smiled her thanks, moving on to her other friends.

'Meg, you look divine! Doesn't she look divine, Tom?' Beatrice nudged him in the ribs.

'No idea,' he grinned, 'you're always telling me not to look at other women.'

'Where's that dress from?' asked Libby.

'Oh . . .' Meg shrugged dismissively. 'I got it cheap up in London when I was on that computer course.'

'I'm off to get some drinks in,' said Tom, 'before you girlies start going gaga over what a bargain it was.'

'Only soda water for me,' sighed Beatrice, patting her stomach.

'How's your flu?' Meg couldn't resist the dig. Then something struck her. 'Where's Yaz?'

'She's making her own way here.'

'And she's bringing a bloke with her,' put in Libby.

'It was a last-minute arrangement,' explained Beatrice. 'I didn't get all her message, the answer-machine ran out of tape.'

'So who *is* he?' Meg was ablaze with curiosity.

'No idea.'

Beatrice giggled. 'She's probably stopped off behind some hedge with him on the way here. Remember when she ended up in the stinging nettles that time with what's-his-face?'

Thierry was watching Meg demolish her rum and coke as if it were water. 'And what about you, *chérie?* Where is the gallant Matthieu Potter this evening?'

All eyes and ears swung in her direction like antennae.

She shrugged, frowning into her glass. 'We had a bit of a barney. I don't think we can count on the pleasure of his company this evening. Which I'm perfectly OK about,' she hastened to inform her audience, glancing up to see why they were so silent.

Her heart and stomach seemed to swap places inside her.

'Hello, Meg,' said Matthew, looking as if he'd just stepped out of a trendy mail-order catalogue. He had his arm behind Yasmin's back. Meg battened down a wild urge to run round and check exactly where on her back his hand was.

'Sorry we're late-ish,' said Yaz. 'I laddered a hold-up, bang where the split in my dress is.'

'She had to nip behind a hedge to change it,' explained Matthew.

Meg tested her voice with a low hum, to check it was working. 'What a nice surprise.' She looked at Matthew. 'I honestly didn't think you'd be here tonight . . .'

'Because of our "barney"?'

Oh hell. He'd heard.

Before she could reply, he leaned over and kissed her cheek. 'Well, it *is* your birthday,' he said, his skin warm and smooth and touching hers so briefly, she was forced to swallow a lump in her throat.

'Now that Yaz is here, you can have your present,' said Beatrice. She frowned at Yasmin. 'You did remember to bring it, didn't you?'

'Of course!'

'This was Yazza's idea,' said Libby. 'We all contributed to it.' She glanced at Matthew. 'Well – nearly all. Unless . . .'

He shook his head.

Meg peeled back the fancy paper, reading the lettering on the jewellery box with huge eyes. '*The* Tiffany's? Like in the film?' She took off the lid with shaking fingers and gasped at the sight of a silver charm bracelet lying in a swirl of velvet.

Yasmin helped her with the clasp. 'I only brought the actual bracelet part back from the States. Everyone added their own charms later. See. Bet you can't guess who that little Eiffel Tower is from!'

Thierry shrugged. 'And I didn't even need to

go to Paris. You English think it is *your* tower now. One day I will make it my duty to steal Big Ben.'

Eyes brimming with tears, Meg thanked her friends.

'If I'd known about the bracelet . . .' Matthew drew her aside as the others went off to find a table.

'Don't be silly.' Meg smiled with forced brightness. 'I wouldn't have expected it. I've known this lot for years. It's different with you. You didn't even have to bother getting me a card.'

'So I'm just your personal punch-bag, is that it?'

'If you're referring to the other day and the petrol incident,' she muttered, 'you just happened to be around at the wrong time.'

'Not the right time?' He arched an eyebrow. 'Meg, I haven't told anyone about it . . . About your mother.'

She stared at him. 'Not even Yaz?'

'Why should I tell Yasmin?' He leaned closer. She caught a whiff of his aftershave again, as she had when he'd kissed her cheek. It was more subtle than the one Jake wore. 'Meg, you can't keep your feelings bottled up like this.'

'Who says I'm bottling them up? How do you know what I've done about this whole business since we spoke? You don't! You're just guessing.'

'I wanted to make sure you were OK.'

'Why should you care?' Annoyed that he'd brought up this subject tonight of all nights, she added, 'Please excuse me. I'd like to enjoy myself, if that's OK with you?' And she headed towards the others, who were settling at a table near the fruit machine.

Just before nine-thirty, Beatrice went off to phone the local cab firm. Matthew sat in a corner, only half-listening to Yasmin chatting away to Libby. He stared at Meg on the other side of the table as she shared what seemed to be an increasingly intimate conversation with Thierry Duval.

She reminded him of a flame hell-bent on burning itself out before morning. Her dress, with its thin straps and short, slightly flared skirt, was dark-blue crushed-velvet, the exact colour of her eyes. Her hair was shorter again, reminding him of that day in the churchyard. She was knocking back her third drink since he'd arrived at the pub, although he wasn't sure why he was even counting. He was just an onlooker, sometimes getting sucked into the action when circumstances spun out of his control. He hadn't asked to be thought of as a friend, so why should he care so much? Her words echoed in his head. *Why should you care . . . ?*

'Better hurry up and finish your drinks,' Beatrice announced, returning to the table. 'The cabs'll be outside in five minutes.'

Meg jumped to her feet, grabbing her bag. 'Back in a mo.' She swayed off towards the loos.

Matthew had to shift his knees as Yasmin wriggled past him, flashing him a smile and heading for the loos herself.

'*He* rang *me*,' was the first thing she said to Meg, who was sandwiched between the hand-dryer and the basin, rummaging through her handbag. 'I don't know why you're so uptight about it.'

'How about the fact that I've never been so embarrassed?' Meg scowled into the cracked mirror and decided her hands were shaking too much to attempt wielding an eyeliner. 'He's supposed to be "involved" with *me*!'

'I'm not going to get mixed up in this smoke-screen business, Meg. I don't want anything to do with it. I was his friend long before you had the time of day for him.'

'And isn't it convenient for you now that Polly's out of the picture?'

Yasmin shook her head. 'I don't believe this! You're the one with the biggest plank in your eye, but you've got the gall to cast stones at me.'

Meg swivelled her lipstick into position, then swivelled it back down again. She would end up with Terracotta Red up her nostrils at this rate. 'You're getting your metaphors muddled,' she said. 'And what I'm trying to say is that you could at least have warned me that Matthew was coming.'

Yasmin was still shaking her head. 'I don't know what's wrong with you these days. You're different. So . . . snappy.'

'I am NOT!'

They stared at each other in the mirror.

'Meg,' sighed Yasmin at last, 'please look at this from my point of view. And Matt's.'

'I do look at it from Matthew's!'

Yasmin sighed again. 'Do you? I like the man for his own sake, Meg. Because he's funny and kind and—'

'Yaz—'

'Stop feeling pity. You'll smother him. Stop thinking of Matt as a man who lost his wife and start thinking of him as just a man. You'll find whatever mess your feelings are in, they'll sort themselves out pretty quickly.'

Meg turned round. 'What are you on about?'

'I'm not sure.' Yasmin narrowed her eyes at her. 'You tell *me*.'

The minicabs were on time, Libby was sent to fetch Yasmin and Meg. 'Get a move on,' she bullied.

Outside in the cool April night, Matthew watched as the largest cab was filled first.

'Come on,' said a voice to his left, and a hand

gripped his sleeve firmly. 'We shall be the over-spill, *mon ami.*'

Matthew found himself sharing the second cab with Thierry.

'Didn't you want to ride with Meg?' he asked.

Thierry turned to look at him as they moved off towards Tockley. 'I should have liked that very much, but I am sure I can put up with you.'

Matthew had a sudden notion that he was about to be the recipient of an amicable 'don't get any funny ideas, she's mine' warning. In the dim light filtering into the cab, Thierry's face was almost piratical.

Matthew hadn't believed what the Frenchman had said on Easter Sunday. He was convinced Meg and Thierry were still lovers, even if it was a fairly casual arrangement, which was perhaps why Thierry had lied. Didn't the evidence point towards it? Matthew had first met her on the edge of Yarleigh Woods, near where Thierry lived – the biggest clue of all. And she certainly hadn't looked as if she'd had access to her own wardrobe that morning.

'Marguerite looks ravishable tonight, *non?*'

This was how these 'amicable' threats nearly always started; by lulling you into a false sense of security.

'Hmm,' said Matthew.

'That dress is new,' Thierry went on, 'it suits her. But perhaps I am prejudiced because I know what is underneath. You do well to be patient, Matthieu. It is worth the wait.'

Matthew flinched. He started to choke out, 'I don't know what you mean,' but only got as far as the 'I don't.'

'I remember when I first saw her,' Thierry was reminiscing, as if to the strains of violin music that only he could hear. 'Life plays strange games with us. If Marguerite had been good at German when she was at school, she would have gone to Frankfurt, or Munich. But she came to Paris because she was good at French . . .'

'When . . . ?' stammered Matthew, because his curiosity had kicked into action.

'I met her the summer she was sixteen, when she ran away from home. She had some money she had saved up, and she lived *la vie Bohemienne* in a modest *pension* for a while. But then one day she lost herself in Montmartre . . .'

'And you found her,' Matthew prompted.

Thierry was staring out of the window. '*Oui.* I find her, standing on a corner, frowning at a map, chewing her plait, which is not good for her I say. I take her to a café; we have coffee, we talk. I show her the way to her *pension*, and then that evening I take her out.'

'So you ply her with drink,' surmised Matthew, finding his tongue again with a vengeance, 'and the rest is history.'

'It was not like that,' protested Thierry. 'I was young too. A student. I did not know I was depetalling her . . . I could not read the signs then.'

'You mean . . .' Matthew hesitated; he hadn't expected to get to the nitty-gritty like this.

'And I did not know I would fall in love,' admitted Thierry. 'When she said she was obligated to return to England—'

Matthew couldn't help scoffing, 'You asked her to marry you?'

'No. I have never asked her that. Perhaps it would have made a difference? Women are unfathomable, *non*? They speak much of freedom, but then expect a man to chain himself down misogynously for a lifetime.'

'Monogamously. And marriage isn't a prison sentence.'

'No. But then I have never been married, unlike you. Perhaps *je suis* – I am . . . timid of the responsibility.'

'So, what happened next? Meg came back to Yarleigh . . .'

'To her family – who needed her too much, she said. And she told herself to stop dreaming. Except that a part of her can never stop, like a reckless child . . .'

The cab was pulling up outside Pilgrims. A queue was already beginning to form in front of the club's electric-blue doors.

'It has been beneficial for me to speak like this,' said Thierry. 'You understand, my friend, that Marguerite does not need another man to make demands from her again, as the rest of us have. All her life, Matthieu, men take, take, take. Even when they are giving, they are still taking something for themselves too. You must remember that. It is too late for me, but for you . . .'

A confused Matthew didn't get the chance to ask Thierry what he meant. The car door was wrenched open and Meg and Yasmin stood glaring in at them. 'Come on, you guys, stop gassing. We're not saving you a place in the queue and then getting a whole load of abuse from the people behind!'

Pilgrims was loud. In his fibreglass booth, the DJ was zealously introducing one track after another. They all sounded the same – like a fly buzzing. No wonder people thought they needed drugs to enjoy themselves, Matthew mused glumly. If the 'music' was anything to go by . . .

'It'll get better soon,' Libby was yelling. 'All the old stuff comes on.'

'A couple of fox-trots and a waltz?' he yelled back, but his feeble joke was lost in the *thump, thump, bzzzz,* of a new hit that had Meg racing on to the dance-floor.

She was a good mover, not afraid to show off.

Obviously, she had practice. Matthew himself would normally have avoided 'the club scene' like the plague, although now and again he had tagged along with Polly and a few old friends; they'd always laughed when he'd trudged after them on to the dance-floor to strut his stuff.

Yasmin came up to him. 'Drink, Matt?'

'I'll get these. G&T again?'

She nodded. Matthew headed for a gap at the far end of the bar, with a last glance back at the birthday girl, now frenziedly waving her arms in the air.

Having bought the drinks, he began to push his way back through the ever-increasing crush. A blonde standing at a chrome rail and looking out over the dance-floor stepped back and jogged his elbow. Gin and tonic splashed up his sleeve. The woman swung round, apologising profusely. Their eyes met. Jacintha Arundel turned away quickly, dipping her head. Matthew hesitated, but realised the time wasn't right to start going on about her son again. For one thing, they would hardly be able to hear each other.

Jacintha was still refusing to take the matter of Timothy's behaviour seriously, even when Edward Nugent had bowing-and-scrapingly telephoned her, requesting that she come up to the school – but only when it was convenient for her, of course, there was no hurry, she must be so awfully busy . . .

In class over the last few weeks, though, Matthew had been discovering ways of getting around the fact that Timothy was an arrogant little devil. The boy was highly imaginative, and if his mind was occupied – more so than the other children – he let trouble come to him rather than deliberately looking for it.

Perhaps, with patience . . . But Matthew knew that Timothy wouldn't be his immediate problem for long; only until the end of the school year.

With a sigh, he moved off to find Yasmin, keeping the emptier glass of gin and tonic for himself.

They spotted Libby and Beatrice on a curved sofa in a relatively quiet corner and headed over.

'I'm too old for this,' Libby was lamenting.

'And I'm too pregnant,' added a sleepy Beatrice. 'I don't think all this noise can be good for Baby either.'

They were joined by Tom, just as the music changed. It was familiar now. Groovily nostalgic according to the DJ, who was insisting that everyone 'get on up and boogie on down'.

'He can boogie on down to hell for all I care,' groaned Libby.

'Where's Meg?' Yasmin echoed the question Matthew was asking himself. 'Is she still dancing?'

Tom was seemingly fascinated by one of the television sets fixed up high in a strategic spot, relaying scenes from the dance-floor.

'I wouldn't call it *just* dancing,' he said, his eyebrows raised.

Everyone turned to look at the screen. Meg and Thierry were visible, draped all over each other and gyrating to the music as if they were joined from the waist down. It also appeared, thought Matthew sourly, as though they were snogging.

Beatrice was the first to recover.

'Well,' she pronounced grittily, 'it gives a whole new meaning to having a frog in your throat.'

Sixteen

When Marvin Gaye started crooning 'Sexual Healing', Meg realised that that was what Thierry had in mind. She pulled away from him, drowning in a sea of flashing lights and dangerously swamped by lust and alcohol.

'Stop!' She pressed her fists against his chest. What had got into him? What had got into *her*?

'*Chérie*—'

'Don't you *chérie* me, Thierry Duval!'

He circled her waist with his brawny arms. 'Perhaps we make the fine Matthieu jealous? He is trying to make you jealous too – with Yasmin.'

She snorted. 'Don't be silly!' Thierry was now nuzzling her neck. 'Thierry . . . please stop . . .' If he carried on picking out her erogenous zones this way, she was liable to do a Meg Ryan in *When Harry Met Sally*, right here on the dance-floor.

Thierry prised himself away. 'Marguerite, I am sorry, I was wrong to try this. I am a hypocrite—'

'Meg . . .' Yasmin was tugging at her dress.

Meg swung to face her with a rush of affection mingled with hostility, although she couldn't recall what she was supposed to feel hostile about. 'How're you doing, Yazza?'

'I came to tell you that Matt and I are leaving. Enjoy the rest of your birthday.'

Meg's reflexes had slowed down considerably. 'You're leaving?' she put in at last, frowning slowly as her memory was jogged. 'With Matthew?'

'That's right.'

'Together?'

'We're sharing a cab, yes.'

Meg glanced over Yasmin's head. 'Where is he then?'

'He went to the cloakroom to collect our jackets . . .'

Turning her back on Yasmin and Thierry, Meg lurched towards the exit, the music lowering in volume as she neared the foyer. 'There you are!' she cried sulkily, spotting Matthew and lurching in his direction. 'Were you just going to go off without saying goodbye? And do you realise you haven't even danced with me?' She pouted. 'It's my birthday and you haven't even danced with me!'

'Meg,' he grimaced, 'you're drunk.'

'Can't hack the pace yourself, huh?'

Abruptly, she felt him grab her hand. 'Come on then,' he said, with an undercurrent of defiance, shoving the cloakroom tickets in his pocket. He steered her through the press of bodies until they reached the dance-floor, turning her to face him and drawing her against his chest. His arms cradled her so comfortably, she sank her head into his shirt, gripping the baggy cotton at the back and scrunching it in her clammy hands.

'I'm sorry,' she whimpered, but it was lost in the song sliding like velvet around them: something slow, soothing, even though the lyrics washed over her without making sense. Meg gave herself up to being held, resting her face against Matthew's neck. She vaguely remembered Yaz earlier that evening, telling her to think of him as a man, not a widower. She lifted her face so she could look at him. Suddenly, in the same moment, they moved closer, their bodies pressing together so that even their feet were touching.

Her brain seemed to sober up in an instant. When she felt the indisputable proof that he *was* a man, the club seemed to fall still, as if everyone had been frozen.

Suddenly, Yasmin appeared beside them. 'My cloakroom ticket?' she mouthed at Matthew, as Meg took the opportunity to extract herself from his hold, swaying through the crowd before he could pull her back.

Beatrice came across her in the Ladies as she frowned miserably into the mirror over the end basin.

'Meg, what is it?' Beatrice was instantly in Agony Aunt mode. 'Is this because of Matthew and Yaz? What the hell are they playing at? I don't blame you for trying to get your own back with Thierry. And it worked. You should have seen Matthew's face—'

'He's a man,' groaned Meg.

Beatrice furrowed her brow. 'What are you on about?'

'Matthew,' she sighed. 'Yaz told me to think of him as one, and then he was holding me so . . .' She couldn't elaborate. She couldn't even understand why she was getting worked up over it. The mingled scents of hairspray and perfume was making her feel sick. 'I've got to get out of here,' she muttered. Leaving Beatrice gazing after her worriedly, she headed for the foyer again.

'Thierry!' He wasn't alone, but Meg ignored Yasmin and shook Thierry's sleeve. 'Has he gone yet? Did he say anything?'

'If you mean Matt,' said Yasmin stiffly, 'he's just left.'

'On his own?'

'Well not with me, obviously. I decided it wasn't a good idea.' Yasmin looked at her long and hard. 'If you hurry, you might catch him. There'll probably be a queue for the taxis—' Before Yasmin could finish her sentence, Meg was hurtling towards the exit.

The queue was short, and Matthew was about to climb into the first cab in the rank. Meg only just remembered to check both ways before running across the road. She jumped into the back seat beside him, slamming into his shoulder as the cab driver turned and gaped.

Matthew gaped at her too. 'What the hell do you think you're doing?'

'I . . .' She sat blinking confusedly. She had wanted to stop him leaving with Yasmin, but it had become almost as imperative to stop him going off on his own. 'Home,' she croaked pathetically. 'Tired.'

'Pissed,' she thought she heard Matthew mutter crossly.

'So where's "home" then?' demanded the cabby.

Meg, shivering uncontrollably, was about to stutter, 'Chaffinch Lane,' when Matthew leaned forwards and snapped, 'Peachtree Crescent, Yarleigh.' He sat back. Meg gazed across at him.

The taxi was already half-way down the road when she realised her cloakroom ticket, purse and house keys were in her handbag – and her handbag was with Libby.

'Cash,' she stammered, 'could – could you lend

me some, Matthew? If you get dropped off first, I won't have any money for—'

'Just this once, can't you shut up and let me hear myself think.' He folded his arms over his chest and glared out of the window.

And that was that, the extent of their conversation until they pulled up outside his house ten minutes later. He climbed out, leaving the door open as he counted out his fare and handed it to the driver with a tip.

Meg couldn't believe it; Matthew was abandoning her! This time round he wasn't going to see his rescue through to its natural conclusion. But before she could decide what on earth to do next, Matthew had reached into the cab, hauled her out and slammed the door.

'You and I need to talk,' he said.

If Meg hadn't been caught so entirely off guard by Matthew's behaviour, she would have revelled in the sight of Sarah-Jane's mouth falling open as they entered the lounge. But Matthew was being bewilderingly offhand about it all, as if he was always bringing scantily-clad women home.

'The kids OK?' he asked Sarah-Jane, as the girl rocked to her feet.

'Er – fine . . . They're fine. I haven't heard a peep out of them since I put them to bed.'

'Just how I like it. Come on then, I'll walk you home.'

Sarah-Jane looked at Matthew, confused. 'Oh! But you don't normally . . .'

'Only because I don't want to leave the kids alone.' He turned to Meg. 'Can I trust you to put the kettle on without doing anything that might result in a national state of emergency? I'll only be five minutes.' And he hustled Sarah-Jane out of the door.

Meg went into the kitchen and filled the kettle with water. She switched it on and then collapsed into the nearest chair, her mind in a tangle.

'I'm going to make us some strong black coffee,' said Matthew when he returned.

'But I don't really feel drunk any more.'

'So you're always leaping into men's taxis when you're sober, are you? Without your coat or handbag? I suppose that's one way of getting a free ride home.' He frowned. 'Are you cold?'

'No.' And I'm not home, she almost added.

'Why are you shivering then?'

'I don't know.'

He unscrewed the lid of the coffee jar and started heaping granules into two mugs. 'Did you actually tell anyone you were leaving the club?'

'Thierry and Yaz saw me go.'

'What about your things?'

'Libby will take care of them.'

He added boiling water to the mugs. 'Do you want sugar?'

She shook her head. This was all so clinical and civil. He brought the mugs over and sat down. 'Meg—'

'Matthew, listen.' She leaned across the table. 'You don't have to say anything. In fact I'd rather you didn't. I know you couldn't help it. Men can't, it's out of your control, like when you drink too much – only in reverse. You don't have to apologise or anything.' It occurred to her abruptly that maybe he hadn't been about to refer to that at all. Since when had a man ever apologised for finding her attractive? 'Listen,' she gabbled, annoyed with herself, 'I haven't gone doolally if that's what you're thinking—'

'Why didn't you and Thierry slip away together when you had the opportunity?' Matthew asked quietly, catching her by surprise. 'Do you enjoy playing games? Keeping everyone wondering?'

'Thierry and I aren't . . . That ended years ago. We might flirt a bit too much sometimes, but . . .' She frowned, tossing her head. 'It's got nothing to do with you anyway.'

'Actually, I think it has. You're sitting here in my kitchen drinking my coffee after sharing my taxi.'

She was working herself into a lather now, because anger, she was discovering, was the safest emotion to hide behind. 'You've got some gall! I asked if you could lend me money so I could get home. I had no desire to sit here in your kitchen, drinking your poxy coffee. You were the one who said something about "talking" and then literally dragged me in here. Well go on then, do your stuff, *talk* for pity's—'

But he had come round the table and jerked her upright, shutting the door with his foot.

Oh Lord, this is it, thought Meg, bracing herself. He was going to kiss her. Matthew Potter the Man, as opposed to Matthew Potter the Man Who Had Lost His Wife, was going to smooch her senseless right here in his kitchen, up against his Hygena oven and grill.

And there was no one to blame but herself!

[illegible] and something about 'nothing' and then finally [illegible]

[illegible] came round the table [illegible] slamming the door with his foot.

Oh, Lord, she thought. [illegible]

[illegible] oven or grill.

And there was no one to blame but herself.

Seventeen

'Keep your voice down,' he said, still holding on to her. 'And why have you got your eyes closed? I'm not going to strangle you, much as I'm tempted.'

She stared at him. 'Wh – What?'

'I don't want you screaming the house down and waking the kids.'

'I've got no intention of screaming. This is all my fault. I practically asked for it, didn't I?' And she closed her eyes again.

Sometimes, thought Matthew, he wondered if she spoke a different language. It *sounded* like English, but the similarity seemed to end there.

'You were already yelling like a fishwife,' he pointed out. 'If we're going to have a reasonable adult discussion—'

'Discussion?' She blinked up at him with a start.

'You can't go on this way,' he said. 'Pretending nothing's wrong and then drinking yourself stupid. I know, Meg,' his tone softened, 'I've tried it.'

'*Discussion?*' she echoed dazedly.

'About how you're going to deal with a problem you don't want to admit exists.'

He led her into the lounge and deposited her on one end of the sofa while he took the other. She was rather pink, as if embarrassed.

'Don't interrupt,' he said. 'Please hear me out, this is important.'

'Get on with it,' she muttered, staring into her lap.

'Meg . . . If I had a chance to talk just one more time with all the people I've lost in my life—'

'You should be a songwriter,' she sniped. 'You'd make a fortune.'

'Meg,' he leaned closer, squeezing her hand, willing her to see that this was serious, 'don't turn this into another joke. You'll regret it later, believe me. This business with your mother . . . You've *got* to go and see her. You've got to sort it out. Before it's too late.'

As he released her hand, having made his point, he found that she was holding on to his sleeve. She seemed to be trying to pull him on top of her. 'Meg!' he spluttered. 'Meg, stop it . . .'

'I've got my bracelet caught on your cuff,' she snapped. 'How am I supposed to get it off if you won't keep still?'

'Your bracelet . . .?' He looked down. Her new charm bracelet was snagged on one of his buttons. He freed it, catching a glimpse of smooth white thigh beneath her rumpled dress.

If they'd been in an unfamiliar place, a room with no memories . . . It still wouldn't have been right; but it could have been so easy.

'Did you think . . .' she was stammering '. . . did you think I was making . . . *advances* just now?'

'Advances?' He choked out a laugh, shifting to a safer distance. 'No, of course not!' he lied. 'I just – I just thought you were mucking about. Trying to side-track me. To change the subject.'

'Good,' she nodded feebly, 'because, Matthew . . . I don't want you thinking that I go around making passes at every bloke I fancy. I mean,' she went on hastily, 'every bloke I'm alone with. Because I don't. I haven't been with that many men. I can count them on two hands, but that doesn't include thumbs.'

'Meg, I don't want to hear this—'

'Men seldom do,' she went on stubbornly. 'Look, I'm sure you were faithful to Polly when you were married to her. But even though I know you've got scruples, you're not a priest, are you? Or a monk. They've got to be celibate, it goes with the territory, but I'm sure that before you met Polly you must have had one or two . . . encounters.'

He didn't know whether she was being outrageously nosy or just trying to make herself feel better about her own past.

'I can't lie to you, Meg,' he said. 'Not when you're being so honest with me.'

'I won't tell anyone,' she promised.

'Right, well, you want to know how many women I've . . . ?'

She nodded.

'I can count them all on one hand,' he admitted.

'There, that's what I reckoned. Below the national average for your age, but men who say they need to use a calculator—'

'In actual fact, to be absolutely accurate, I can count them all on one finger.'

'Oh . . .' Meg stared at him. She shrank against the sofa, as if wishing she could vanish into it.

'I'm not a freak,' he said quietly.

But she was still looking at him as if he was.

Meg had never met a man in his thirties who had only ever slept with one woman. Or if she had, then they'd certainly never bragged about it. She had definitely never met a man who was more than willing to let her have the whole of his bed to herself while he contorted himself on his sofa. On the whole, she found it a bizarre experience, as if discovering that Father Christmas did exist after all.

'The sheets are fresh from yesterday,' he said. 'But I can change them again for you.'

She shook her head. 'Thank you for letting me stay. It saves me waking Dad or Pug and explaining what happened to my keys. And I don't mind crashing out downstairs . . .'

But he wouldn't hear of it. 'We'll talk more in the morning, we're both too tired now.' And he backed out of the bedroom at full throttle.

On her own, Meg took off her dress and laid it carefully over the back of an armchair cluttered with old books. She picked one up: *The Thirty-nine Steps.* Beneath that was *Swallows and Amazons* and a couple of Cold War thrillers. *Great Expectations* had been dipped into so much it was dog-eared, propped up against an ancient leather-bound Bible that was probably a family heirloom.

So, what could she deduce from all this, she wondered idly.

Simple. He was in dire need of a book shelf.

She toppled into bed. The duvet cover wasn't the one she had stained; she hoped that hadn't been ruined. The duvet itself was the lovely heavy variety. She snuggled into it, opening one eye to look at the photograph of Polly on the bedside table beside the alarm clock.

'I was wrong, Pollyanna,' she murmured, 'you

were a lucky woman. A bit of a bummer about the dying part though.'

It was such a large bed for one man to be alone in; it must make him even lonelier, she thought. Hugging a spare pillow, Meg flipped over to face the window. Her eyes drifted shut, and her last conscious thought was that she was glad he hadn't changed the bed-linen . . .

Daylight was already creeping in when she woke with a start. A track-suited dwarf was standing in the doorway. Blinking several times through the fog of sleep and the first dull pangs of a hangover, she realised that it was Freddy in his pyjamas.

'Hiya, kiddo,' she muttered with a yawn. 'Are you after your dad? He's downstairs on the sofa . . .'

She listened to the boy hurrying down the stairs. 'Daddy, Daddy! Meggy's in your bed! And she hasn't got any clothes on!'

Matthew swiftly pulled on the trousers he'd been wearing the night before, shut his son up with a banana milkshake, and then put him back to bed, making the supreme effort of not glancing in through the open door of his own room as he did so. He went back downstairs, but knew he wouldn't be able to sleep again; not that he'd slept much before. Padding into the kitchen, he rubbed his stiff back and slipped on his crumpled shirt without doing it up.

During the night, tossing and turning awkwardly on his cramped sofa, he had stopped running from the way he felt and confronted his emotions head-on. It was almost a relief to admit the truth, if only to himself. If Meg *had* been making advances at him yesterday, Matthew was aware he wouldn't have been able to fend her off for long. He would have smoothed down that provocative curl sticking out above her right ear, would have kissed her slender neck, her luscious mouth . . . long and slowly, knowing exactly where it would lead. But this had been Polly's house as well as his; Polly's bed upstairs. It was one thing for Meg to sleep in it alone, another to . . .

Matthew knew that he wanted Meg in the most physical way a man could want a woman. Beyond that though . . . That was too hazy and undefined, a part of him he'd been so sure had died with Polly.

Meg had thrust herself into his life unexpectedly, and he had stopped questioning the whys and wherefores the instant he had realised that he *needed* an adult like her in his world. Someone completely different. Someone unpredictable. Someone who didn't treat him with kid gloves.

So what if people in Yarleigh had jumped to

the wrong conclusion? It wasn't his fault, and he'd stopped caring about the petty-mindedness of village life a long time ago.

But Meg had made him feel things he hadn't felt since Polly. He had denied that realisation for a long time, and then – last night – when denying it had become impossible, he had resisted it instead. There was a distinct difference.

And now . . . ?

Upstairs, as Meg wriggled back into the dress, she noticed something unusual about it for the first time. There was a small embroidered motif by the back seam, near the hem. In the same colour as the crushed-velvet, it was easy to miss. Meg pulled the dress off again and examined the motif more closely. It was either a sunrise or a sunset: tiny rays splaying out over a flat horizon . . .

The dress had been another birthday present from Jake. Laid out in a rustling sea of tissue paper in a long pink box, there had been no tag, no label, not even washing instructions. Of course, she had told herself, washing instructions were too tacky. It was obviously dry clean only.

The motif, she realised, was a sunrise. At the back of her mind, a memory stirred fretfully. Meg had read about this discreet embroidered 'signature' sometime last year. It wasn't so much ingenious as logical.

The rising sun represented dawn.
And the Roman goddess of dawn was Aurora.

When Meg finally shuffled into the kitchen, Matthew was sitting at the table eating toast and reading a newspaper.

He looked up and pulled a face. 'Sorry about Freddy. I should have warned you.'

'Doesn't matter,' she mumbled.

'You look a bit . . . odd.'

'If you mean the blotchy skin and the eyes like doughnuts, I think we both know why.'

'You don't have to rush off anywhere, do you?' he asked. 'I can drop you off on my way to church later.'

Meg sank down at the table. 'Church? On a Saturday?'

'Actually, I'm seeing Father Ben, about Freddy doing his First Holy Communion. Would you like cereal or toast?'

'Just coffee, I'm not hungry.' She twiddled a finger in her hair and watched him as he made it. His chest was on show: smooth and taut but not hairy. He looked so at ease, as if having breakfast with her was commonplace.

'It's what Polly would have wanted,' he said.

Meg swiftly transferred her gaze to his face. 'Huh?'

'Freddy – his First Holy Communion.'

'Oh, oh right.'

Once he'd put the coffee in front of her, Matthew grew serious. 'Meg – I've been thinking . . . You said that Aggie was willing to go up to Yorkshire with you to see your mother.'

Meg cupped her hands around her mug. 'I told her I wasn't going. But I wouldn't take Aggie with me, even if I did decide to see Mum. She's too much a part of it.'

'And you're the one who needs a shoulder to lean on, not her.'

'But shoulders to lean on when it comes to this are in short supply. I can't tell Dad. Or Pug, or William. I've never really been able to talk about my mother much since she left. The only people who know she's been in touch are you, me and Aggie.'

'Well, now that I'm involved, I was wondering . . . would it help if *I* went with you to see her?'

Meg's ears were still buzzing from the music in Pilgrims, but she was certain she had heard him correctly. She gaped across the table. 'You're – you're saying you'd come with me? All the way to North Yorkshire?'

He nodded. 'If it would help.'

'But that's such an imposition . . .'

'Not really. I wouldn't mind getting away from Yarleigh, even if it's just for a weekend. The kids are great, but even a Superdad like me could do with a break.' He smiled.

She couldn't smile back. Her thoughts felt as if they were passing through a spin-dryer, but there was one thing she was certain of. Her voice was almost childlike as she murmured desolately, 'I can't go alone, Matthew. I can't.'

He gazed straight at her. 'You don't have to.'

Eighteen

'Sorry I'm late.'

'Run out of petrol, did you?'

'I thought that was your prerogative, Miss Oakley?'

She sniffed. 'Do you have any idea what it feels like to wait around in a bus station while all these buses go in and out but you don't actually get on one?'

'It was you who said we shouldn't be seen leaving Yarleigh together. And I've told you I'm sorry, but Georgie suddenly decided to call me Daddy and cling to me like a limpet.' Matthew hoisted Meg's holdall into the boot with an 'Ooof' of disbelief.

'I couldn't decide which clothes I might need,' she said sullenly.

'I should be charging you excess baggage. How did you manage to get it this far?'

'I came by taxi.' She clicked on her seat-belt. 'Has Georgie never called you Daddy before?'

'Not properly.'

'Why don't you look happy about it then?'

He frowned. 'I am happy.'

'Are you upset about leaving her? Is this the first time you've been away from her for so long?'

'Meg, I'll miss both the kids, but as I've told you before, I could do with a break.'

They left Tockley behind and wound their way along hedge-flanked country lanes. In half an hour, they would be on the A1 heading north. Meg had started the journey with her fingers gripped around the edge of the seat, but soon she began to relax. Matthew wasn't such a lousy driver after all. She must have caught him on a bad day that first time. But then the anniversary of a beloved wife's death was hardly going to be good, she reminded herself irritably.

'Did you sort out the insurance so that I could drive?' she asked. 'I really thought I'd be covered on my own.'

'I rang them up. They said no problem.'

'Fine. When you get tired, let me know and we'll swap over.'

But Matthew wasn't going to relinquish his hold on the wheel quite that easily. 'If you'd had a car with more leg and head room, we could have gone in yours,' he pointed out.

'I love my car! It's an extension of my personality.'

'Meg, you're not mini in any sense. Why didn't you choose something larger?'

'Because when I went to the second-hand car dealer in Tockley, it was the only vehicle in my price range with MEG in the registration.'

'Other people buy the personalised plates separately; you had to buy the entire car.'

'And it was red,' she stated grumpily. 'I love red.' She didn't give him the chance to remark that that part *was* an extension of her personality. She switched on the radio and turned up the volume.

They hit the Friday evening traffic just as the news report warned drivers that the roads were congested.

'Could have figured that out for myself,' grumbled Matthew.

'It always reminds me of noses,' Meg murmured.

He looked at her askance. 'Noses?'

'When they start talking about congestion, I always imagine . . .' She changed the subject. 'So, what did you tell your in-laws in the end? About where you were going this weekend.'

'I said I was going to York to visit an old friend who'd trained with me, which is true in as much as I do know someone who trained with me who just happens to live in York. But I said his phone was out of order, so I'd have to call home from a pay-phone now and again, to check on the kids. I'd have preferred it if I could have left a number in case of emergencies, but . . .'

'I'm sorry . . .'

'What about you? What did you tell your lot?'

'I told them I was going on another computer course.'

'So you've been on one before then. Was it any good?'

Meg fiddled with a loose thread trailing from her shirt. 'Er – it was – interesting, I suppose.'

'You must be well practised in this kind of thing.'

'What kind of thing?' she asked sharply.

'You've been so meticulous about keeping this trip a secret.'

'I couldn't tell anyone the truth about where I was going, and it would have looked dodgy if we'd said we were going together . . .' She hesitated a moment. 'Do you mind what people say about you?' she asked, trying to sound nonchalant.

'Tongues always wag, especially in a small place like Yarleigh. You can't stop them.'

'But' – her own tongue felt bone-dry – 'going away for the weekend together – *not* that we are together in the sense that people might think we are – it *was* best to keep everyone in the dark, wasn't it?'

'I suppose.'

'So,' she said, after a long pause, 'were your in-laws OK about coming down to Yarleigh to look after the kids?'

His smile was grim. 'They would have preferred it if I'd taken Freddy and Georgie to London, but I said that wasn't convenient; I would have wasted too much time. Daphne dithered a bit until I quietly pointed out that Freddy had missed seeing his granny and grandad at Easter and he'd really appreciate a longer than normal visit from them to make up for it.'

'Very crafty.'

'A three-bedroomed sixties semi isn't their idea of an idyllic weekend retreat, but they'll feel a lot less guilty by Sunday night.'

'It'll do Daphne good to slum it for a while,' smiled Meg.

' "Slum it"? Are you implying . . .'

She bit her lip and turned the radio up another notch.

They were already lost by the time they had to stop for petrol. Walking around the car to stretch her legs, Meg watched Matthew bending to remove the petrol-cap. He had a few grey hairs, she noticed now, hoping they weren't all her fault.

'If I go and pay,' she said, 'I can phone the bed and breakfast and say we're going to be late. The landlady might not keep our rooms if I don't warn her.'

Even worse, the landlady might give one room to someone else. Meg appreciated that it wasn't fair on Matthew if she landed him in a compromising pickle.

He didn't look up, just grunted.

'I told you I wasn't a brilliant navigator,' she said. 'If only you'd let me drive—'

'OK. Fine. You take over the last leg.'

He looked worn out already. Meg went to pay and then ferreted out the public telephone.

When she returned to the car, Matthew was strapped into the passenger seat. His eyes were shut. Meg got behind the wheel and after a few false starts eventually found her way around the unfamiliar controls. Matthew didn't stir. For once – when she actually needed to bow to his superior knowledge – he wasn't going to help her out. She would have to drive *and* attempt to decipher the road signs all by herself.

Drat, damn, bugger. The car jerked out of the service station and stuttered into the slip-road. She frantically built up speed before they could be crushed by a HGV.

A dark sports car roared past. Meg scowled, gripping the wheel tighter. With each mile she put between her and Jake, it gave her a chance to think more clearly, to approach the situation logically. He had been away on business in the States. There hadn't been a chance for explanations or excuses. He had kitted her out in one of his fiancée's designs, but he wasn't even aware that Meg knew.

What would he say? she wondered miserably. How would he squirm out of it?

'Are we alive?' asked Matthew, yawning and glancing at his watch. It was almost midnight. 'Oh heck, I can't be dead, I'm starving.'

Meg rested her head on the steering-wheel. 'I think we've arrived. I think this is the place. I just want to turn around and go straight home again.'

As if afraid she'd do precisely that, Matthew quickly lugged their things inside. They both followed the landlady – who always stayed up late watching repeats on the telly, she reassured them amiably – up the stairs to the attic floor of the large Georgian house full of creaking floorboards and chipped antiques.

'There are only two rooms and a bathroom up here,' Mrs Baker was saying. 'It's nice and quiet. Now,' she beamed, 'are you hungry? Shall I bring up a couple of plates of sandwiches?'

Meg couldn't believe their luck. This plump woman in the frilled pinny was straight out of an Enid Blyton story. *Meg and Matthew's Holiday Adventure.* She'd be offering them ginger pop next. 'I'd love a quick bath first,' said Meg. 'Matthew's starving though, he'd better have something to eat before his stomach caves in.'

'No problem, lovie. And you'll find clean towels in the bathroom.'

Twenty minutes later, Meg was sitting cross-legged on a lumpy bed in her favourite nightshirt – two sizes too large for her – munching ham salad sandwiches and distractedly picking out the watercress, when there was a knock on the door. 'It's me,' said Matthew.

'Come on in!' she called. 'The more the merrier.'

Matthew poked his head tentatively around the door. He was still dressed in jeans and a shirt; not in his pyjamas or whatever he wore to bed. Tucked under his arm, oh bliss, was a silver hipflask.

'I thought we might need this – in small doses.' He handed the flask to Meg. 'It's whisky.'

'Neat, I hope.'

'On the rocks.'

'Think you're such a comedian, don't you?' She took a sip. It warmed her to her toes, which were hidden by pink towelling bed-socks. Matthew was staring at her, seemingly fascinated by the embroidered bear on her nightshirt.

'What did you expect?' she challenged recklessly. 'A Janet Reger teddy?'

'Who?'

He hadn't a clue what she was talking about. 'Never mind. Just park yourself somewhere. You don't have to stand to attention.'

She examined the hipflask. It looked expensive. There was a name engraved on one side: Adam Charles Frederick Stewart.

'My mother's father,' explained Matthew, sitting on the bed and leaning against the scrolled wooden headboard. 'He died when I was a baby, but my grandmother told me all about him, including what size feet he had. The same as me apparently.'

'Large,' smiled Meg. 'And was he Scottish by any chance?'

'He was.' Matthew reached for the flask and took a grateful swig himself. 'But as far as I know, not related to the royal Stewarts.'

'What if you were a long-lost heir to the Scottish throne? Bonny Prince Matthew!'

'Oh right.' He made a face. 'I can really see that. Maybe if you dropped the Bonny part.'

'But that's the best bit,' she said, and then looked bashfully down at her plate, empty now except for a few crumbs and strands of watercress. She thought she heard Matthew mumble something under his breath about courage and the Dutch. She looked up again. He was fiddling with one of the arms of his glasses, adjusting it over his ear. She studied him more closely. 'You look as if you're having an argument with yourself.'

'What?'

'It's just something my dad says. You just looked . . . Oh, I don't know. I can't think how else to put it. Can I have more whisky, or have I exceeded my ration?'

He gave her the flask, his fingers brushing against hers. She saw him gulp. '*Carpe Diem*,' he said.

'"Seize the day."' She echoed the toast. 'There's no need to look at me like that! I'm not a Latin scholar, I just cried buckets during *Dead Poets' Society*.'

'Sometimes you can't though,' he said quietly.

'What? Cry buckets?'

'No. Go around seizing the day whenever you feel like it.'

She wondered what he was talking about.

He slid off the double bed and made for the door. 'I'd better let you get some rest. What time do we have to be at your mother's?'

'Three o'clock,' she reminded him. 'I wrote and told her we could go in the morning, remember? But she wrote back and said the afternoon was better.' Meg had explained all this to him before. He had agreed it was best that she didn't phone her mother; it would be emotional enough hearing her voice again when they were face to face.

'Maybe we can go for a drive up on to the moors in the morning then?' Matthew suggested.

Meg nodded. She'd need the diversion.

'Goodnight then.' He closed the door softly behind him.

Meg suddenly felt very alone, and terrified, as if she was carrying the weight of the world on her shoulders.

All this way . . . All this effort . . . Just to find out something she wasn't even sure she wanted to hear.

The clouds were so near, he felt as if he could touch them. They were ivory, flecked with grey, like the sheep on the opposite hillside. Matthew closed his eyes, the breeze scudding through his hair. He sat on the grass and thought about Meg. She had emerged from her room this morning looking like a different person. Her make-up was barely noticeable, her flowery dress swishing around her ankles, the outfit made complete by a pair of plimsoll-type shoes with thick soles and white ribbons for laces. She wore a denim jacket to ward off the brisk May chill, which was nippier up here on the green and purple moors.

'I wish I could stay here for ever,' she said. He opened his eyes. She was gazing into the distance towards the sea. 'If you could freeze just one moment in your life,' she murmured, 'what would it be?'

It was the hardest question she could have asked. Only a short while ago he wouldn't have hesitated over his answer. It would have been achingly clear.

He turned to stare at her, her cheeks pink from exertion, her hair wind-blown. They had parked the car in a small vale and walked up here to the top of the world.

'I don't know,' he mumbled.

She was still looking out to sea. 'Would it have been when you first met Polly? Or when you got married? Or when Freddy was born? Or—'

'I said, I don't *know*.' Impossible to escape. Whatever was pursuing him had followed him up here. 'It would have been our wedding anniversary this week,' he said suddenly. 'Polly's and mine. We would have been married ten years.'

'Oh!' Meg turned to look at him, pressing her hand over his on the bristly grass. 'I'm sorry . . .'

'Maybe that's why I needed to get away from Yarleigh.'

'Is it helping? Am I enough of a distraction?'

There was a pause. 'You know, if you were going to be stuck up here for ever,' he said crustily, 'you'd want better company than an old misery-guts like me.'

She didn't reply, just took her hand away from his and stared out to sea again.

They delayed it as much as they could, but eventually they had to return to the car.

'Matthew . . .'

'Getting nervous?'

She nodded, chewing her lip. 'Matthew . . . when you look at Georgie, do you see Polly? I mean, do you think to yourself: if I didn't have this little girl, I might still have my wife?'

He stopped walking and faced her. 'Meg—'

'I know. It's got nothing to do with me. It's just . . . you didn't seem happy about Georgie calling you Daddy. You ought to be over the moon. And I know how it happened – how Polly got worse because she didn't have the treatment she needed—'

Matthew cut her short, his voice like sandpaper in his throat. 'I've never agreed with abortion. But there I was, day and night, *begging* Polly to have one . . .'

'Matthew—'

He interrupted again, desperate to explain. 'There were never any guarantees, though, that she would have pulled through after treatment. Somehow, that was supposed to make me feel better.' He squeezed his eyes shut. 'Georgie is my daughter. I love her. But sometimes I think I can't love that little girl enough to make up for how much I hated her.'

Arms were sliding around him, pulling him close. He slid his own arms around Meg, swaying with her half-way down the gusty deserted hill-side, struggling with the realisation that this hug of mutual support was more terrifying than making love to her could ever be.

The house where Meg's mother lived looked tiny from the outside. It was red-brick, on the end of a terrace, across the road from the sea.

Matthew turned to Meg. 'Do you want me to come in with you?' But he already knew the answer before she nodded.

He stood behind her, his breath in her hair as she rang the bell.

The door opened. But it wasn't a woman who stood there.

It was a man, in his fifties, tall, with greying red-brown hair curling in a wind-blown fashion above dark-blue eyes. Matthew had stared into eyes like those only a moment ago.

'You must be Margaret,' the man said to Meg, giving Matthew just a cursory glance. 'I'm Colin Oakley.' And he stood back to let them in, his whole manner grudging.

Matthew felt Meg start to tremble. He imagined he could hear her heart beating faster, her mind racing to take this in, to make sense of how a dead man could be answering her mother's front door. For a moment, Matthew even thought that she might faint, crumpling against him like a Victorian heroine whose corset had been laced too tightly.

But she just stared at Colin Oakley and gasped incredulously: '*You're* the heart-throb?'

As if all these years she had been picturing Elvis Presley.

Nineteen

Seagulls wheeled noisily overhead. Meg pulled her denim jacket around her and leaned against the sea-wall, the smell of salt in her nostrils, the breeze cold against her face. She shifted slightly to look at the fidgeting mousy-haired woman on the bench a few yards away. A woman so like Pug, so small-boned, like a sparrow; Meg felt as if she were gazing at an older faded version of her sister.

'Let's walk along the promenade,' her mother had said, back at the house, just a short while ago.

'Are you sure you ought to, Kathleen?' Colin Oakley had been against it, but she had waved his protests aside. He had glared at Meg as if it was her fault.

The woman in the armchair by the window had turned to Matthew then. 'Will you come for a walk with my daughter and me?'

Meg had looked desperately at Matthew, but with a shake of his head he had excused himself.

'You two should be alone. I'd only be in the way. If I come back in a couple of hours—'

'An hour,' Meg had interjected.

'You can have tea with us, Mr Potter.'

Matthew had nodded, seeing himself out. Meg had felt as if her last defence had been stripped away.

'Your Matthew Potter seems a fine young man,' her mother was saying now, staring out to sea.

Meg heard her own voice from far away. 'He's not mine! He wouldn't touch me with a barge-pole!'

'A strapping lad like that? He wouldn't need any help from a barge-pole.'

'We're friends,' stressed Meg. 'Strictly platonic. And besides, he's married.'

'He wasn't wearing a wedding ring.'

'Wasn't he?' Meg frowned. She'd always thought the plain gold band had been welded to his finger. 'Men don't always bother,' she said quickly, wondering when and why Matthew had prised it off. 'Anyway, by "married" I mean that he had a wife but she . . .'

'Left him?'

'In a sense,' said Meg, after a pause. 'He's got two young children to look after.'

'And you help him, do you? You're always there for each other?'

'I didn't come all this way to talk about *me*. In

fact, it was Matthew who persuaded me to come. He told me I'd regret it if I didn't.'

'Then he's got a wise head on those broad shoulders.' Kathleen patted the space beside her on the bench. 'Won't you sit down, Meg? Won't you let me explain? You were just a girl when I left. You would never have understood.'

'What makes you think I'll understand now?' Years of suppressed anger billowed to the surface.

'Because you've grown into a beautiful young woman. You must know something about love.'

Huh, thought Meg scornfully, I know sod-all.

Aloud, she retorted, 'You can't *make* me understand. Not if I don't want to. You can't make me forgive you.'

The woman shook her head, her eyes watery. 'I just want you to listen to me. Just listen. I don't expect you to forgive—'

'Like hell you don't!' said Meg, blinking back her own tears. 'I mean, what's all this in aid of? Is it for my benefit or yours? So you'll feel a little less guilty for walking out on me? For walking out on your husband and a three-year-old daughter and a young step-son who'd already lost one mother—'

'Oh Meg . . . don't make this any harder, don't turn away . . . Haven't you worked it out yet?'

'Worked what out?'

'I was never a Heybridge. I was never married

to Robert. He was kind, older than me, understanding. His wife was dead, he had a baby son to look after. I did care about him . . . It wasn't love, though. Nothing close to what I'd felt for your father. But Robert was *there*. He took care of me when I needed him, when pretending to be something I wasn't just stopped being enough. And he said it didn't matter about Colin, and for a time it didn't. But, Meg, honestly, I never thought your father would come back for me . . .'

Meg stared at her mother in disbelief. 'You told me he was dead. For as long as I can remember you must have been feeding me lies. Weren't you even the slightest bit afraid that they'd catch up with you?'

'Every day. Every single day. But your father *was* dead then, in a way. I didn't want him anywhere near you. I found it so hard to face up to what he'd done by walking out, and I didn't want you to grow up thinking it was all your fault. He'd married me because I was pregnant, but then he started feeling trapped by the thought of fatherhood. We were both still young, we loved each other, but he wasn't ready for you, for everything you represented. He tried to pressure me into agreeing to give you up for adoption. As soon as you were born, they'd take you away from me. He said we'd have other babies one day, when we were ready. But I *was* ready. We were always arguing. And then one day . . . the ultimatum. The baby or him.

'We were renting a small flat in Durham back then,' her mother continued without faltering, as if she had rehearsed this a thousand times. 'He packed his bags one day and left, and I knew that was it. We'd both made our choice. I went down south to Yarleigh to start again. It was where my mother, your grandmother Hermione, had been raised. Agnes Widdicombe had been a friend of the family; I had no one else to turn to. She seemed to understand. She helped. And then, after years of pretending to be a heartbroken widow, I met Robert Heybridge . . .'

Meg filled in the gap. 'And fell pregnant again – another accident.'

'Robert and I went away to Scotland. When we came back, we said we were married. It seemed logical. I didn't want a divorce; I'd never stopped loving Colin.'

'So,' said Meg caustically, 'where *was* he all that time? Doing a Peter Pan and refusing to grow up?'

'He had grown up, Meg. For years he worked on the oil-rigs, trying to forget what he'd done, to run away from the past, until he couldn't run away any longer and came to find me. Now he's doing what he loves best, taking tourists fishing. That's where he was this morning, why I wanted you to come this afternoon, to meet him. He's calmed down so much. He isn't the boy I knew. There've been other women, I know that, I haven't fooled myself, but he never stopped loving me either. We've been happy. As happy as we could be after what I did, and we've been closer than ever since I found out I was . . .'

'Kathleen.' Colin Oakley was suddenly looming over the bench, his hand on his wife's shoulder. He glared at Meg. 'I knew this was a mistake. I knew Kathleen should never have got in touch with you again. You ruined everything nearly thirty years ago, and you've been in the bloody way somehow or other ever since.'

'Colin—'

'No, Kathleen. You know I didn't want her to come here. I knew it would turn out like this. I knew she'd upset you.'

Meg looked at her father. It felt as if a band around her ribcage was growing tighter and tighter with every passing second. Because of her, Colin Oakley had walked out on her mother. Then, years later, her mother had walked out on another family. Meg had felt guilty all this time; somehow responsible, without knowing why. Now, her sense of guilt was ten times more profound.

'D'you know something,' she said slowly to Colin, 'you're right. I wish she had left the past alone. At least when you were dead I didn't hate you.' And at least you didn't hate *me*, she thought dizzily. She stared down at her mother. The woman couldn't even meet her gaze now. Meg pulled a photograph wallet out of her bag. 'Here, these are of the other daughter you abandoned. I thought you might at least have asked how she was.' Meg looked at Colin Oakley again but couldn't bear to see what was in his eyes. 'I wish Robert Heybridge was my real dad,' she added raspily. 'I'm glad my half-sister has that consolation at least.'

And without glancing back, without expecting her mother or father to call out after her, she turned and fled along the gusty promenade towards the small pier.

Matthew was well aware that he had a short temper. But those moments in the past when his fuse had blown now seemed inconsequential compared with the way he felt about Colin Oakley. Matthew didn't doubt that the man cared for Meg's mother. But wasn't there a possessive element to it, something egocentric demanding that she return his adoration just as exclusively?

Standing outside the small terraced house, Matthew looked both ways along the street and then headed towards the promenade. He could scarcely believe Meg's parents had left her to come to terms with all these bombshells on her own. Kathleen Oakley – not Heybridge after all – had tried to explain. But she'd been interrupted so many times by her husband that Matthew had struggled not to lash out at him.

Pounding along the promenade towards the pier, panic tightened Matthew's throat as he wondered where Meg had got to. Then he spotted her, alone on a bench.

'Meg . . .' She was ashen. He had to get her somewhere warm, somewhere they could talk. In silence, she let him take her hand and steer her across the road into a clinical white café where the only other customers were an elderly couple by the window. She allowed him to sit her down at a stark Formica table in the furthest corner while he went up to order two teas and a currant bun, the only thing behind the counter that looked edible.

'I'm not hungry,' said Meg, when he placed it in front of her.

'Just try to eat something,' he coaxed. 'And drink your tea.'

He watched as she sat picking out the currants from the bun. 'I don't like them,' she muttered. But nothing except the tea reached her lips.

'I've just come from your mother's,' said Matthew. 'She told me everything.'

'Everything?' Meg's eyes filled with scorn.

'Even how she kept up to date with stuff that was going on in Yarleigh? It was the first thing she told me on our walk. As if it would make a difference.'

'She mentioned something about this bloke your father knew who used to go down south on business . . .'

'And while he was at it, he'd visit Yarleigh and nose about, except that you don't need to nose about very hard in a place like that to find out what it is you want to know.' Meg put her cup down so fiercely that tea splashed over the edge. 'I feel as if I've been spied on. Violated in some way.'

Matthew started fidgeting with the plastic ketchup bottle in the centre of the table.

'I've been trying to make sense of it all,' Meg went on. 'Going round and round in circles. You know, I think Mum feels that Pug doesn't belong to her, that she's Robert's and no one else's. But me – I think she wanted Colin to take one look at me and discover all these paternal feelings he never thought he had . . .' Meg paused and shuddered. 'But it's too late. He doesn't want to know. He never did.'

Matthew squeezed the ketchup too hard. Red sauce squirted into the air like a distress flare.

Meg let out a laugh, but it was hollow. And then suddenly, plaintively, she asked, 'Can we go back to the B&B now?'

'What about your mother . . . ?'

Meg shook her head. 'I can't. I can't face either of them again. Not ever.'

'You'll feel differently when you've had time to take it all in.' But the words were feeble to his own ears. 'Finish your tea,' he muttered.

'Matthew, your car . . .'

He wiped the ketchup from the table with a paper napkin. 'I had to park in a side road. You won't have to walk past the house, there wasn't room in front this time.'

They left the café and drove back to the bed and breakfast in silence. As they stepped into the entrance hall, the landlady spotted them through the door of the large dining room where Matthew and Meg had forced down porridge and toast that morning.

'Nice day out, was it?' she beamed at them.

'We went up on to the moors and walked for miles,' said Matthew. 'Meg's exhausted now.'

'Are you, lovie?' The landlady looked at her sympathetically. 'What you need is a nap and then a long soak in the bath. It'll do you the world of good, and come seven or eight o'clock you'll feel bright-eyed and bushy-tailed again. I hope this young man is taking you out for a nice dinner this evening? You don't have to go anywhere too fancy if your pocket won't stretch to it. I know this cosy little seafood restaurant just round the corner from here, but as it's a Saturday you really ought to book. If you like, I can give them a call right now—'

'No,' said Matthew quickly. 'No thanks. That's very kind of you, but Meg's. . . . um . . .' He could hardly say that she'd just discovered her father was stone cold alive rather than stone cold dead. 'She's allergic to fish,' he muttered.

The landlady turned to Meg. 'Really? But this restaurant, it's not *just* seafood, it does do a couple of meat dishes too.'

'I'm a vegetarian,' fibbed Matthew, clutching at straws.

'A vegetarian? But – I gave you ham sandwiches last night!'

'Did you? I didn't even realise. Just goes to show.' He hustled Meg up the stairs, turning to her as they reached the attic landing. 'I'm sorry. It was the first thing that came into my head. The thing is, all that talk of food . . .'

'If you're hungry I saw a chippy just down the road,' said Meg. She fumbled for her key and opened the door to her room.

'Meg—'

'I'd like to be on my own for a while.'

He nodded, although he didn't want to leave her. 'Of course.'

She closed the door behind her.

* * *

For the first time since losing Polly, Matthew was experiencing someone else's pain as acutely as his own. He walked along the seafront again, in the other direction though, as far as the harbour, and sat in a small, dark pub, staring out at the fishing boats. He had tried to eat something from the chippy after he'd left the bed and breakfast, but the chips doused in vinegar had stuck in his throat. He was still hungry now, but the actual process of chewing and swallowing was too much hard work. He abandoned what was left of his lager and started walking again, without knowing where he would end up. Women had no idea how hard it was to act macho, he reflected.

Dusk was already blanketing the town when he trudged back to the B&B. He climbed the stairs to the attic floor and knocked softly on Meg's door. There was no answer. He went to the bathroom and then to his own room, but he was too uneasy to rest.

He rapped on Meg's door again. There was still no answer. She could be asleep, but . . .

Matthew turned the knob; the door wasn't locked. He opened it cautiously. As his gaze fell on Meg, he panicked. She was so still, so pale. Then he realised her eyes were open, staring at him in recognition. It seemed to Matthew that she had collapsed on the bed and hadn't stirred from the position she'd fallen in. She was still wearing the long flower-print dress. The duvet was rumpled around her bare ankles, her plimsolls lying beside her bag and jacket on the floor.

Suddenly, she stretched out a hand to him. 'Matthew . . .'

'It's all right.' He sat down on the bed. 'I'm here now.'

'I'm sorry,' she said.

He frowned. 'What for?'

'Today. All this stuff to do with cancer. It can't have been easy for you.'

This was so typical of her, he realised, insisting aloud: 'It's you we should be worrying about.'

'Aggie must have known, mustn't she? Mum couldn't have kept it from her. Aggie must have known my father hadn't died. And Dad – my stepdad – all these years . . . he knew too. Don't you see? I should never have been born. I was always in the way . . .'

'Don't say that. I'm glad . . .' But he couldn't say it, couldn't get the words out, even though they were true.

'I've only messed up your life,' she was moaning. 'I mess up everyone's lives.'

'Meg, why don't you try to get some rest. If you won't eat, then—'

She reached out for him, clutching at his sweater. 'Hold me,' she whispered. 'I'll be all right if you just hold me.'

He pulled the duvet over her. With his arm around her waist, he kicked off his shoes and swung his feet up.

'You're trembling,' she said.

'I'm OK.'

She lifted her face and blinked at him.

'I'm just tired,' he muttered. 'It's been a long day.' Her lips were so close, it would be so easy . . .

Meg rested her head against his chest, pulling his left hand further around her, threading her fingers through his. 'Why did you take your ring off?' she asked softly.

The buttons of her dress were wide enough apart to . . .

She lifted her face again. 'Why, Matthew?'

'So people up here wouldn't get the wrong idea about us.'

A married man and his bit on the side.

'The wrong idea?' Meg played with the phrase on her tongue, her eyes growing deeper, shadowy.

Suddenly, Matthew understood what Thierry had meant – those words, spoken in confidence in the taxi on the way to Pilgrims nightclub. Even when men were giving, they were taking. It was all Meg had known.

She would accept his need, Matthew was certain of it; she would accept it without question, even if he was taking advantage of the situation.

For a brief interlude, Matthew would have what he knew he had wanted for weeks now. But then, when it was over, he would be the same as all those other men. Something – more than pride, more than ego, more than morality – something told him he had to be different.

'Try to get some sleep,' he urged, drawing Meg's head down on to his shoulder, stroking her hair as if she were a child. Her body relaxed against him until eventually her breathing grew deep and even and calm. Matthew continued holding her, fighting to stay awake as long as possible just to feel her sleeping in his arms, as if, in some strange way, she belonged there; as if – and this was even more preposterous – she had come home.

Meg woke first, stirring slowly to consciousness. It was late, almost eleven. She extricated herself carefully from Matthew's embrace. He had forgotten to take his glasses off; they were crooked across the bridge of his nose. She watched him as he slept, his light-brown hair curling over his brow.

What must it be like, Meg wondered, to be loved the way he still loved Polly – faithful to her even when he wasn't bound to his marriage vows any more? She could hardly imagine it.

'Oi . . . sleepy-head.' She brushed the hair back from his brow.

He stirred, his eyes fluttering open.

'Good morning,' she murmured.

'What's the bloody time?' His words slurred into a yawn. He tried to sit up, but landed back against the pillow with a groan. As he rubbed a hand across his face, he realised he still had his glasses on. 'Bugger. Could have broken them.'

'Are you very short-sighted?'

'Enough to be up the creek without a sodding paddle if anything happened to these.' He straightened them on his nose.

'You should have a spare pair. Or contact lenses. Do you always swear a lot when you first wake up?'

He raked a hand through his hair. 'Sorry. Polly always said I needed to rinse my mouth out every morning.'

Meg stared down at a loop in his sweater where the wool had snagged. 'She was very brave.'

'Had to be. I normally bit her head off.'

'I meant . . . about what happened to her . . . Would she have done things any differently if she'd known how it was going to turn out?'

Matthew attempted to sit up again. This time he succeeded, leaning against the headboard. 'Meg, you ask the most intrusive questions' – she was surprised to find at this point that he appeared to want to hold her hand – 'but for the simple reason that you don't usually tip-toe around me like everyone else, you can have a straight answer.'

She regretted having asked him in the first place. 'Matthew—'

'No. Polly wouldn't have done things differently. Not the Polly I knew. At the time I called her selfish, which was big of me, wasn't it? But she'd dreamed of Georgie too much and for too long to pay any attention.'

It was becoming more and more incomprehensible – how could Polly have taken the risk of losing a man like Matthew? Of course, there was all that heaven and hell business to consider; perhaps that had played a significant part in her decision. 'She was a Catholic,' Meg mused aloud. 'Was she scared of—'

'Meg, even if she hadn't been a Catholic, it wouldn't have made any difference. In Polly's mind, she was Georgie's mother before Georgie was even conceived.'

Meg wet her lips; she didn't have Polly's courage, but she had to go through with this anyway. She had to speak the truth now that she knew how it felt to be lied to for so long.

'Matthew,' she said, 'I can't put it off any longer. There's something I have to tell you. I can't go on pretending. It isn't fair to you. I can't cope with it any more. I should have told you ages ago, about where I was that night – the night before we met in the churchyard. And about why I kept interfering in your life after that.'

His hand slipped away from hers. 'What are you on about?'

'Aggie saw us together, when you dropped me off that morning. Everyone started getting the wrong end of the stick. They thought that you and I were . . .' Meg knew she had to be glowing like tungsten. 'And I didn't correct them, not exactly, because I needed a sort of alibi . . .'

'Alibi?'

'A smoke-screen, to draw attention away from . . .'

'From what?' He was already sardonic, because he could guess what she was going to say. She had denied it the night of her birthday, and he'd wanted so much to believe her, but now . . . 'Your affair with Thierry Duval?'

'No.' Meg swallowed hard. 'My affair with Jake Arundel.'

Twenty

It had been the worst journey Meg had ever known, the atmosphere oppressive. Matthew had driven fast and determinedly. They had stopped once to fill up with petrol and buy sandwiches. Meg had tried to eat but couldn't. Now she felt faint with hunger, yet she knew she wouldn't be able to force anything down; her throat was tight with unshed tears.

It was raining as Matthew pulled up outside her house. An eerie darkness had closed in like a shroud. Meg glanced up and down the street, but no one was about.

'I'll give you a hand with your things,' said Matthew, climbing out as she just sat there in the passenger seat. She sprang to life as he yanked open the door.

'Matthew—'

'Go on in or we'll both get soaked.'

'But—' She bowed her head. 'I'm sorry . . .'

'So am I.'

'And you're angry, I know—'

'And tired. I don't want to say things I'll regret.' He paused, the rain streaking his glasses so that he raised his sleeve to wipe them clean. 'No one likes being used, Meg. I thought I was a friend, but . . . I don't enjoy being part of the game you're playing.'

'It isn't a game—'

'No,' he said slowly, 'you're right. It's real life.' He heaved her holdall out of the boot. 'And that makes it so much worse.'

It was just gone six o'clock. Daphne and Hugh ought to be sitting the children down to tea now, thought Matthew, parking the car in front of his house. He felt humiliated, like a fool, but he was already regretting the way he had acted with Meg. Regardless of how she had used him, she didn't deserve what she was going through over her parents. No one did.

He jumped out of the car, grabbed his own bag from the boot and was heading towards the front door with his keys at the ready and a pensive frown set into his brow when the door swung open as if of its own volition. His mother-in-law stood blinking up at him, arms folded over her long pearl necklace, frosted-pink nails tapping against the sleeves of her plum silk blouse.

'Matthew – you're home.' Her lips were apparently too stiff to curl into a welcoming smile. 'How was your friend in York?'

'Um, fine.' He closed the door behind him with more force than was necessary. 'Where are the kids?'

'They've had their tea and they're playing in the nursery with Hugh . . .'

Matthew was already bounding towards the stairs.

His son and daughter flung themselves at him.

'Daddy, Daddy!' cried Georgie, who seemed to have grown a couple of inches.

'When are Granny and Grandad going home?' whispered Freddy. 'They think I'm a baby.'

Hugh looked tired. 'Daphne and I would like a quiet word with you, Matthew,' he said, suggesting that they leave the children playing upstairs.

A few moments later, Matthew found himself in the living room with his in-laws. 'Shall I make us a pot of tea?'

'No, thank you,' said Daphne. 'I'd be grateful if you could just sit down and hear me out.'

He sat.

'Just after you left here on Friday, there was a phone-call,' continued Daphne.

'A phone-call?' he echoed blankly.

'From your insurance firm.'

'Oh . . . really? What did they want?'

'To check the details of a driver you'd asked

them to temporarily add to your policy. I would have mentioned it when you called on Saturday morning, but . . .' She frowned at Hugh.

Matthew gulped.

'The additional driver was a Miss Margaret Oakley, of Twenty-six, Chaffinch Lane, Yarleigh.' Daphne tugged at the cuffs of her blouse. 'Or "Meggy", as Frederick seems to have a penchant for calling her.'

The morning was so bright and clear, the abysmal weather of the night before might have been nothing but a dream. Meg had hardly had a wink of sleep though. The revelations of the weekend and her need to confess all to Matthew had left her feeling sick, drained and unable to work out exactly what was hurting the most.

She left the house at eight, on auto-pilot, with a million chores to catch up on as usual, none of which she wanted to do. She trudged to the general store in the High Street, which opened early. It was small but well stocked. Mentally ticking off her shopping list, she was just delving around in the freezer when she spotted Matthew and the children entering the store.

She simply couldn't face him today.

Ducking behind the nearest row of shelves, she prayed that he wouldn't need to come to this section of the shop.

'Meg?' The voice was familiar – but female. 'Meg, what on earth are you doing down there?'

She blinked at a pair of strappy silver sandals, her gaze following sun-bed-tanned legs upwards to an A-line mini and a silver cropped T-shirt.

'Oh . . . Hello, Savannah.'

'What on earth—'

'Meggy!' Freddy had run around the corner and was now showing off his gappy smile. 'Meggy, are you doing exercises? Is that one like a bunny-hop?'

Matthew appeared, carrying Georgie and a shopping basket. His face crumpled into a frown.

Meg winced. 'I – um – was just bobbing down to get this, so I don't strain my back.' And she grabbed a tin from the bottom shelf without reading the label.

'I didn't know you had a dog,' said Freddy.

Dammit, thought Meg, neither did I. She glanced at the tin of pet-food. 'I, er, thought I might get one. I was watching this programme about the RSPCA, and I reckoned I could go to an animal shelter and . . .' She tailed off lamely.

'What kind would you get?' asked Freddy.

'What kind? Oh, a sort of labrador, maybe, or a red setter type.'

'You'll find the tin you have in your hand is for smaller dogs,' said Matthew.

Meg shuddered inwardly. 'Is it? Maybe I'll get a

Yorkshire terrier then, or—' Hell, she'd said Yorkshire. 'Maybe a Staffordshire, or a West Highland . . .'

'I saw that programme too,' sighed Savannah. 'It was all about these poor pets that their owners don't want any more and try to get rid of. Do you know, some people are actually cruel enough to flush dear little puppies down the—'

'Yes,' interjected Matthew, 'we get the idea.'

'Daddy,' said Freddy, 'can I have a dog?'

'No.'

'Why not?'

'Because you can't.'

Meg popped the tin back on the shelf. 'I'll come back for that another time, I think.'

'When are you going to come round to our house again, Meggy?' asked Freddy.

'I explained to you,' said Matthew, 'Miss Oakley's a very busy person. Things to do, people to see.'

Meg couldn't bear this. Matthew had seemed wounded enough yesterday, but today . . .

'Excuse me,' he was saying now. Hustling Freddy along in front of him, he moved off towards the counter.

Meg stared after them, her heart like lead. She couldn't avoid him for ever. They had to sort things out once and for all.

'I don't mean to pry . . .' said Savannah, who

had been pretending to examine a packet of dog biscuits, even though she didn't have a dog either.

'Please don't,' muttered Meg. 'It's too long a story.'

'What you need is to come into the salon and cheer yourself up. I've finally been on that eye-lash perming course.' Savannah beamed. 'And how about if I give you a discount on a facial, seeing as you're such a valued customer?'

The suggestion was made with such seriousness, Meg battened down a compulsion to throttle the beautician. She took a deep breath.

'Maybe I'll call and make an appointment,' she said, remembering that she had found solace in beauty therapy once, but knowing that those past troubles were nothing compared to her present ones. 'I'm really busy now though. You'll have to excuse me too . . .'

Forgetting about the last few items on her list, she rushed to pay just as Matthew was leaving the store. Hurrying out after him a few moments later, she spotted him loading the children and shopping into his car. Without hesitating, she ran over.

'Listen,' she began to gabble, as he closed the door quickly on Freddy so that the boy couldn't hear, 'I'm going to have to keep saying I'm sorry, even though you don't want to hear it. You can't begin to imagine how bad I feel—'

'Freddy,' he hissed, 'close that window.'

Meg nodded at the boy. Freddy did as he was told. Meg looked at Matthew again. 'I *know* I started off using you to divert attention away from what was really going on—'

He glanced at his watch. 'Meg—'

'Whatever my original motive, it doesn't mean to say that I didn't come to value what we had. I'd do anything to go back and change the reasons why I did what I did, but I can't. I can't go back. And with everything the way it is now . . .' She thought of her mother and father, the pain sweeping over her in waves.

Matthew was silent for a moment, then he said quietly, 'The damage is done, though.'

'Damage?' she stammered. 'Can't we just forget—'

'It isn't about my hurt pride. Not any more. It's about Daphne and Hugh, and how I lied to them. But for your sake I couldn't tell them the truth, could I? I couldn't tell them *why* we'd gone up north, because I'm not supposed to breathe a word of it to anyone. So I just had to let them think what it must have been perfectly natural for them – for anyone – to think.'

'Matthew . . .' Meg frowned. '. . . Are you saying they've found out that we went away together? How? When?'

'My insurance firm rang up. There'd been

some sort of mix-up. They wanted to verify your details.'

'Oh no . . .'

'Plus I knew there might be trouble from Freddy. I had no real control there, although I kidded myself that I'd dealt with it. I asked him not to mention your name in front of his grand-parents. I said it might upset them. But my son couldn't be fobbed off with the reasoning that he was too young to understand *why* it would upset them, so . . .'

Meg groaned. 'He came straight out and asked them.'

'After that, it was only a matter of time before he told them everything he knew. And Hugh being a High Court judge—'

'A judge?' Meg gulped. 'He was only a barrister when Polly was at St Dominic's.'

'A QC, to be precise. And Freddy gets more like him every day, but with a lot still to learn, because once Hugh started offering him extra ice-cream, the boy stood *no* chance.' Matthew closed his eyes briefly. 'A "chat" with the Elliotts was the final nail in my coffin,' he continued, his voice ragged now. 'Sarah-Jane was very forthcoming. Apparently she'd been terribly shocked the night of your birthday when she babysat for me. If you recall, I started the evening off with one woman and ended up bringing a different one home. Suddenly I'm Yarleigh's answer to Don Juan and – how did Daphne put it? – "an unsuitable parental influence".'

Meg was shaking her head. 'Matthew, you're the best dad ever! Anyone with eyes can see you love those kids to bits. And of course you're not Don Juan! I mean, I'm not saying that you *couldn't* be, in a different set of circumstances . . .'

He put his hand to his brow. Suddenly he seemed very young and vulnerable and . . . lost. Meg wanted to stroke his hair and tell him everything was going to be all right. But maybe Polly had reassured him in that same way too, once upon a time, when he would have had the faith to believe her.

'Matthew . . . the children . . . Daphne and Hugh aren't going to try . . . they don't intend . . .'

'I don't know what they intend. All I know is that I was never really approved of as a son-in-law. Maybe they haven't tried ousting me from their lives before now because they didn't have the right ammunition.'

'Are you saying . . . ?'

He turned towards the car, indicating that the conversation was drawing to a close whether she liked it or not. 'Thanks, Meg.' His shoulders slumped. 'Thanks for everything. You're just the sort of bullet they've been waiting for.'

* * *

It was only nine o'clock in the evening, but Linden Trees Villa was in darkness except for the outside lamp over the porch. Meg stabbed her finger down on the doorbell until lights came on inside and her godmother shuffled to the door and peered out through the letter-box.

This was the first chance Meg had had to break away from her daily grind, and she couldn't put off what she had to say any longer.

'I'll speak to you from out here if you won't let me in,' she warned.

The door opened. Her godmother stood there in dressing gown and curlers. 'What is it? What's wrong?'

'Aggie,' gasped Meg, feeling about eight years old all of a sudden, 'I saw her. I saw Mum.'

Instantly, the old woman drew Meg inside, ushering her along the corridor towards the kitchen. To Meg's amazement, Aggie opened the fridge and started milking a carton of French white wine into two glasses.

A while later, cross-legged on the Persian-style rug in the living room, Meg felt exhausted and yet strangely calm. She had told her godmother everything about the meeting with her mother and father; there were only questions left, but suddenly they weren't as urgent.

Aggie was settled in a winged-back chair with jonquil-yellow upholstery and carved mahogany legs. 'Why didn't you want me to come with you to visit her, Meg?' she asked weakly.

'Because I couldn't have handled seeing all the pain Mum had caused you. You wouldn't have been able to hold it in. You wouldn't have been able to pretend.'

'For your sake . . .'

Meg looked up, staring at the old woman's lined face.

'We've had our differences,' said Aggie. 'I know that. But I only ever wanted what was best for you.'

Anger churned in Meg's stomach. 'So you and Mum concocted this lie between you, about my father being dead.'

'It seemed right at the time. I was convinced he had no intention of coming back into your lives. Some men are like that. They can father a child and have no regard for it whatsoever. But your mother loved you. She still does. You were her first born, Colin's baby. She gave him up for you, and then later she gave you up for him. She's had to live with that. Why do you think she wanted to see you, even though your father was against it?'

'To ease her guilt. To die with a lighter heart. But I didn't forgive her. I didn't give her what she wanted.'

'Didn't, or couldn't?'

'What's the difference?'

'Perhaps you should write to her, maybe even telephone. You can't just leave it like this. When she . . .' Aggie hesitated. 'It will be your turn to feel guilty.'

'You're harping on at me like Matthew does.' Meg shivered. 'Like he *did.* Oh God!' She put down her wine glass and buried her face in her hands. 'What am I going to do about him?'

Her godmother paused for a long moment. 'What do you mean?'

'If it wasn't for me, Matthew's life would be running without a hitch!'

'So being a widower who's bringing up two children isn't a hitch?' Aggie sighed. 'You've obviously become very close, Meg, and you certainly managed to drag him out of his depression—'

'Only to plunge him straight into another! People aren't going to believe that Matthew's an innocent party in this, are they? It's gone too far for that now. They're going to think that I lead him astray.' She spilled out the whole Daphne and Hugh story while her godmother listened patiently.

'I'm sure,' said Aggie at last, 'that once the Hancocks have had a chance to think things through properly . . .'

'Matthew lives for those kids, you know he does! What if there's a custody battle? Who do you reckon's going to win? Respected High Court judge and la-di-da wife, or lowly primary school teacher who's been running around with the wrong sort of girl and parading her in front of his impressionable young children while their virtuous mother is barely cold in her grave?'

'Don't be so dramatic. Polly's been dead for almost a year and a half now. And the Hancocks would have to prove that Matthew's a lot more than just a young man susceptible to a pretty face before any court would take Frederick and Georgina away from him, even if Hugh Hancock does have friends in high places.'

Meg despaired. If only it was that simple! A friend in a high place could work all manner of dark magic in the Hancocks' favour. Matthew would have lost before the case was even heard. The ideal solution had to be to nip it in the bud, Meg mused. A plan – still very hazy – was beginning to take shape. But she couldn't tell Aggie about it. Her godmother would probably dismiss it as a terrible idea. Meg knew she had to do something, though. Without those kids, Matthew would give up on life altogether.

She drained what was left of her wine and unfolded herself stiffly, swaying to her feet. 'It's late. I'd better go.' As she reached the living room door, she hesitated. 'Aggie . . . why are you being so nice to me? Is it because of this thing with Mum?'

The old woman wasn't looking at her now, she was just staring into the empty fireplace. 'Partly,' she said at last. 'It helped me see your life from your point of view, and I even mulled over my own past, particularly when it came to how I'd felt about a certain RAF officer who lost a leg in '44. Although perhaps,' she was smiling now, 'what I felt then was just the same sort of sympathy and pity you feel for Matthew . . .'

Meg had often tried to imagine her godmother as a young woman. It had been virtually impossible, especially as there seemed to be a shortage of photographs with which to prove it.

'Nothing ever came of it,' said Aggie with a sigh. 'He was engaged to another girl. I never interfered. But I'm ashamed to say that if it wasn't pity or sympathy . . .'

'You mean you might have had the hots for him?'

'Coveting may have come into it somewhere, yes.'

Meg shook her head. 'You wicked, wicked girl, Aggie Widdicombe.' And she went over to the winged-back chair and dropped her first kiss in years on the old woman's crêpe paper cheek.

* * *

Tired and discouraged, Meg flicked shut the telephone directory and glanced around the reference section of Tockley Library. She stood up and lugged the heavy volume back to its spot on the shelf.

There was nothing for it: she would have to resort to Plan B.

She went outside into Tockley High Street and found a vacant telephone box. Somewhere in her bag there was a wallet with a phone card in it, but everything else seemed to be surfacing instead: a pencil with a Teletubby on the end, furry orange organiser, keys . . . wallet!

The phone card in its slot, Meg punched out a number. The mobile phone was switched on. Within seconds, it was answered with business-like efficiency: 'Jake Arundel.'

'It's me – Meg. Can you talk?'

'I'm busy at present. Are you calling to arrange a meeting?'

'The thing is—'

'Tomorrow? Around eleven-thirty, usual place?'

'Jake, I only wanted to ask—'

'Any problems, give me a buzz, OK?' And he was gone.

Perched on a low wooden chair, Meg frowned and gazed around her at 'The Usual Place' – the old Gamekeeper's Lodge in Yarleigh Woods. Her watch was ticking towards midnight. She shuddered, even though the night was warm. The decrepit little cottage seemed to have lost its charm; there was nothing romantic about the oak beams any more, or the flagstone floor.

The front door clicked and creaked open. Meg jumped up. 'Jake?'

He stooped to cross the threshold. A second later, Meg found herself crushed in his arms. 'I've missed you so much,' he moaned, kissing her. 'And we've got weeks of catching up to do.'

He looked as virile as always but she pulled away from him as he tried to steer her into the bedroom. 'Jake, I actually came here tonight because we need to talk.'

'Talk?'

The quivering light of the oil-lamp threw ghostly shadows against the walls.

'Why did you give me one of Aurora's designs for a birthday present?' asked Meg, as calmly as possible. 'Didn't she ask who the dress was for?'

'I got a friend's PA to order it. Rory never suspected a thing.'

'Did it give you a kick, Jake? Or was it because you wanted to help your precious Rory out financially, without her knowledge, so her pride wouldn't be wounded?'

'Meg—' He tried to reach out for her, but she

took a step back. 'Meg, listen, I knew the dress would suit you. It was perfect. Does it matter where it came from? You're worth every penny. And Rory isn't precious to me, *you* are.' This time he caught hold of her before she could step away. 'Meg, listen. You're in my head. You've been in my head for a while now and I can't get you out. Believe me, I've tried.' He sounded almost resentful. 'That's one of the reasons why I went away, as far as I could get, I felt so out of control. In the beginning, when we started this, I admit I just thought we could have some fun together for a while, you know how it is. But then something happened. Something that's never happened to me before.'

She blinked up at him, realising that she had longed to hear these words for months, even though she had told herself countless times that their relationship had been serious from the start. Yet even as her heart flipped over at the thought of him loving her, she suddenly panicked. This wasn't how she had imagined it. Something didn't seem right. But what?

He leaned down to kiss her. Unconsciously, she turned her head at the last instant so that his lips landed on the side of her jaw. 'Something's wrong,' he frowned, 'apart from the dress.' His breath stirred her hair. 'Tell me, darling,' he whispered. 'Tell me so that I can make it up to you . . .'

'Jake,' she muttered, 'I need your help.'

'Of course you do, darling. Why don't you tell me all about it in bed?'

'No!' she snapped. 'I mean . . . this is important, I don't want to get distracted.'

'Fine then,' he smiled indulgently, sitting on the chair she had vacated and pulling her on to his lap. 'What's the problem?'

She took a deep breath. 'I need to find out an address. Before the weekend. I've got Saturday off and I thought I'd go up to London and sort it all out before it gets any more out of hand. You've got contacts, all that Old Boy stuff. You must know how to find out where someone lives, especially a High Court judge. There seem to be about a million H. Hancocks living in London and—'

'Sort what out?' Jake frowned. 'What the fuck's going on?'

Meg told him as much as she dared, neglecting to mention where she had been last weekend, and who she had been with. She merely explained that Daphne and Hugh Hancock had been visiting in Yarleigh and had heard unsavoury rumours about their son-in-law. 'And Matthew's hardly going to come straight out and tell me where they live, is he?' she concluded.

'Just think, Jake, it's because of us that he's in this mess.' She scowled. Jake was laughing.

'You're going to make even more of a hash of it,' he choked. 'I can see you now, sitting in a chintz armchair, ankles crossed, looking demurely through your lashes and murmuring, "Please, Mr Hancock, Mrs Hancock, Matthew's such a good boy really, he's never laid a finger on me, he wouldn't know where to start."' Suddenly, with an unnerving abruptness, Jake stopped laughing. 'He hasn't, has he, Meg? Laid a finger on you? You'd tell me if he had?'

'He hasn't. Not the way you're thinking.' She focused on a freckle by Jake's ear. 'Like you said, he wouldn't know where to start.'

'Exactly.' Jake grinned. 'OK, so he's got two sprogs, he must know something. But his wife was just a tiny speck of a thing, wasn't she? It probably didn't take much to satisfy her physically.'

'Jake . . . you've heard the gossip about Matthew and me. It was what you wanted, to divert attention away from *us*. But that's all it ever was. Just gossip. The thing is, if I don't try to convince the Hancocks that nothing's going on, I'll feel awful.'

'OK, OK, leave this with me; it shouldn't be too difficult. A couple of calls tomorrow morning and I'll have that address for you. Matthew Potter seems to have outlived his usefulness anyway. We can let the poor sod settle back into obscurity.'

Meg nodded, forcing herself to smile. Who else did she know who could help her as speedily as Jake? Speaking of which . . . Somehow, without her being aware of it, he had undone most of the buttons of her cardigan, his hot-blooded hands now in direct contact with her flesh. She wasn't in the mood for this, but she'd never refused him before.

'Come on, darling,' he coaxed, when she was slow to respond, 'I don't want to have to do all the work.'

'Actually,' she rasped, 'I've a bit of a headache . . .'

'My poor love. I know just the medicine.' He stroked her cheek. 'And besides, you want to keep me happy, don't you?' Easing her off his lap, he stood up and started leading her towards the bedroom and the bleak expanse of sagging grey mattress. 'Show me how badly you want me to be happy, darling. Show me . . .'

[illegible]

Mrs [illegible] arranged to [illegible] [illegible] as [illegible] Speaking [illegible] [illegible]

[illegible]

[illegible]

[illegible]

Mr [illegible] was the [illegible]

Twenty-one

A heat-wave had set in, rather an intense one for May. The temperature in London was a couple of degrees hotter than Yarleigh. Meg noticed it as she tramped up the King's Road with an A-Z and a swarm of doubts and reservations. She had decided to walk this last leg of the journey rather than relying on a taxi, which gave her more time to go over her lines, as if rehearsing for a play. She could have come in the Mini, but she wasn't used to driving in big cities; her navigational skills being what they were . . . Even walking, with plenty of time to pause and consult her map without getting tooted or gesticulated at, she was still having difficulty.

She paused a moment to adjust the strap of her bag on her shoulder, glancing around and suddenly missing Yarleigh like mad. The navy-blue top she was wearing was short-sleeved, but it had a high neckline: a bugger in this heat. Her long white and navy sarong-style skirt fluttered in the breeze; she tugged it firmly across her legs and continued up the road.

Sod's law the Hancocks wouldn't even be home. Phoning them beforehand would have been pointless, though. They were hardly going to say, 'Of course, dear, do come over, we can hardly wait!' It was more likely to be a case of: 'We're going to be out. In fact, we've moved. Sorry about that. If you want to get in touch with us, speak to our solicitor. He's the best money can buy.'

Because that was another thing: Matthew could never afford to hire a renowned brief to fight his custody battle for him. Which left Meg no choice. She had to go through with this.

Consulting her A-Z, she turned left and then right. A tasteful plaque informed her she was in the correct street at last. She gazed at the houses with their white façades, and gulped. She walked a few paces, and there it was, Number 3. Before she could change her mind, she charged up the stone steps and jabbed her finger down on the doorbell.

A few seconds later, the door swung back in a stately fashion and a vaguely familiar man with white hair and a pleasant enquiring smile stood staring out at her. 'Yes?'

Dammit, she'd forgotten what she was going to say!

'Are you a Jehovah's Witness?' he asked, still smiling pleasantly.

'No,' she said, without thinking, 'I'm a Roman Catholic.'

'Really. So was my daughter. She was going to marry one, so she thought she might as well become one.'

'Oh, I didn't realise—'

'Hugh!' trilled a voice Meg had heard before but wished she didn't have to hear again. 'Who is it?'

'I don't know, she hasn't told me yet.'

A woman popped her head around a door along the hall. Meg recognised her instantly. Daphne Hancock came out, her brow drawn over sharp green eyes, pale golden hair waving gracefully around her slim face. 'Can we help you?'

'No,' said Meg. 'That is, yes. Or rather – it isn't me who needs helping.'

Daphne frowned. Hugh rubbed his hands together. 'Jolly good. I love a conundrum. Give me another clue.'

Meg couldn't detect any sarcasm in his tone, but she was certain he was teasing her.

'I'm Meg Oakley,' she said.

'Oh!' Hugh's eyebrows shot up.

'I suppose you'd better come in then, Miss Oakley,' said Daphne, through barely-moving lips, as if she was a ventriloquist. The Hancocks obviously didn't want a scene on their doorstep. Meg found herself ushered into an imposing drawing room. The bottom half of the walls was panelled with wood, the top half decked out in rose-patterned wallpaper. Silver-framed photographs of Polly at various stages of her life stood clustered on the mantelpiece. At the far end was a wedding picture, identical to one Meg had seen at Matthew's house. As she stared at the bridegroom, her throat constricted.

'Please' – Hugh gestured to a dusky-pink armchair – 'do sit down, Miss Oakley. Would you like tea? Coffee?'

She shook her head.

'What's this about?' asked Daphne, settling on the sofa. 'Did Matthew send you?'

'He doesn't know I'm here,' Meg managed to utter. 'He'd kill me if he knew.'

'So, Miss Oakley,' Hugh perched beside his wife, 'why *are* you here?'

'I thought,' she stammered, 'I thought I ought to explain. You've got things all wrong—'

'Are you or are you not having an intimate relationship with our son-in-law?' demanded Daphne.

Dazed by the bluntness of the question, Meg just stared at her. 'No,' she mumbled at last.

'So you didn't go away with him last weekend?

And my grandson lied about seeing you in his father's bed?'

Indignation surged into Meg's vocal cords. 'Did Freddy also mention that his father slept downstairs on the sofa that night?' she challenged.

'Well, actually—' began Hugh, but his wife interrupted him.

'It wasn't just that particular episode which led us to draw our own conclusions, Miss Oakley. It was common knowledge in the village . . .'

Meg sat up straighter. 'You know what villages are like. Gossip spreads like wildfire.'

'Are you saying that it's all been one huge misunderstanding?' Daphne looked at her incredulously.

'Mrs Hancock, I've never met a man with more integrity than Matthew.'

'So what exactly are you denying or confirming then?' asked Hugh, still remarkably good-natured. Any moment now, thought Meg warily, he would whip out a gavel, a wig and a red cape. This chummy act was probably just a ploy to catch her off guard.

She took a deep breath. 'I suppose – I suppose I'm just confirming that there have been a few men in my past, although I would like to state for the record that none of them were ever one-night stands.'

'No one's taking any of this down,' said Hugh mildly.

She felt cheap, with an IQ of minus eighty. 'Matthew was never one of them though,' she continued. 'He was a friend, purely platonic, all above board. I've been having a few personal problems lately. He was there when I needed a shoulder to cry on. I know it sounds clichéd—'

'These personal problems' – Daphne leaned forwards – 'were they drug-related?'

'Sorry?' Meg's bottom lip trembled.

'Are you a junkie, Miss Oakley?'

'Daphne—'

'I'm sorry, Hugh, but if she's been in contact with the children . . .'

'I don't do drugs,' Meg said hurriedly. 'I never have.'

'A drinking problem then?'

'I admit that sometimes I drink a bit more than I should . . .'

Hugh smiled and nodded. 'Love a tipple myself.'

'But it isn't a problem,' said Meg, who would have jumped at the chance of a sherry if it had been offered. 'And this doesn't have any bearing on why I'm here. Right now Matthew's furious with me, and he has every right to be. Because of me, and through no fault of his own, you accused him of being an unfit parent.'

'Miss Oakley—'

'But he isn't!' Meg clenched her fists, her voice rising tremulously. 'He's the best father I've ever seen. He lives for Freddy and Georgie. Wasn't losing Polly enough? Does he have to lose all he's got left of her? I'm not disputing that you haven't suffered too. Polly was your daughter, your only child, but at least you've got each other to turn to. Can't you just leave Matthew to get on with things the best way he knows how – quietly and unambitiously – without sticking your noses in and making all these threats and—' She stopped short, realising in mortification that her ankles were no longer crossed in a lady-like fashion, and that she had ceased peering imploringly, demurely or otherwise through her lashes. In fact, she was on the edge of the chair, grinding a fist into the crocheted doily thing draped across the arm.

Daphne was blinking at her in stupefaction.

It was Hugh who spoke first. 'Miss Oakley, do you honestly wish us to believe that Matthew has never made any advances, of any description, towards you?'

'Yes,' said Meg. 'He's behaved like a perfect gentleman.' She sat back in the chair, ankles crossed, hands folded neatly in her lap, wondering if this was how Polly had conversed with her parents.

'He hasn't ever – what's the phrase nowadays? – asked you out?' Hugh persisted.

'Matthew would never dream of asking me out,' Meg said weakly, trying to recall what judges were addressed as in all those courtroom dramas she'd watched. Your Honour? Mi'Lord? Your Worship? 'You see,' she went on, 'I'm not girl-friend material in his eyes, let alone the stuff a potential wife or step-mother would be made of.'

'Ideally, she'd have to be flesh and blood,' said Hugh, scratching his head. 'Hope this isn't too personal, Miss Oakley, but what are you made of? Somehow you don't strike me as the sugar and spice variety of female.'

'Er,' said Meg, 'how many varieties are there?'

Hugh shrugged. 'My father used to say there were only the two.'

'Oh.' Meg frowned, totally thrown now.

'Miss Oakley,' put in Daphne, recovering at last, 'I'm not entirely sure what you hoped to gain by turning up here uninvited and losing your temper.'

'I didn't mean . . . I never intended . . .' Meg bowed her head. 'I only wanted to help.' Jake had been right to predict she would screw this up big-time. 'It's just . . . you want to make out that Matthew's guilty by association with me. People always see it that way. Everyone's so cynical. Why can't they think that maybe it's the other way round? That maybe I'm innocent by association with him? Or maybe that's not the best way of putting it. Maybe what I'm getting at is that if something's pure and it gets corrupted by something corrupt, why can't it work in reverse? Why can't something corrupt get *un*corrupted by something pure?'

'Why not indeed?' Hugh squinted at the glass-fronted bookcase to the right of the fireplace. 'Have you ever studied law, Miss Oakley?'

'Law?' She barely contained a derisive hoot. 'I'm afraid I never got around to it.'

'Pity,' sighed Hugh.

'Miss Oakley,' said Daphne, 'have you quite finished what you came here to say?'

Meg felt cut down to size again, which at that moment was floor level. 'Er . . . yes.'

Daphne stood up. 'Well then, we won't take up any more of your time.'

'But,' mumbled Meg, rising to her feet too, 'Matthew—'

'—is none of your business. As you said yourself, it's not as if you were or ever will be his girlfriend.' Daphne smiled at her, but it was brittle. 'Don't worry, I won't tell him about this visit, we'll keep it our little secret.' She ushered Meg out into the hall again and flung open the front door. Hugh remained in the drawing room, having distractedly nodded his goodbyes.

'Mrs Hancock,' Meg was desperate, 'about Freddy and Georgie . . .'

'As I told you, Miss Oakley' – Daphne frowned, nostrils flaring as if she suddenly remembered being called a snooty cow all those years ago and who precisely had done the calling – 'this really has nothing to do with you!'

And on that charming note, she closed the door in Meg's face.

'What's wrong with the lad?' mused Hugh, looking across at his wife, who was restlessly flicking through the latest trend-setting cookbook.

'Pardon?'

'Matthew. What's wrong with him, do you think? Has he gone blind? Or maybe he's deaf? God help him if it's both.'

'What are you wittering on about?'

'Doesn't seem five minutes since Polly was sitting in that same chair defending the lad too, although she wasn't quite as colourful about it. Then again, she was practically a child. There we were, with all these expectations of her, how she'd go to Oxford or Cambridge, how she'd meet a decent chap, perhaps the son of someone I went to school with, one of those likely candidates we kept introducing her to, remember?'

'Hugh . . .' Daphne leapt to her feet, pacing to the drinks cabinet and pouring herself a sherry.

'And then,' Hugh took up the thread again, as if oblivious to his wife's discomfort, 'one day, instead of turning up to Sunday lunch with a Hector Billington, or a Roger Delaware-Hunt, or an Honourable Charles Henry Smythe, she brings home an English student she'd met in some backstreet library. A Matthew Potter, who wants to be a *primary school teacher.* And the next thing we know she says she's going to marry him and forget about Oxford or Cambridge or getting that First we'd always dreamed she'd get because she was so damn bright.'

'Your blood-pressure, Hugh,' hissed Daphne, the sherry glass rattling against her teeth.

'But no,' he went on with a shrug, ignoring his wife, 'our Polly wanted to be "ordinary". She wanted to settle for a second-hand car, and a cramped semi, and a simple little secretarial job, and d'you know why, hmm? Because they were the last things on earth we'd ever wanted for her!'

'I never pushed Polly into anything. I never drove her to marry that boy. You know I did everything in my power to dissuade her!'

Hugh shook his head pityingly. 'Exactly, Daphne . . .'

She frowned at him.

He sighed. 'Polly was a teenager doing what teenagers do best. In the long run, she must have been surprised to find she'd rebelled so wisely, because I don't think she dared believe she would actually be happy. I don't think she even knew what happiness was until then.'

'Hugh!'

He stood up, walking to the rear window, staring out into his small but carefully tended garden. 'She never humiliated herself for the lad though, did she? Although, back then, we thought the humiliation was in marrying him. But that was her master-stroke.' Hugh was pensive and far away, remembering his golden, ingenious daughter. 'She never had to embarrass herself for his sake. She never had to squirm, or make herself look bad merely to cast him in a good light. And now, I wonder,' he turned and stared at his wife, his expression lined with curiosity and something else, something Daphne couldn't define, 'did she ever love him enough to have gone quite that far?'

Twenty-two

'We'll order a takeaway,' said Libby decisively, searching through a drawer in her kitchen. She walked over to the sofa brandishing a Pizza Perfecto menu.

Meg was pouring out the wine. She placed a glass in front of Libby. 'Thanks for inviting me to stay over tonight. I needed a break. Things have been so tense at home lately. Pug's being a typical teenage nightmare.'

'It's been ages since I've had a girly night in,' sighed Libby. 'Maybe it's because I'm not such a girly any more.'

'Nonsense!'

'You say the sweetest things.'

'That's what friends are for.'

Libby was poring over the pizza menu. 'Not the Blow-out Chilli Meat Spectacular,' she muttered with a sniff. 'I remember the last time I had it. I think I'm going to try the Hula Hula. It's got ham and pineapple.'

'One huge Hula Hula for both of us then?' suggested Meg. 'And masses of garlic bread, yep?'

Libby nodded enthusiastically. 'Oh, yep.'

Meg rang Pizza Perfecto and repeated the order.

'About half an hour to forty minutes,' she told Libby, hanging up. Sighing, she grabbed a fashion magazine from a pile on the coffee table. 'This is old. It's the March issue.'

'I've been meaning to sort through them all.' Libby reached for the TV remote and started flicking from channel to channel. 'I think there was an article in that one about Aurora Lloyd. I never got around to showing you.'

Meg stiffened. 'Oh? And – um – what was the article about?'

'Fashion, you plonker.' Libby rolled her eyes and snatched the magazine away. 'Here it is: "*More Than Just A Famous Name*". Very clever.'

'Clever?'

'A "Lloyds' Name" – get it?'

'Er . . . no.'

'Well, I don't suppose you read *The Financial Times*.' Libby sighed, and went on to explain.

Meg gazed at a glossy photograph of Aurora holding up a shimmering ballgown.

'"*With her supermodel looks*,"' read Libby, '"*her spectacular talent and her inherited business acumen, Aurora Lloyd – Rory to her closest friends – is going for gold in a major way. Business in the South Ken boutique and the design studio above is clearly booming*"—'

'Bastard,' muttered Meg under her breath, realising Jake had been lying to her all along.

Libby looked up in surprise.

'I mean, bitch,' Meg said quickly. 'But only in a mildly derogatory way, like you call me hussy.'

Libby carried on. '"*Even Aurora's personal life reads like a fairytale. Her fiancé is City high-flyer Jake Arundel, owner of a sprawling country estate, in his family for generations. When asked if they'd set a date for their wedding, Aurora smiled affectionately. 'Jake and I are perfectly happy to keep things as they are for now. Maybe next year, but we'll just have to wait and see.' Rest assured, whenever she ties the knot, this stunning and successful young lady will be walking down the aisle in a million dollar dress.*"'

'Yikes, who writes these things!' Meg cringed.

Libby grimaced. 'Jake's the only bit of her life I don't envy. I'd call that Stephen King territory, not a fairytale.'

'Oooh, look, it's that comedy I like!' Meg pointed at the telly, anxious to change the subject.

'Did you see it last week? I was in stitches.'

'Um, last week?' Meg tried not to dwell on the journey back from North Yorkshire. 'No, must have missed it. I don't think I was home from my computer thingy.'

They sat and watched TV. Just as the comedy was ending, the door buzzer went. Libby did a hula out of the flat, but when she returned she was pizza-less.

'It's Thierry for you, Meg. He didn't want to come up.'

'Why not? Silly beggar.'

Meg found him waiting outside. He had two small old-fashioned brown suitcases with him. Meg stopped short. 'Are you going on holiday?'

He shook his head. She couldn't recall ever seeing his eyes this red, or his face so ashen. 'I have been bagged,' he said.

'Bagged?'

'Sent packing. Given my trotting orders.'

'You mean *sacked?*'

He nodded.

'Well you can't just stand around out here all evening.' Meg was adamant. 'Come upstairs and tell me what happened.'

He hesitated as he picked up his cases. 'You mentioned to me that you were coming here tonight. I do not want to disturb—'

'You're not disturbing anything.' Meg bullied him up the stairs to the flat. 'Sit yourself down. Would you like some wine?'

Libby was already reaching for the bottle, but Meg got to it first. 'You can have my glass.' She handed it to him, replenished. 'Now tell me from the beginning – what happened?'

'Lately, nothing I could do was right,' murmured Thierry. 'Faults are picked everywhere. Today, I was told to leave. To pack my belongings and go.'

'Who exactly fired you?' asked Meg.

He paused. 'It was Jacintha Arundel.'

'But your cottage,' said Libby in horror, 'you had to pack everything and leave – just like that?'

'I was only a handyman.'

'*Only* a handyman!' Libby frowned. 'I wouldn't be surprised if you had to wipe the Arundels' blinking bottoms for them!'

Thierry stared at his feet. 'It was simply work. Something to do.'

'So what now?' asked Meg.

'I am not sure . . .'

'Where are you going to stay until you get yourself sorted out?' Libby was being practical.

'He can stay round mine,' said Meg. She had never seen Thierry so depressed. She was certain that there was more to all this than Jacintha – or anyone else – picking fault with his work. 'William's not home at the moment. I'm sure he wouldn't mind you kipping in his room.'

Thierry nodded. 'That is kind of you, Marguerite.'

'Don't be silly, it's the least I can do.'

By the time the pizza arrived, Meg had lost her appetite. Thierry didn't seem to have much of one either. They needed to talk, but she knew he wasn't going to open up in front of Libby.

'Would you mind if we made a move, Libs?' she asked. 'I know I was supposed to stay over . . .'

'Actually, to tell you the truth, I'm getting rather sleepy.' Libby yawned. Meg knew it was put on. Smiling at her friend's tact she lifted one of Thierry's cases, promptly plopping it back down again. 'Maybe we ought to get a taxi.'

'I will leave the cases here, if that is all right with you, Libby?' He looked at her for reassurance. She nodded. 'Then I will fetch them tomorrow,' he went on. 'Tonight I would appreciate a walk, to clear my head.'

'Well, come on then,' said Meg, leading the way downstairs.

'See you both tomorrow.' Libby closed the front door after them. Meg linked her arm through Thierry's and slowly they started walking in the direction of Chaffinch Lane.

'Now, Monsieur Duval, are you going to tell me the truth?'

He looked away, but she could still see his left eye twitching. 'The truth?'

'What did you really do? None of the Arundels would sack you without a strong enough reason. You've been with them too long.'

'And you, *mon ange*, you think you know the Arundels well, no?'

It was Meg's turn to look away. 'Everyone in Yarleigh knows them.'

'But they do not all know about the old Gamekeeper's Lodge.'

Meg swung round. 'What?' She tossed her head haughtily. '*What* old Gamekeeper's Lodge?'

'Do not pretend with me, Marguerite. I have known about you and Jake Arundel for a while now. Sometimes, when I cannot sleep, I take a stroll through the woods on my own, to let air into my brain. One night, I see a light in the little cottage no one lives in. I go to the window, and—'

'No . . .' Meg pulled away from him, stepping into the shadows of the nearest shop doorway.

Thierry followed her, turning her to face him, lifting her lowered chin. 'I told nobody about what I saw.'

She couldn't think of anything to say. Suddenly, there was no defence.

'I was not surprised,' he went on. 'I know what you want from life, all those fantasies in your head, those fairytales. But I remember I was sad for Matthieu because I believed that you were in love with him. But you are in love with your dreams, *non*? And Matthieu, however good a man he is, cannot give them to you.'

'Thierry—'

'All these years,' he continued, 'you thought I stayed in Yarleigh because of you . . . for no other reason . . . But do not underestimate the ties between father and son.'

Father and . . . ? What was he on about? She frowned, then realised what he must mean. 'You argued with your father. And now . . .'

Thierry sighed, hesitating. 'Now he has been dead three years, and I wish that we had made the argument up. It is why I will never argue with you.' The omission of '*chérie*' or '*mon ange*' only made his words pierce deeper. 'I have learned my lesson.'

She took his hand. 'I wish I could have loved you the way you wanted me to.'

He stroked her fingers. 'It would only have made everything more confused.'

'You make it sound like the end of an era.'

For that matter, so was she, she realised.

'Perhaps it is good bye,' he said. 'Perhaps this has happened for the best.'

'Thierry, what are you saying? You're not going to leave Yarleigh? You can't! I don't know what I'd do . . .'

'I would miss you too, Marguerite. But my uncle, you remember I have told you about him, he is running his vineyard by himself, he is no longer a young man.'

'Why now though?' She pulled him closer.

'Why are you getting all grown-up and responsible *now*? You're only thirty! Can't you put off being the prodigal nephew for a few more years? Your uncle would still get the fatted calf out for you. In fact, he'd be even more pleased to see you if you kept him waiting a bit longer.'

'Some things are destined, Marguerite, and others are not, however much you want them to be.' His black eyes, once so merry, so fiendish, were swimming in sorrow.

Had she done this to him? Reduced him to a shadow of the boy she'd met in Montmartre, keeping him on a short leash for whenever she wanted him to jump through hoops for her?

'Oh, Thierry . . .' As she clung to him, she knew she was really clinging to the past, *their* past, because the future was a place she couldn't bear to go to alone.

'*Chérie*,' he gently extricated himself, 'we were never meant to be. You know that. You have always known it. I was the one who needed to learn it for myself.' He sighed. 'Now, come on, do not cry. We will walk and we will enjoy the night. No need to explain anything to each other, no judgements, no recriminations.'

Wiping her face with the back of her hand, Meg mustered a smile. 'D'you know, your English has got better lately, Frog.'

He smiled back just as thinly. 'It was about time, *non*?'

'Are you sure Meg won't be coming home?' asked Giles.

'Positive.' Pug flopped on to the sofa beside him. 'She's staying at Libby's.'

'Come here then.' Giles pulled Pug into his arms. She squealed and then surrendered. This was the fourth time they had kissed this way. Pug knew this because she had been counting ever since she had finally let him kiss her the first time.

Giles drew back, his breathing loud and shallow, his fingers hovering over her buttons. 'Are you sure you want to do this?'

Her heart was huge in her chest, pumping away so violently she was certain he could hear it. All those girls at school who picked on her, especially Sarah-Jane Elliott in the sixth form; wouldn't their eyes just pop if they could see her now?

'Yes,' she nodded. 'Yes, I'm sure.'

'I love you,' he said.

'I love you too,' she muttered, suddenly ashamed of her small chest. Why couldn't she be big and bouncy like Meg? Giles would laugh at her; she was afraid to look at him. They both heard the key turning in the front door, just as Giles' hand—

Oh *hell*! It was only just gone eight. Dad wasn't

due home for ages. Pug grabbed at her flapping blouse, but it was too late to do up the buttons again.

Meg and Thierry walked into the lounge and came to an abrupt halt.

'What's going on here?' Meg frowned.

Pug frowned back. Why did people ask that when they'd obviously already guessed? 'What does it look like?' she snapped.

'I thought,' said Meg, 'that you had no intention of turning out like me?'

'I won't! Giles and I love each other. We'll probably get married one day.' Beside her, Pug noticed Giles flinch.

Meg paled. 'Is this the first time?'

Pug held her chin high and pulled the blouse tighter around her. 'It would have been, if you hadn't barged in here treating me like a child.'

'You're only sixteen!'

'And how old were you when you met Thierry?'

Right on cue, Meg turned scarlet.

Thierry gave her arm a gentle squeeze. 'I will go and make us all some tea,' he said, and escaped to the kitchen.

'Er,' Giles edged forwards, 'if you're concerned that I wouldn't be careful . . .'

Meg's eyebrows somersaulted. 'It's got nothing to do with being careful; it's got everything to do with being ready. Or being taken advantage of.'

'I really do care about her,' mumbled Giles.

'Then don't pressure her into something she's not emotionally equipped for.'

'Shit,' said Pug, 'you've been reading my magazines.'

'Don't you swear at me, young lady.' Meg grabbed her arm, steering her towards the hall and the stairs. 'Where's Dad?'

Pug's eyes were beginning to sting. This was the most appalling moment of her life. 'He went out to the pub.'

'And he trusted you to behave, didn't he? He didn't imagine you'd be getting up to *this* the moment his back was turned!'

It was just too much. Pug fled up the stairs, yelling over her shoulder, 'You're a hypocrite, Meg Oakley! A sodding bloody HYPOCRITE!' And she slammed the door to her room.

Meg blinked several times and crumpled on to the bottom stair.

'I should be going.' Giles crept backwards, his gaze pinned to her as if he thought she might blow up in his face again.

'Listen,' she said tiredly, 'it isn't that I don't like you, Giles. I do. These past few months, you've brought Pug out of her shell. I just don't think she's ready for this.'

'I wasn't pressuring her,' he stammered, ducking behind his naturally streaked hair.

'Maybe it wasn't you. Maybe it was the girls at school, or maybe it's just the way things are these days.' Meg rubbed her eyes. 'Pug should be concentrating on her GCSEs right now. And in the autumn when you go to university, Giles, you'll probably try to keep in touch. But you're young, you don't know how quickly things change. There'll be other girls, they'll practically stalk you, and you'll end up resenting Pug for holding you back, for being too involved. And she would be. We both know she would be if you made love to her.'

'I just wanted . . .' Giles looked at the ceiling in despair. 'I wanted her to understand that she's beautiful.'

Meg sighed. 'I know she is.'

Giles hesitated, and then let himself out quietly. Meg sat hugging her knees and staring at the closed door, *all* the closed doors of her life, for what seemed an eternity, until Thierry appeared in the kitchen doorway.

'I have made tea,' he said.

Meg nodded. 'In a minute. There's something I have to do first.'

She went upstairs and stood outside her sister's room, pausing a moment. 'Pug?' There was no answer. Meg turned the knob gently.

The teenager was lying on the bed, her face in a pillow. 'Go away.'

'Not until we've had a talk. We haven't done enough of that lately.' And before Pug could protest, Meg had pulled her into her arms and was embracing her tightly. She let the girl sob until gradually, inevitably, silence fell and Pug stopped trembling. 'I'm sorry if I humiliated you,' said Meg. 'But I still think I was right to interfere.'

'You're not my mother. Why did you act as if you were?'

Meg couldn't look at her. Instead, she stared down at a photograph on the bedside table of a woman holding a baby; a woman who looked like Pug but who wasn't even smiling for the camera. 'Do you remember Mum?'

'I remember *you.*'

'I'm really the only mother you've ever known, aren't I? Your mother, your sister, your friend. And I want you to know that I'm proud of you, and William. And I love you both very very much.'

'Oh God, Meggy!' Pug flung her thin arms around Meg's neck. 'I've been such a cow to you! But I was so scared. I thought all those awful things, did all those awful things, but I never hated you.'

'Scared?'

'Scared I'd wake up one morning and you'd

have gone. You'd have gone and you wouldn't be coming back.'

'Why would I do that?'

'Because he was different from the others. Matthew was different. If anyone was going to be a catalyst, it would be someone like him. Things were going to change, *you* were going to change.'

'Oh Pug . . . When William went off to university, do you remember how you thought the world was caving in? But he comes home, you still argue like you always did, he's still your brother.' Meg smiled and smoothed her sister's mousy hair into a pony-tail. 'And in a couple of years, you'll probably go off to university too, and Dad will be the one crying on my shoulder.'

'Sometimes I wish we could all stay together, just the four of us, how I always remember it.'

'What about Giles? Where does he fit in?'

Pug didn't answer. Meg stared down at her. Why did children always want to grow up so fast? Why couldn't they be children for a while longer?

'What were you trying to prove, Pug? And to who?'

Silence.

'Do you love him?'

Pug looked up. 'I think so.'

'Because he makes your heart pound and your

pulse race and you feel as if you can hardly breathe?'

'Yes.' Pug pounced on this. 'Yes!'

'But does he also make you feel so safe you wish you could hide yourself away with him for ever? When he puts his arms around you, do you feel as if you've come home?'

Pug hesitated. 'Is that how you feel about Matthew? Is it love?'

Meg turned to gaze out of the window, a rush of heat flooding through her.

'Is it, Meg?'

'I . . . I don't know.'

'How does Matthew feel about *you*?'

Meg had tried to suppress the memory for days – of the way he had looked at her the last time they had spoken – but now it charged back through her consciousness until there was no evading it.

'I haven't the faintest idea,' she said at last, with a strained air of calm.

It was a lie. She knew very well. It had been written all over his face.

The dawn chorus would start soon, thought Meg, tossing and turning in her bed. She hadn't had a wink of sleep.

Love. *Love.* LOVE. The word echoed in her head. It seemed to grow more persistent each time. Thierry had used it, and now Pug. They had both been talking about her and Matthew.

'Love,' Meg whispered, as if saying the word aloud to herself would make everything clear.

But it didn't. It only made everything more complicated.

She arrived at Best Bib and Tucker early that morning, but with a wan complexion and bags under her eyes. When she dropped her second slice of quiche on the floor, Libby took her to one side. 'You look terrible.'

'I feel it.'

'What happened last night? Did you get anything more out of Thierry?'

Meg shrugged and shook her head. 'I had an argument with Pug, though. We made up afterwards, but I just couldn't get to sleep.'

'Well you're no use to me in this state.'

'What are you saying?'

'Don't worry. I'm just trying to tell you that Bee and I can cope for the rest of the morning. Why don't you try and have a nap upstairs?'

'Really?'

'You'll have more peace and quiet here than at your place. And I won't dock your pay. Mind you,' Libby wagged a finger at her, 'I won't be making a habit of this, so take advantage of my good nature while you can.'

Meg shuffled gratefully up to the flat and collapsed on Libby's sofa. 'Don't think,' she told herself. 'Don't think about anything or anyone. Just sleep, *sleep* for pity's sake.'

Within five minutes she was doing precisely that.

It was the middle of the afternoon by the time Meg woke up; far later than she'd intended. She went downstairs to make her apologies and ask why no one had woken her, but Libby, looking pale, bustled her back up the stairs again.

'What is it?' asked Meg. 'What's wrong?'

'It's Thierry—'

'What about him?'

'He came round earlier to collect his suitcases. He seemed relieved when he saw you were asleep. He wrote you a note . . .' Libby handed Meg a folded piece of paper. 'And he asked me to give you this too.' She picked up a twilight-blue winter scarf that had been lying on the breakfast bar behind her.

'Why didn't you wake me up, Libs?'

'I'm sorry . . . Thierry begged me not to. You were really out of it, you know. He said it was better this way.'

Meg's fingers seemed to swell and multiply as she unfolded the sheet of paper.

'I'll be downstairs if you need me . . .' Libby slipped out discreetly.

'Marguerite,' read Meg, *'I could not bear to say goodbye in person. Perhaps that was unfair of me, but I think you will understand. I thank you again for everything you have done for me. I have no choice but to go back to France. Call it duty or destiny, or whatever. My uncle is waiting, and my new life, the vineyard that one day will be mine and which I hope in turn to pass down to my son. And you have your own life to find and lead, one that does not include me, but where I sincerely hope you will not forget your friend.*

I am leaving you this scarf that my father gave me many years ago, and which you always had your thieving eye on. It is cashmere, but remember that it is not what it is made of that is important, but who gave it to you, and how for so long you made everything "rosy", as you English say, when he had no one else to turn to.

Whatever happens, I will always carry a part of you with me.

T.'

Typical of him, sniffed Meg. Typical of him to make her smile through her tears. Chauvinistic pig, she thought, knocked sideways by a rush of affection and pain. How did he know he would be passing the vineyard on to a son one day? What if he only ever had daughters? Typical Latin male, she snorted. Typical male full stop.

She stared down at the scarf and shook her

head, missing him already. 'Oh Thierry, you sod . . .'

The silence wasn't unnerving, as Meg had expected it to be. The large oak doors creaked open at her touch. The pews were all empty. Ahead of her, the light of the stained glass window scattered gem-stones of colour over the marble altar. In an alcove on the left was a statue of the Virgin Mary holding the Baby Jesus. Below that was the stand with the candles. Meg popped a few coins into the slot in the wall and picked up an unlit candle, using one that was already burning to light it. She made the sign of the cross, wondering if she'd done it the right way round; it had been so long since the last time. Then she put the candle in a space on the stand.

She couldn't say what had most influenced her to come to St Dominic's Parish Church today, or what she had come here to pray for. Was it one huge miracle, or just lots of tiny ones? Incense lingered in the air. Meg closed her eyes for a moment, vowing that as soon as she got home she would put pen to paper and wrench out all those words she knew her mother wanted to hear. Perhaps, through the physical act of writing, she would gradually come to mean them.

A sudden draught sent the flames flickering

sideways. Spooked, Meg looked over her shoulder, but it was only Father Ben Holmes, who had come in through the main entrance and was now proceeding up the aisle towards the altar. Abruptly, he stopped, turning slowly in her direction as if spooked himself. His apple-cheeked face broke into a smile as he came towards her.

'It's Margaret Oakley, isn't it? Miss Widdicombe's god-daughter?'

Meg nodded, shaking the proffered hand.

'I didn't think anyone was in here,' he said. 'It's usually locked at this time of the afternoon.'

'I thought churches were always open?'

'In an ideal world, Margaret. May I call you Margaret?'

He had kind brown eyes, she thought, a shade lighter than Matthew's.

'You can call me Meg,' she said.

'Not Meggy, like little Freddy Potter?'

'How . . . how did you know that?'

'I've come to know him quite well. He's a bright little lad. Jabbers away about everything and nothing. In my opinion, he has a crush on you.'

'He's only seven!'

Father Ben chuckled. 'Maybe he qualifies as your youngest ever admirer then. But what brings you to St Dominic's today, Meg, when it's such a lovely day outside? That's where I was, you know, in the orchard behind the presbytery.'

Wasn't he supposed to say, 'Delightful to see you here at last,' and glue her to a pew?

'I came to light a candle,' she explained.

'Really? Splendid. I won't ask why. Unless you'd like to tell me, but it won't make any difference if you don't, He won't hold it against you.'

'Who won't?'

The priest raised his eyes towards the vaulted ceiling.

'Oh, Him Upstairs. Sorry, you mean . . .'

Father Ben chuckled again.

'Actually, while I'm here,' Meg broached, 'I wanted to ask you about nuns.'

He nodded. 'What about them?'

'Well,' said Meg, 'how would I go about becoming one?'

Twenty-three

'So what did Father Ben say next?' demanded Beatrice, on tenterhooks, leaning over the back of the sofa as far as her bump would let her.

'He said he wasn't convinced I had the right . . . "temperament" for it.'

'That's putting it politely,' smirked Yasmin. 'Whoopi Goldberg stood more chance. You weren't really serious about it were you?'

Meg shrugged. 'I was just exploring my options, that's all. Father Ben suggested I watch *The Sound of Music* if I hadn't already seen it. And even if I had, he said there wasn't any harm in watching it again.'

Beatrice came around the sofa and sat down, glad to take the weight off her ankles. 'Everybody's seen *The Sound of Music*, unless they've lived on Mars for the last forty years.'

'So why,' frowned Yasmin, 'do we have to sit through it again tonight? Can't we watch—'

'I'm not exposing my unborn child to gratuitous sex, violence or bad language, thank you very much,' huffed the mother-to-be.

'What about gratuitous 'Doh-ray-me'ing?' muttered Yasmin.

Meg went to fetch the popcorn from the kitchen.

'I play classical music to Baby every day,' said Beatrice, rubbing her bump. 'Although he seems to prefer my *Now* compilations.'

'After all this, it'll turn out to be a girl.' Meg sank back down on the sofa. 'Have you picked a name for him yet, seeing as you're so convinced it's a boy?'

Beatrice grabbed Meg's hand and spread it flat over her stomach. 'Feel that!'

'Wow! You should call him after a famous boxer.'

'He's kicking, dipstick. Tom wants to call him Pele.'

Julie Andrews warbled away obliviously.

'Bee,' warned Yasmin, 'you're making Meg broody. You'd better stop it. She's got an awful gooey look on her face.'

'No I haven't!' said Meg defensively. 'And we'd all better concentrate on the film. That's why we're here!'

They sat and watched, munching their way through the popcorn and pretending to drool and swoon whenever Captain Von Trapp appeared.

'Hunk.'

'Beefcake.'

'And a widower too,' sighed Beatrice.

Meg and Yasmin both sat up straighter. 'So?'

'So, um,' Beatrice squinted at an unpopped kernel, 'how is Matthew these days?'

'He's fine,' said Yasmin, gazing fixedly at the TV screen. 'At least, he was last night.'

A coldness stole over Meg. 'What happened last night?'

'We just shared a bottle of wine and a chat,' said Yasmin, 'nothing special.' She shrugged. 'It's not as if you could call them dates or anything.'

' "Them"?' echoed Meg. 'It's happened before?'

'Nothing's happened. Matt and I are just friends. There isn't anything in it. He just needs someone to talk to.'

Meg stared down at her nails. 'So,' she began, wetting her lips, which were suddenly rather dry, 'how are Freddy and Georgie?'

Yasmin looked at her askance. 'They're fine, although I haven't seen much of them really, they're usually in bed by the time I arrive.'

Dammit, thought Meg, what time did she usually *leave*? 'So Matthew's still got them, has he?'

'Of course he's still got them! Why shouldn't he?'

Meg was pensive, experiencing a trickle of optimism, although the feeling had been in such scarce supply lately she wasn't sure if she was identifying it correctly.

'Shut up, you two,' reproved Beatrice. She pointed at the TV. 'We're just getting to the soppy bit!'

Another bouquet of orchids and lilies on the kitchen table.

Meg gritted her teeth, hooking the strap of her bag over a chair and switching on the kettle. Fishing in the caddy for a teabag, she heard footsteps on the stairs. A moment later Pug clattered into the kitchen.

'Afternoon,' she grinned. 'Stick another bag in a mug for me, please?'

Meg did as requested. 'How's the revision going?'

Pug pulled a face. 'OK, I suppose.'

'You'll do fine. Don't worry.' Meg finished making the tea and put the two mugs on the kitchen table, sitting down opposite her sister, the flowers in her peripheral vision just begging to be referred to. She sighed, attempting to forget they were there by *not* referring to them. She didn't want to have to think about Jake; she needed to distance herself, to work out what her next step would be.

'D'you know what happened to me at Best Bib and Tucker today?' she began, realising that she didn't sound quite as excited as she ought to.

'What?'

'I only got promoted.'

Pug's eyes grew wide. 'What to?'

'Basically, I'm in charge of the shop now. My rate's still the same, only I'm working full-time. Libby says the responsibility's getting too much for her on top of the café. She wants to concentrate on the kitchen side of things. And because Bee says she's not going to come back to work after the baby's born, Libby's bringing in a new part-time assistant. She's even going to buy a PC to run the accounts on – and she says I've got to teach her how to use it!'

Pug jumped up, rounding the table and hugging Meg with a congratulatory squeal. 'So now you've got all that extra responsibility, you have to keep up to date with stock and that sort of thing? Chase after suppliers? Come up with new ideas? Think up special offers?'

Meg nodded.

'Well then,' Pug frowned at her, 'why don't you look ecstatic about it? I thought you wanted to be a career woman, or isn't this glamorous enough for you?'

'It's perfect,' said Meg. 'I don't want to work behind a desk all day, or trek up to London every morning . . .'

'So what's the problem?'

Meg shrugged, her gaze sliding unwittingly towards the flowers. There was a long pause.

'I put them in water for you,' said Pug.

'Thank you.'

'They're virtually the same as the ones you got when all this business with Matthew began . . .'

'You think these are from him?' Meg wrinkled her nose. 'They're not his style at all.'

'Are they from Thierry then?'

'I'd be a lot happier if they were.'

'But . . . the way he left Yarleigh like that . . .'

'He wanted a fresh start. I'm not going to hold that against him.'

'So, who *are* the flowers from then?' Pug would definitely get an A if there was a GCSE for persistence.

Meg hesitated. 'I can't tell you yet. Maybe one day . . .'

'Not this again!' Pug rolled her eyes.

'Trust me,' said Meg. 'Trust me, and I might even begin to trust myself.'

As it happened, Meg's chance to start trusting herself came sooner than she had expected. She was just checking through the shop inventory on her own the following evening, long after Best Bib and Tucker had closed for the day, when she lifted her head with a start at the sound of urgent knocking.

'Jake . . .' She grudgingly unlocked the door and let him in. 'What are you doing here?'

'What does it look like? I came to see you.'

'But you're broadcasting it to the entire village!'

'Don't exaggerate, there's hardly anyone about. Besides, it doesn't matter any more.'

Meg positioned herself so that the counter was between them.

'I've something to ask you,' he said.

'Ye-es?'

'Mother and Jacintha are taking Timothy up to London for the weekend. I've got the Hall to myself, and I was wondering—'

'I can't. I'm busy. Loads to do, you know how it is.'

'Meg—'

'Jake, really, I can't.'

'We've got to talk, Meg. But not here, not now.' He sounded serious as he took something out of his suit pocket. A slim velvet box. He opened it, and placed it on the counter. 'I bought you a little something . . .'

A row of diamonds twinkled up at her, ten times more sparkly than her charm bracelet.

'Oh my Aunt Fanny!' blinked Meg.

'Come to the Hall,' said Jake. 'Saturday evening, when you finish work. I'll be expecting you.'

The pub doors swung shut behind Matthew and Yasmin, semi-darkness closing in around them as they turned and headed in the direction of the small cottage she was renting. The night was warm, the breeze heavy with the mingled scents of late spring.

Matthew felt his palms grow clammy and a blush inch its way upwards along his throat, the silence unnerving him. If this wasn't a date, what was it? And if it was, then what precisely was Yasmin anticipating?

Back in the Spread Eagle, among the lights and the chatter, they had talked effortlessly about Yarleigh Primary and Yasmin's own job covering the assistant history teacher's maternity leave at Tockley Comp. They had discussed Freddy and Georgie and plans for the summer holidays. They had even smiled over a few collective memories of Polly. Now though, alone together and in an atmosphere conducive to romance, Matthew didn't know what to say.

They reached the cottage, the thatched roof hunched over its single storey whitewashed walls like an old rustic's hat, the garden a tangle of long grass and wild flowers that suited Yasmin perfectly because she had no time or inclination to take care of it.

'It reminds me of you,' Matthew heard himself remark.

'Overgrown?' she giggled, indicating that she could easily get through her front door while he would have to stoop.

'No. It's just . . . you've shied away from being cultivated – in a figurative sense. You said yourself that people have tried to prune and tame you one way or another since you were a child, but you've always gone your own way.'

She shrugged, reaching up to pick lint off his shirt. 'I come from a family of miserable sods who wanted me to conform and be a miserable sod too. So I suppose you're right – I am rebelling. Just like this garden.'

He bent instinctively to kiss her lips, but at the last moment swerved and brushed his mouth against her cheek.

'Would you like to come in for a drink?' she murmured. 'It doesn't have to be coffee. I can be more imaginative than that.'

'I said to the babysitter I wouldn't be home any later than midnight.'

'Which gives you forty minutes. And it would only be a five-minute walk for me if I had legs as long as yours. Besides,' she smiled, 'I want to see how you fit through this door.'

He managed it.

Opting for tea, although brandy was on offer, he perched on a stool in Yasmin's tiny oak-beamed kitchen, watching her make it. 'What time do Dopey, Sneezy and the others get home?' he teased.

She ruffled her red-blonde curls. 'Actually, it's the three bears. D'you take sugar? I haven't made you a cuppa since my stint at Yarleigh Primary.'

He shook his head.

'Not like Meg then,' sighed Yasmin. 'She takes two teaspoonfuls in tea. I don't know how she can. I can't stand any.' And she passed Matthew his mug, which he promptly dropped because his hand was a couple of manoeuvres behind his brain.

'Oh heck, I'm sorry!' He grabbed a cloth and started picking up the fragments of china. 'Your mug! it wasn't part of a set, was it? Yasmin, I'm really—' But he couldn't continue, because she had bobbed down beside him on the wet floor, cupped his face in her hands, and was kissing him so passionately he forgot to breathe until they both tore away gasping for oxygen. He stared at her for what seemed minutes rather than seconds.

'Matt—'

'I'm not ready for this,' he gulped.

'Matt, you're looking at me, but who are you really seeing?'

He was silent, various parts of his anatomy assuring him that he was more than ready, his mind casting up a suspicion that he was being tested somehow; and as for the misshapen lump in his chest that passed for a heart nowadays . . .

'Is it Polly?' asked Yasmin.

He wrenched a hand through his hair, nodding . . . shaking his head. 'You know it isn't, don't you?' he groaned. 'You *know* . . .'

'Are you sure you don't want that brandy?' she said softly.

The moment her Mini crunched gravel beneath its wheels, Meg knew she was entering fairytale territory. Staring up in awe, she parked in the shadow of the sprawling country house and switched off the engine.

She unfolded herself from the small car, biting her lip at the sight of a concrete jardinière by the main flight of stone steps. If she wasn't mistaken – she bent down to examine it more closely – there was a scraping of blue paint . . . just . . . *here*. She touched it lightly with her finger.

'Darling!'

She straightened up. Jake was coming towards her, cool and casual in white jeans and a pale-blue shirt. Kissing her cheek, he led her indoors.

Everything seemed to stretch for miles, exactly as Meg had imagined when she'd gazed up at

Arundel Hall from the outside as a trespassing child.

'I've got the champagne on ice already,' smiled Jake, leading her into the drawing room. It was decorated in creams and sky-blues, with watered silk drapes and a carpet so deep and soft Meg seemed to sink into it up to her ankles. Three pairs of French windows were all open on to the sun-washed terrace, the lawn sloping away gently towards the spinney. Meg felt as if she were a kid again, scruffy-clothed, with tousled hair and a face glowing through the grime.

She turned back to the dazzling boy she had spied on so often while he'd frolicked on the terrace with his dazzling twin and his dazzling friends. But the boy was now a man, and there were lines around his eyes, and grey roots beginning to show at his temples.

'I'm going to spoil you rotten,' he was vowing, passing her a glass of champagne. 'You'll be sick of all this pampering by the time I'm through.' He stroked the back of his hand against her cheek. 'Oh hell,' he murmured, 'I do love you, Meg Oakley. I didn't want to, but there's something irresistible about you I can't quite put my finger on.'

'Really?' she said quietly. 'What about Aurora?'

Jake hesitated. 'What about her?'

'Did *you* break the engagement off, or did *she*? Assuming, of course, that it is broken off.'

'Does it matter how it ended?'

Meg couldn't believe his gall. 'Of course it does, Jake.'

He paused again. 'It was mutual.'

'Did she find out about me? Did you tell her?'

Jake sipped his champagne. His hand seemed to be shaking slightly. 'It had nothing to do with you. It was something else.'

'What?'

He sighed, and met her gaze again. 'I've been offered a job on Wall Street. It's too good an opportunity to pass up. Rory doesn't know about you. We broke things off because she didn't want to move to the States with me.'

Meg was thrown off guard.

'She doesn't want to take the business out of London. Not yet, at least,' Jake went on. 'And she wouldn't leave anyone else in charge. We reached a deadlock, and she knew it was over. In the end, I didn't have to rub salt into the wound and tell her I wanted to be free for other reasons.'

Meg stood clutching her champagne, paralysed with shock.

'Do you understand what I'm saying?' There was an urgency in his voice. 'I want you to come with me. You can have everything you've ever wanted. And in time, who knows, we might even think about making things more permanent . . .'

She gazed around her, letting Jake's words sink in. 'But what about this place? How can you just give it up?'

'I'm not giving it up. I'm reaping the best of both worlds. Mother and Jacintha will take care of the estate. They'll probably hire a manager, although it's about time my sister started pulling her weight around here.'

She already *had* with regards to Thierry, thought Meg.

'I can't believe this, Jake . . .'

He put down his glass and drew her into his arms.

'No.' She pushed him away, and it struck her that to a degree he was still that boy she remembered, living in his own private Never Never Land. She actually felt sorry for him.

He was reaching into his pocket. 'You can wear the bracelet now. What's to stop you? I can't keep looking after it for ever.'

But as he went to clasp it around her wrist, she pressed it back towards him and closed his hand around it. She couldn't bear to see it, just as she couldn't bear to see the apprehension in Jake's eyes. Each of those tiny diamonds was a reminder of everything she had once coveted. The apprehension was even worse.

'I need a cigarette,' he said, slipping the bracelet back in his pocket and tremulously lighting a Silk Cut with his silver monogrammed lighter.

Meg watched him drift towards the French windows. She knew he wouldn't want to believe that she was turning him down. He was already fearing it, but it wasn't in his nature to accept defeat graciously, without a fight. However much he tried to charm her, though, he wouldn't get his own way this time. It was an ironic revenge, and one that Meg had never intended. She was all too aware of how much it would hurt. She was in the same position, wasn't she? Because she knew now what it was she wanted. It wasn't a dream but a certainty she knew she couldn't have; not that that made any difference.

She loved Matthew. She loved him in ways she had never loved anyone: so silently and deeply that she hadn't recognised what she was feeling until it was too late.

'Stupid bitch,' she muttered bitterly under her breath.

Blinking back tears, steeling herself for the matter at hand, she joined Jake on the terrace.

Twenty-four

'Miss Widdicombe! Mrs Sopwith! Lovely to see you! Come and sit here by the window, it's our best table.' Beatrice was in a good mood, and definitely blooming.

As soon as the mum-to-be had taken the order and returned to the kitchen, Meg ambled over to say hello. It had been a relatively quiet morning at Best Bib and Tucker, and her tongue was in need of exercise.

'I was hoping to have a word with you,' said Aggie. 'I was wondering if you'd like to come over for a spot of supper tonight.'

'Supper?'

'Perhaps we could send for an Indian take-away?' Aggie's eyes were hopeful. Even Edith seemed vicariously thrilled.

'Never say no to a korma,' smiled Meg.

Edith leaned forwards, wetting her lips, as if about to impart a priceless pearl of wisdom. 'I hear,' she murmured, 'that tikka massala's rather nice too.'

'Wine?' offered Aggie, once Meg had telephoned the Pride of Bombay and repeated their order three times to the timid new waiter, before having to ask for the big boss himself.

'I'd love some.'

She played with her glass as they waited. Every so often she would glance at the kitchen clock, willing the food to hurry up. It was clear that Aggie had something important to say, but why wouldn't she get around to it rather than just making small talk?

'Meg, a letter came here for you this morning,' she said eventually, once the food had arrived and they had spooned out their respective portions.

'Oh?'

'I believe it's from your mother.'

Meg dropped a forkful of pilau rice.

'Did you write to her? Is this a reply?' Aggie reached for the letter.

'I did write,' admitted Meg. 'I must have thrown away half a dozen attempts though . . .'

'Well, there's no need to open this now. Take it home, read it when you're alone.'

'You don't mind?'

'It's not a question of minding.'

Meg nodded, smiling weakly and clearing up the spilled rice.

'I ran into Matthew yesterday,' remarked Aggie, a few mouthfuls of tikka massala later.

Meg sat bolt upright. 'Matthew?'

'He was telling me about his plans to take the children to Scotland during the summer holidays. He wants to show Freddy his childhood haunts and his grandmother's cottage, from the outside at least; the cottage was sold years ago. His in-laws may even be joining them up there, so it seems that your anxieties turned out to be unfounded. Matthew and the Hancocks are clearly on good terms again, although I think Matthew finds it hard work. They can't be his favourite people.'

Meg gazed out of the window into the garden. In the fading light, each blade of grass seemed brushed with gold paint. It even looked as if someone had spray-painted the old oak tree bronze and amber.

'I'm afraid,' said Aggie, 'that I have to confess to interfering in your life again, Meg.' She smiled, her taste-buds clearly in heaven. 'May I try a bhindi bhajee?'

'Help yourself.' Meg gestured to the foil container full of okra. 'What have you done this time, Aggie?'

Did it have something to do with Matthew?

Meg's heart was in her throat along with a lump of naan bread.

There was a sparkle in the old lady's eye. 'You know that I have no family left – no next of kin, as my solicitor likes to put it. Although I have a few small bequests in my will—'

'Don't be morbid! You've got years of go in you yet.'

'I like to hope so, Margaret.'

Meg snapped to attention at the use of her full name. This was serious.

'Now that I've reached my twilight years,' said Aggie (a hardship for the old lady to admit, Meg realised), 'I've come to the conclusion that this house is rather too large for me. When I was younger, it didn't seem to matter. But, anyway, since Edith's husband passed away last year, she's slowly been bringing me round to the notion of the two of us becoming "house-mates".'

It struck Meg as an inspired idea. 'You're going to suggest she moves in here with you?' Two lonely old women wouldn't be so lonely if they lived under the same roof.

Aggie shook her head. 'On the contrary, I was planning to move into her bungalow. I wouldn't have any infernal stairs to climb, for one thing.'

Meg glanced around her, her eyes widening in shock. 'You mean – you're going to sell this place?'

'Margaret, when I pop my clogs, as the saying goes, the majority of my worldly goods, including Linden Trees Villa, passes to the main beneficiary in my will. However, I spoke to my solicitor the other day and told him I didn't want to wait to pass on this house; I want to see it put to good use now.'

Meg had a vision of domesticated moggies of all shapes and sizes spilling out of the attic, the airing cupboard, the utility room . . . Didn't old ladies love leaving everything to animal sanctuaries, especially feline ones?

'You're turning this place into a cats' home,' she said.

'You really can be very obtuse at times,' sighed her godmother.

Freddy's birthday fell on Father's Day this year. To Matthew, it seemed only last week that he'd first held his tiny bawling son in his arms, but the boy was going to be eight, and was having a party for a dozen playmates who'd been permitted to tear themselves away from their own dads to come and harass someone else's.

With a sigh, Matthew finished pushing all the furniture in the lounge back against the walls. He ought to have booked an entertainer, although they weren't cheap. A magician, perhaps, who could knot long thin balloons into giraffes and dachshunds. Or a clown who would squirt you with water if you tried to smell the flower on his lapel. There was only so much time the darling little revellers would be prepared to spend on jelly and ice-cream before looking around rapaciously for something else to demolish.

'You should have booked an entertainer,' tutted Daphne, upon her arrival with Hugh. 'Really, Matthew, you of all people ought to have known better.'

Hugh peered over the top of the large colourfully wrapped box that was obviously Freddy's birthday present. 'Probably thought he could sit them in neat rows and teach them their times table,' he chuckled.

Matthew suppressed a groan. 'How did you guess?' he uttered instead.

Minutes later, Freddy was running in excited circles around the lounge. 'Wow! Dad, look at this! It's awesome!' His grandparents had given him a radio-controlled Jeep. 'Can I play with it now? Can I? Can I?'

'In the garden,' sighed Matthew, who had only bought his son a Manchester United duvet cover and matching waste-paper bin.

'We were toying with the idea of getting him a computer,' Daphne was saying, inspecting the food on the kitchen table. 'But all that business about processors and hard-drives put me off. It's so confusing. Hugh says we'll look into it properly for Christmas.'

The doorbell rang. Matthew went to answer it. 'Thank God you're early.' He hustled Yasmin into the house. 'They've only been here five minutes and they're already driving me—Daphne! Er, I'd like you to meet Yasmin Bradley.'

Daphne smiled and took hold of Yasmin's arm. 'Matthew's talked a lot about you, my dear. Come through to the kitchen and have some tea, before bedlam breaks out.'

Hugh stood up courteously as Yasmin was propelled through the lounge. 'Very pleased to meet you, Miss Bradley.' He smiled and shook her hand. 'Sugar and spice and all things nice, eh?'

'Sorry?'

'Don't mind me, don't mind me . . .' And shaking his head, he drifted into the garden to join his grandson.

'Where's Georgie?' asked Yasmin.

Matthew jerked his head upwards. 'Asleep. Though how long that'll last—' The doorbell rang again. ' 'Scuse me.'

This time it was Jacintha Arundel and Timothy. 'Sorry,' she hazarded a smile, 'we're a little early.'

'Don't worry, everything's more or less organised. And at least the weather's held up.'

Jacintha looked sky-wards. 'Gorgeous day,' she mumbled. 'Super.'

Timothy tugged at Matthew's sleeve. 'Can I call you Matt?' he asked. 'We're not in school now.'

His mother ruffled his dark hair. 'You'll show some respect and call him Mr Potter.'

Timothy's black eyes flashed piratically. 'OK.'

'Go on,' smiled Matthew, 'the birthday boy's in the garden. He's got something to show you.'

Timothy strode on in as if he owned the place. Matthew turned awkwardly to Jacintha. For a while now she had been making the effort to pick her son up from school. Matthew didn't know what had changed, but he didn't think it was anything he'd said.

'Would you like to stay for some tea?' he asked her now.

She looked surprised. 'Oh! Oh, I really don't think . . . That's very kind of you, but I'd better go. Shall I pick Timothy up around five?'

Matthew nodded. When he returned to the garden, he found Timothy playing with the radio-controlled car.

'My mother's got a real Jeep,' said the boy, directing the toy into the pansies.

'So I've noticed.' Matthew had seen her drive away in it with the roof off and her blonde hair flailing about in a dangerous fashion.

Yasmin sidled up to him. 'Matt,' she broached hesitantly, 'have you got around to calling—'

'No.'

'Are you going to?'

He looked at her dolefully. 'I don't know.'

'Coo-ee!' called Daphne, poking her head around the patio doors. 'I think you've got some more arrivals.'

Matthew and Yasmin raised their eyebrows at each other, and didn't get a chance to attempt meaningful conversation again that afternoon. Within half an hour the garden was strewn with cup-cake crumbs, the crusts from the sandwiches, jam from the doughnuts and a litre or so of spilled lemonade.

'Why don't you take them to the playing fields by the river?' suggested Hugh, as a child on all fours barged between his legs and dived into the house. 'There's more space. They can play rounders or something.'

'By the river?' gulped Matthew. 'Is that a good idea?' He pictured calling in the Coastguard complete with rescue helicopter.

'I'll come with you,' said Hugh. 'I'm sure we can manage between two of us. And besides, you've got practice.'

As the Jeep crashed into his ankle for the umpteenth time, Matthew decided Hugh was right.

Yasmin and Daphne remained at the house, along with Priscilla, a small freckled girl from Freddy's class who had carroty pigtails and wanted to play Mummies and Daddies all the time. She had appropriated Georgie and was calling her her baby. Freddy, who had been named as the father, was mortified.

'I wish I'd never invited her,' he confided in his dad as they trooped to the river.

'If Georgie was really your baby,' Timothy informed him loftily, 'it means you must have done it with Priscilla.'

'I can't have!' snapped Freddy. 'She isn't old enough.'

'I'm warning both of you,' said Matthew, wishing he could ban his son from watching TV ever again, 'stop talking like that, it isn't nice.'

' "Nice" is a very boring word,' Timothy reminded him. 'You said so yourself in class.'

Matthew glared at the boy.

Once at the playing fields, Hugh set about organising the children into two teams. He caught Matthew's eye and smiled oddly. 'Funny, I'd expected Miss Oakley to be around today.'

Matthew dropped the bat he'd been holding. 'Shit! I mean, ow!' He scowled as it landed on his toe.

'Meg Oakley,' went on Hugh, 'was she busy?'

Matthew handed his son a ball and told him to start bowling.

'Meggy's *always* busy these days,' Freddy informed his grandfather, giving his dad a grumpy look before rubbing the ball on his trousers and marching off.

Matthew stared after him, then turned to Hugh. 'I didn't invite her.'

'Oh?'

'I didn't want any more trouble.'

'She is rather a handful, isn't she?' Hugh winked.

Matthew crimsoned. Then something struck him. 'You sound as if you know her.'

'I've only really met her the once. Quite recently. But I've always prided myself on being a good judge of character.' Hugh snorted. 'Judge – get it?'

'What do you mean you've met her recently? When?'

'When she came to London to plead your cause.'

'*What?*'

'Mmm, had an inkling that you didn't know about it. I was sure she wasn't the type to rush back and boast about what she'd done. I should have told her there and then that I wasn't part of Daphne's "crusade". It's not as if you beat the children, or starve them; in fact you're raising them exactly as Polly would have done, I'm sure of it.' Hugh sighed. 'You've got to forgive Daphne for thinking no one's ever going to be good enough to take her daughter's place. But this business with Meg Oakley; it was going to be damn hard proving she was a detrimental influence. Especially when Frederick didn't have a bad word to say about her. And then when a salt of the earth type like Agnes Widdicombe writes to tell us what a blessing her god-daughter has been to you and the children—'

'Aggie did *what?*'

'Got our address from Mrs Sopwith. You know her – Edith – lives opposite you. I played golf now and again with her husband, God rest him. He was in the RAF, did you know that? Lost a leg in the war, though to see him walk you wouldn't have thought it was that serious.' Hugh tapped his nose. 'He didn't like to broadcast the fact. Anyway, Miss Widdicombe wrote to us saying she'd heard a rumour that we planned to sue you for custody of Frederick and Georgina – these molehills can become mountains so ludicrously quickly in a place like this, can't they? – and she was utterly emphatic that her god-daughter had been a tonic for you and the children, and that you'd been a good influence on her in return. She quoted St John's Gospel, "let he who is without sin" and all that. Said none of us should be casting stones. Always thought that argument would cause anarchy in court myself, but that's not the issue.'

'I don't believe this!' said Matthew.

'Mr Potter,' demanded Timothy, 'are you umpiring this game or not?'

'Er, in a minute.'

The boy strutted off again. Hugh stared after him with raised eyebrows. 'There's something very Napoleonic about that boy. Who's his father? Would I know him?'

'I hardly think so. Rumour has it he was someone Jacintha Arundel met on her last night on a kibbutz. Listen, Hugh—'

'Polly had her faults, Matthew, but you always loved her in spite of them. Maybe you didn't even see them. This image you have of my daughter, by all means hang on to it, the children need something of their mother to cherish as they grow up, but don't start comparing every woman you meet with a memory. It isn't a competition.'

Matthew looked away towards the river. Hugh was the last man on earth he'd ever thought he'd hear this from.

The élite of Yarleigh Rowing Club were out on the water today, practising for the Regatta in a fortnight. The oars dipped fleetingly and rhythmically as the long narrow boat skimmed the Yarl in the direction of the old stone bridge.

Matthew turned back to his father-in-law. 'Let's get this rounders game properly organised, shall we? We have to be home in time for Freddy to blow out his candles. He wanted to leave it till last.'

'Wonder what the boy will wish for this year?' remarked Hugh, humming nonchalantly as he trailed after Matthew.

It had been a gorgeous Midsummer's Eve, and now a whole night stretched ahead of Meg, when anything, even magic, seemed possible. The kitchen windows of Linden Trees Villa were open wide on to the garden. Spring had collided with summer this year rather than gently fusing into it. The confetti blossoms had vanished and suddenly everything was lush, a riot of colour, like a Mardi Gras.

'I don't expect you to keep Linden Trees exactly as I had it,' Aggie had assured her one afternoon last week, over tea at 26 Chaffinch Lane. 'I've always thought a country farmhouse theme would look rather good. Anyway, the annuity I'm going to give you will help with any changes you might want to make, as well as with other expenses; it's a large house to run, after all.'

Meg had consulted her sister. 'What do you think? I'm not making a decision about moving out without talking it over with you, Dad and William first.'

'Frankly, the sooner you go the better.' Pug

had been insistent. 'I can have your old room and use mine as a study rather than that poky cupboard.'

'Charming!' Meg had been hurt. 'I thought you didn't want me to leave?'

'I don't want you to leave Yarleigh, and now you won't,' Pug had explained brightly. 'For goodness' sake, don't look at me like that! You're only going to be down the road. I'll be popping in so often you'll get sick of me.'

And Dad? He had reacted with less enthusiasm, but when he had helped her move her things last Sunday, he had given her a house-warming present of a wooden key-box to hang in the hall. A modest gift. Symbolic. And he had gathered her up into a hug for the first time in years. 'It's never easy to let go of a daughter,' he had muttered gruffly. 'That's what you are to me, Meg, never forget it – my daughter.'

Meg had clung to him as if she was never going to see him again. 'And you're the only father I'll ever want!'

William, an inadvertent witness to this scene, had stuck two fingers into his mouth and wandered off again to continue with his thorough nose around.

Now, on this sublime evening, Meg sat on her own at the kitchen table, flicking through an interior design magazine and allowing her imagination a free rein. What colour was 'absinthe' exactly, and which room would it look best in? And what was ragging? Or marbling? Or all those other techniques she'd heard of but couldn't remember anything about.

This large old house, which had seemed so dull and musty once, was now her refuge, a distraction from everything that had gone wrong in her life. It couldn't fill the emptiness inside her, but that was the price she had to pay for her mistakes, however hard it was.

She turned her attention to the garden; she'd always had a fetish for plant names: honeysuckle, azalea, wisteria, clematis . . . Brier-roses were wild, weren't they? So did that mean she couldn't cultivate them herself? And what about a couple of goats? They could keep the lawn trim and supply her with milk to make cheese. Or was that taking the country farmhouse theme too far? She would be conjuring up chickens next, or even pigs. Just as she was imagining how geraniums in clay pots would look on the windowsill – a more down to earth idea – the doorbell chimed 'Auld Lang Syne'.

Meg hadn't been expecting anyone and wasn't in the mood for company. As she debated whether to be in or out, the bell chimed again, just as imperiously. With a sigh, she went to answer it.

'A woman on her own should always use the security chain,' said Matthew, stepping inside before she'd invited him in. 'I could have been anybody.'

Twenty-five

Feeling herself break out in a flush, Meg closed the door behind him. 'What are you doing here?'

'Hoping you'll offer me a stiff drink.'

Decaffeinated Gold Blend was about as stiff as it got. 'I'll, er, have a hunt about and see if Aggie left anything alcoholic behind.'

'You haven't got anything of your own?'

'I haven't stocked up yet.' She pointed him in the direction of the kitchen – her favourite room – and went and ransacked the sideboard in the dining room in the vain hope . . .

But the hope did not turn out to be entirely vain. There was a bottle of sherry, with a drop left that might just about fill a thimble. Matthew watched with a puckered brow as she dribbled it into the smallest glass she could find.

'There wasn't any brandy or Scotch,' she muttered, putting the empty bottle to one side for recycling. 'Sorry.'

'Doesn't matter.' There was a pause. 'Are you going to sit down or just stand there?'

She sat.

Matthew drained the sherry in one sip, looking surprised to find it gone so fast, as if he hadn't noticed it shoot past his lips. In her role as hostess, Meg jumped up, too nervous to stay still. 'Would you like some coffee? It's decaff, but at this time of the evening—'

'Meg, please sit down. I don't want coffee.'

She sank down slowly into the chair again. 'What *do* you want, Matthew?'

'To apologise.'

'What for?'

'You know what for. The way I acted . . . The things I said . . .'

'You were perfectly justified.'

He shook his head. 'No, I wasn't. How I felt . . . it was nothing compared to what you were going through.' He looked at her pensively for a moment, before saying, 'I know what you did, when you went to see Daphne and Hugh.'

She blinked. 'How . . . ?'

'Hugh told me.'

'*Hugh*?'

'The ins and outs aren't important. Let's just say it's sorted out and I appreciate what you did for me.'

She looked down at the table. 'It was all my

fault in the first place,' she mumbled. 'I had no choice.'

'Yes, you did.' He stared at her glossy red-brown curls, desperate to stretch a hand across the table and touch her. With the light shining on her from behind, it seemed as if she had a halo, albeit a crooked one. Matthew – his heart thumping harder, his throat tightening – was seriously doubting that someone this beautiful, this extraordinary, could have romantic feelings for him. Surely Yasmin had got things wrong? She hadn't been sure, after all, had said it was only a hunch. And yet, she'd been right about the way *he* felt.

'Meg—'

'So, what did you think when you heard I was living in this house?' She looked up, a feeble smile on her lips. 'How did you find out?'

'Oh,' he shrugged, 'Aggie told me. The way she explained it, it seemed to make sense.'

'I wish it made sense to *me*. I can't help thinking it's crazy. She might want to change her mind about the whole thing one day.'

'I doubt it.'

'But she might,' Meg stressed. 'I understand how this house felt too large for her, and that she's probably happier living with Edith in that bungalow. And I know I was born here and lived here when I was a kid, but it still doesn't feel as if it should be mine.' She hesitated, and Matthew instinctively predicted what was coming next. 'I don't deserve it,' she added.

He wanted to reach across the table and hug her until she melted into him, until all her guilt and feelings of worthlessness were squeezed out and she understood how much people cared about her. But he couldn't. He was too terrified.

'Aggie obviously felt you deserved it,' he said. 'And what else was she going to do with it?'

'Sell it, of course. I even offered to rent it from her, not for very much, but she said that wasn't the point and that she didn't need the money. Her mother's father was quite well off apparently. He left her all his dough when he died. She told me she's been living off it half her life.'

'Well she's hardly the big-spender type.'

'I asked her why she hadn't just gone off around the world when she was younger. She was an heiress, she could have done anything. Why had she settled for working in a small village library.'

'And what did she say?'

'She said she'd enjoyed her job and Yarleigh had always been her home; she'd never contemplated leaving. And the funny thing was, I understood what she meant. It was slightly different for me: there *was* a time when I wanted to go off and see the world. I wanted to make my fortune doing something glamorous and exciting. But now . . .'

Matthew didn't say anything for a moment. This village had its attractions, but he hadn't been born and bred here.

'Speaking of leaving,' he began, playing with his empty sherry glass, 'I've been thinking of trying my luck elsewhere.'

'Trying your luck?'

'I mean,' he coloured, 'moving away and making a fresh start.' He waited for her reaction.

She just stared at him in silence.

'I'm sure you've heard those rumours about Yarleigh Primary closing down,' he went on. 'I thought I'd try somewhere with a bit more job security.'

'Oh,' was all she said.

'Yes.' He felt his stomach start to sink. 'It makes sense, doesn't it? Before the kids get any older. They won't feel so uprooted if I make the move now rather than later.'

She was nodding. 'I suppose so . . . But—'

'What?' he asked quickly.

'I've always thought that as long as the Leigh Farm Estate kept expanding, Yarleigh Primary would be perfectly safe.'

Matthew was convinced it would be too, but he couldn't tell her that. If she didn't want him to leave, why wasn't she throwing more obstacles in his path? Why was she being so matter-of-fact? So unemotional?

Because she'll probably be glad to see the back of you, scoffed the voice of reason.

'If you're certain that leaving Yarleigh is a step in the right direction,' she murmured, rising to her feet and switching on the kettle, 'then I can only wish you the best of luck. Are you sure you wouldn't like a coffee? I quite fancy one myself.'

He shook his head, his heart in his boots. There was nothing to stay in Yarleigh for now. He had lost Polly here; that had been bad enough. But having to live with the daily possibility of running into Meg and not being able to talk to her the way he longed to, or . . .

'Do you still have feelings for Jake?' he asked, wondering how, perversely, he had the audacity to bring *that* up.

Meg didn't look at him; she continued making coffee for herself. 'Jake and I are over. I broke it off with him.'

'I presumed the relationship had ended when I heard he'd gone to the States.'

'That wasn't the reason I ended it.'

Matthew realised that she wasn't going to elaborate. 'Did anyone else ever find out about you two?' he asked.

Meg hesitated, then shook her head. 'I don't suppose you told anyone?'

'You asked me not to.'

'Yes, but . . . You were so angry back then. I wasn't sure . . .'

He knew now that he'd been more jealous than angry. 'I never mentioned it to anyone and I never will,' he said, not even wanting to think about it any more himself.

'Thank you,' she nodded.

'I – um – heard about Thierry leaving too,' Matthew added.

'He's gone back to France at last. It seems as if everyone's lives are changing,' she said, turning back to face him, leaning against the sink. 'Yarleigh will never be the same again.'

No, thought Matthew gravely. He realised there was one more thing he had to bring up tonight. He grew even more subdued. 'Listen, there's something else Aggie told me. About your mother . . .'

'Oh.' Meg bit her lip and put down her coffee mug.

'I came to tell you I'm sorry.'

'Thank you.'

'Aggie said that your father had been in touch.'

'Sort of . . . It was just a note. He'd enclosed it with the last letter Mum wrote to me.'

Matthew scraped back his chair and went to Meg's side.

'Her writing wasn't very legible,' she went on shakily. 'The tumour was advanced; apparently she found it difficult to hold a pen. The gist of it was that she'd received my own letter, and she was writing back to say she'd always loved me, even if she hadn't always faced up to her responsibilities.'

'Aggie said something about the funeral.'

Meg's eyes filled with tears. 'My father didn't want me to be there. He didn't want to have to explain who I was. He only wrote and sent Mum's letter to me after it was all over.'

'I'm sorry . . .' Matthew coaxed her into his arms. She wrapped her own around him and clung fast.

'I suppose I'll have to tell Dad and Pug,' she murmured huskily. 'I can't face it yet though.'

'When you feel up to it, you owe it to them,' said Matthew.

Meg nodded. 'You're right. You're always right. I should have gone back to see Mum that day . . .'

'You can't think like that, Meg. And I don't always get things right.' He pulled away, before she could sense how much he needed her. Before he could make a prat of himself. He had to get out of there. He had to be able to breathe. Trying to comfort her like this had been a mistake. 'Will you be OK?' he asked, pretending to glance at the kitchen clock.

'What?' She looked dazed.

'It's just – I didn't realise it was getting so late . . .'

'Oh . . .' She glanced at the clock herself.

'I told the babysitter I wasn't going to be long,' he lied. 'But I can't leave you like this . . .'

Quickly wiping the last of the tears away, she shook her head. 'Don't be silly. I shouldn't have started blubbering all over you, I'm sorry . . .'

'There's no need. I understand. Are you sure you'll be all right?'

'I'll be fine,' she said, suddenly looking almost bouncy. A smile breezed across her face. 'Really. I'm sorry for being such a wimp.'

'You weren't.' He turned and walked down the corridor towards the front door. Meg was a couple of paces behind.

'Matthew—'

He stopped, his hand on the latch, but he didn't turn round. 'What?'

There was a long pause. 'Nothing,' she mumbled.

He opened the door. 'Are you sure you'll be—'

'I'll be fine, honestly. I just need a bit of time on my own.'

She had all the time in the world, thought Matthew, in a house like this, with no one else for company.

'Goodnight,' he said.

'Goodnight,' she muttered. 'And thank you . . .'

He walked down the path to the gate without looking back.

Meg sank into the bath. The water lapped around her, warm and cleansing. But it couldn't reach into the core of her. It couldn't calm the despair that had overtaken her as she'd watched Matthew walk away.

And yet – what would have been the point of telling him how she felt? Aside from the fact that she was a coward, how could she have tried persuading him to stay in Yarleigh without letting slip that she cared? She had his forgiveness; that was the best that could be salvaged from this whole mess. It was too late for anything else. When he'd embraced her, downstairs in the kitchen, she had felt how much he wanted her physically. But he'd been embarrassed by it, enough to make the excuse of having to rush off.

And so, she had gone along with it.

She had made it easier for him to say goodbye, when what she had really needed – what she still longed for – was to curl up in his arms and cry her heart out.

Twenty-six

Meg woke to find the sun shining on the first morning of Yarleigh Regatta, but she had no desire to go this year. Her friends had accused her of becoming a hermit. What of it? Hermits didn't have to bother fussing with their hair or putting on make-up – such a hassle lately. Meg wouldn't even have made the effort to look good for work (she wouldn't even have bothered *going* to work if she didn't have to) but it wasn't fair to scare Libby's customers away.

She sat in the kitchen and forced down some breakfast. Afterwards, still wearing the baggy shorts and T-shirt she'd slept in, she went into the study. There was a small old bookcase in there, but Meg planned to put a newer one on the opposite wall, along with a desk by the window. She would get around to it eventually, once the image of who might have sat at the desk, pushing up his glasses and marking exercise books, faded into a less painful blur rather than the sharp agonising picture it was now.

A few days ago, Aggie had asked if Meg wouldn't mind packing up the books from the bookcase and bringing them over to Edith's place. Meg realised it was about time she got around to the job.

Most of the volumes were ancient hardbacks, some were even leather-bound: *Tess of the D'Urbervilles*, *Pride and Prejudice*, *Vanity Fair* . . . Meg began putting them carefully into a cardboard box, moving on to an empty one once that was full. When she started to sneeze, she opened the window to let out the dust. It *was* a gorgeous day: the sun shining balmily, birds twittering, the hum of a lawnmower . . . She felt a pang at being cooped up in the house, but stubbornly ignored it and carried on with the task at hand until she came to what turned out to be a photograph album, its thick leather spine designed to resemble an old novel.

Turning the first protective sheet of crackling tissue paper, she saw a sepia photograph of a group of children hanging like monkeys out of the oak tree in the garden, the white house in the background. Without exception the children were knobbly-kneed and grubby-cheeked, as if to prove that in the circle of life and death, very little changed.

Intrigued, Meg continued turning the heavy pages . . .

A girl with a heart-shaped face and a mass of long hair caught back in combs grinned up at her. '*13th October 1943. My sixteenth birthday. (Italy declares war on Germany!)*' Meg stared at her godmother. 'Nowadays, Aggie, they might say the same thing about a football match.'

After a long pause, she carried on looking through the album, lingering over the young men in uniform who had been carefree boys just a few pages previously, and pausing in fascination at a picture of Aggie laughing alongside a slightly older girl – a bit of a bombshell – who just had to be Edith by the potty glint in her eye and the familiar distinguishing fuzz of hair, so pale in the photograph it was almost white. Behind them, tall and proud and grinning, was a young man in RAF uniform. '*Off to the Regatta with Pilot Officer Sopwith, July 1943,*' read the caption. '*Another one in the eye for Adolf!*'

Why don't I have an indomitable British fighting spirit? wondered Meg, poking at her upper lip and checking for signs of stiffness. With a sigh, she studied the young man in the photograph. So this was Edith's late husband in his youth. He didn't look much like the old man Meg remembered having seen around the village. He was actually quite dashing. He must have been considered a catch in his day.

As she turned to the next page, a scrap of paper fluttered to the floor. She picked it up and frowned. There was only a faded signature on it, written out several times in slightly different ways, as if someone had been practising.

'*Agnes L. Sopwith . . . A. L. Sopwith . . . Agnes Sopwith . . .*'

Oh my God! thought Meg, the pieces of the jigsaw falling into place.

Had Aggie meant her to find out? she wondered. Had that been her intention when she'd asked if Meg wouldn't mind packing up the books for her?

Meg stood in front of the mirror in the bathroom and tugged a comb hurriedly through her hair. Being disappointed in love, she mused, was like learning a completely new language and discovering you could understand people who had been an enigma to you for years beforehand.

She recalled what Aggie had said to her about the RAF officer who'd lost his leg in the war. He'd been engaged to another woman. Aggie had never interfered. But what if the man you adored *wasn't* engaged or married or unavailable in some other way? What if he was just brooding over a past relationship? What if he needed someone to yank him into the present and tell him how wonderful he was *now*, right this very minute?

Of course, thought Meg, contorting herself in order to zip up her dress, she wouldn't come out and say it quite like that. But she knew now that she had to tell Matthew how she felt. Even if all he did was stare at her in dismay. Even if she humiliated herself totally . . . So what? So bloody *what?*

Perhaps Aggie had no lasting regrets; she'd been loyal to her best friend after all, had done the right thing. But Meg knew it wasn't the same in her own case. She would be kicking herself for the rest of her life. Haunted by 'what ifs' and 'if onlys'.

I can't live like that, she realised. I can't go on paying for my mistakes forever.

'Well hey there, look at you!' William was at the Regatta with Pug and Giles. They all stopped short when they spotted Meg.

'Have you seen Matthew?' she asked.

Pug shook her head. 'Nope.'

'He wasn't answering his phone at home, so he's probably around here somewhere, don't you reckon?' Meg didn't wait for an answer. She rushed off into the crowd again, stopping at the Best Bib and Tucker stall in the refreshments tent to interrogate Libby, who hadn't seen him either.

A few minutes later, Meg stumbled across Beatrice, Tom and Yasmin. They were sprawled on a picnic blanket in the shade of a large cedar.

'Meggy! I thought you weren't coming!'

'You look great!'

'Very bride-like,' sniggered Tom.

Meg shot him a withering look and smoothed down her cream dress. 'Have any of you seen Matthew?'

Yasmin peered over the top of her sunglasses. 'No . . . Is something wrong?'

'It's just—'

A booming voice over the loud-speaker cut short Meg's reply.

'Ladies and gentlemen, the first race will commence . . .'

But another voice, calling Meg's name, made her jump and spin round. All of a sudden she was suffering from stage fright.

'Meg,' Matthew was saying, 'have you seen Freddy?'

She realised he was looking rather haggard, and right behind him was Jacintha Arundel dragging a sullen Timothy.

Meg's blood ran cold. 'Freddy?' she echoed.

'Have you seen him?' Matthew articulated the words as if she didn't understand English.

'No.'

He was asking the same question of her friends now, but they were all shaking their heads. He beckoned to Jacintha. 'Let's try the clubhouse.'

'What's going on?' demanded Meg, hot on their heels.

'He's gone missing,' said Matthew hoarsely.

'The boys were playing, you see,' explained Jacintha. 'They went off on their own, but only Timothy came back. He said the last time he'd seen Freddy—'

'—Freddy had been talking to a man and woman by the ice-cream van,' continued Matthew. 'When Timothy looked round again, Freddy and this couple were gone.'

'Vanished,' gulped Jacintha.

'I think he's been kidnapped,' said Timothy, adding his penny's worth.

The first race had already ended by the time the steward made another announcement over the loud-speaker, this time asking if anyone had seen eight-year-old Frederick Potter. He gave a description of the boy, including what he'd been wearing.

'Shorts,' Matthew was repeating, for the benefit of the police sergeant who had turned up at the clubhouse with a po-faced constable. 'A biscuit sort of colour, and a T-shirt with blue and orange stripes.'

The constable took down the details. 'Are you sure the boy couldn't just be lost in the crowd, sir?' he asked, suppressing a yawn. 'Has he got other family here today?'

'His grandparents are away in Jersey. And if Freddy was around here somewhere, someone would have recognised him by now.'

'Well,' the sergeant was trying to be reassuring, 'children go missing at events like this all the time. I'm sure your son won't be the last today—'

Matthew gestured towards Timothy. 'This boy can describe the couple Freddy was last seen with. Shouldn't you be asking him about that?'

The sergeant drew Timothy to one side, accompanied by Jacintha and the constable.

'Look, there's Aggie with Georgie.' Meg pointed as her godmother came towards them pushing the buggy.

The old lady looked a hundred years old. 'Has Freddy . . . ?'

Meg shook her head. 'The police are on to it now though. They say this kind of thing happens all the time.'

'It does!' choked out Matthew. 'You hear about it on the news, you read about it in the papers. A child goes missing, there's a search mounted but no one seems to have seen or heard anything. Then days, sometimes weeks later, the body's found in a ditch less than a mile from—'

Meg couldn't bear it. 'Don't say that! He'll be fine. Freddy will be fine!' She moved closer to Matthew, her hand on his arm. 'Everything's going to be all right,' she whispered, 'I just know it . . .'

And suddenly, clinging to her so desperately she could scarcely breathe, he burrowed his face in her neck, his glasses digging into her as she stroked his hair and soothed him as tenderly as she might have soothed Freddy.

'I feel as if I ought to be out there *doing* something,' huffed Jacintha.

'Waiting around is never easy,' said Aggie tensely. 'But the police were right. Don't you think it would have been better if Matthew had stayed put here rather than getting under their feet?'

'He couldn't have stayed put if you'd paid him,' said Meg, who had only agreed to stay put herself because Matthew had asked her to.

'In case Freddy turns up and I'm not around,' he'd said. 'In case he's scared. I want you to be here.'

Meg looked across the table in the clubhouse at Timothy Arundel, who was sitting opposite her swinging his feet, his Nike trainers kicking a chair-leg in a perpetual thud, thud, thud, that jarred on her frayed nerves. She studied him carefully, having never been this close to Jake's only nephew before. The lad had the Arundel twins' bone structure, but not their fair colouring. And there was something about his petulant pout that drew Meg's attention. Something about the twitching of his left eye . . .

Oh my—

Her jaw dropped. Feeling Sherlock Holmes-like already for having solved one mystery after the discovery of the photograph album that morning, she stared hard at Jacintha, the woman who had supposedly fired Thierry. Meg had always thought there was something dodgy about that whole business, something left unsaid.

Old memories, and more recent ones too, floated to the surface. Meg could remember Thierry talking about Timothy over the years, recounting the lad's latest antics. And then . . . the night before Thierry had left Yarleigh, what was it he had said? Something to do with the ties between father and son. And the note he had written her – that reference to passing the vineyard on . . .

She couldn't believe he had never confided in her! Years ago, not long after he had first come to Yarleigh and when things hadn't worked out romantically between them, Meg had been surprised when he'd told her he was going to stay anyway. She recalled the day when he had started working for the Arundels. She had known he could do better. But he had been happy in that cottage, never wanting to be anything or anyone important. It was one of the reasons he had fallen out with his father.

Although she was still in shock, Meg recovered her wits enough to lean across the table towards Timothy. Wetting her lips and keeping her voice calm, she asked, 'Is there anything more you can remember about Freddy's disappearance? Anything that might be of use to the police? You've been incredibly helpful so far.'

The boy shrugged. 'I think Freddy might have had an ice-cream bought for him, although we're always being told not to take anything from strangers.'

Meg stared at Timothy's left eye. It was still twitching. 'An ice-cream. Really. What kind?'

Timothy shrugged again. 'Vanilla. In a cone.'

Meg glanced at Jacintha. 'How long has Freddy been missing now?'

'Almost two hours.'

Meg turned back to Timothy. The lad squirmed in his chair.

'Is there anything more you might be able to tell me about these two people Freddy was with?' she probed further. 'The ones buying him an ice-cream?'

The boy shrugged a third time. 'They were tall, and blond, and fat.'

'Fat? I thought you said they were tall and thin?'

'No.' Timothy shook his head. 'I didn't say that.'

'Oh,' Meg pursed her lips, 'my mistake. Is there anything else you can remember? Please, Timothy, you know how important you are to the case. One of the policemen might even take you for a ride in his car.'

'D'you think so?' He perked up, thinking a moment. 'They had baseball caps on,' he said. 'New York Yankees.'

'Goodness!' gasped Jacintha. 'Darling, is there anything else you can remember, anything at all?'

'They both had beards,' he said. 'Really bushy ones.'

'Beards,' repeated Meg. 'I see.' She stood up, came around the table and took Timothy's hand. 'Come on, we're going for a little walk.'

'I don't want to.'

'Beards?' frowned Jacintha. 'But I thought one of them was a—'

'Your mother's going to come along too,' Meg assured the boy sweetly, 'because something tells me she'll want to hear what's really going on as much as I do.'

'Why can you never find a policeman when you need one?' gasped Meg, returning to the starting point of her sprint around the clubhouse.

Jacintha sighed in irritation. 'There's no sign

of that constable that was supposed to stay posted here.'

'He's probably in the loo.' Meg frowned, scratching her head. 'Thinking about it though, the last thing Freddy needs is half the Yarl Valley police force cornering him gung-ho style, lights flashing, sirens blaring.'

'It would be just like on TV!' said Timothy, not realising that Meg was exaggerating to try to make him feel guilty.

His mother tightened her grip on his arm. 'This was all your idea, my boy. I can see your hand in this as clear as day, so don't think you're getting away with it!'

'I did it for Freddy,' pouted Timothy.

'It doesn't matter who you did it for,' snapped Meg. 'You're putting a father through hell and wasting valuable police resources – you could even get charged for it.' She turned to Jacintha. 'Did you walk to the Regatta this morning?'

'Well, *I* don't mind using the footpath through the estate, but Mummy wouldn't hear of it. Her Merc's being serviced so I gave her a lift in the Jeep.'

'Is it parked nearby?'

'Not far. We get special privileges. We're meant to be presenting some of the prizes later.'

'Good,' said Meg, 'then you're driving. Wait

here a mo.' And she dashed back into the clubhouse to leave a message with Aggie.

Jacintha's latest fad was parked in a patch of field set aside for the use of VIP guests, one of whom was the Mayor of Tockley. There was even a lad employed to keep an eye on the two modest rows of immodest motor vehicles, so Jacintha hadn't bothered putting the top on the Jeep.

Within a short while, the two women and Timothy were whizzing along the hedge-flanked lane leading south out of Yarleigh. The wind whistling through their hair, they sped past St Dominic's Parish Church. Meg glanced at the gravestones, reliving the morning of February sixteenth as if replaying an old and much-watched video.

'Did you ask Miss Widdicombe to tell the police exactly where we were going?' asked Jacintha.

'No. They'd only have come charging after us. Freddy will be frightened stiff if he realises how much trouble he's caused. I just said that I had a pretty good idea where he was, and that Matthew wasn't to worry because we'd gone to fetch him back.'

'Won't Matthew be annoyed that you were so cryptic?'

'Probably,' sighed Meg, holding on tight as Jacintha swerved through a pair of familiar iron gates and careered up the winding drive towards Arundel Hall.

The Jeep squealed to a halt. They all leapt out, the gravel crunching underfoot as Timothy broke into a run towards the lawn. Meg and Jacintha followed suit, hoisting up their dresses. The boy led the way to the spinney, stopping at the foot of what seemed to be the tallest tree in the little wood. The branches were low enough to the ground to be reached by a child.

'He's up there.' Timothy pointed at a wooden platform visible through the leaves. 'It's the tree house Thierry built for me.'

Meg had to bite her tongue to stop herself asking twenty questions and letting on to Jacintha that she'd guessed the truth. 'We've got to try to coax Freddy down,' she said instead, looking at the tree and wondering if it was one she had climbed as a kid. 'Freddy!' she called. 'Freddy, it's me, Meggy – are you up there?'

No answer.

Timothy craned his neck back. 'Freddy, you should have seen the police turning up at the Regatta!' he yelled. 'There must have been—' His mother's hand cupped itself firmly over his mouth.

'It's all right, Freddy,' Meg called assuagingly, 'it's just Timothy and his mother with me down here, nobody else.'

Still no answer.

'Freddy?' Meg was growing panicky again.

What if he wasn't up there any more? 'Freddy, I just want to talk. Your father's looking for you by the river. He's really worried about you. He thinks you may have been kidnapped.'

A small face appeared over the edge of the platform.

Meg thanked God in relief. 'Freddy, are you going to come down?'

'I can't,' he whimpered.

'Of course you can, kiddo. I'm not here to tell you off. And your dad isn't going to either. In fact, when he sees you, he's going to give you the biggest hug—'

'I can't come down,' said Freddy, louder and more plaintive. 'It's too high.'

Jacintha groaned. Timothy squirmed in her grasp. She removed her hand from his mouth but stood poised to reapply it.

'I'll go up and help,' he said. 'It's always harder to come down the first few times.'

Meg had a vision of both boys breaking arms or legs, or even worse, necks.

'There's nothing for it,' she sighed. 'I'll have to go up myself.'

Jacintha blinked at her. 'Are you sure?'

'It's been a while since I climbed a tree,' she admitted, taking a deep breath.

'How long?'

'Um – about twenty years.' She was already

unbuckling her sandals. 'But it must be like riding a bike,' she said, with more optimism than she felt.

Jacintha was doubtful. 'Maybe we *should* call the police and wait till they get here . . .'

'It's OK. There's nothing to it.' Meg hitched up her dress. 'Freddy needs someone up there now.' And flashing a smile full of bravado, she began her ascent.

'It's a bit like being a bird in a nest up here, isn't it?' Meg smiled at Freddy as he sat huddled in the furthest corner of the tree house.

'Dad has these Secret Seven books,' said the boy. 'They're about this gang who solve mysteries. They've got a tree house too.'

'I remember reading those when I was your age. The Famous Five were my favourite though.' She nodded towards the plastic bag beside Freddy. 'Did you bring provisions with you?'

'Pringles,' he said. 'And Lucozade.'

She grinned. 'I ran away from home once too, you know.'

'Did you?' Freddy's eyes widened. 'Why?'

'I was sixteen, which probably seems old to you, but when I look back I was really very young. I wanted an adventure, like the kind I'd read about in books.'

'Where did you go?'

'Paris, in France.'

Freddy's eyes grew even wider. 'But that's miles away! Did you have an adventure there? Why did you come home?'

'I had lots of adventures. And I came home because my family was missing me and I was missing them. I realised that they must have been worried about me, just like your dad's worried about you now.'

Freddy bowed his head. 'Dad wants to leave Yarleigh, but I don't want to. I like it here. Timothy said that if I ran away for a while, it would be a sort of protest. Dad would have to listen to me then.'

Meg ached to hug the boy, but he was still in a defensive huddle.

'Timothy heard him saying something to Mr Nugent, the headmaster,' Freddy went on. 'Before school broke up. He was outside the office one day, he heard them talking. Dad was going on about "his options", and that maybe Yarleigh wasn't the right place for him.'

Meg's stomach knotted. 'But has your father actually said anything to you properly?' she asked.

'Not properly.' He hesitated. 'Meggy, if you talk to him, maybe he won't go.'

'Why do you think that would make any difference?'

'Because Grandad told me Dad fancies you.'

Meg gripped the nearest branch. She couldn't get her hopes up. Lots of men 'fancied' her. 'How d'you mean exactly, Freddy? Did your grandfather explain . . .'

'He said Dad thought you were a cracker. But not a Christmas one or the kind I like with cheese. He said Dad would be a goon if he let you get away. What's a goon, Meggy?'

'An idiot,' she murmured, hardly daring to believe what she was hearing.

'Meggy, do you fancy my dad? If you do, you could get married and we could go and live with you in that house with the big garden. I said to Grandad I wouldn't mind. He asked if I would because of Mummy. But I said I still loved Mummy anyway. She's in heaven where people are really happy, so she'd want Dad to be happy too, wouldn't she?'

The logic of children was the most astonishing thing in the world, thought Meg, realising that she had never felt this broody or maternal before. 'Oh, Freddy, come here . . .' She opened her arms. He crawled across the platform and snuggled into them. Tears rolled down his cheeks leaving clean streaks through the dirt. 'Listen, Freddy, I'll speak to your father and explain how you feel. And, to be honest, I think he's a bit of a cracker himself.'

'Are you going to tell him that?'

'I'd be a goon if I didn't.'

Freddy smiled. 'Can we go back now then? I don't want Dad to be worried any more.'

The tree house seemed much higher looking down, but it was soundly constructed among a mesh of sturdy branches. Thierry wouldn't have been irresponsible enough to make it a major hazard, especially when his own son was going to be the one using it. But to an adult who was no longer the daredevil tom-boy she used to be, and to a child unaccustomed to climbing higher than two branches, it seemed an eternity until they were both on solid ground again.

As the boys ran ahead to the Jeep, Jacintha watched Meg slip on her sandals and dust down her snagged dress. 'I couldn't have climbed up there the way you just did,' she admitted, her voice small. 'I was always against that bloody tree house, but men can be so . . .' she tailed off.

'You look like you need a holiday,' Meg heard herself say. 'I hear the Loire Valley is lovely at this time of year.'

Jacintha blanched.

Meg frowned pensively. 'There wasn't a one-night-stand on a kibbutz, was there? You made that up as your cover story. But the fling, or whatever you want to call it, must have happened quite soon after you came back to England, when Thierry was new in town and things weren't working out between him and me.'

'How – how did you . . . ?'

Meg suddenly felt sorry for her. 'This isn't the time.' She started leading the way out of the spinney. 'I shouldn't have brought it up.'

'Did Thierry—'

'He kept your secret safe, don't worry. I only guessed it today, when I was looking closely at Timothy. Maybe it was because I knew Thierry so well myself. I just wish I understood—'

'When I first found out I was pregnant,' Jacintha said, an urgency in her voice, as if she was desperate to explain it to someone, 'Thierry wasn't in love with me.'

'You mean, he is now?' Meg, kicking herself for having brought up the subject, wished there was more time to discuss it.

'I thought he might have been. Until I saw you both together that night in Pilgrims.'

Meg stopped in her tracks. It all became horribly clear. 'You thought that we were . . .'

'I knew he'd been head over heels about you once, and I knew you were still friends. He used to tell me that was all it was. He said he'd been drunk the night of your birthday party, and he'd been trying to help you make Matthew jealous. I was a bitch to him for weeks afterwards though.'

'You didn't believe him,' said Meg, adding intuitively, 'But you didn't sack him, did you? He left of his own accord.'

Jacintha's eyes were misty. 'He said he'd had enough, and that if I ever came to my senses . . . If I ever decided to tell Timothy the truth . . .'

Oh lord, thought Meg, Jacintha was another goon.

'Mummy!'

'Meggy!'

Timothy and Freddy, impatient as only two boys their age could be, were running over to see what the delay was about.

'Come on,' said Meg, galvanised into action, hustling everyone towards the Jeep. 'We've got to get back to find Matthew.'

'I've never been in a car without a roof before,' Freddy confessed to Meg as they careered up the driveway towards the road. 'It's windy.'

Meg smiled, then leaned forward as far as the seat-belt would allow, addressing Jacintha: 'It's the school holidays soon,' she said, raising her voice so that it carried to the front. 'If you go over to France and sort things out . . .'

Jacintha flashed Meg a heated look in the rear view mirror. 'I can't leave Mummy alone. Now that Jake's gone, she needs me here more than ever.'

'I'm sure your mother could survive without you,' said Meg. 'She has employees to look after the estate, and a manager now too. It's not as if she's in Yarleigh that much anyway. She seems to prefer the giddy social whirl of London. And then there are all those charitable committees to keep her busy. I bet you hardly see her as it is.'

Jacintha didn't reply. Meg had clearly hit a nerve.

'Mummy, are we going on holiday?' asked Timothy. 'Are we going to France? If we do, we can visit Thierry's farm where they grow grapes and make wine. He used to tell me all about it.'

'We'll see,' mumbled Jacintha.

The Jeep was turning into the road leading to the river and the clubhouse. The crowd had thickened. Jacintha had to drive at a crawl to get through, cursing volubly under her breath, vehement with her hooter. Finally, the crowd seemed to part like the Red Sea. Aggie, with Georgie sleeping through the drama in the buggy, was standing beside Matthew. Her strained face broke into a smile. Meg waved. Freddy was already climbing out and tumbling into his father's arms before Jacintha could even apply the hand-brake. Matthew crushed him to his chest and swung him round in a dizzying circle.

Meg wiped the tears from her eyes, then leaned forwards, squeezing Jacintha's shoulder. 'If you can at least be civil to Thierry, and if there's any sort of spark between you, make the most of it, build on it, don't get bogged down by what's gone before. You've got an incredible son who needs a father in his life. Can't you at least give it a chance?' And with that, she climbed out of the Jeep, only to be accosted by the police sergeant.

'Miss Oakley, would you mind explaining what all this has been about? You left a rather obscure message with' – he consulted the notebook – 'a Miss Agnes Widdicombe. Your godmother.'

Meg couldn't deal with an interrogation right now, but Timothy interrupted anyway, striding up to the policeman and holding out his wrists. 'Go on then,' he said defiantly. 'I wasted valuable resources. You'd better nick me.'

Meg spotted Yasmin and beckoned her over. 'Yaz—'

'Oh, Meg, it was so awful! Everyone was saying Freddy had been abducted!'

'Yaz, listen, this nice policeman here would like a word with someone who has a vague idea of what's going on. Basically, Freddy ran off and hid in Timothy Arundel's tree house because he didn't want to leave Yarleigh. It was a sort of protest – all Timothy's idea. But maybe if you fill the sergeant in on the story leading up to it . . .'

Yaz tilted her head back to look at the tall policeman, giving him her best schoolmarm frown.

He looked humbled. 'Miss—'

'Bradley. Miss Yasmin Adele Bradley . . .'

Meg took the opportunity to blow her nose.

Timothy Arundel – miffed because the copper wouldn't arrest him – watched his mother being bombarded with questions by his grandmother, who was wearing a hat like a meringue. Kicking at a pebble, he drifted over to where Freddy was still being hugged by a relieved-looking Mr Potter. Absorbed by the sight, Timothy wasn't aware that his mother had come to stand beside him until she took hold of his hand and turned him to face her.

'Would you like a father of your own, Timothy?' She bobbed down in front of him, tidying the collar of his polo shirt.

'A real one?' he asked quietly, after a pause. 'Just like Freddy's got?'

She tweaked his nose, her smile small but resolute. 'I think something could be arranged,' she said.

'Meg Oakley, why didn't you tell Aggie exactly where you thought Freddy was?'

Meg looked up from the basin with a start. 'Matthew, these are the Ladies' toilets! What are you doing in here?'

He leant against the door frame, his hands thrust casually in his pockets. 'I've been looking for you. Why did you vanish? You weren't worrying I'd bite your head off or something? Because—'

She grabbed his sleeve and steered him outside. 'Everyone's staring,' she hissed.

'Good. There's something I'd like them to see.' And before Meg could snatch her breath, he'd taken her into his arms and was kissing her thoroughly and passionately. Fireworks after fireworks went off in her head. If this was how smooching would be between them . . .

'So,' he muttered throatily, a moment later, 'how was it?'

'Clichéd,' she moaned.

'Is that good or bad?'

'It's perfect.' She felt dizzy, and incredibly brave. 'I love you,' she said.

'Freddy told me you thought I was a cracker.' Matthew smoothed back her tousled hair, his eyes speaking volumes. 'I don't think he really trusted you to tell me something that important yourself.'

'Does this mean you're going to stick around in Yarleigh?'

'Well, seeing as you like it so much, I might be persuaded . . .'

She pinched him, and then pinched herself in case she was dreaming. There was so much she wanted to say still, so much she needed to ask; such as when he had first realised how he felt, and what it was about her (apart from the glaringly obvious) that had attracted him, and—

He was practically lifting her off her feet. 'You're a miracle!' he laughed. 'I love you too, Meg Oakley. You'd never believe just how much!'

'Are people going to make it difficult for us though?' she asked, suddenly apprehensive. She was aware that some of them would approve, but there were others whose opinion probably hadn't changed.

Matthew glanced around, still keeping a tight hold of her. 'Why don't we ask them? They might think it's high time someone made a respectable woman of you.'

'Oi!' She pinched him again, then realised the full extent of his words. 'Are you saying—?'

'It's a tough life, kiddo,' he murmured into her neck. 'But I'm willing if you are . . .'

'All I mean was you [illegible] it, I mean, I might be [illegible].'

She [illegible] him, and then [illegible] herself [illegible] as he was [illegible]. There was so much she wanted to say still [illegible] she wanted to ask [illegible] had first [illegible] him, [illegible] and what it was about her [illegible] the [illegible] had [illegible] him, and –

It was [illegible] her [illegible] 'I love you too, Miss [illegible]. You [illegible] [illegible] [illegible] [illegible] to [illegible]. [illegible] tonight' she asked [illegible] [illegible] [illegible] [illegible] [illegible] changed.

[illegible] [illegible] [illegible] still [illegible] [illegible] [illegible]. Why don't we [illegible] them? They might [illegible] [illegible] [illegible] [illegible] of [illegible].'

'Oh' she [illegible] him again, and [illegible] the [illegible] of his [illegible]. 'Are you [illegible] [illegible] [illegible] [illegible] [illegible] [illegible] [illegible] [illegible]'